Praise for

Author Joni M. Fisher

A gifted story-teller, Joni Fisher writes with energy and passion that comes to life in her characters. *North of the Killing Hand* is an intricate and suspenseful read that grips the reader from start to finish."
> – John Foxjohn, International, *USA Today*, and *New York Times* bestselling author

"*South of Justice* is a multilayered, intricate, and suspenseful page-turner you'll want to read in one sitting."
> – Diane Capri, *New York Times* and *USA Today* bestselling author of the Hunt for Jack Reacher thrillers

"Past secrets test the bonds of family loyalty and a fledgling love affair. The unwavering strength of the protagonists, their commitment to the truth and to each other will have you cheering for *South of Justice*."
> – Melissa Hladik Meyer, Author of *Good Company*

"Bottom line is: *South of Justice* is a multilayered romantic book that will grasp your attention and lure you to read it in one sitting."
> – SeriousReading.com

"*South of Justice* is fantastic and fun—a crisp and suspenseful story. Fisher makes a wonderful entrance as a crime fiction writer. I can't wait for *North of the Killing Hand*!"
> – Timothy D. Browne, M.D.

"Joni M. Fisher weaves a tale of passionate love, undying loyalty and enduring friendship between strong characters bound together and tested by deep-rooted principles. Curl up in your favorite chair with a tasty snack and a refreshing beverage—you won't want to move until you've turned the last page of *South of Justice*."
> – Donna Kelly. Author of *Brass Chains*

"A fabulous start to an intense series with a large cast of characters I couldn't help but love and cheer for. Fisher is a master weaver of intrigue and strong characters willing to go the distance to get things done while keeping their love strong."

    – K.D. Fleming, Author and Golden Heart Winner

"Tightly written, complex characters, intriguing plot—all the ingredients for a great read! This debut book is a winner, and I am looking forward to more books in the future."

    – Diane Burke, award-winning author of inspirational romantic suspense

"I was intrigued from the very first chapter. It grabs your attention, and I loved the characters immediately. I believe I have found my new favorite author."

    – Kindle Customer

"Long-held secrets kept me turning the pages to the end. This is a great book to read for anyone who enjoys crime stories with a touch of romance. Also, the book has loyal friends, moral values and strong faith to make this an enjoyable and clean read. I appreciate books like this one."

    – Joann R. Greene, Goodreads Giveaway Winner

"*South of Justice* has an intricate plot with several twists and turns. Long-held secrets keep the reader turning pages all the way to the end. I really enjoyed reading *South of Justice* and recommend it for anyone who enjoys crime stories with a touch of romance."

    – Luv2read

"I really enjoyed this book. It was well written and the twists and turns had me turning pages deep into the night."

    – Vicki W Tharp, Author of *Don't Look Back*

"Well written book with great details and informative. The trial and the back story of the crime make me not want to put the book down. Great read, can't wait for the next one."

    – C. Riecke

"Intricate plot with totally believable characters that draw you in and don't let go! Suspenseful and real."

    – Clara Jane Sweet

Also by Joni M. Fisher

South of Justice

To August,
*   May you enjoy this on a*
quiet evening.

North of the Killing Hand

Joni M. Fisher

North of the Killing Hand

Copyright @ 2016 Joni M. Fisher

North of the Killing Hand is a work of fiction. Names, characters, places, and incidents are the product of the author's imagination or are used fictitiously, and any resemblance to actual persons, living or dead, business establishments, events, or locales is entirely coincidental.

ISBN-13: 978-0-9972575-2-6 (Trade paperback version)
ISBN-13: 978-0-9972575-3-3 (eBook English version)

Original Cover Design by Damonza
Interior Formatting by Author E.M.S.

To Jessica Nicole Fisher Crisostomo,

a gift from God.

ACKNOWLEDGMENTS

Deep thanks to critique partners from Kiss of Death and the Tampa Area Romance Authors who encouraged, corrected, and occasionally laughed at my flailing transition from non-fiction to fiction writing. Special thanks to authors: Jamie Beckett, KD Fleming, John Foxjohn, Donna Kelly, Mary McGuire, Melissa Hladik Meyer, and Carol J. Post for their unflinching, wise advice. Special thanks also to brave beta readers: Dawn Anderson, Kim Addington, Doris Arrington, Cyndi Boswell, John M. Esser, Carol Faulkner-Davis, Chuck Davis, Caryn L. Frink, Terri Johnson, Audrey Nettlow, Cheryl Riecke, Suzanne Roustio, Carol Speyerer, and Martha Walker for taking my long journey to publication as seriously as I do.

North of the Killing Hand

. 1 .

Fourteen-year-old Nefi Jenkins settled into her perch thirty-four feet up a strangler fig tree, shaded by the canopy of the top branches. From her favorite place, she enjoyed a bird's eye view of the Amazon from the Juruá River that wrapped the west and northern boundaries of the tribe's territory, to the denser jungle to the east, and the swamp to the south. Her parents didn't know of this place because they had not asked. Experience had shown her that forgiveness was easier to gain than permission. She did not want to be lectured about every injury and fatality from falls suffered in human history.

On a clear day, she could locate other tribes by smoke columns where women cooked at the center of other settlements. At the center of her village, surrounded by a dozen wooden huts with palm-frond rooftops, Mali cooked for Nefi's family and her own.

Nefi longed to travel, even just to visit other tribes, but in August, the river ran low. Father said he refused to go out in August because the boat was too heavy to tow, but Nefi believed the real reason was his fear of anacondas that draped themselves on branches over the river like braided hemp ropes thrown from a ship. Father said anaconda did not live back in the states. He

1

promised to take her there, but every year changed to 'next' year.

Nefi sighed. Each year grew longer, and this was the longest month of the year.

Birds scattered from trees along the riverbank west of the village. Nefi dug her father's binoculars from her satchel to investigate the disturbance. A human-made bird call sounded. A warning. Moments later the seven other children of the village dashed to their hiding places.

Had the Matis crossed the river to hunt?

She leaned forward to see around leaves into the center of the village where three men with rifles faced Mali. The small elderly woman turned toward Mama and Papa, who walked toward the strangers. The shortest man pointed to Papa. Nefi focused the binocular lenses on the stranger's face. The Pirarucu Man.

What kind of fool came to trade this time of year? He probably got his boat stuck in the shallow river. City dweller.

The Pirarucu Man pointed to the ground. Mama and Papa knelt. A chill ran up Nefi's spine. He did not seem like a man who would ever ask for prayer. Nefi widened her view to see Mali step toward Mama and Papa. The Pirarucu Man raised his rifle and shot twice.

Nefi sucked in a deep breath. Mama and Papa slumped over. A tiny cloud of smoke rose from the rifle. A howl roared out of Nefi as if by sound alone she could scare off the Pirarucu Man.

She lost her balance and fell four feet onto a wide branch below, striking it hard enough to cut off her scream. Clinging to the branch, she watched Papa's binoculars fall thirty feet before the rare and unmistakable sound of breaking glass marked the impact.

She shimmied to the tree trunk, hugged it, and slid to the next lower branch. The tree blurred, forcing her to blink repeatedly. Her mind spun. Her feet and arms worked on sense memory as her body scrambled down the familiar smooth-skinned fig tree into the cavernous wall-like folds in the trunk. Gasping and wobbly among tree roots that arched waist-high around her, she rubbed her eyes to clear away the nightmare images flashing in her mind.

Stepping over the shattered binoculars, she ran. Crashing through knee-high ferns and tree roots, she tore a fresh path back to the village. Her bare feet slapped the hard-packed mud. She trampled ferns and flowers, sending small creatures scuttling out of her way. She panted. Her heartbeat drummed in her ears. Small branches scratched her arms and her face. Stumbling over roots and vines, she groped her way upright and charged on. She raced to her village, to home, to Mama, to Papa, praying the binoculars lied.

. 2 .

The more twenty-one–year-old Vincent Gunnerson thought about his mission, the more heroic it sounded. He and two others were tasked with a privately-funded mission to go to the Brazilian jungle to pick up the fourteen-year-old niece of U.S. Senator Jenkins. The girl's parents had been murdered, leaving her stranded. Four hours into the jungle it seemed a tame assignment.

Vincent was second in a line of three men hiking northeasterly through waist-high brush and towering trees in Serra do Divisor National Park on the Brazilian side of the Amazon rainforest. Ruis Ramos led the way along a worn pathway. Vincent waved off a cloud of gnats, caught the toe of his boot on a tree root, and stumbled. He gasped, inhaled a bug, and then his rifle barrel smacked him in the back of the head. Good thing only Blake saw it.

Being that kind of friend, Blake Clayton laughed.

Vincent coughed out the bug.

"Just a walk in the park, eh?" Blake muttered from behind Vincent.

Their leader Ruis Ramos had suggested this mission would be fairly easy.

4

So far, Vincent believed him. "Did you expect paved walkways?"

"I expected something better than a critter trail in a national park."

Ruis called back, "We're almost there."

There being that spot on Ruis's map labeled Queimado Hill. *There,* where they were to meet the Brazilian officials for a briefing and to plan their combined search for the girl who disappeared from her village right after the shootings.

Vincent had accepted the mission immediately though he spoke neither Portuguese nor Spanish. If anyone asked, he was prepared to say he was in it for money, for bragging rights, for something to do before starting college in September, and for a letter of recommendation from Senator Jenkins. Though he would never admit it, his true motive was to be like his father, a man who daily risked his life to save others as an officer in the NYPD. Rescuing a recently orphaned American citizen from the heart of the Amazon rainforest seemed like the most heroic use of the summer.

He didn't know Blake Clayton's reasons for going, but he was glad to have him along. After serving in the Marines with him, Blake was like the older brother Vincent always wanted. At six foot even, age thirty, redheaded, with 220 compact pounds of bone, muscle, and integrity, Blake had the soul of a poetic clown. They had separately applied to Berkeley College and were accepted. So why not take on one last mission before starting college?

Ruis, a former U.S. Navy lieutenant with special operations training, was five foot nine and thirty years old. Though shorter than Blake and Vincent, Ruis had movie-star good looks and justified confidence. He had assumed leadership of the mission because he spoke Spanish and a smattering of Portuguese. Vincent just knew Ruis was the kind of guy who slept in Kevlar.

The men arrived at a trailhead that opened onto a hilltop.

Standing at the peak of Queimado Hill along the bank of the Moa River in Southwestern Brazil, Blake set his backpack on the ground. Vincent followed suit, keeping his M-16A2 rifle hanging from its strap over his shoulder. He walked to the cliff's edge.

Blake approached Ruis. "How do the park rangers know when to meet us?"

Ruis planted a hand on Blake's shoulder. "Let's not call them that."

Blake raised his eyebrows. "Okay."

"IBAMA," Ruis said, "stands for the Instituto Brasileiro do Meio Ambiente e dos Recursos Naturais Renovaveis."

How anyone got the acronym IBAMA from *that* mystified Vincent. Even in Portuguese, the letters didn't add up right.

"This agency is chronically underfunded and outmanned," Ruis added. "It fights poachers, slash-and-burn farmers, squatters, drug runners, fires, illegal loggers, guerillas, and eco-terrorists over an area larger than California and Texas combined. Occasionally they also rescue lost tourists and arbitrate quarrels between tribes." Ruis's hand dropped off Blake's shoulder. "If nothing else, let's respect them for their high mortality rate."

When Ruis returned to the trailhead, Blake bowed his head.

Vincent didn't believe Blake meant to insult the local officials. If given a few more minutes, he too might have called them park rangers.

Blake stepped up to the cliff edge beside Vincent.

The foliage had been thicker on the trail side of the hill than it was looking eastward. From this vantage point, the Amazon terrain had widely-spaced trees. The Adirondacks looked more like a jungle than this. Morning fog rose from the land like steam, as if the land itself was sweating, but the breeze at the cliff chilled. It felt like one-hundred percent humidity. The sun glowed with blurry borders through drifting layers of smoky fog.

Ruis's voice caused Vincent and Blake to face the trailhead. There Ruis greeted two short, solidly-built men in uniform. They shouldered ancient, dusty rifles that looked unreliable in a firefight. Everything about the two Brazilians seemed gritty and dust-covered except for their brightly colored IBAMA agency patches.

Ruis introduced Officers Raposo and Machado.

IBAMA Officer Raposo came up beside Vincent and waved his arm out toward the expanse of the sparse forest below. "*Mirante.*"

Vincent scanned the flat valley below. "That's *Mirante*?"

Raposo spoke rapidly with Ruis in Portuguese that sounded like Spanish with a German accent which made Vincent all the more grateful Ruis handled the translation.

Ruis said something that made the IBAMA officers laugh then he said, "*Mirante* means overlook."

Vincent nodded at Ruis. "And a beauty it is."

The two IBAMA officers smiled at the view. Unlike Vincent and Blake, the officers had not broken a sweat. A chorus of trills, twitters, whoops, hoots, whistles, squeaks, and squawks, clicks, and chirps sounded as birds and frogs joined in to celebrate the day. Despite the variety of noises from the trees, Vincent couldn't spot a single creature in the dense vegetation.

Ruis handed cold bottles of water to the IBAMA officers. While the officers drank, Ruis told Vincent and Blake, "I'm going to plan our search with these gentlemen. It'll go faster and smoother if I don't have to translate."

Vincent could take a hint. "That works for me."

Blake nodded. Ruis then spread a topographic map on the ground in the center of the clearing. The IBAMA officers each took a knee along the edges of the map.

Vincent used binoculars to scan the area below. "Brazil," he said to Blake, lowering his binoculars, "has seven thousand miles of beach."

"Try not to think about it," Blake said.

They were almost too far inland for Vincent's imagination to conjure coconut-oiled women sunning themselves on topless beaches hundreds of miles away. Almost.

Blake sighed. "Maybe we'll see some genuine Indians."

Images of male Indians in loincloths obliterated all fantasies of beach beauties. A flash of color flitted overhead toward the trees. Vincent located it in the canopy where a branch swayed. There in black, gold, and orange glory, a toucan repeatedly snapped his oversized beak. The bird looked just like Toucan Sam on the cereal box. His father had loved that cereal.

A squeal from Raposo's radio scared off Toucan Sam. Raposo tuned his radio until a voice came through weak but clear. The device looked like an ancient field phone, like the kind shown in old war movies. Perhaps this *was* old war surplus equipment sold to an agency in a third-world country. Lowering his radio, Officer Raposo spoke to Ruis.

Vincent raised his eyebrows.

Ruis asked Vincent and Blake, "Do you want the good news or the bad news?"

Maybe they found the girl. "The good news," Vincent said.

"IBAMA officers have arrived at Nefi's village," Ruis said. "They are interviewing the villagers and searching for evidence."

"And the bad news?" Blake asked.

"The investigating officers will probably be gone by the time we reach the village." Ruis resumed studying the map.

To locate a fourteen-year-old girl in the vast Amazon River basin was a daunting challenge. They were starting out with disadvantages of time and distance. The murders had occurred five days earlier. But how far away was this village? Vincent stepped up behind Ruis to get a better look at the map.

The two IBAMA officers knelt on either side of Ruis around the map. A penciled line ran from *Cruzeiro do Sul*, where they had landed earlier that morning in the southwest part of Brazil, to their present position at Queimado Hill in the Serra do Divisor National Park.

On the map, Officer Raposo swept his hand toward settlements along the Moa River, a tributary of the Juruá River. It flowed north-northeast into the Solimoes, which emptied into the great Amazon River. Officer Raposo pointed to a settlement on the Juruá River labeled in the smallest letters on the map. He then set his fingertip farther northeast along the river, to an area surrounded by dark green, and then Officer Raposo said the only thing Vincent understood. *Casa* Jenkins.

Of all the places in the Amazon, this area looked the least inhabited. On the flight to Brazil, Vincent learned from Ruis that the rivers were the main form of transportation in the rainforest, but as August was winter—the dry season—the shallow river meandered through six-hundred miles of canyons and flood plains. The river was too low to navigate by boat from their starting point to the smudged fingerprint that marked *casa* Jenkins; however, the river was deeper downstream from the target village to the north. How long would it take to hike *that* far?

Ruis and the IBAMA officers pointed to different spots on the map. Officer Raposo spread his hand over the map of an area west of the Juruá River and spoke in emphatic tones. The other officer had crossed himself before he sat back on his legs. Vincent stepped up to the map. The discussion continued in Portuguese or Spanish, he couldn't tell the difference. The men then stood.

The officers offered Ruis one of their ancient field radios. Ruis then removed his Motorola 9500 satellite phone from a waterproof bag.

Ruis had briefed Blake and Vincent on it during the flight to Brazil. It uplinked to a series of sixty-six satellites, and it had a twenty-hour battery life. Ruis, of course, carried two fully-charged backup batteries along with the satellite phone in a waterproof bag.

The officers admired Ruis's fancy phone and put away their relic radios.

Both officers shook hands with Ruis, Vincent, and Blake then they headed back down the trail. Apparently, the Brazilians and

Americans were conducting separate searches. It made sense considering the vast ground they needed to cover.

After the IBAMA officers had left, Ruis pulled a pencil from his shirt pocket and dropped to one knee by the map. "This," he said, jabbing at a place on the Juruá River, "is where the Jenkins lived. The villagers report that Nefi ran off on August third and left her family's boat behind. In that terrain, she could have traveled anywhere in this area." He drew an eighty-mile-wide circle on the map.

Vincent sighed. They were south of the area Ruis circled on the map.

"Both officers say she probably headed north along the river," Ruis said. "The water is deep enough there for a boat."

"Why did that officer genuflect?" Vincent asked.

"This area on the west side of the river is the Matis tribe territory." Ruis scowled. "Hostiles."

Vincent checked the scale on the map and estimated their position. "The girl has a two-hundred-mile head start on us."

"How can we catch up?" Blake asked.

Ruis smiled. "I'm hiring a seaplane to take us to Nefi's village."

Blake paled. The poor guy despised flying more than dental work. "Forgive me, Lord. I shouldn't have complained about the hike. So we go back to the park station?" Blake tucked a thumb under the shoulder strap of his backpack.

"The park we just hiked from?" Vincent asked pointing west to the trailhead.

Ruis reached up and gently nudged Vincent's arm southwesterly. Vincent dropped his arm to his side.

Blake shouldered his backpack. "I don't mind going back. I forgot bug spray."

"The seaplane can pick us up here, tomorrow." Ruis stabbed the map with his pencil to indicate a place downstream on the Moa River a day's hike away.

Vincent crouched by the map, casting his shadow over it.

Ruis tapped the map. "Officer Raposo believes her parents took her to Manaus for immunizations. If she heads for a city, this northern city is the most likely choice. Copies of her description have been transmitted to authorities all over the country. He said he'll contact us if he gets any news."

Vincent resigned himself to a day's hike to the spot on the map where the seaplane would pick them up. He set his expectations low for the reliability of a seaplane in the Amazon. The nearest airport with a mechanic had to be a couple of hundred miles away. Commercial flights were spooky enough, but the idea of riding in a seaplane gave him chills. They were so small, like a car with wings.

Vincent waved his open palm over the north half of Ruis's drawn circle. "So we hike to the pickup point and fly to her village. After that, we follow the trail northeast and look for signs of her?"

Ruis nodded. Vincent and Ruis waited for Blake to weigh in. Blake nodded.

Vincent found encouragement in the fact that a girl raised here should fare okay if left on her own, but where were the men who killed her parents? And why did she leave the village?

Rising to stand, Ruis shook the dirt off his map. He folded it and tucked it in a plastic bag that he stuffed in his shirt pocket.

"I'm sorry to say we don't have any photos of the girl. Based on photos of her parents, she's probably tall for her age." Ruis dug something that looked like a string of beads from his backpack. He held it up. "Senator Jenkins said this is something the girl should recognize."

Vincent examined the leather and stone bead choker up close. "Looks handmade."

Ruis handed it to Vincent. "Show it when we encounter any girls."

Vincent said, "I'll be glad to." With that, he fastened the

leather and stone bead choker around his neck for safekeeping.

"Maybe I should take it," Blake said. "We don't want to scare her off. Females trust me." Blake waggled his eyebrows. He had a kind of boyish Southern cowboy charm women responded to, but still...

"She's fourteen," Vincent reminded him. "Can you say jailbait?"

Blake patted Vincent's shoulder. "And you just turned twenty-one. Legal age here too, I bet."

Ruis cleared his throat. His glare sent chills through Vincent. "I have to make a call." He stepped away from Vincent and Blake.

Vincent overheard Ruis arranging for more supplies and the seaplane. Vincent took a swig of water and tucked the bottle back into his pack. After adjusting the straps comfortably over his shoulders, he waited beside Blake for Ruis to finish his call.

Ruis swung his machete up to his shoulder as he led the way back to the trailhead. Vincent and Blake fell in line behind him. At the mouth of the trail head, Vincent elbowed Blake and cut in front of him, leaving Blake at the end of the line.

They were going deeper into the road-less nowhere. They could encounter poachers, guerillas, drug runners, hostile Indians, and who knows what kind of vicious wildlife. Vincent didn't know which he dreaded most, the flight in a seaplane or the idea that their connection to the outside world depended on a satellite phone.

They had brought along a few days' worth of food and water. He hoped it was enough to last until they caught up with the teenager.

Why did she leave her village?

An hour after they left Queimado Hill while hiking parallel to the Moa River, Blake launched into conversation. "Two years ago, I learned that Vincent has a fierce intuition that's worth trusting. Tell him, Vincent. Tell him about the Osprey."

Vincent shook his head. *Not this again.*

"Ah, don't be modest," Blake said. "So we're stationed in Yuma, Arizona, in the spring of two thousand, and this brand-spanking new airplane arrives. It was one really ugly contraption, half helicopter, half airplane."

"The Osprey?" Ruis asked.

"Yeah," Blake continued, "And about that same time the Osprey arrives, we ended up escorting Senators around the base. Seems Congress wanted to close some bases, so the Senators went on a look-see tour to decide which bases to keep and which to close."

Ruis ducked under a low-hanging branch. "Heads up."

Vincent stopped and backed up a step. The vine on the overhanging branch moved. He pointed it out to Blake. It looked like a pale green vine wrapped around the branch until it lifted its head and stuck out its forked tongue. Vincent stepped off the trail, crushing a small bush under his size fourteen boot. He took two more steps to resume the trail and Blake followed.

A few strides ahead, Ruis glanced back.

Blake resumed his story. "One Senator asked Vincent what he thought of the plane. So with his usual New Yorker diplomacy, Vincent tells him, 'Sir, it doesn't look aerodynamically sound. It looks like it was designed by a committee.'"

Vincent said, "You know Senator Jenkins was on that tour."

"Was he the tall Senator or the fat one?"

Vincent answered, "The tall one."

Ruis said, "Is that where you first met Senator Jenkins?"

"Yeah, yeah, but what I'm trying to say is that Vincent's intuition was dead on. The Osprey took off with a full crew and a group of Marines. It crashed west of Tucson."

Ruis scowled. "How bad?"

"Killed nineteen Marines."

Ruis shook his head and resumed hiking.

"The other important thing to know about Vincent," Blake said elbowing past Vincent, "is that he's a living, breathing, two-hundred-pound human magnet for dangerous females."

Ruis grunted. As he walked, his head swiveled slowly left to right, right to left, ever watchful.

"I'm telling you if we walked into a bar in Rio," Blake said, "the craziest, most dangerous woman in the place would rise from her stool and stagger toward him. It's uncanny."

"How do you know Senator Jenkins?" Vincent asked Ruis in a blatant attempt to change the subject. Maybe Blake would take the hint.

"My father played poker with him. They served on the same ship," Ruis said.

"Wait a minute," Vincent called out. "Is your father Admiral Ramos?"

"Yes."

Vincent felt a bit slow-witted that he had not made the connection earlier between Admiral Ramos and Ruis Ramos. Having a Navy Admiral for a father was a big deal.

Blake sighed, no doubt resigned to having his story about the Osprey crash ignored. "So," Blake said to Ruis, "why aren't you going for a Navy career?"

"People would expect too much of me or nothing at all," Ruis added, "I applied to the U.S. Marshals Service. Senator Jenkins said he'd write me a recommendation letter."

"Sounds like a better plan than Blake's," Vincent said.

"Better than joining the rodeo?" Ruis asked deadpan.

Blake snorted.

"Blake said he was going to apply to colleges," Vincent said, "under affirmative action."

Ruis stopped and glanced at Blake. "Since when does being a red-head qualify as a minority under affirmative action?"

"If I didn't get in on the first try," Blake said with an accompanying glare to Vincent, "which I did, by the way, I was going to re-apply under affirmative action. I'm a white Christian gentleman. Whites are fast becoming a minority. And on television and in movies gentlemen and Christians are universally portrayed as hypocrites, wimps, and fools. If y'all ask me, it has all the hallmarks of discrimination."

Ruis took out his canteen.

Vincent said, "Be grateful colleges don't require passing a psych test."

"I should add *Southern* to the discrimination list. Southerners get treated poorly, too, if you ask me. My own friend," Blake said, taking out his canteen, "himself a big-city Yankee, insists that rural Southerners are natural-born crazy."

"As proof," Vincent said, uncapping his water, "I offer a game called Cow Bingo."

"That's only once a year." Blake downed a deep swallow of his water. "For a New Yorker, you sure have a long memory." In a flagrant attempt to redirect the conversation, he said, "Ultimately, I plan to work for the FBI."

"Get this," Vincent said, waving his canteen, "after their high school homecoming football game, they mark squares on the field. Grown adults buy deeds to sections of the field. Then they bring out a cow. Yes, a cow. Crowds sit for hours watching the cow, hoping he'll crap on their section of the field."

"She," Blake said.

"What?"

"Cows are female; bulls are male."

"Excuse my ignorance of livestock." Vincent placed his canteen over his heart.

"You're excused," Blake said.

Ruis swallowed a swig of water. "Why?"

"Raised in New York City," Blake said, "the closest poor Vincent ever gets to livestock is at a barbecue."

Ruis glowered at Blake. "*Why* would you pay to watch a cow defecate on a football field?"

Blake said, "The section with the biggest cow pie wins."

"Wins what? Fertilizer?" Sarcasm did not look good on Ruis.

"In defense of my sanity as well as the spirit of the band booster's fundraiser," Blake said, "Let me explain that the winner gets a new pickup truck. It's a fundraiser for the band geeks."

Ruis glanced from Vincent to Blake, as if waiting for a punch line.

Pleased at making his point, Vincent smiled.

Blake's shoulders slumped. "Y'all go ahead, mock small-town Southerners. Call us uncivilized, but we don't shoot each other in traffic. No, siree. In my part of the country, if you're stranded on the roadside, don't be alarmed if a complete stranger stops to help."

Speckled sunlight pierced the high canopy. The three men hiked over knee-high thick tree roots and vines, through waist-high ferns and flowers, and emerged onto a wide flat plain dotted with trees. The lowlands smelled of rotting plants and smoke. Near the river where wildlife gathered, the stench of decay intensified. Blake pointed out a variety of animal tracks and scat in the muddy trail leading northwest. At day's end, at their pick-up point, they camped for the night. Ruis ordered Blake to serve as a lookout while Vincent gathered firewood. Ruis strung up hammocks and mosquito netting.

As Vincent dropped a pile of gathered wood, he noticed Blake standing stock still, staring at something large roiling the murky water in the shallows. A small branch fell into the water ahead of the disturbance. The ruffling of the water's surface stopped. Water flowed over the thing in the water, rippling over the uneven contours of its back. Crocodile. Blake slowly lowered his rifle to aim. A nose broke through the water. A second ridge appeared behind the nose. Two wide-set eyes opened half in and half out of the water.

"Hey, Ruis." Blake kept his sights lined up on the beast. "Is crocodile edible?"

Ruis's voice sounded about twenty feet away in the trees. "Tastes like chicken. The meat under the jowl is the best."

Of course, Ruis would know that. Vincent knew that unlike alligators, crocodiles were fiercely aggressive. He wondered how aggressive as he attached a flash muzzle to his own rifle barrel.

"Are you using the suppressor so you don't alarm the crocodile's friends?" Blake asked.

Vincent said, "What do you think the IBAMA officers would do if they heard gunshots?"

"Arrest us for poaching." Blake attached a bayonet to the end of his rifle. "I don't suppose anyone thought to get a hunting license."

"Is this for sport or food?" Ruis's tone suggested he questioned his colleagues' sanity.

"Survival," Vincent said. "Don't tell me these things are an endangered species."

"Okay, I won't tell you," Ruis said.

"If he charges, shoot through the eye," Blake offered. "They're thick-skulled."

Taking aim, Vincent chuckled.

"Yeah, yeah," Blake said, "It takes one to know one."

The crocodile slapped its tail in the water then it bared rows of sharp teeth. Ruis fast-pitched a clump of mud into the crocodile's mouth. Its jaws snapped shut with alarming speed and force then it backed into the deeper water.

"Is a group of crocodiles called a nest?" Blake asked.

All three watched the croc ease downstream and sink out of sight. Vincent breathed easier.

Ruis holstered his handgun. "I believe it's a bask of crocodiles. Or maybe a float."

Shouldering his rifle, Vincent stared open-mouthed at Ruis and Blake. Their discussion had become absurdly academic. Ruis arranged sticks for a fire.

"I wouldn't mind bringing back a souvenir claw or skull." Blake removed his bayonet and tucked it back into his backpack. "Then again, those boys in U.S. Customs are not very sporting."

Vincent suspected Blake was speaking from experience.

The men dined on MREs, the instant meal-ready-to-eat substitute Ruis brought. The MREs tasted slightly better than their packaging. Vincent ate facing the river. If there was one crocodile, there were more unseen, lurking in the murky river. Blake kept a lookout. High in the canopy across the river, a loud guttural call sounded.

"What is that?" Vincent said squinting in the direction of the sound. It sounded like a large animal.

"That," Blake declared, "is a howler monkey."

Ruis and Vincent traded a glance.

"I watched a lot of National Geographic specials." Blake sat on a fallen log and placed his rifle across his lap. "Got the magazine, too. Here in the scenic Amazon you got your poison dart frog," he said, opening his left thumb from his fist, "you got leeches," he counted on his pointer finger, "you got tarantulas," he raised his middle finger, "you got goliath bird-eating spiders," he raised his ring finger, "you got Colombian giant spiders," he counted on his pinky. Switching to his right hand, he said, "and electric eels, piranhas, vampire bats, Caiman crocodiles, and anacondas," and having run out of fingers, he opened both hands. He stared at his hands as if trying to remember something.

"So you're saying we're not at the top of the food chain here?" Vincent said.

Blake dropped a hand to his rifle. "I'd say we're in the middle." His expression brightened, the way it did when he finished solving a puzzle. "I think *jaguars* are at the top."

"Looks like a leopard?" Vincent might have seen one at the Central Park Zoo.

"Kind of. Leopards aren't in South America," Blake said. "Jaguars are bigger. They can grow up to your weight class."

Vincent struggled to imagine a predatory cat that large.

"They kill with one leap." Blake gestured with both fingers splayed like claws.

Grateful for his rifle, Vincent stared at the river in the fading light. This reminded him of camping trips in the Adirondacks with his family when they told scary stories by the fire. Ghosts, zombies, and the unknown creature under the bed featured largely in his father's stories.

"I'm more concerned about mosquitos," Ruis said.

Vincent and Blake stared at him. Mosquitos?

"You are a strange man," Blake said.

"They spread Yellow fever, Hemorrhagic Dengue Fever, parasites, equine encephalitis, and other you-don't-want-to-get diseases," Ruis said. "I'd rather die from a jaguar attack than Hemorrhagic Dengue Fever."

"Bigger bragging rights for your obituary," Blake said.

"Exactly," Ruis told Vincent.

"And here I was," Vincent said, "watching out for poachers, drug runners, and savage natives."

Having heard so many dangers in the jungle, Vincent sobered at the unspoken truth that a fourteen-year-old girl could be wandering alone through it. The most likely outcome, the one they avoided discussing, was that she was already beyond the reach of earthly dangers.

He looked up at the small clearing over the river. Blood red and orange streaks reflected the dying sunlight. With the new moon, the night was going to be pitch dark. The cacophony of bird calls faded to creepy silence. The sudden quiet set the men on alert. With one hand on his rifle, they listened. Time slowed in the darkness. Logs crackled in the fire, spitting sparks. A single frog started the night chorus. Moments later more croaks sounded off from low in the trees.

Vincent drew the short twig for the first watch. He climbed up roots and branches to a strong perch on a thick tree limb ten feet above the ground.

Blake lifted the mosquito netting tented over his hammock and climbed into the hammock facing the jungle. He set his rifle diagonally across his torso so that the barrel angled away from his thigh and the rifle butt rested on his chest. He pulled the netting over himself from boots to scalp.

"What does *Cruzeiro do Sul* mean in English?" Blake said.

"The city is named after a constellation." Ruis climbed into the other hammock. "We call it the Southern Cross."

"I take that as a good sign." Blake nodded in the dark. "I'm gonna sleep like a baby 'cause I know there's no way a New Yorker will nod off to the sounds of the great outdoors."

"Thanks, buddy." Vincent noticed Blake and Ruis kept their boots on. Was this a cowboy thing, like dying with your boots on? He thought fungus would be a problem in this sweaty, damp environment. "Why are you guys keeping your boots on?"

Ruis and Blake answered in unison, "Tarantulas."

"Oh, great. Yeah, we're having fun now."

A buzzing summoned Ruis from his hammock. He wadded mosquito netting on his way to his backpack. Digging into his pack, he lifted out the bag containing his satellite phone. After a few exchanges, he ended the call with *gracias,* but he didn't sound at all thankful. He secured the device back into its waterproof bag and jammed the bag in his backpack.

"IBAMA officers at the girl's village found two more bodies. Shot." Ruis grabbed a corner of the mosquito netting. Dragging it to his hammock, he half-heartedly tossed it over the line strung over his hammock.

"The girl?" Vincent said.

"Two men. But they also found a severed hand."

Vincent quietly mourned. Why bring a child into such a dangerous, remote place? For all the many natural dangers in the jungle, humans remained the most ruthless predators. He hoped against the odds that the hand did not belong to Nefi Jenkins.

. 3 .

The next day, on August 9th, Vincent, Ruis and Blake did not speak for the duration of the damp, noisy, cramped seaplane ride. They couldn't have heard each other over the engine noise anyway because the pilot wore the only working headphones. Vincent's thoughts became somber. He dreaded the probable news that the girl was dead. Really, what chance did a teenage girl have against armed men? It took five days for the IBAMA officers from the north to reach the village after the murders were reported. *That poor kid.*

The jungle grew thicker as they neared the nameless village. Vincent hunched in the back seat, trying not to crowd Ruis amid packs of gear. Blake had begged to ride shotgun, pleading that he hated to fly and might need window access to puke if they survived the trip. Riding in the co-pilot's seat, Blake had an unobstructed view of the terrain ahead while Vincent had only glimpses of the river through the thick jungle.

As the ride grew bumpier, Vincent sympathized with Blake's fear of flying. Vincent had been nervous about flying, but his fear kicked in when the pilot asked for everyone's weight. The man muttered something about being over gross before they climbed in. It didn't sound like a good thing. Maybe the engine was over taxed, maybe the weight of the extra gear and supplies Ruis had ordered caused the plane to strain as one pontoon, then the other pontoon lifted off the water. But here they were airborne in a claustrophobically small plane. Even slouched over, Vincent whacked his head on the headliner with every bump of turbulence.

An emergency landing out here, he decided, would be a two-stage crash. If they crashed over land, they'd hit first into the tree canopy and second they'd fall from the canopy to the ground as the branches broke. It could, he reasoned, also be a two-stage crash over water, or maybe three stages if they hit trees before the water. If they crashed into the water, first the plane would slam and flip, then sink, drowning them as they scrambled to climb out. Cramped as they were, they wouldn't stand a chance.

The wood frame and cloth-covered wings completed the impression of flying in a glorified kite. Factor in combustible fuel inside flammable wings and the whole contraption seemed an accident in the making. *How long would it take to find our bodies?*

Water glinted through an opening in the trees. The plane spiraled down and entered the narrow gap in the tree canopy. Vincent inhaled sharply and held his breath. One duct-tape covered wingtip snapped off small tree branches overhanging the river. The pontoons skipped and settled on the water before the plane taxied toward the pale gray riverbank. The engine stopped, leaving the plane to glide toward shore sideways, drifting in slow motion.

Vincent exhaled.

"Amen. Looks like we cheated death again," Blake announced. He glanced at the pilot and added, "No offense."

"None taken." The pilot tapped a gold medal dangling from a chain strung around the compass on the windshield.

Vincent recognized the medal of Saint Christopher, the patron saint of travelers. Being a pilot here must regularly push the limits of faith.

Blake said, "Just so you know, I pray directly to his boss."

"You must be an American."

Blake climbed down to the pontoon, rocking the whole plane

as his weight shifted, then rocking again as he hopped to the riverbank. The pilot climbed out, followed by Ruis. Vincent handed backpacks and gear to Ruis. Ruis passed them along to the pilot, who piled them on shore. Blake stood facing the embankment. Why wasn't he helping? Was he puking?

Vincent squeezed his shoulders through the doorway and climbed down onto the pontoon. Shouldering past a metal strut between the wing and the body of the plane, he stepped off the pontoon onto the hard-packed mud. "You okay, Blake?"

Blake twisted his head and shoulders around. "The *village* is a bit...underwhelming."

Twelve wooden huts on stilts lined the top of a small ridge fifty yards from the river. Just below the ridge sat two metal canoes and a motorboat. Weathered gray palm fronds, lashed in rows, served as roofing. Beyond this line of huts, an open area of bare dirt separated another scattering of huts nestled on the edge of the tree line.

A vile smoky smell assaulted him. He covered his nose and mouth with his hand.

"Whoa." Blake pinched his nose. "Are they roasting something with the fur still on?"

Vincent and Ruis hauled the gear uphill toward Blake. Ruis looked uphill at the village. He was frowning when he handed them their rifles. What was Ruis upset about? The men then shouldered their overstuffed backpacks and their rifles and ascended the riverbank toward the huts.

"No one came down to greet us." Ruis's observation alerted Vincent that this was unusual. Ruis wasn't the type to talk to himself.

The pilot spoke to Ruis, "I've got another pickup so I can be back tomorrow if you need me."

"Thank you," Ruis said. "I'll call if we need a ride."

Vincent watched the pilot climb back into the plane. He sent a silent prayer for the man's safety.

They wandered up to the center of the village and piled their gear in the clearing. Ruis made a show of opening the map he'd used with IBAMA Officers Raposo and Machado. The only villager visible was an elderly woman stirring a pot over an open fire. Were the others hiding? Had the village been abandoned? Perhaps the others died from the old woman's cooking. What a stench.

"Keep your rifles on your shoulders and look bored," Ruis said softly.

Vincent sat beside his backpack with his back to Blake, letting the sun warm his face. Looking bored and feeling alert, the men had nothing to do but wait for information from Ruis. The seaplane revved up and taxied against the current until it disappeared into shadows. Minutes later, it roared back, taking off through the narrow gap in the trees. In the plane's wake, twigs and leaves showered the river.

Portuguese/English Dictionary in hand, it took Ruis an hour to win the trust of the elderly woman by the fire. She stirred while Ruis talked, upwind of the fire, wiping his eyes. While Ruis coaxed information from the old woman, a boy cautiously circled Vincent and Blake. Barefoot, clad in a red loincloth tied with a leather string at his waist, the boy approached Blake.

"I got a boy at my twelve o'clock," Blake muttered. "Looks like his momma cuts his hair in the shape of a bowl."

"How old would you say he is?"

"At home, I'd estimate three. They grow 'em kinda short here, so it's a tough call. He could be six."

"Need backup?" Vincent rose to his knees to search through his backpack pocket by pocket. After finding a roll of hard candies, he tossed it to the boy who caught it and raced away.

The old woman left Ruis. Yelling, she headed toward Vincent. Ruis kept pace alongside her. The boy showed the candy to the woman, who promptly took it from him and thumped him on the head with her fingers. The woman nudged the boy aside and waved the candy in front of Vincent. Ruis plucked the candy from her grip. He then unwrapped the candy and put one piece in his mouth. The woman watched Ruis intently. She tugged at his chin. He opened his mouth to show the partly melted candy greening his tongue. He then crunched the candy and swallowed it. The woman then nodded, took the candy roll from Ruis. She pressed it into the boy's hand. He dashed away with it.

She then leaned close to Blake's face, squinting at him. Suddenly she jerked away from him, pointed at Blake, and laughed revealing a collection of crooked teeth. She held her hand, fingers up, over her head. Blake glanced at Ruis as if for an explanation of the old woman's mocking.

Ruis tried to suppress a laugh which caused a sound like an odd cough. Vincent chuckled just because the woman was so entertained by Blake. But what set her off?

"All right," Blake drawled, "I'll play. Five words. The first word sounds like crazy."

"She has never seen hair like yours before," Ruis said.

"Vincent has the same cut."

"I wear it better," Vincent said.

"Redheads and blondes," Ruis said, "are rare."

Blake rubbed his copper-colored bristle cut, causing the woman to laugh harder. She reached over and rubbed his scalp. After glancing down at Blake's lap, she said something to Ruis between guffaws.

"Please," Blake said, "don't translate that."

Vincent laughed. He had heard women ask Blake very rude personal questions before about whether or not he had red hair everywhere.

Laughter attracted other villagers from their hiding places. While Ruis conversed with the villagers, children converged on Blake to touch his head. Blake handed his rifle to Vincent, who stood off to the side to watch the crowd. Women and children found Blake irresistible. Vincent had handed out candy, yet the children still flocked to Blake. Ah, well. It was fun to watch him interact with them. Maybe they liked Blake because he gave off a playful vibe.

A toddler climbed up on Blake's thigh and stuck a finger in his ear. At this point, Blake swept his arm around the toddler's waist and stood, causing the children to back up, squeal and hop in place. Vincent could not decide whether it was Blake's height or the fact that he picked up the child that caused such amusement.

"What's the news, Ruis?" Blake asked, casually holding the toddler sideways under his arm like he did it every day.

By size, Vincent estimated the boy was four years old. The giggling child waved his arms and legs in a mock struggle.

"The two bodies were adult males wearing clothes just like the men who killed the Jenkins," Ruis said.

Vincent stepped closer to hear Ruis. His presence caused the toddler to stop moving. Blake bent down, setting the toddler's feet on the ground. The child looked up and up and up at Vincent until he lost his balance and fell against Ruis's legs.

"The hand doesn't belong to the corpses," Ruis said, absently placing a hand on the boy's shoulders, nudging him to stand.

Vincent's heart sank. Killing was one thing, but mutilation... Were other body parts out there?

The boy playfully tapped the inside of Blake's knees and then he tried to pry them apart. Grunting, the boy wedged his shoulder between Blake's knees and squirmed between the legs to emerge behind Blake. This entertained the other children, who responded with shouting and more hopping in place. Vincent remembered when his little brother was a toddler. He, too, was a climber.

The old woman clapped her hands, causing the children to scatter. Vincent noted he had not seen another teenager in the village. Did Nefi Jenkins have friends here? The old woman led Ruis to a hut and after a few minutes, she and Ruis returned.

"That hut," Ruis said, "belonged to the Jenkins. This woman Mali lives in it now. It has rustic furniture and a knee-high stack of Bibles in Portuguese."

"Were they missionaries?" Blake asked.

That would explain why they'd be here. This place pretty much met Vincent's definition of the ends of the earth, where the apostles were told to bring the Word of God. His sense of duty to find the girl grew stronger.

Ruis shrugged. "Mali showed me bloody footprints on the wood floor that lead to the back window. She says they're Nefi's."

Vincent and Blake traded a knowing glance. Something caused Nefi to flee or sneak out away from the line of sight of the other villagers. A severed hand. Bloody footprints. Whatever happened here had been brutal. That accounted for the initially cautious behavior of the villagers.

"Why wouldn't the girl come back after the danger passed?" Vincent asked.

Ruis scowled. "Maybe she couldn't."

Blake's voice wavered when he asked, "Did Mali get a look at the hand?"

The old woman tugged on Ruis's khaki shirtsleeve then she pointed to Vincent's neck. Ruis asked Vincent to show the woman the leather and stone necklace that Senator Jenkins had given him. The Senator had said that Nefi would recognize it. Vincent knelt, putting him almost eye-level with Mali. She touched the necklace and then she placed her calloused hands on Vincent's face. Ruis and the woman conversed for a few minutes. Ruis consulted his dictionary. The names Jenkins and Nefi popped up in the conversation. Mali looked wistfully at the choker.

"Mali said three guerillas came and left," Ruis said. "The hand had short wide fingers, nothing like Nefi's. She said it looked like the killing hand of the ugly Pirarucu Man."

"What's the Peer-a-roo-ku Man?" Blake asked.

Ruis consulted his dictionary. "*Pirarucu* is a fish. Maybe he was a fish seller?"

"So Nefi Jenkins' parents were murdered by a man named after a fish," Vincent said, "and he left behind his own hand?"

Blake whispered as if the Indians might understand English, "So are we thinking maybe the locals exacted a little jungle justice?" He looked at Vincent.

"I got nothing," Vincent said. "That makes more sense than the bad guys fighting each other to the death."

"In either case, why wouldn't the girl come back here?" Blake asked. "I'd think one of the boats belonged to her family."

"The motorboat," Ruis said.

It would have taken every man in the village to pull that boat to the water. Maybe it didn't run. She was a teenage girl, after all, so asking for logical behavior might be too much to expect. Vincent hoped Nefi wasn't in shock wandering the jungle.

Ruis announced it was time to go. He led them to the back of the Jenkins' hut where they discovered a footpath to the river that ran northeasterly along the riverbank.

After two weeks of hiking alone and foraging for fruit, Nefi heard the outsiders from a mile away by the rhythmic *crunch* of their boots and *whack* of a machete. Three of them at least. She climbed a sturdy strangler fig to the uppermost branches to watch for them.

If they were IBAMA, she could ask for help. If not, she would hide.

As she peered down, the first one passed beneath her, slashing at underbrush like he was angry at it. He had reddish hair, thick arms, and broad shoulders. The second one had dark hair and moved more like a native. They wore camouflage pants, dark t-shirts, rifles, and soldier's boots, but they were not IBAMA. Then she saw the third.

Oh, the third.

The moment *he* appeared tromping shirtless through the

underbrush took her breath away. He was far too tall and pale to be an Indian and he dressed like a soldier. He stopped as if he had sensed her watching. He even twisted to face the tree where she hid high in the shadows of the tree trunk. She feared he heard her heart banging like a trapped bird against her ribs. Tingling spread through her insides. Breathing through her nose, she stilled herself.

The third man raised his powerful arms, baring his muscled chest and belly that glistened in a shaft of sunlight. Was he basking in a shaft of sunlight? After a few heart-racing moments, he lowered his arms and walked away. She stared at his broad shoulders until the jungle settled back in place.

When her brain functioned again, her first thought was that he was magnificent; her second, that he had to be dangerous.

The seventeenth of August marked a week and a day since they last saw any other humans, the day they left the village to search along the murky, shallow Juruá River. Vincent was taking his turn at the end of the line behind Ruis while Blake merrily chopped a path. Vincent would have been encouraged by any evidence of the girl, even a footprint in the mud, but the intermittent misting rain could have erased shallow indentations.

At mid-day, he sensed a presence watching him. There had been no snapping of twigs, or sudden quieting of animals to alert him, but he froze at the sensation. Thanks to Blake, he was tense about getting jumped by a jaguar. Up ahead, Ruis reminded Blake to cut down and outward. His voice faded while Vincent paused on the path. His neck tingled.

The sensation of being watched grew stronger, like breath on the back of his neck. Was it a jaguar or howler monkey? Indians? Guerillas? Poachers? He became acutely aware of his bare chest.

Earlier in the heat of the day, he had pulled his arms out of his green t-shirt and left the shirt hanging around his neck. Maybe there was an Indian spying on him. He hoped his size and height would intimidate whoever was watching. If Indians wanted to attack, they would, but perhaps they were merely curious about strangers cutting through their hunting grounds.

He held out his arms in what he hoped would be interpreted as a gesture of peace. A warm wave of sensations passed through him. Though too fleeting and conflicting to identify, the sensations left a lingering feeling of...nakedness. Gooseflesh rose on his bare chest and arms despite the sweltering humidity. After a moment, he dropped his arms and followed the trail of hacked greenery to Ruis and Blake.

. 4 .

Damiano Guerra awakened to rocking motion. Pain shot through his head. He was in a small dark room with little to see except the outline of a door, lit from outside. What was this place? Was he a prisoner? The door opened, revealing a man in silhouette who set a battery-operated lantern on a shelf just inside the door.

The stranger spoke in Portuguese. "You are still alive."

"Where am I?" Damiano rasped. His heart banged faster while his limbs ached.

"We're docked at Macapa."

At the mouth of the Amazon River? Why did this man help? His dry throat ached, so he chose his words carefully. "Whose boat is this?"

"That depends on who you ask." The man stepped into the room enough for the lantern to illuminate his face. He had weather-beaten skin with a scraggly gray and black beard and thick black hair.

Damiano tried to push himself into a sitting position, but pain shot up his right arm. Looking down at a bandage where his hand used to be, he fought the urge to vomit. His recurring nightmare

31

slammed into his consciousness as real as pain. He roared, *"My hand!"* As his nightmare reality flashed before him, he angled as far away from his hand as he could. Squeezing his eyes shut he shook against the onslaught of images.

The bearded man backed to the door. "I'll get the captain."

Soon after the bearded man left, a round, squat man swung his bulk sideways to fit through the doorway. He wore civilian clothes. "What's your name?"

"Damiano Guerra. I work for Alexander Cortes." Surely that would give the stranger fear about harming him.

"I thought I recognized that Seabee you were in. We found it adrift."

Damiano touched the bandaged stub at his wrist. The name Cortes usually worked as a strong warning.

The captain shut the door, leaving the bearded man in the corridor. "I'm supposed to ask you what happened."

"Why?" Damiano scowled at the man. *What did he want?*

"I'm a friend of Mr. Cortes."

"He doesn't have friends."

The captain laughed. "Let's just say that Mr. Cortes and I are in business together. I told him we found a man and one of his boats adrift. He wants to know which man you are and what happened."

That made sense. A tingle of pride rose at the idea that Cortes might be glad to learn his best worker was alive. "I was attacked at night in the jungle. Someone cut off my hand," Damiano said, grimacing at the blur of images of a machete and blood. *So much blood.* How many Indians were there? *The ring!* The Indian who cut off his hand was the one who stole his jeweled jaguar head gold ring. Took it right off his bloody hand. Damiano shook with fury and pounded his good hand on the bed.

"Take your time," the captain said.

Damiano remembered images from that night's chaos. The blood. Shouting and screaming. Crawling to hide behind a tree in the darkness. Tying his wrist tight with a bootlace. Giant shadows running around the fire. Finding his rifle.

"I found my rifle in the dark." He remembered picking up a rifle, slippery with his blood and trying to hold it. A dark figure suddenly appeared in front of him, so he shot it. Then another. He fired until the rifle clicked and clicked. After all movement had stopped, he crept out for a look. Did the Indians have guns? He found the bodies of his men. Fools! They should have been keeping watch. *It was their fault.*

"What happened to your men?" The captain's stare seemed to probe for the truth, so Damiano gave him a portion.

"They're dead." Damiano studied the captain's weathered face. "We were attacked by Indians." Let him tell Cortes that. Maybe Cortes didn't like his lazy cousin. That idiot was supposed to be keeping watch.

The captain nodded. "We found you at the mouth of the Juruá. The cook cleaned and dressed your wound. Looks like you were lucky to escape. The big white pills," he said, pointing to two bottles on the shelf at the head of the bed, "are antibiotics to stop the infection. Take one every day. The blue pills are for pain."

"What day is it?"

"August twentieth. You have been awake at times, but delirious."

Fifteen lost days! Had Cortes written him off for dead? Would Cortes forgive him for losing the custom-made gold ring?

"You have been in shock. We fed you soup, but I'll bet you could take something to chew on now. Stay put. Your dinner will be right up. I'm going to call Cortes now that I have a name to give him. Is there anything else you want me to tell him?"

"Tell him the foreigners are dead."

The captain left Damiano alone. His thoughts fell back on the foreigners—his first kills. He wanted to make Cortes proud.

It had not bothered him to travel three days by boat and on foot deep into the rainforest, because the most recent target of his hatred waited at the end of the journey, unarmed. He marched into the village to avenge a wrong and, backed by two men and rifles, he felt empowered. It was time to show everyone this territory of Brazil belonged to him. It was time to punish the Americans for interfering.

The Indians kept a respectful distance as he led his men into the village. He called out for the Americans. The Indians understood the superiority of guns over machetes. He didn't consider them to be fellow Brazilians any more than he thought of them as humans just because they walked upright. Did they even understand Portuguese? As far as he could tell, they grunted at each other to communicate. When the American couple stepped out of their hut, he ordered them to kneel on the dirt path between two rows of huts for all to see.

He waved away a flying bug that circled his head. Sweat trickled down his back to his waist, where his shirt and pants absorbed it. He believed his use of English elevated him above the likes of the half-naked villagers. "Do you know who I am?"

"I know what you are," said the kneeling man.

Damiano sneered. He took his rifle off his shoulder. He slid his hand into place around the trigger guard and with the other he flipped the safety switch. "Then you know why I am here."

"*Pirarucu*?" The kneeling man taunted. He held his wife's hand.

The woman whispered to herself, eyes closed, her body rocking gently in a slight bowing motion.

Damiano raised his rifle barrel. These foreigners were dumber than the Indians; they thought they were invincible. Worse still, they taught the Indians their way. *He* was the powerful one here, not their god. The villagers cried out and stepped toward the kneeling couple. He swung the barrel toward the Indians, stopping them and then he aimed the rifle down at the couple and fired two short bursts. Colors exploded from the nearby trees, followed by frantic flapping. The husband, with his last energy, flung his arm over his wife as both bodies slumped over. A sharp, high-pitched shriek rang down from the tree canopy. All pivoted east toward the eerie sound. He calculated the source as a howler monkey less than a kilometer away. A young one, by its high-pitched call. Even the wild animals feared him. He flipped the safety back on as the stench of gunpowder drifted by him. It was so easy, it was slightly disappointing.

The villagers encircled the bodies and swayed in place as they wailed.

He pivoted on his heel and casually slung his rifle strap over one shoulder. His two men followed, backing toward the trail. He wiped the blood off his large gold, jewel-encrusted jaguar head ring onto his pants. He did not want to ruin the shine of the valuable ring his boss had given him. He glanced behind from the trailhead to make sure no Indians followed.

Standing near the huddle around the bodies, an old woman pointed a crooked finger at him. She shouted in Portuguese, "*O Deus puni-lo-a.*"

Snorting at the threat of God's punishment, he had stepped back into the cool shadows.

He reasoned it wasn't God's punishment that took his hand. It was Indians. *Animals.*

On the morning of August twentieth, Vincent awoke to light rain and the rasping barks of a howler monkey. The call started off like barking and changed to a deep throaty growl. The exotic primal noise roused him from a deep sleep. Monkeys. Even at the zoo, they were smelly, vile creatures that threw excrement at people. Why on earth did these monkeys howl every time it rained? What's their deal? He considered himself in excellent health, yet the rain and oppressive humidity consumed him. His feet burned. His arms ached from using the machete. He estimated his weight loss at eight pounds, maybe ten. Ruis claimed this was winter, the dry season, so the expected rainfall was between two and six inches for the whole month. *Yeah, right.* Perhaps Ruis didn't consider the misting, dripping fog actual rainfall, but after hours of it, it drenched just as sure as a downpour. And it made the stupid monkeys howl.

Much more of this and Vincent suspected he might start howling. He opened his eyes to shades of green in all directions. It was still dark in this part of the jungle because of the thick canopy of kapok, strangler fig, Brazil nut, banyan, capirona and other trees Ruis and Blake had taken turns pointing out, as if anyone could discern where one ended and another began in the endless tangle of roots, branches, and vines. Eleven days of slogging through the thickening vegetation and mud challenged his hope of finding the Jenkins girl alive. They had hacked through animal trails northward along the Juruá River shoreline at a rate of twenty miles a day. The Juruá River zig-zagged so much that, on the map, it looked like a cartographer's joke. They had consumed most of their MREs. The remaining food was rationed. They had found no definitive sign of the girl, no proof of life. As a matter of pride, the men refused to stop until they had something to offer Senator Jenkins about the fate of his niece.

Vincent had noticed that they spoke less and less about Nefi Jenkins as a person and more and more about their strategy for finding signs of her with each passing day. Ruis argued for staying by the river. Blake occasionally called out her name. Since leaving her village, they had found only one human footprint in the mud. Such prints showed no gender differences, so it could have been left by any of the thousands of elusive Indians who inhabited the rainforest. Maybe IBAMA officer Raposo had been right to pity them for trying to find a girl in a rainforest of one *billion* acres. Vincent could not imagine a million acres let alone a billion. The vastness was like counting stars.

Vincent nursed the hope that they had not found a body. During their daily hikes, he watched for carrion eaters. He also sniffed for that distinct smell of decomposition. Each night he prayed she was alive. Each morning he struggled against a sense of futility. Longing for a solid, soft bed, he wobbled out of his hammock.

Blake stood by the fire where he boiled water for coffee. He held out a handful of something toward Ruis.

"Did you know Brazil nuts are pollinated by bats?" Ruis said, taking a few from Blake's hand.

Blake paused in his chewing to inspect the nuts more closely. "If I get rabies will ya put me down?"

Ruis nodded.

Vincent wondered if Ruis was kidding. He hoped they would never need to put Ruis's word to the test.

Blake continued chewing and swallowed. He looked around and jerked his chin up at Vincent by way of greeting.

Vincent nodded back. According to Blake's *National Geographic* studies, tarantulas sought warm, dark places to sleep, so Vincent picked up his boots by the heel and banged them together. Dirt fell out. He tugged his boots on and laced them up. Maybe there were tarantulas in the Amazon, or maybe Blake and Ruis were teasing, but it didn't hurt to take precautions. He would rather look stupid banging his boots together than be heard screaming over a boyhood fear realized.

Vincent touched the homemade cord and stone necklace Ruis had given him. It was supposed to be something Nefi would recognize. To keep it visible, he simply wore it around his neck. It comforted him to touch it, like a rosary. He remembered his dark days after losing his father. His mother kept a rosary in hand.

He headed toward Blake, who handed him a hot mug of coffee that smelled like civilization.

"Thanks." If someone hadn't made coffee, he might have chewed the grounds to get caffeine into his system.

Blake also gave him a plate of shucked Brazil nuts. The men

sat facing the glowing embers as smoke swirled gently upward like prayers. Blake's generally enthusiastic nature seemed dampened lately. He looked scruffy with his reddish beard. He told fewer jokes each day in their grim search. When would the rescue mission be openly called a recovery mission?

"What does your personal radar tell you?" Blake's green eyes gave Vincent a searching look.

Again with the intuition thing? Vincent warmed his hands on the mug. Finding the girl had dominated his thoughts and his dreams for the last three days, but he kept that to himself. He scratched his own beard and wished he had thought to carry along a razor. If he discussed his intuition with Blake and it proved to be wrong, maybe Blake would let it go. "For three days I've had the feeling we're being watched."

"From where?"

Vincent pointed up.

"God?"

Vincent shrugged. He preferred to rely on reason and evidence instead of hunches or intuition. Feelings were fickle, and his faith waned. "Or monkeys."

"Scavengers." Blake scowled. "I once read that they're full of mischief and prone to stealing. I suppose they're the Amazon equivalent of raccoons."

Blake scratched his red buzz cut and his pale beard stubble. His freckled face gave him a boyish look. Though he claimed he was known in school as the fat kid, Blake played four years of football in high school. By the time Vincent met him in boot camp, Blake was a square-built, six-foot-tall force of nature. Vincent was grateful for his company on this bleak mission.

Nearby Ruis combed his thick hair. He tucked the comb in his back pocket then he sat on his backpack across the fire from Blake. Ruis moved like an athlete. Special operations training had prepared him to handle working in darkness and shadows like this endless jungle. Surefooted as a tight-rope walker, Ruis had so far avoided tripping and falling during the long hikes over the roots and vines that choked the footpath. Whereas Blake laughed whenever Vincent stumbled over a root, Ruis did not. Perhaps Ruis's feelings were tempered by the concern that he might have to help carry a heavy klutz out of the jungle.

Fog snaked up the riverbank between the tree trunks. Though the sun was up its warmth and light did not penetrate this part of the jungle. The ground rose from the river to a low hill covered with towering trees, blocking sunlight.

"Maybe we're going about this search backward." Blake stared into his coffee cup as if it held the answer to the great mysteries of the world.

"Oh, really?" Ruis said.

"I'm just saying, how about considering another option?" Blake looked up from his coffee, the spell of it broken.

Ruis said, "I'm listening."

"How about instead of chasing around the jungle — why don't we try to attract the little PK to us?"

"I'll bite. What's a PK?" Vincent said.

"Preacher's kid," Blake announced as if to suggest that everyone knew that.

"And what," Ruis dared to ask, "would attract a preacher's kid to three unbathed, armed male strangers?"

Blake opened his mouth and shut it. He pursed his lips as if to hold back something he might regret saying.

Vincent had seen him hold back his immediate response before in conversations, mostly with superior officers. "Say it," Vincent challenged.

Blake smiled at Vincent. "I don't think your uncanny ability to attract dangerous females applies to this situation."

Ruis smirked. There was no point arguing about Blake's opinion though Vincent regretted it had spread.

"Hear me out," Blake said. "Those Howler monkeys can be heard for what? Two miles or so?"

Ruis nodded. A flicker of a grin passed over his face. He, too, kept a thought to himself.

"Can either of you carry a tune?" Blake asked.

Ruis answered, "Yes."

Vincent nodded.

"I think if the three of us can belt out even a mediocre rendition of 'Amazing Grace' she might hear it."

Vincent raised his eyebrows at Ruis. Ruis slowly nodded. The concept had merit. Anyone could call her name, but guerillas, poachers, and indigenous Indians would be unlikely to sing a hymn. The leap of faith in this theory, of course, rested on the assumption of Nefi being alive.

"We'd have to sing it in English." Blake shrugged.

"It's worth a try." Ruis stood, clearing his throat. "If nothing else, it will confuse poachers and guerillas." He raised his hand palm up at Blake.

Blake stood.

Vincent asked Ruis, "And you're standing because…?"

"Standing," Ruis said, "opens up the diaphragm, providing more room for the lungs to expand."

Oh, why not? Vincent stood. Memories from sixteen years of Catholic school and Wednesday morning mass rushed back to him. It had always lifted his spirit when the choir broke into four-part harmony as if it opened a window into heaven itself. Besides, singing couldn't do any harm.

"Back to back to the fire," Blake said, "so the sound carries out in different directions."

The men faced away from the fire.

Blake started it off in a clear, strong baritone that surprised Vincent. "Ama-a-azi-ing Graaace how swe-e-et the sound that saved a wretch like me-e-e."

Vincent and Ruis joined in. "I once was lost, but now am found; was blind but now I see." Since the intention was to sing loudly, Vincent set aside insecurities about the quality of his voice.

"Twas grace that taught my heart to fear, and grace my fears relieved; how precious did that grace appear the hour I first believed."

Their voices rose into the tree canopy's shadows. Vincent closed his eyes through the next verse. A detective had sung this song at his father's funeral. The words resonated in his heart.

"Through many dangers, toils and snares, I have already come; tis grace hath brought me safe thus far, and grace will lead me home."

Ruis broke off to harmonize in the tenor range, suggesting voice lessons in his past.

"The Lord has promised good to me, His word my hope secures; He will my shield and portion be, as long as life endures."

The back of Vincent's neck tingled. His intuition often showed up as a sensation of touch and at other times like *déjà vu*. He sensed a presence listening or watching. The sound of men singing had to be rare in the jungle. Even birds had quieted. Vincent opened his eyes. He stopped singing because he believed he had sung all the verses.

Blake continued, "Yea, when this flesh and heart shall fail, and mortal life shall cease, I shall possess, within the veil, a life of joy and peace."

Then Ruis stopped singing. Blake continued solo. Apparently, they sang *all* the verses at Blake's church. According to Blake, Baptists didn't do anything halfway. Years ago when Blake had learned that Vincent was a Catholic, he said Baptists believed that Jesus got dunked, not sprinkled to demonstrate His pledge to God. All or nothing.

"The world shall soon dissolve like snow, the sun refuse to shine; but God, who called me here below, shall be forever mine," Blake said, "I'm sure you recognize the next part." He resumed singing, "When we've been there ten thousand years, bright shining as the sun, we've no less days to sing God's praise than when we'd first begun."

Vincent looked through a gap in the tree roots at the river. A pile of leaves flowed downstream. A solemn silence fell in the camp, as quiet as hope receding. Still holding his coffee, he watched the river. Behind him, embers crumbled and crackled, warming the back of his legs. He drained the last sip of coffee and held it in his mouth. Even lukewarm it tasted comforting.

Bird calls resumed in full force. Were they calling out to their lost ones?

Blake's voice rumbled softly, "Hey Vincent, want to bet fifty bucks that our girl shows up in the next few minutes?" Blake rarely bet on anything but horses.

Vincent faced Blake, who jutted his chin toward the hill. To see what Blake saw, Vincent pivoted. A slender silhouette emerged from the trees in short hesitating steps. A tall, thin girl, she wore a satchel messenger bag style strapped across her torso from her right shoulder to her left hip. Her stained yellow top and dark blue pants hung loose and boxy on her slender frame. Her long brown hair dangled to her elbows. She stepped barefoot into the firelight. Her forehead was blood red and a broad stripe of black marked one-third of her face like the mask of Zorro. Tribal markings? A glint reflected from something in her hand. Is that a *machete?*

Ruis said, "Nefi Jenkins?"

She took two fast steps toward the fire then leaped over the fire at Vincent. Startled, he dropped his coffee cup to grab the girl's machete hand. He tripped, falling backward. As he fell, he fought training that urged him to toss her overhead. He didn't want to injure her. The girl crash-landed on top of him with her hair draped onto his neck and jaw. He had been tackled plenty of times before, but always by men. This was vastly different and alarming in many ways.

She said something in urgent gibberish. Her attention was focused on his neck. Did she want to slit his throat? He looked at the girl's machete. What if she was crazy? What if the trauma had triggered a dormant personality disorder? *What if this wasn't Nefi Jenkins?* He looked to the others for help.

Blake had his handgun pointed at the girl. Ruis snatched his *Portuguese/Spanish Dictionary* from his backpack. A dictionary? *Really?* Vincent focused his attention back on the girl and her machete.

"Easy now," Vincent said in soothing tones. "Let's not do anything permanent."

Blake said evenly, "She has another blade at your ribs."

Her left arm quivered in his grip. He glanced down to his right. She held the point of a small hunting knife against his t-shirt. After he had grabbed her other wrist, he pulled the second knife away from his ribs. An angry armed teenager, she was determined about something. Her warm breath blew on his neck. She had wild, golden-colored eyes that contrasted with the black stain on her skin. Was she crazy enough to stab him? A stab wound, even a shallow one, would be serious this far from civilization.

Vincent tried to calm Blake. "This could be Nefi."

At the sound of the name, the girl's eyebrows furrowed.

Ruis called out something in Portuguese.

The girl repeated her demand. She spoke to Blake. Vincent looked up at the bottom of Blake's pistol and the two steady hands that held it.

"What did she say?" Blake said. His voice was as steady as his hands.

Ruis spoke rapidly, "She said 'shoot me or tell me.'"

The statement cut Vincent to the core. *Huh? Did she want to die?* Outnumbered three to one, facing a gun, she demanded an answer. Any one of them could have overpowered her but, like Vincent, no one wanted to hurt her.

"Tell her what?" Blake asked.

Ruis spoke to her using the name Jenkins.

Pulling the girl's arms away from his torso, Vincent knew he had the advantage. Her arms were long; his, longer. As he demonstrated he had control of the girl, Blake stepped back and raised his pistol near his shoulder. As Blake stood down, Vincent tightened his hold on the girl's wrists.

The girl spoke again. Ruis answered.

The girl's eyes met Vincent's, the fire in them faded, and she relaxed, releasing her weapons. Her face dropped onto Vincent's chest. Surely she must have felt his racing heartbeat through his thin cotton t-shirt just as he felt the warmth of her face and her tears on his chest.

"I take it back," Blake said, coming up alongside Vincent, "You belong in the *Guinness Book of World Records*." He holstered his gun. "She's probably the only armed female in five hundred miles. You *are* a crazy magnet."

Vincent reached around his attacker, gently draping his arms on her back with one hand on her waist and the other hand between her shaking shoulder blades. "You're safe now."

"Are you okay, Vincent?" Blake's hands shook.

Vincent nodded. Blake collected the girl's weapons and placed them on the far side of the campfire.

Nefi breathed raggedly. She drew her arms in like wings. Ruis knelt beside her and spoke to her in a calming, slow, soft voice. He pulled her up and off Vincent and set her by the fire. She dropped in a heap, tucked over her legs. Vincent sat up. Ruis patted the girl's back. Fleeting expressions passed across Ruis's face. His eyebrows bunched. He rubbed his hand down her back. He spoke to her, his inflection rising at the end.

Nefi pulled up the back of her loose yellow cotton shirt. A dozen quarter-size leeches spotted her pale skin. She wiped her eyes with the back of her hands, smudging black war paint down her cheeks. Whimpering, she then crawled on hands and knees to the fire where she drew up her navy blue pant leg, exposing more leeches. She picked up a stick that she lit in the embers of the fire.

Pulling the stick to her face, she blew out the tiny flame. She pressed the red stick end on a leech, causing it to twitch and fall off. She used another small stick to flick the leech into the fire where it sizzled and emitted a stench like burning hair. She repeated this procedure, burning the leeches one by one from her legs, her stomach, and her sides. Though tears dripped into her lap, she had stopped whimpering.

Blake stoked the fire with more branches. Ruis asked Nefi questions. She answered him briefly in a soft voice. When she hiked up the back of her shirt again, Vincent knelt beside her and took the smoking stick from her hand. Imitating her procedure, he removed the leeches from her back. Nefi's passiveness was more disturbing than her rage. Her slouching posture, her resigned expression, and her soft voice all suggested soul-weary exhaustion. After he had finished, she eased around to stare at his neck.

Ruis dug into his backpack. Drawing out a waterproof bag, he fished around in it. After a brief search, he found a tube of ointment and an antiseptic wipe that he handed to Vincent. Ruis talked with Nefi while Vincent cleaned his hands. He tossed the used wipe into the fire. It sizzled and emitted the acrid alcohol smell mixed with smoke. Vincent then gently dabbed ointment on each bite mark on Nefi's bare back. Nefi's eyes watered though she neither cried nor flinched. Between her grief and simple fatigue, it was a marvel she could function. Vincent was amazed.

Meanwhile, Blake prepared food.

After all the leech bites on her back were dotted with ointment, Vincent pointed to Nefi's legs. She drew up her loose cotton pants to her thighs. Her bare feet had muddy black soles and toenails with jagged edges. Vincent dabbed each red spot on her legs with white goo from the tube. After placing the ointment on the bites, he paused, trying to decide if he should hand her the ointment for the leech marks on her stomach and ribs. He was about to ask Ruis to talk to her when Nefi raised her shirt on her own.

Nefi pulled her shirt up enough to expose her leech bites, but not her chest. Vincent quickly dabbed ointment on the bites on her belly and sides. Nefi let her shirt hem fall. By the stains of her clothes, Vincent suspected she was wearing what she had on the day her parents were killed weeks ago. Either she didn't smell of sweat or her smell was overpowered by his own.

"Why did she attack me?" Vincent recapped the ointment tube and handed it to Ruis.

"The last time she saw the necklace was on her father's body." Ruis tucked the ointment into the waterproof bag.

"Oh, man," Vincent said. He removed the cord and stone choker from his neck and handed it to Nefi. "Did she think *we* killed him?"

Nefi examined the choker, tenderly touching the thin leather laces. She put it on her neck then she bowed her head and hugged her knees. Her hair fell like a curtain around her.

"I explained her uncle gave it to us," Ruis added, "She said she didn't know she had an uncle. The only relatives she knows about are her mother's parents. She was going to Manaus to call them."

"She was going to walk two-hundred miles?" Vincent could not imagine taking such a journey in this terrain alone.

Ruis nodded.

"How was she going to cross the rivers?" Blake asked.

Ruis conferred with Nefi for a moment, before answering. "She was going to walk until she saw a boat."

Vincent backed away from Nefi to sit on a fallen tree. Blake held a steaming plate of hash and a fork in front of Nefi. He cleared his throat, causing her to look up. Her eyes watered again. She spoke to Ruis. He answered.

"*Gracias,*" she said to Blake. She took the plate and set the fork on the plate and the plate on her lap. She inhaled steam with her eyes closed. A moment later she bowed her head and clutched her hands together under her chin. Her lips moved silently. She opened her eyes and picked up the fork.

Blake looked away, blinking repeatedly. He went through the motions of cleaning up. Vincent felt a tightening in his throat and his chest. The starving girl had paused to pray.

Ruis had a stricken expression. He absently rubbed his left shirt pocket over his heart. "She's the same age as my sister Martina. She starts high school this year." He watched her eat. As if he suddenly remembered something, he hefted his backpack onto a thick tree root. After rummaging around in the backpack, he lifted out a clean shirt and a pair of pants.

Vincent gazed back at Nefi. She finished eating and sat in a daze with the empty plate and fork on her lap. Her head drooped slowly forward. Her eyelids flickered open and shut and open again. Vincent remembered watching his younger brother Oscar nod off at the table when he was a toddler. That had been entertaining. Watching Nefi nod off nearly broke his heart.

Blake eased the plate from her lap, accidentally rousing her.

Ruis held out his hand to her and spoke. He helped her stand then he handed her clean clothes. Wearily, Nefi headed toward the hillside and disappeared out of view with the clothes.

"I'll take the first watch," Vincent said. "I'll take every watch when she's sleeping." For an exhausted teenager, she was deadly fast on her feet. He wasn't sure she was mentally stable.

Nefi strode back into camp wearing the clothes Ruis had given her, carrying her clothes bundled under one arm, and bearing her satchel over her shoulder. She handed her clothes to Ruis. She was almost as tall as Ruis; Vincent estimated five feet eight. Ruis set the bundle on the ground near his backpack. He then pulled his sleek satellite cell phone from his backpack.

Nefi and Ruis exchanged a few more words. Ruis pointed to two hammocks strung up on trees. Nefi sniffed them like a dog, then said something to Ruis, who pointed to Vincent and Blake.

After shaking her head, she chose Vincent's hammock and climbed in. Ruis pulled the mosquito netting over her. Within minutes, she was asleep.

Nefi settled into the hammock that smelled like the beautiful one. If they spoke the truth, the men would take her to America. Whether or not the uncle existed, she knew she could dial the numbers to reach her grandparents in America. They still loved her and wanted her. They would take her in. They wouldn't send her away as the villagers had. Though her heart stung, she was too tired to cry.

She needed sleep as much as she dreaded it. When the nightmares came this time, the hammock should save her from falling. Her body relaxed with the sway of the hammock as the comforting smell of smoke lulled her to sleep.

As she fell asleep, she dreamed of falling.

Screaming, she dropped four feet from her perch in the towering strangler fig tree's canopy onto a wide branch below, striking hard enough to cut off her breath. Clinging to the branch, she watched her father's binoculars fall out of sight. Why did the Pirarucu Man kill mama and papa? The question cut like shards of glass.

She awoke to a hand patting her shoulder. Ruis spoke to her in soft, soothing tones.

Still weary, she wanted to ask Ruis a question she felt was urgent. Her eyes wanted to sleep. Her body was so tired, she feared she might be dying. Her words tumbled from her brain to her mouth. If she died tonight, she would refuse to enter heaven until she knew this one thing. She asked Ruis if Vincent was an angel, a mortal, or a demon.

Ruis's eyebrows arched so high they wrinkled his forehead. His mouth opened, shut and opened again. He asked why she asked. His emotions were easy to read. He was amused and shocked at her.

Nonetheless, she wanted her answer. She deserved an answer. Did he hesitate because the answer was hurtful? *"Demonio,"* she guessed, deeply disappointed. Father warned that temptations tend to look beautiful or easy and almost always appear to satisfy a selfish want. Vincent was such an intensely beautiful *man*. In his presence, Nefi felt alive and full of want.

"Americano," Ruis said. He glanced at Vincent for a moment as though checking whether or not Vincent could hear their conversation.

She argued that many people called America, the land to the north, *heaven*, and since she was finally going there, she must be dying. America was a dream her parents promised she would see one day.

Ruis explained that America was a country north of Brazil, north of Venezuela, north of Guyana, north of the island of Cuba. He reminded her that America was on the world map. Ruis's words matched his thoughts and his manner.

Nefi asked that if Vincent was mortal then why did his presence feel so...strange?

Ruis's expression changed from amused to serious. His voice edged with discomfort, he asked her to describe how she felt.

Suddenly self-conscious that Vincent might hear her, she switched to Portuguese, whispering that Vincent caused her to be calm and excited, hot and cold at the same time.

Ruis relaxed slightly. He asked if she felt this way with him or with Blake.

She shook her head.

She knew Ruis could translate her words for the others, but Vincent had sensed her presence in the jungle when he could not have heard her, seen her or smelled her from her vantage point thirty feet above him. Yet, at the very moment she thought of him, he had stopped still. He even turned toward the tree where she hid. The sight of him warmed her blood, stirring new sensations in her chest and belly. He had a cloth around his neck. His muscular chest and arms looked slick with sweat. She held her breath and blanked her thoughts to whiteness. Clearly, he had the gift like she did. He raised his powerful arms as if offering himself before walking away. She had pressed her back to the tree and closed her eyes to sear his image in her memory.

Ruis explained in whispered Spanish that Vincent was mortal, just like everyone else.

Nefi insisted Vincent was different. She yawned.

Ruis placed his left hand over hers and patted it. In Spanish, he told her, "You feel different about him. That's all. It's natural, little sister, to have these feelings. Be careful to keep them to yourself or some men will trick you or lie to you."

"I can tell when someone lies," she said in Spanish. She knew when a person's words and thoughts disagreed. Liars revealed themselves in a thousand tiny, fleeting expressions if one watched for them.

"You think so." He slid his hand to her wrist. He squeezed it for emphasis to mark his words. "Remember this—when someone tells you a lie you want to believe—it is still a lie."

She nodded, sealing the promise to remember his advice.

Nefi closed her eyes. She wanted to believe she had an uncle. But her father and mother never spoke of him. Was this a lie? There were other things that she desperately wanted to believe were true. She wanted to believe her mother's parents would welcome her to live with them. She wanted to believe that tall, beautiful, magnificent Vincent might love her. She wanted to believe someone still loved her.

Yes, love is as real as death. I will find it.

She surrendered to a great peacefulness.

Vincent, Ruis, and Blake gathered on the far side of the fire, near enough to keep an eye on her, but far enough away to talk without disturbing her.

"She didn't like the hammocks?" Vincent asked.

Ruis said, "She said they are jaguar height, so I told her we take turns keeping watch."

Vincent doubted height would matter much. Surely the big cats could climb. He hoped the hammock was too unstable to support the weight of the big cat.

"Why didn't she go back to her village?" Blake asked.

"I asked her that. She said, 'Why return?'"

"Poor kid." Blake, still holding the plate and fork, looked down as if to see what was in his hands.

Ruis turned his satellite phone over and over in his hands.

"Do you think the villagers killed the guerillas?" Vincent asked.

"That would explain their unwillingness to talk to us," Ruis said.

"How did she get leeches?" Vincent leaned toward Ruis. Just thinking about leeches made him itch.

"From bathing in the river," Ruis spoke softly. "She told me she spotted us three days ago."

"Three days ago, you say?" It was Blake's way of reminding Vincent of their earlier conversation.

Vincent groaned. Okay, so he had felt the sensation of being watched three days ago. No doubt Blake considered this iron-clad proof of intuition. First the Osprey incident and then this. Blake will be insufferable about it. So if Nefi was watching them for three days, he continued his thought aloud, "Why did she wait so long to make contact?"

"I suppose because guerillas carry rifles and wear camouflage." Ruis deadpanned.

Vincent looked down at his camouflage pants. To Blake, he said, "Perhaps it was your intuition that paid off this time since you came up with the idea of singing a hymn." *A brilliant idea for a redneck.* Vincent mentally flinched. Blake was right. People do underestimate him because of his southern accent. Chagrined, Vincent realized he was one of those people.

"Looks like we're staying." Ruis poked numbers on his satellite phone. "It's time to notify the Senator and IBAMA she's alive."

Blake scowled. "Why'd she risk going in the river?"

Looking at the fire, Ruis said softly, "She said she had to wash off blood." He carried his cell phone toward the river.

Ruis's statement stopped the conversation dead in its tracks. Vincent and Blake simultaneously leaned back as if to distance themselves from unsavory questions. Whose blood? Her parents? Her own? The poor teenager had been out in the jungle for weeks. In this environment, the smell of blood would attract predators, so she risked encountering other predators in the river to clean up. Or had she washed up to be presentable to strangers who could have been killers? That required a special courage or pride. Or perhaps she made the decision to enter the camp because she was too weak to continue on her own. Vincent found hope in the fact that she attacked him. She still had some fight left in her. Though traumatized and possibly unstable, she was alive after traveling for weeks alone in the jungle.

Vincent nodded at the sleeping girl. "When I grow up I want to be as tough as this girl."

. 5 .

The next morning Vincent paused during his watch to check on Nefi. She had slept twenty-four hours. The fire died to embers, but it illuminated her enough to allow him to see her sleeping in his hammock. In this, the quietest part of the day in the jungle, night predators had gone off to digest their kill, and it was too early for monkeys and birds to announce the dawn with their usual racket. He missed the honks and hum of traffic and the endless construction of the city. The silence felt so unnatural to him it kept him alert.

The plan for the day was to travel north along the shoreline of the Juruá River to the Solimoes, the western part of the great Amazon River. Ruis had confirmed by phone that the U.S. Consulate in Manaus expected Nefi and would have a Brazilian passport waiting for her. She had one issued when she was ten. A copy of her U.S. birth certificate would also be waiting there.

Nefi whined in her sleep again. Ruis had comforted her last time, but he was asleep. Her face contorted while her feet moved, causing the hammock to sway. She might have been running in her nightmare, so Vincent approached to comfort her. He couldn't speak Portuguese or even much Spanish, but he expected a soothing tone of voice would transcend the language gap.

"It's all right, Nefi. You're safe now."

Her eyes fluttered open. The firelight caught her golden irises.

She looked up at him, causing him to feel flushed and light on his feet then she closed her eyes. The moment sparked something deep and dormant in his heart. Such trust and innocence, after all she had been through, stirred in him a fierce protectiveness.

He marveled at her resilience. How would he have fared at her age alone in the jungle? This double tragedy forced her to grow up too quickly just as it had forced him, at age sixteen, to take on adult responsibilities after his father was killed. Knowing his mother could not afford to send him to college, he had signed up for the Marines at seventeen to take advantage of the G.I. Bill. This freed up savings for his younger brother's education. Oscar excelled in school so he deserved to go to college; good looks would not be enough to carry Oscar though life. His mother had called it a noble decision. Vincent considered it practical. He also believed his father would have been proud to have a son serve in the Marines.

The service had been good for him. It reinforced his father's principles of character. It also forced him out of his own emotional bubble while giving him the skills to challenge himself. In his years of service, he had witnessed dozens of brave acts. He witnessed men running into the line of fire to rescue fallen friends. He saw injured men struggle to walk so their rescuers would be less exposed to gunfire.

This fourteen-year-old girl survived an attack from armed men, witnessed her parents' murder, and fled alone and unprepared into the Amazon. That was memorable, too. This girl survived the most ferocious predators of all—armed humans. In Vincent's estimation, she deserved to live a rich, full life after being robbed of both parents. He breathed in the moment to lock it in his memory. He was proud to help her, this resilient PK, in any way he could, whatever it took.

He circled the campsite, past Blake and Ruis in their hammocks, past the pile of gear, past the line where Nefi's clothes hung to dry, and back to the clearing by the river. The Juruá River ran slow, murky, and wide. Trees poked up through the water like small islands, making it difficult to delineate the river's boundaries. Their campsite sat on the high ground at the base of a low ridge, placed high enough to challenge crocodiles, and on a ridge so rain would drain.

A rustling brought Vincent back to the campsite. Nefi shook out mosquito netting from the hammock. She folded it into a neat shoebox size rectangle and looked around. She spotted Vincent. At a glance, she looked like a native in facial war paint, but the quick smile she flashed on her way toward him transformed her into a teenager. She stopped in front of him. Her hair tumbled over her shoulders as if in protest of the sudden stop. She held up the folded mosquito netting.

"*Gracias,*" he mumbled, hoping Spanish was close enough to Portuguese that she would understand. He took the netting.

"*No hay de qué,*" she said and pivoted on her bare heel in the dirt. Her voice was as soft and natural as leaves rustling in the wind. She headed off to a thicket of bushes just out of sight.

In her wake, a slight dizziness washed over him. He didn't know what she had said, but it sounded like "you're welcome." He checked his watch. If she was not back in three minutes, he would call out for her. If she didn't answer, he'd run in the direction of the thicket.

He mused, under that frightening war paint was great bone structure. She would probably grow up to be a heartbreaker, the kind whose presence brought out good manners in some men and no manners in others. Her smile would open doors and cause men to walk into posts. Her unique, startling, honey-colored eyes and long, lean limbs would be a stunning combination one day.

They had only a few days to protect her. In a month, she would be safely stateside, surrounded by hormonal high school boys who don't speak her language. Perhaps having a U.S. Senator as an uncle would scare off the riff-raff. A year from now she would be old enough to drive with a learner's permit. In four years she would be old enough to vote. In seven years she would be his age, old enough to drink and buy property.

Vincent sat on his backpack. He checked his watch. Nefi knelt in front of him and said something. He flinched at her reappearance and chided himself for allowing her to sneak up on him.

Ruis translated Nefi's words. "She said you worry." Ruis climbed from his hammock.

"I was thinking. Is she ready for high school?"

"She survived for weeks in the Amazon on her own with a knife and a machete," Ruis said. He made no attempt to hide his amusement. "I wonder if high school is ready for her."

Blake sat up in his hammock and stretched his arms.

Nefi bent over, putting her face near Vincent's. Her eyes seemed oversized this close. She gently touched her fingertip to his forehead, pressing the furrows between his eyebrows. "No worry."

Vincent stood and gave Nefi a one-armed hug around the shoulders. "Okay." It was only after he hugged her that he realized she spoke English. "Hey, did you guys hear that?" He looked at Ruis, but Ruis did not look at all pleased. Neither did Blake, who was looking at Nefi. "What?" Vincent looked down.

Nefi had her eyes closed with her face pressed against his chest. She looked like she was nuzzling a puppy.

Uh oh. Vincent released her and stepped around the fire to take down his hammock. Why did she look at him like that? Why him? He unfastened the hammock from the trees and wadded it up.

Ruis took the hammock from Vincent and handed it to Nefi. He gave her an order. When she headed off with the hammock toward the backpacks, Ruis stepped up beside Vincent. "You don't have sisters, do you?"

"A younger brother."

Ruis's gaze was direct but friendly. "At this age, girls are extremely responsive to attention from older men."

Blake's voice sounded from behind Vincent and Ruis. "There weren't any older boys in her village."

Vincent raised his hands to stop the advice. "I get it." We're probably the first men she's met taller than her.

The men broke their huddle. Vincent took their conversation less as a warning to watch his behavior and more as a gentleman's agreement to be on guard. Nefi could become infatuated with any of them. She was emotionally vulnerable. Man, it would have been so much easier to rescue a boy.

Ruis spread his topographic map on a knee-high stand of ferns. He determined their campsite's position on the map. Vincent and Blake stood on either side of him to read the map. Nefi stood by the north end of the map. Ruis marked their current location with a fingertip. He then pointed to the nearest city, Fonte Boa, on the Solimoes River.

"If we follow the Juruá to the Solimoes and backtrack the riverbank of the Solimoes upstream, it would take eight days," Ruis said, tracing the route with his finger, "But if we cross the Juruá now, where it's shallow, we could head northwest straight to Fonte Boa in four."

Nefi leaned over the map. Ruis and Nefi conversed and pointed to areas on the map until Nefi nodded. Nefi pointed to the circled area on the map that had caused the IBAMA officer to genuflect. North of that, she pointed to the area along the shorter path to Fonte Boa. The proposed river crossing point bordered the danger zone.

Nefi said, *"Marawa selva."*

"Okay, Nefi said we can cut through the Marawa Indian territory. We're safely north of Matis territory."

"What?" Vincent said, "The Matis would try to use bows and arrows against rifles?"

"I believe the local weapon of choice is poison blow darts," Blake said.

"Okay, then." Chastened, Vincent said, "From Fonte Boa can we hop a boat to Manaus?"

Ruis smiled. "Fonte Boa has an airport."

Vincent rubbed his hands together. "That's more like it."

Blake groaned.

The men broke camp. They divided the remaining gum, granola bars, and matches left from the MREs into three backpacks. They carried trash in the outside pockets of their backpacks. For Nefi, packing meant putting on her satchel and picking up her weapons. She followed Vincent around with her hunting knife strapped to her leg and her machete in hand. He told himself that she followed him because she was bored. Perhaps she was afraid to be alone. Was she following him for protection? His bulk made him a sizable shield from attack. She probably would not believe that Ruis was the most skilled protector. Feeling crowded, he told himself she needed something to do, so he pointed to her clothes hanging on a line.

Nefi sauntered over to the clothes and pulled them down with one hand. Setting down her machete, she folded the clothes into a bundle that she tucked under her arm. Picking up her machete, she carried her clothes to Ruis, who stuffed them in his backpack. Blake took down the clothes line. Vincent picked up his backpack, his rifle, and Ruis's machete.

Ruis poured water on the fire. He then kicked dirt on it with his boot, all the while looking at Vincent. The actions and the staring seemed somehow connected, like a message to stamp out whatever hidden fires burned. After the last smoke had puffed off the hissing fire, Ruis gestured for Nefi to follow him. He glanced one last time at Vincent before heading down to the riverbank.

Blake followed. Vincent fell in at the end of the line, separating himself from Nefi as far as safety allowed. Ruis's quiet mood spread to the others. They hiked for a few hours to a bend in the river that created a wide beach. Nefi tagged along without question or complaint. At the beach, Ruis checked his map against the topography to the north, south, east and west. Apparently satisfied with the location, he folded the map and put it in a plastic bag that he placed in his left front shirt pocket.

Vincent stood on the riverbank with his rifle and his backpack. He suspected that if he sat, Nefi would park herself right up next to him. Standing kept him mobile. He searched the gurgling river for signs of other people. After attaching his bayonet to his rifle, Blake checked the shallows of the riverbank that curved around them. He then plopped down on the beach. He set his rifle across his lap and pulled his backpack straps off his shoulders, letting the pack drop to the ground behind him. Ruis kept his backpack on.

Blake handed Nefi a granola bar. She sat beside him, unwrapped the bar, and tossed the wrapper over her shoulder. Blake snatched the wrapper off the riverbank.

"No, no, no." Blake then stuffed the wrapper in his pocket. "No littering."

Nefi furrowed her eyebrows at Blake while she chewed. She seemed at ease with Blake and Ruis.

Listening to the birds, Vincent noticed that the birds highest in the canopy gave short, loud, simple calls. The birds in the lower parts of the tree sang more complicated warbles, whistles and melodic groupings of chirps. At ground level, the humans made few communicative sounds. He would have welcomed small talk. Even Blake remained silent. They waited on Ruis.

Ruis said. "This is where we cross."

"Too bad we can't hitch a ride on a boat," Blake said.

"August is the dry season." Ruis pulled a long nylon rope from his backpack. "The river is too low for big boats. See where it narrows down there? It moves faster. If we make a raft, we can bring the gear across dry."

Vincent tramped away from the river to search the ground for a fallen tree or large fallen branches. Nefi followed him. Finding a fresh looking log, Vincent set his machete on it and reached down to pick up one end. Nefi shouldered him aside. She hacked at the log with her machete. Two long black snakes raced from underneath the log into the underbrush. Though barefoot, she didn't move out of their way even though one squirmed within striking distance of her. Maybe they weren't dangerous snakes. Maybe they were, and she knew enough to hold still. Maybe, like Blake and Ruis, she wanted to point out how seriously uninformed he was about all things in this jungle.

"*Gracias.*" Vincent kicked the log for good measure. He then dragged the log down the riverbank toward the river. He dropped his end of the log near Ruis. He then hauled three more logs to Ruis.

Ruis cut his rope into sections while Blake placed the two longest logs parallel, three feet apart. He then set a shorter log across the long ones, lashing them together with tight knots. Since his father was a Navy Admiral, Ruis probably learned to tie a variety of knots while the rest of the kids were learning their letters. Sweat ran down Vincent's back, tickling and annoying him. Gnats buzzed his face. While Blake shoved the loose logs together, Vincent set the second short log alongside the other top log. Ruis secured this log to the others. Blake dug his hammock from his backpack then he and Ruis wrapped the hammock around their backpacks and rifles to the center log.

Blake and Ruis grabbed one side of the raft, so Vincent grabbed the other side. Together they lifted the front end of the raft and dragged the whole thing toward the river. Ruis pointed to a corner of the raft and gestured for Nefi to hold on. Nefi balked in rapid Portuguese.

Ruis sighed and closed his eyes as if to hide the fact he was rolling them. "Nefi can't swim."

That made sense to Vincent. "I've seen what's in this river. A child would be little more than bait learning to swim here."

Ruis took Nefi by the hand and directed her to sit on the backpacks. Nefi complied. Ruis moved his backpack to the top of the pile. "Can't get the phone wet."

Nefi steadied herself by grabbing handfuls of hammock

webbing. The men towed the raft into the water and waded in. Nefi whimpered once when the raft yawed in the current. She twisted around until she saw Vincent. He nodded at her. Her shoulders relaxed. At one point, all three men lost footholds on the riverbed, so they switched to kicking while they towed the raft to the western shore of the Juruá.

The instant they reached the other side, Nefi hopped off to help haul the raft onto the beach. After they offloaded their gear and caught their breath, the men stripped off their shirts. The men cleaned their guns while Nefi strung one hammock between two trees. She draped the men's shirts on it to dry in the sun. Meanwhile, Vincent checked himself for leeches. Blake and Ruis did too. A collective sigh signaled they were leech free.

A prickly sensation spread across Vincent's scalp. They were being watched. He glanced behind at Nefi, who sat near the tree line by the clothesline. She had her eyes closed, and her chin raised, a bit like a dog alerted by a strange sound. Nefi aimed her face toward Vincent and opened her eyes.

Nefi said something to Ruis.

"We have company." Ruis then said something to Nefi with a rising inflection at the end.

Nefi slowly stood and stepped close to Ruis. While keeping her back to the tree line, she opened her hand like a fan close to her belly. Was she signaling five? She and Ruis exchanged a few words. Nefi whistled a bird call Vincent would have sworn came from a bird if he hadn't seen Nefi make it.

Three short silhouettes appeared in the shadows between trees. When the strangers stepped into the sunlight, Vincent blanched. Wearing only face paint like Nefi's and thin white objects pierced through their noses, the Indians were naked and uncircumcised. Their short straight black hair hung from the crown of their heads to the tops of their ears. Each man held a long spear, point up, like a walking stick. One man had a dozen fish strung on a line from his spear.

"Well, now," Blake said with a drawl, "Looks like we got ourselves an Amazon meet and greet. We are so overdressed."

Nefi sauntered to Blake's backpack where she pulled out the last few granola bars. She carried them to the Indians who backed up a step as she approached. She unwrapped a granola bar and took a small bite, offering the rest to the oldest man in the group. Standing a head taller than the tallest Indian, she moved in a graceful manner and slow movements that demonstrated fearlessness or familiarity in approaching these naked strangers.

The oldest Indian stepped forward and took the granola bar. He sniffed it then bit it. Nefi held out the other granola bars for him. He had accepted them before he tapped the youngest naked native who then spoke to Nefi in what sounded like vowels strung together searching for consonants. His voice quavered.

"Fonte Boa," Nefi answered.

The oldest Indian reached for Nefi's hair. The moment his hand touched her hair, Nefi swatted his hand down. She said something to the old one that made him back away.

Vincent's hand dropped to his rifle just in case. If he had to, he could lean left for a clear shot at the old man. After the old man and Nefi had stared each other down, the old man whistled a bird call. Two men dropped from trees and walked to their colleagues. Lookouts. And that made five. Nefi was right. Vincent was impressed with their tactics. The Indians didn't trust strangers. Did they trust Nefi?

Vincent was about to stand up when Nefi pivoted and glared at him, then at Blake and Ruis as if warning everyone to stay put. Nefi then faced the Indians.

The older Indian handed the string of fish to the youngest native, the one who spoke first to Nefi. The other Indians faded back into the forest, leaving behind the one holding the fish. Nefi stepped up to the hammock. She picked her bag off the dirt and strung the strap over her head and one shoulder. She then strolled to Ruis and sat on the riverbank. Ruis and Nefi talked in tones just above a whisper for a minute.

Ruis said sitting, "we have permission to cross Marawa territory. That man will lead us to Fonte Boa."

Blake brushed the dirt off his rifle. "Is he going to wait for our clothes to dry?"

Ruis nodded.

"Why'd she swat the old man?" Vincent asked.

Ruis talked to Nefi, who responded by blushing and talking in a whisper. Ruis glared at the Indian left behind. Nefi pointed to the jungle and said something else.

Ruis translated. "The Marawan chief invited Nefi to be their shaman. She declined."

"Why on earth would they think she's a shaman?" Blake asked.

"My Portuguese is weak, but I think it has something to do with her eyes." Ruis pulled out his *Spanish/Portuguese Dictionary* and paged through it. "I take that back. The word Nefi used suggests second sight or clairvoyance."

Blake chuckled. "That figures. Those guys don't want to admit a girl detected them sneaking up on us. They want to write it off as supernatural."

Vincent stared at the Indian left behind, whom he believed would take them to Fonte Boa on a path that avoided Indian settlements in the territory.

"Could be," said Ruis. "The IBAMA officers told me there are seven-hundred-thousand Indians in the state, and they dislike contact with outsiders."

"That works for me." Vincent had seen more of the Indians than he ever wanted to see again. The sooner they returned to civilization, the better.

The Marawan planted his spear handle in the sediment near the tree line. He gathered kindling into a small pile.

"Do you think the locals have seen the magic of lighters?" Blake patted his left chest pocket.

Ruis asked Nefi, who answered.

Ruis said, "It would insult him. Nefi says they take pride in traditional ways."

The guide eventually started a fire. He then cleaned and cooked the fish. He served it on leaves that he handed to Nefi. Hours later, after they had eaten the fish, dried their clothes and dressed, the group resumed their hike toward civilization.

Vincent assessed the threat level of the naked Indian. He was a wiry, agile five footer. In New York City, Vincent had seen a variety of tattoos and piercings, but this guy sported six parallel lines on his left cheek that, at a glance, looked like whiskers. His eyes, lined in black, definitely detracted from the tough-guy look. Top that with a five-inch thin bone that curved up into one nostril and out the other and his look exemplified exotic. He moved through the dense growth without hacking away foliage along a footpath, so Ruis and Nefi followed without using their machetes. Vincent and Blake stooped to clear the overhanging branches. The Indian kept pace like a bored trail guide leading a pack of lost tourists.

On their three-day journey to the outskirts of Fonte Boa, a city of forty thousand, Vincent lost track of Nefi one evening near dusk. His first thought was that the guide had kidnapped her for his chief. His heartbeat slowed to normal as soon as he spotted the guide by the fire wearing shorts Ruis had given him, secured by a rope belt. Vincent called out for Nefi. She whistled back from twenty feet above them on a smooth tree branch where she was rubbing something on her face. Ruis nimbly climbed up after her. Vincent stepped back to watch.

Ruis and Nefi had a brief conversation that ended with Nefi climbing back down. When she reached Vincent, her face appeared freshly painted in brilliant red and deep black in the same pattern as when they first found her. Nefi, petulant and brooding, stomped to the fire and plopped down beside the Marawan guide. She dug what looked like fruit and spiky blowfish from her satchel and handed them to the guide. He shrugged. Nefi tugged open the cargo pocket on the side of the guide's shorts and stuffed the items inside. She demonstrated the snap on the flap of the pocket. The guide entertained himself by opening and closing the snap.

Ruis climbed down to Vincent. "She was reapplying war paint made from urucum and Jenipapo fruit."

"Why?"

"She said the world is a dangerous place." Ruis let out a sigh through his teeth.

"How long will it take for the paint to wear off?" Vincent asked.

"Good question." Ruis strode to the campfire and talked with Nefi.

Nefi answered him then crossed her arms and propped her elbows on her knees.

Ruis shook his head as he walked to Vincent. "The thicker it is, the longer it takes to fade. She said her bare face will show through in two weeks."

Vincent shook his head. Won't the Senator be surprised?

The rest of the muddy trek continued until their guide stopped a mile short of the city on August 24th. When he stopped, the others stopped. Nefi spoke to their guide and pointed, reciting the full names of Vincent, Ruis, and Blake. The guide stood by them one by one, placing his spear in front of them and marking their heights on his spear handle with his fingernail. Lastly, the

Marawan stepped in front of Nefi. Nefi straightened her posture, like a child trying to measure taller. The Indian pointed to her.

"Nefi," she said pounding her fist over her heart like Tarzan. Nefi said something to Ruis, who answered 'no.' She held out her machete to the guide and said something to him.

"Tepi," he answered, slapping his bare chest. He crossed his arms and said something to Nefi.

She gasped and flung the machete into the ground hard enough to bury the point a few inches. The handle swayed. Nefi then swatted Tepi on the shoulder and spoke sharply to him.

Vincent feared for the guy and held his breath.

Ruis cleared his throat and shook his head at Vincent. "Let them settle this."

Tepi took a deep breath and stepped toward Nefi. After a moment, he reached out and patted Nefi on the sternum. Nefi patted his chest. Tepi pried the machete from the mud and pointed northwest with it.

Vincent, like Blake, looked northwest. When Vincent looked back, Tepi was gone, and Nefi passed Vincent in the direction Tepi had pointed. Blake, Ruis, and Vincent fell in line behind her. Ruis and Nefi talked for a few minutes. Ruis laughed. After Ruis had handed Nefi his machete, Nefi slashed through the foliage with a vengeance.

Ten minutes into their hike, Vincent broke the silence. "Care to share with us what happened back there?"

Ruis translated, "I told Nefi she won't need her machete in America."

"Okay, but what about that business with the spear?" Blake said.

"Tepi, our guide," Ruis said, "measured us and got our names so he could tell our story."

"No cable television to keep them entertained at night?" Vincent asked.

Blake snorted. "That didn't sound like Nefi was speaking Portuguese."

"It was one of the native dialects." Ruis then spoke to Nefi.

"Arawak," Nefi answered. She spread her fingers apart and waved her hand over her head as if to say more or less.

"What was the problem with the machete?" Vincent asked.

"Tepi interpreted her offer as a dowry. He said he didn't want her." Ruis cringed. "Because he didn't want her in his head. Seems the locals consider her psychic. Mysticism is big here."

"Maybe it's her eyes," Blake said. "Golden eyes have to be rarer than red hair."

Vincent understood why Tepi would be fearful of her. Her eyes were startling, especially framed in a stripe of black war paint. Though Vincent no longer feared her, he knew she was already anchored in his head.

"Our girl doesn't talk very much," Blake said. "I wonder if she's usually this quiet."

Ruis asked Nefi a question in Portuguese.

She answered briefly.

Ruis nodded. "She said silence makes words meaningful."

When they reached the airport at Fonte Boa, Ruis asked to charter a plane one-way to Manaus. The thirty-something-year-old male Asian attendant stepped around the reception counter and invited them to the hangar to see the charter plane. Vincent followed Nefi into the hangar. He was hungry and longed for a shower, but he was even more eager to see what passed for an airplane in this remote jungle village. He gaped at a gleaming, metal twin-engine plane.

"Now that," Vincent said, slapping his right hand over his heart, "looks like a real airplane."

"I'm so relieved we can die in style," Blake muttered.

"The Beechcraft King Air three-fifty is a load-and-go dream," the airport attendant said. "Pressurized, full-fuel, she can go nine-hundred nautical miles packed to the windows. Pratt & Whitney engine. Cruises at three hundred knots easy. She's beautiful, but she's not cheap. I'll have to charge you five-hundred-fifty American dollars per person." He popped open the rear door and pulled down the steps. "Double cabin seating for eight."

No one moved toward the plane's open door.

"What do you say?" the attendant asked.

"How soon can we leave?" Ruis asked.

The attendant grinned. His expression changed when he encountered Nefi face-to-face. "Is she...housebroken?" He waved his hand at her face. "We just installed new upholstery."

Ruis talked briefly with Nefi then he addressed the attendant. "She's been in seaplanes."

"Huh. Well, I'll call the pilot." He led them back to the office where he scooted behind the counter.

Ruis pulled a handful of good old U.S. bills from his wallet, the top one displayed Ulysses S. Grant's face. Ruis wasn't the kind of guy to do anything by half, so the whole stack was probably fifties. As the saying goes, money talks. He didn't have to say more to convince the man.

The attendant hefted a large invoice book onto the counter. He rapidly completed the form down to the passengers' names. "Your names?"

"Ruis Ramos," Ruis paused between names while the man wrote, "Blake Clayton, Vincent Gunnerson, spelled with two Ns, and Nefi Jenkins."

"Give me two hours to fuel the plane and get the pilot here. You're welcome to sit in the lounge, or you could try the restaurant down the road."

The attendant assured them they should be able to leave soon after the pilot arrived. This was the clearest weather they had enjoyed since they landed in *Cruzeiro do Sul* earlier in the month. The clock on the wall behind the counter read nine a.m. local time.

A clock beside it read Zulu time. Regardless of how one measured time, two hours remained two hours. Vincent hoped the restaurant served something edible, something he could identify, something not qualified as road kill. What kind of meat did locals eat? He had not seen a cow or a chicken on his way through the town to the airport. Did they eat monkeys? Crocodiles? He decided to stick with fish.

Ruis removed trash from his backpack and dumped it in an open barrel lined with a black trash bag. Blake and Vincent cleaned out their backpacks as well to lighten the load.

"Where can we stow our gear?" Vincent, tired of lugging his backpack and rifle, let his backpack slide down his arm to the floor.

"Right there's fine." The man pointed to the floor. "You have to unload the rifles for the flight."

Blake, Ruis, and Vincent unloaded their rifles and stuffed the bullets in the outside pockets of their backpacks. All three men removed the firing bolts from their rifles and pocketed them. Without their firing bolts, the rifles were useless and, therefore, unlikely to be stolen. Ruis pocketed his passport, so Blake and Vincent dug theirs from their backpacks as well. By silent agreement, they also kept their handguns then they left for the restaurant.

They were back an hour and a half later to wait in the lounge for the pilot. A small television in the corner blared news in Portuguese. Vincent longed for news of the outside world in English, even scores of the NFL preseason Giants games. Anything. Three long plain, brown, sweat-stained, fabric sofas lined the waiting room. Wary of the decrepit furniture, Vincent itched just thinking about whether or not the sofas housed fleas.

Who knew how much longer it would take for the pilot to show up? He sighed and sat. A musty stench rose off the fabric.

"I want a hot shower and a cold beer," Blake declared, slouching on a sofa across the lounge from Vincent and Nefi.

Ruis said, "Just so you know. Faucets marked 'C' stand for *caliente*." He plugged a charging cord into his satellite phone. He sorted through a collection of electrical adapters.

"So?"

"*Caliente* means hot."

"That's very sporting of you, Ruis," said Blake. "Thank you."

"I hope the hotel bed is big enough that my feet don't hang off the end," Vincent said.

"I made reservations at the Tropical Manaus," Ruis said. Having found an adapter, he plugged it into an outlet on the wall.

"How big a city is Manaus?" Blake leaned back, propping his elbows on the sofa's back.

"One and a half million," Ruis said, "They have an opera house and a zoo."

Having seen enough wildlife to last for years, Vincent said, "Let's skip the zoo."

"And the opera house," Blake said.

"Tomorrow," Ruis said, "we go to the consulate and then...."

Nefi's face became animated. She spoke to Ruis rapidly in Portuguese while poking him in the arm. Very few people could get away with poking Ruis like that.

"*Vinte e quatro*," Ruis answered.

"*Augusto?*" Nefi's demeanor collapsed, her face contorted in what Vincent interpreted as a great disappointment.

Ruis and Nefi conversed. Ruis shrugged. "Brazil's Independence Day celebration falls on September seventh. I told her we won't be here that long."

Nefi slouched. It encouraged Vincent that she cared about resuming life. It also saddened him that she stopped keeping track of the date while alone in the jungle. He understood. In the weeks after his father had been killed, the days blended together in such emotional darkness that day and night held no meaning. He drifted through school like a zombie, unaware and unconcerned until his mother told him that his younger brother needed a new role model. Once he focused his attention outside of himself, he recovered his involvement in the world. He was sixteen when he lost his father. Nefi, at fourteen, suffered a double tragedy. How resilient would she be starting over in a foreign land?

"You okay, Vincent?"

Vincent raised his attention from the gritty tile floor to Blake. "Yeah." He glanced at Nefi's red and black stained face. Won't she wake them up at U.S. Customs?

A shadow passed over the doorway to the office. From his position in the lounge, only Vincent could see into the office. A short square-built woman leaned over the counter and whispered to the man behind it. She looked like the waitress from the restaurant. The attendant glanced at Vincent then back at the woman. Suddenly nervous, the woman darted from the building.

What was that about? "Ruis," Vincent said, "Is there much anti-American sentiment here?"

Ruis rearranged items in his pack. "No. Brazil and the United States are allies."

The attendant appeared in the doorway. "The pilot should be here soon." He stole a glance at the weapons piled on the floor.

Maybe Nefi spooked the locals. Did they distrust Indians? Vincent watched the news but was unable to decipher much beyond video coverage of a riot somewhere in the world.

Two men in uniform, one fat and one lean, rushed into the lounge. Fatso aimed a handgun at Ruis. Slim waved his gun at Vincent and Blake. Local police? Federal police?

Seated, Vincent slowly raised his hands. What did they want?

"Hey, guys," Blake said, raising his hands, "did we forget to pay for lunch?"

71

Ruis glanced up from his pack. He raised only an eyebrow at the uniformed men as if eyeing children with water pistols.

Slim, whose gun pointed at Vincent, quaked slightly at the knees. His gun shook. Certainly, Ruis would clear up whatever had the locals upset, Vincent thought as he once again wished he had taken Spanish in high school.

Fatso shouted at Ruis.

"Nefi Jenkins?" Ruis said. His voice had a calming quality.

"*Si!*"

Nefi stood, so Vincent stood to block her from the armed strangers. Slim inhaled sharply. His eyes widened, and he stepped back as if he couldn't decide where to aim at such a large target. He tried to steady his gun with both hands, but it did not help. Was this a shakedown? Did these guys assume all Americans carried loads of cash with them like Ruis?

Ruis spoke softly. "Stand down, Vincent. Let Nefi talk to the officer."

Nefi eased around Vincent's right side. Nefi spoke to Fatso, pointing to herself and saying her name. She pointed to Ruis. "*Meu amigo*, Ruis Ramos." She pointed to Blake, "*Meu amigo*, Blake Clayton." She then placed a hand on Vincent's chest. "*Meu caro amigo*, Vincent Gunnerson." She stood in front of Vincent, facing Slim's unsteady gun.

Vincent suspected that she had called him more than a friend. Ruis and Fatso confirmed the suspicion with a scowl. The officers talked with Nefi for a few more moments, though they did not lower their weapons. Vincent's heart raced. He took long, slow breaths. Though it bothered him to face the business end of a gun; it alarmed him to face one held by an unsteady hand.

Fatso addressed Ruis.

Ruis and Fatso argued. As Fatso got louder, Ruis's voice grew quieter, forcing Fatso to listen. Ruis reached for his satellite phone so Fatso shouted and aimed his handgun at Ruis. Vincent considered disarming the smaller officer, but Nefi stood too close.

A stray bullet would be a disaster. Ruis nudged his phone with his foot while he said something about Raposo and IBAMA.

Fatso shouted something at Nefi, so she unplugged and picked up Ruis's phone and held it up to Fatso. After more argument between Ruis and Fatso, Nefi followed Ruis's instructions to place a call. When a voice answered, Nefi held the phone up to the overweight officer's cheek.

Fatso's voice changed as he spoke with IBAMA Officer Raposo. Nefi then held the phone to Ruis's face. After Ruis had talked, Nefi talked into the phone and then held it up once again to Fatso. Fatso relaxed, ended the call and holstered his gun. The guns lowered. Hands lowered. A collective sigh sounded in the room.

Fatso addressed Ruis respectfully.

"The captain apologizes for the misunderstanding," Ruis translated. "He heard that the daughter of the murdered American missionary couple was missing. He had to be sure we were not kidnapping her."

Captain Fatso said more that Ruis translated. "He said good people must challenge evil, or there will be lawlessness."

Vincent nodded. Blake exhaled loudly and leaned back on the sofa.

The captain shook hands with Ruis. He nodded at Vincent and Blake. He tenderly pulled Nefi's hair from her face while he whispered something to her. The officers left.

Sniffling, Nefi sat beside Vincent with the satellite phone in her lap. Ruis asked Nefi a question. She wiped tears from her face with the back of her hand, leaving black smudges on her hand.

Sitting beside her, Vincent draped an arm around her shoulders. "Did they scare her?"

"The captain," Ruis said, taking the satellite phone from Nefi's lap, "told her many people have been praying for her."

The airport attendant leaned into the doorway. "Sorry, the pilot's running late. I expect him within an hour."

Hurry up and wait. Patience was a virtue nurtured by places like this. Vincent took his arm off Nefi. Crossing his arms over his chest, he slouched into the sofa to nap. Soon, the television's drone put Nefi to sleep, leaning against his shoulder. Her mouth was open. Her long arms dangled, one beside Vincent's leg and the other between her knees. At one point in her nap, she snored lightly. Vincent tried to hold still while acting as her human pillow. Her face warmed his shirt right through to his skin. Against all odds, she was alive and on her way to safety.

Blake whispered, "Even in her sleep she's drooling over you."

Feeling his wet sleeve under Nefi's face, Vincent rolled his eyes.

An hour and a half later, the pilot arrived, whistling. It was enough to wake Nefi. She opened her eyes and pushed herself off Vincent's shoulder. She left a wet red and black stain on his shoulder that made her laugh. It was the sweetest sound Vincent had heard in weeks. She rubbed the spot, spreading the stains. She covered her mouth with a hand and laughed.

"Sure," Vincent muttered, "pull knives on me, ruin my shirt."

Blake, who looked fast asleep, spoke without opening his eyes. "Now, now, the good book admonishes us to forgive one another."

"Really," Vincent said, "which part is that?" Blake's reputation for being a walking Bible concordance dared Vincent to test his knowledge.

Blake opened one eye at Vincent. "I would think even good Catholics like you have heard the part about turning the other cheek."

"Done that."

"If you want to be specific," Blake said opening both eyes, "in Matthew chapter eighteen, verse twenty-two, Jesus tells us to forgive not just once or twice but seventy-seven times."

"She has sixty-nine to go."

"And then what?" Blake sat up.

"Then I'll be entitled to get mad," Vincent said.

"I don't believe the verse meant we should keep score."

"She didn't pull a knife on you."

Blake grinned. "I don't have that effect on women."

. 6 .

The next morning in Manaus, rested, showered, shaved, and dressed in clean clothes, they gathered their gear and weapons and climbed into a taxi van to ride to the U.S. Consulate. Vincent appraised Nefi's partial transformation from a savage to a young lady. Except for the slightly faded face paint, Nefi was transformed. Ruis's influence on her wardrobe reminded everyone she was a minor. Wearing a modest short-sleeved flowered top, navy pants, and navy socks, she smelled of lavender. Her hair hung shiny, clean and straight, unlike the previously matted mess. She fidgeted in navy low-heeled shoes. How long had it been since she had worn shoes?

"She looks dang near ladylike without a machete in her hand," Blake said.

"We can take the girl out of the jungle," Vincent said, "but can we take the jungle out of the girl?"

"We just need to get her home," Ruis said. It felt like he was reminding Vincent that Nefi was simply their temporary responsibility.

Too late. Vincent had already grown attached to the brave young teenager. Possessiveness had also crept in during their travel from the middle of predator-infested nowhere to civilization. How would Nefi adjust to life in the suburbs of Washington D.C. in the home of a powerful politician?

On their ride to the U.S. Consulate in a taxi van, they passed a pink building with a yellow dome that the cab driver identified as the opera house. The driver, a self-appointed tour guide, told them that the city was built on the rubber industry. The real rubber, he said, from trees. He asked in English if Nefi was familiar with the Chicle tree, where chewing gum comes from.

Ruis informed the driver that they had a schedule to keep.

The man gave a quick, forced smile.

Ruis told him that they would like to hire him for the day to keep on schedule. The driver's mood brightened. He took two sharp turns to the right to deliver them to the front entrance of the U.S. Consulate. Ruis handed the driver a colorful bill that drew another large smile from him. The group climbed out. The aging van squawked in relief as Vincent climbed out, unfolding himself at the curb.

Vincent wondered if it was safe to leave their rifles in the van. He still had the firing pin, and Ruis didn't seem concerned, so Vincent headed to the consulate gates with Ruis, Blake, and Nefi.

While Ruis showed his papers to one guard, the other guard looked at Nefi as if assessing her threat level. The guard near Ruis opened the gate. Ruis took charge of the business at hand switching between English and Spanish with ease. They were led to the office of a compact well-groomed man in a suit, who searched his desk for Nefi's immunization record. A phone call and a FAX later, another paper was added to the stack on Nefi's file. Within half an hour, the doctor himself arrived with a black medical bag and a nurse. He greeted Nefi with a tearful hug then he and the nurse took Nefi to a room. Vincent did not have to understand Portuguese to interpret the doctor's condolences. They returned fifteen minutes later to hand two pill bottles to Ruis.

Vincent recognized the prescriptions, one killed parasites, and the other was a strong anti-anxiety drug. In English, the doctor explained that Nefi suffered from exhaustion. He urged Ruis to give Nefi one anti-anxiety pill so she would sleep on the flight to the U.S. Ruis nodded then he introduced Vincent and Blake to the doctor, who greeted them before he warmly bid Nefi goodbye.

The interviewer led Nefi and Ruis to another room. They came back with Brazilian and U.S. passports with Nefi's picture in them. It struck Vincent that the whole process had been fast-tracked by someone in authority. He assumed Senator Jenkins had prepared the way. The clerk then handed a small box in bright red gift-wrapping to Nefi. The tag on the gift read 'to Miss Nefi Jenkins from His Excellency, Brazilian Ambassador Alfonso Morales.' Nefi seemed more interested in the conversations around her than in the gift as if she had been asked to simply hold it for someone else.

A clerk stepped into the interviewer's office, said something and left.

The interviewer handed papers to Ruis as he stood. While Ruis quickly shuffled through them, Vincent spotted a U.S. birth certificate. The interviewer nodded at Vincent and Blake. He shook Nefi's hand and gave her a slight bow at the waist. Nefi surprised everyone by giving a short curtsy as she shook his hand. The interviewer beamed.

"Gentlemen, members of the press have gathered at the front gate. While you were traveling through the jungle, Miss Jenkins' safe recovery became international news. Would you permit me to escort her to the gate for a photo?"

All looked to Ruis for an answer so he placed a call to Senator Jenkins. While Ruis was on his phone, two IBAMA officers entered the corridor. Vincent recognized Officer Raposo and his partner. Wearing clean uniforms, they walked straight to Vincent and Blake and shook their hands.

After conferring with the Senator, Ruis shook hands with the

IBAMA officers. He then took the waterproof bag that contained the accessories for the satellite phone and the phone and handed them to Officer Raposo. Raposo gasped and hugged Ruis. The officer then placed the phone in the bag and tucked the bag under his arm.

Patting the bag Officer Raposo said, "Thank you. Thank you most kindly." He then he asked Nefi something in Portuguese.

Her answer made Ruis, the interviewer, and the IBAMA officers nod and smile.

"What did she say?" Vincent asked.

"Some Indians," Ruis said, "believe that having your picture taken steals part of your soul. Nefi said nothing can steal her soul because she gave it to God."

The interviewer addressed Ruis, Blake, and Vincent, "Would you like to speak to the reporters?"

Ruis shook his head, so Vincent and Blake also declined. Nefi handed the gift to Ruis.

"Then we shall be right back." The interviewer took Nefi's hand and placed it in the crook of his arm. The IBAMA officers followed Nefi out to the gate while Ruis, Blake, and Vincent watched from the windows.

The interviewer made a quick statement to the gathered reporters. Two television cameras and eight photographers stood among the reporters who fired off questions. The interviewer answered a few questions and deferred others to Officer Raposo. After a few minutes, they headed back to the consulate doors. At the doorway, Nefi looked back over her shoulder. One news photographer captured that moment.

The camera's flash struck Vincent like a blast of cold air. The hair on the back of his neck stood at attention. He watched the photographer gaze down, more interested in his camera than Nefi. Vincent fought anxiety until Nefi stepped inside the building. He silently argued with his intuition. Whoever murdered her parents would probably not risk killing her in such a public place. She had witnessed two murders, but the rest of the village had probably witnessed it as well.

After the journalists had dispersed, Ruis, Vincent, Blake, and Nefi left the embassy for their taxi. Vincent scanned the rooftops for snipers. He inspected the inside and underside of the van. Due to the lack of space in the back, the guns were placed in the front seat with their barrels pointed down. The cab driver raised his eyebrows at Vincent.

While they stood by the cab, Blake elbowed Nefi. "Go ahead. Open it."

Vincent performed a visual sweep of the area. An Asian couple bearing cameras strolled by, so he watched them. When Nefi twisted toward the couple, the woman gasped, and the man raised his camera. Vincent stepped between the couple and Nefi before the man could remove his lens cover. The man froze. Intimidated by Vincent's presence, the couple rushed on down the sidewalk.

Blake swatted Vincent's shoulder. "What was that about?"

"She's not a tourist attraction." Vincent hoped the red and black face paint would wear off quickly.

The cab driver slid the van's side door open. His attention fell on the red wrapped box in Nefi's hands. "Oh, a present."

It became clear that they would not move until Nefi opened the package so she tore off the bow and handed it to Blake.

"Atta, girl," Blake said. "No littering."

Nefi ripped off the paper and handed it to him. This revealed a box with a picture of a digital camera on it. Nefi pried the box apart to get to a small camera nestled in a form-fitting plastic cradle. A pamphlet of instructions fluttered out of the box. Ruis nabbed the papers mid-air.

The driver held out a plastic trash bag to Blake, who wadded the wrappings into it. Nefi handed the box, camera and all, to Vincent as if she didn't know what to do with it.

Vincent removed the camera from the protective packaging

and handed the waste to Blake. With his right hand, he pressed another button, causing the shutter cover to spiral open. He aimed at the cab driver whose face appeared on the back of the camera on a small screen. Nefi peered at the small screen. To demonstrate, Vincent placed his right pointer finger on the button on the top right of the camera, he held it down until it flashed.

"I am your first picture." The driver laughed. "May I take your picture?" He directed them to line up by the van around Nefi. He took two group photos. After he had handed the camera back to Vincent, he asked, "Now where would you like to go?"

"The airport."

Thirty seconds into the taxi ride, Vincent groped the end of the bench seat for a seatbelt. Driving in Manaus was a high-speed sport. Larger, faster vehicles bullied for the right of way. Signaling meant honking or waving. Drivers treated traffic lights as a suggestion. They passed on blind curves. They drove on pure faith or stupidity. They drove at whatever speed they wanted. The speed signs listed numbers in kilometers, but the car's speedometer showed miles per hour. On the fifteen-minute ride from the hotel to the airport, the driver never used his signals and only once used his brakes.

"So this is where New York cabbies train," Vincent muttered.

Meanwhile, oblivious to the dangerous ride, Nefi read the Spanish version of the instructions on her new toy. Vincent believed that the differences between Spanish and Portuguese must be minor. It did not occur to him that Nefi understood both because, in his mind, if she was bilingual her parents would have taught her English as the second language. Had they ever intended to bring her to the United States? Didn't missionary families visit home once in a while?

Vincent asked Ruis. "Has she ever been to the U.S.?"

Ruis asked Nefi. She said something back to him. She took photos of Vincent, Blake, Ruis, passing cars, buildings and, by accident, her feet.

Ruis's downcast reflected expression in the window amplified the message in his words. "Her parents promised to take her to the United States for her sixteenth birthday."

At nightfall and at last in the United States, Nefi gawked at the traffic and the neighborhood while Ruis drove. Everything moved faster than raindrops, like a blur of color and the noise! Oh, the loud noises here. She tried to understand the arrangement of roads, hills, buildings and trees, but Ruis drove too fast. How did he know which road to follow with so many choices at this speed?

He slowed in an area of bright green clearings framed in an explosion of flowering plants and shade trees. Nestled within these green spaces sat giant stone structures with ornate windows and rooftops that looked sturdy enough to withstand fierce storms. Was one of these beautiful buildings where grandma and grandpa lived?

The van pulled into a driveway and stopped. Nefi couldn't see the whole building from the van window. She staggered out last and stared up at the home whose walls were lined with pink, white and red flowers, and purple clusters of flowers bobbing on the ends of branches.

Ruis stepped beside her and told her this house belonged to her Uncle Hamilton and Aunt Louise Jenkins. Nefi memorized *tio* Hamilton and *tia* Louise. Why not go to grandma and grandpa's house? Nefi froze in place.

Vincent carried the small red suitcase Ruis had bought for her to check her clothes and knife through the airports. Ruis carried a large manila envelope. Standing as tall as Ruis, Nefi twisted the hem of her shirt in one hand.

In Spanish, she asked if her grandparents were here.

Ruis shrugged.

What if they don't want me? Her heart thumped in her chest like a small trapped bird.

Ruis took her hand in his and asked for her to trust him. Even though the air felt thin and her body heated up, she let him lead her toward the house.

Ruis, Nefi, Blake, and Vincent strode up the stone walkway to the large cut glass front doors. Ruis pointed to the doorbell button. She loved to command the elevator and the television by pressing buttons. What would this button do?

She pressed it. Chimes played a nonsense song her father had loved called "Yankee Doodle."

The door opened to reveal a short, plump woman with black and silver hair framing her smiling face. She opened the door wider and stepped aside to invite them in. Nefi entered and took in a spiral staircase that framed a massive crystal chandelier.

Ruis introduced Nefi to the woman whom he addressed as Mrs. Jenkins.

"*Ola*, Nefi." Louise hugged the towering girl.

Nefi's voice came out as a whisper, "*Ola, tia* Louise." Had they met in her village, Nefi would have greeted her by patting her on the chest and shoulders, but Ruis had explained hugging as an appropriate greeting between family members, so hugging it was.

While Ruis introduced Vincent and Blake to *tia* Louise, Nefi took in her surroundings. The stairway emptied into an open space where a large round black rug, adorned with a pattern of colorful swirls and flowers, covered most of the floor. It was too beautiful to walk on yet someone in large shiny shoes was walking on the flowers toward her.

Nefi looked up the legs of the man who dared walk on the artwork and saw her father's face. It couldn't be! Wide-eyed, she staggered backward into Ruis. He caught her by the elbow and back.

Hamilton glanced at Ruis, "So, my brother didn't tell her he was a twin."

Ruis explained what a twin was. Nefi went through the motion of nodding as if she could so quickly grasp the concept that the man her father never mentioned looked exactly like him. Father and this man *had* to share the same blood. Brothers. Twins. In that instant, she understood. Nothing could have stopped her from wrapping her arms fiercely around Hamilton. He kissed the crown of her head. She knew this could not be her father raised from the dead, but for a glorious, healing moment time stood still while this hug felt like her father's. Like hope. Ruis had told the truth.

Nefi sniffled. Her tight hold eased. She lifted her face from his chest and stepped back just enough to pat his chest repeatedly with both hands. *This is real. This is real. This man with father's face is real.* Her throat tightened and her eyes burned. When she realized she was greeting him tribal style, she dropped her hands to her sides.

Ruis said, "The Indians believe what they can touch."

She glanced at Ruis, who nodded as if granting his approval.

"I see," Hamilton rasped, "thank you." He cleared his throat.

Louise hugged Ruis. "Thank you, Ruis." To Vincent and Blake, she said, "Ruis is the oldest son of my dear neighbor and friend, Gloria Ramos."

"Vincent Gunnerson," Hamilton said offering his open hand to Vincent.

Vincent stood as tall as *tio* Hamilton. To be the size of her father was to be a man in Nefi's eyes. All grown up.

Louise and Vincent shook hands.

"Pleased to meet you, Ma'am," Blake said as he shook hands with Louise.

"And you must be Blake Clayton," Hamilton said, waving toward the solid-built redhead.

"Good to see you again, sir." Blake shook hands with Hamilton.

Tio Hamilton's voice matched her father's. Nefi wanted to listen to the perfect musical rumble of it forever.

Vincent followed as the Senator led the group into a formal sitting room on the right from the foyer. Why hadn't Nefi's parents told her about her aunt and uncle? Was it a matter of twins striving too hard to develop separate identities? Vincent carried his concern into a comfortable room set up with a deep cushioned pale green leather sofa against the back wall, and a taller than usual coffee table ringed on three sides by four soft brown leather wing-back chairs.

Mrs. Jenkins said she had insisted on the arrangement and comfort of the furniture because she said too many sitting rooms in town were filled with showy antiques that people were afraid to use. "Why bother having a sitting room," she said, "if people feel unwelcome in it?"

Mrs. Jenkins had a maternal plumpness that reminded Vincent of his grandmother in her younger years. Her dress hem fell modestly below the knees as she carried herself gracefully on low heels. In contrast, Senator Jenkins towered head and shoulders above her and walked with long strides.

The Senator settled into one of a pair of armchairs facing the sofa, with his back to the window. Ruis took the far chair facing the foyer and Blake sat across the table from Ruis. Left with the choice of sitting beside Hamilton Jenkins or Nefi, Vincent chose to sit by Nefi on the sofa. The sofa was both stylish with just the right balance of support and cushion.

"Please, make yourselves comfortable," Louise Jenkins said, standing in the doorway. "I'll be right back with refreshments."

Blake, ever the southern gentleman, stood and stepped toward Mrs. Jenkins. "May I help?"

She reached a manicured hand around Blake's elbow, and the two of them disappeared into the foyer.

"Where would you like this?" Blake's voice carried from the foyer.

They had left Nefi's suitcase in the middle of the foyer.

"By the stairs for now," Mrs. Jenkins answered. "I don't approve of leaving objects in the traffic pattern." Her voice drifted off to another room in the house.

Hamilton Jenkins addressed Ruis. "How did it go?"

"We found Nefi exhausted, but in remarkably good health," Ruis said. "She has about a dozen small puncture marks from leeches. Her immunizations are up to date. Her medical records are from her pediatrician in Manaus." Ruis handed the manila envelope to the Senator. "Her papers."

The Senator opened the envelope and tipped the contents out onto his lap. A Brazilian passport landed on top of the papers. He opened it. Nefi's photo showed a solemn red and black face stamped with a seal. He then found the U.S. passport. "You have dual citizenship," he said to Nefi.

Ruis translated. Nefi nodded.

Vincent thought it must seem like more paperwork to her. Thousands of refugees from South America risked their lives to come to the United States. Did she realize how much more privileged her life would be here? Perhaps she suffered from future shock. So much change so quickly would disorient anyone.

Senator Jenkins sorted through the papers. Medical records in Portuguese or Spanish. Three handwritten military-style mission reports: one from each of them. It seemed he was busying himself to keep from staring at Nefi's face paint, which he glanced at often. Vincent had mentioned in his report that the fruit-based stains on Nefi's face were fading a little every day. As the Senator sorted through the other papers, an ornate gilded card slid to the carpet. It had a message on it in Portuguese, signed by

Ambassador Morales. The Senator picked it up from the ornate plush rug.

"She received a gift from the Ambassador," Ruis said. "A digital camera."

"Alfonso," the Senator held the gilded card, "He was a classmate of ours at Harvard. My brother and sister-in-law also graduated from Harvard."

Ruis nodded. Vincent glanced at Nefi, who seemed spellbound watching her uncle speak. What a shock it must have been to see her dead father's lookalike. *The poor kid.*

Mrs. Jenkins carried in a tray of glasses filled with iced tea. She served the drinks by carrying the tray around the room. Blake followed with a tray of cheese squares and crackers and cut fruit. He set his tray on the coffee table in front of Vincent and Nefi as directed by Louise. He then took the empty seat across from Ruis.

Mrs. Jenkins sat in the last empty chair by her husband where she smiled lovingly at Nefi. "I can't tell you how much it means to us to have Nefi here." Her eyes welled up, threatening tears. She blinked rapidly and then looked at Ruis, prompting him to translate.

Ruis translated. Nefi smiled.

Nefi eyed the food. The girl had a serious appetite. At the hotel in Manaus, she'd downed a large pizza on her own.

"Please go ahead, dear." Mrs. Jenkins opened her hand toward the tray of food.

Nefi plucked a cheese cube from a neat row of cubes, first sniffing it then nibbling it. After the taste nibble, she popped the rest of it in her mouth. As the cheese bulged in her cheek, her gaze took in the chintz curtains and Oriental rug then it ran up the walls to the oil paintings and framed photographs. Nefi's home in Brazil was a wood and palm frond structure with two rooms with a wood slat floor.

Vincent believed Nefi might be in culture shock. He was impressed as well by the size and elegance of the house. He drank the Southern-style syrupy sweet tea and imagined that the Jenkins' primary residence had giant white columns supporting a wraparound porch overlooking a cotton plantation. An aftertaste of mint lingered on his tongue.

"Louise," Senator Jenkins said, tucking the papers back in the envelope, "the men have written reports about their journey."

Mrs. Jenkins nodded. "I look forward to reading them." She probably had questions she might be hesitant to ask in Nefi's presence. She sipped her tea. Suddenly her face brightened. "So, how did you manage to find her?"

The men exchanged a glance. Ruis and Vincent smiled at Blake, volunteering him to speak for the group.

"To be honest," Blake said to Mrs. Jenkins, "we were kind of surprised to find her alive. All she had was a machete and a hunting knife. She's a real survivor. Somebody has been praying her through."

Mrs. Jenkins nodded at Blake. "God is good."

Vincent was convinced that Southern Baptists recognized each other by signs invisible to all others through holy radar. He knew Blake's Southern Baptist background. Had Mrs. Jenkins read Blake's record? Or did she just sense it?

"In the second week, we were on the Juruá River, north of the settlement where Nefi lived. Vincent suspected we were being followed. So I suggested something to signal to whoever was shadowing us that we were the good guys." Blake picked up his sweating glass of tea. "We sang 'Amazing Grace' at the top of our lungs." He sipped. "Truth be told, Nefi found us."

Hamilton laughed. "Brilliant. Resourceful and brilliant."

Mrs. Jenkins clapped her hands together. "You sang?"

"In two-part harmony." Blake grinned. "Ruis sings a mean tenor."

Vincent nodded. Perhaps Ruis had been a choir boy.

Nefi took a long drink of her tea while peering over the glass rim at the other faces in the room. She fished an ice cube from her glass and examined it while it dripped from her hand to the Persian rug. She had done the same thing at the hotel restaurant. Vincent understood her fascination with ice. He had dreamed of it when he was stationed in Afghanistan. People in the States took such luxuries for granted.

Ruis tapped his glass, attracting Nefi's attention. His look prompted her to return the ice to her glass. She then wiped her hand on her pant leg. She stole a shy grin at Vincent. He smiled back. *No harm, no foul.*

Mrs. Jenkins had a great deal of work ahead in teaching this wild girl how to behave in civilized society. Advanced technology, cell phones, toilets, television, ice, shopping at the mall, wearing normal makeup, these were things girls her age took for granted, things Nefi would need to discover and master to fit in. Learning English would help only so far in communicating with other teenagers, who had a language all their own.

A portrait of a teenage boy hung in an ornate gilded frame set prominently on the side wall. Ruis had briefed them on Senator and Mrs. Jenkins. Their son had died of a drug overdose four years ago. Wealth and position did not protect families from tragedy, which was the great equalizer. Vincent turned his attention back to the living.

Nefi talked to Ruis, who translated. "She wants to know where Grandfather and Grandmother Wright are."

"They'll be here this evening. They're very excited to see you." Senator Jenkins smiled at Nefi. To Ruis, he added, "We were relieved they didn't argue about custody. Honestly, the idea of seventy-year-olds trying to raise a teenager, well, it doesn't merit debate."

Nefi's gaze darted from the Senator to Ruis and back as if she expected Ruis to translate. Perhaps she sensed she was the topic of discussion.

Mrs. Jenkins sniffled and tugged a lace-trimmed handkerchief from her pocket. Nefi sat up and watched her aunt.

"It won't be easy for her," Mrs. Jenkins said dabbing her eyes. "Starting over from tragedy. None of this will happen quickly." Her eyes welled up but did not spill over. "Thank you, gentlemen, for giving her...for giving all of us, this fresh start."

"You're welcome, Ma'am."

"It's our pleasure," Ruis said. "If you'd like me to help tonight—"

"Would you?" Louise asked.

"Of course." Ruis took a long drink of tea. "Thank you for your hospitality. I need to get Vincent and Blake to the airport."

Everyone stood. Nefi bolted from the room. The others followed her to the foyer. She was digging in her suitcase for something that she stuffed in her messenger bag before she picked up her messenger bag and stood.

Senator Jenkins shook hands with Vincent, Blake, and Ruis. Mrs. Jenkins hugged them one by one, sniffling as she did. The Senator handed his business cards to Vincent and Blake with an admonition to call him if he could help them in any way. Vincent tucked the card in his dress shirt pocket. When he applied to the FBI, he would call in the favor from Senator Jenkins. Since Ruis had paid them already, their business with the Jenkins family was complete.

Nefi pulled the leather and stone choker from her bag and held it out to Vincent.

Her father's choker? "Thank you, but you should keep it." He raised his hands. She would no doubt regret this impulsive decision later when she realized she had nothing of her father's.

Nefi patted Vincent's chest, rattling his dog tags. She pointed to them bulging under his shirt.

He was no longer the property of the government. Why not? He had been honorably discharged two months ago, so he reached into his shirt near his collarbone. He pulled a long shot bead chain up over his left ear and his head. The dog tags clinked as he tugged the chain from under his shirt. He dropped them into Nefi's cupped hands. She put the chain on over her head and let the tags dangle down her front. She pressed her father's choker against Vincent's chest until he took it. She hugged him so fiercely he thought he might cry.

During his good-bye hug, he momentarily rested his chin on Nefi's head to lock her height into sense memory. He also locked into his brain that Nefi was fourteen years old. Seven years his junior. He almost wanted to be fourteen again, at that moment, to surrender his years of education, experience, training and knowledge to be near her during her transition from childhood to adulthood. He wanted to protect her from tragedy. It was too late for that. Her childhood ended with murders. His father's murder had ended his childhood at sixteen. When he released her from their hug, their parting felt like an audible tearing away, like Velcro. Proud that she gave him the stone and leather necklace she had made for her father, he was equally proud she wanted something of his. He hoped Nefi would find joy in her new life. He also hoped that one day she would read his dog tags and remember him fondly.

Next, she reached into her bag and pulled out her sheathed hunting knife.

Mrs. Jenkins sucked in air.

Nefi gave the knife to Blake. They hugged. Her words were somewhat muffled by Blake's chest.

Ruis said, "She said it's a good snake knife."

Blake hugged the knife to his chest. "*Gracias.*"

Nefi then pulled a tiny leather pouch from her satchel and handed it to Ruis.

"*Gracias*, Nefi." Ruis took his *Portuguese/English Dictionary* from his shirt pocket and gave it to her.

She pointed to the pouch. Taking her cue, Ruis opened the pouch and tipped it over his open hand. Three green, pea-size stones fell into his hand. They were beautiful like sea glass with rough edges. Ruis tucked them back in the pouch.

A brief discussion ensued between Nefi and Ruis. It ended when Nefi pushed Ruis's hand and the pouch to his chest.

Ruis looked pleadingly at Senator Jenkins. "Sir, these are uncut emeralds."

Were emeralds common in the rainforest? Is that what the Indians used for currency?

"She wants you to have them," the Senator said in a decisive tone.

Ruis embraced Nefi while he whispered something in her ear.

It took a few minutes to make another round of goodbyes, during which tears rolled down Nefi's face as she watched the men leave. The Senator reached around Nefi's back to wrap his hand around her bony shoulder. Vincent, Ruis, and Blake descended the front porch steps and crossed the paved driveway where they climbed into their rental van.

When the vehicle pulled out of sight Nefi pressed her face against her uncle's shoulder. She was afraid to ask how far away Vincent and Blake lived because she wanted to believe they lived nearby.

Uncle Hamilton patted Nefi's back as he said to Louise, "I can't believe my brother didn't teach her English."

Nefi sniffled then said, "Papa tried."

Uncle Hamilton and Aunt Louise gaped at her.

Aunt Louise recovered first. "Can you understand us?"

Nefi nodded.

"Then why didn't you speak to the men in English?"

"Strangers have to earn trust." Nefi's bottom lip quivered.

Aunt Louise patted Nefi's back. "Did they earn your trust?"

Nefi's eyes stung. Tears popped from her eyes and rolled down her cheeks. She nodded.

Uncle Hamilton laughed and kissed the top of Nefi's head. "You're very smart to judge people by their actions instead of their words."

"Thank you for taking me. I do my best to be part of your tribe."

❦

On the road back to the airport, Vincent's curiosity compelled him to ask Ruis, "What did you say to her?"

"I told her to read Romans, chapter twelve." Ruis glanced in the rearview mirror as he drove.

From the front passenger's seat Blake said, "I would have suggested the study of First Corinthians thirteen since she's near dating age."

Feeling surrounded by Bible scholars, Vincent promised himself to look up those verses.

"Fourteen is too young to date," Ruis said.

Blake asked Ruis. "And how old were your sisters before you let them date?"

"The youngest, Martina, will be eighteen before she's allowed to go out without a chaperone," Ruis added, "I think Nefi's in good hands. And my family is one street away."

"Big Brother Ruis," Blake said.

Ruis nodded.

"Okay," Vincent said, "What's in chapter thirteen of Romans?"

"It's about love, about living right, about not conforming to the world, and it warns against revenge," Ruis said. "It ends with a command—do not be overcome by evil, but overcome evil with good."

. 7 .

Two weeks after welcoming Nefi into her new home, Uncle Hamilton announced he was expecting a visit from a long-distant friend from college, His Excellency Ambassador Alfonso Morales. When a black limousine decorated with a small Brazilian flags on the front bumpers pulled into the driveway, Nefi was the first person in the house to see it as she spied down from the second-floor window of Aunt Louise's sewing room. The driver, a handsome dark-haired man in his early twenties, hopped out and opened the back door. An older dark-haired man climbed out from the back of the limousine, buttoning his jacket. He stood five feet eight and every inch of him from his dark gray suit to his shiny black shoes announced his presence as a man of importance.

Nefi dashed to the banister overlooking the foyer.

Uncle Hamilton welcomed the Ambassador with a back-slapping hug. "It's so great to see you, Al."

"Thank you for inviting me to your home."

Perhaps he brought news of the investigation or an arrest. Nefi tingled with anticipation.

"What is it, Al?"

"Is there somewhere private where we can talk?" the Ambassador asked.

Uncle Hamilton's face tightened. "I believe you once said the study was your favorite room." He and the Ambassador disappeared into the sitting room which connected to the study.

Aunt Louise called the study the man cave. The dark room, lined with cherry and mahogany bookshelves, held sturdy leather furniture and a massive desk. It also muffled sound unless one knew just where to stand to eavesdrop. Nefi tiptoed into the master bedroom, directly over the study, and settled down beside the air vent between the closet door and the dresser.

"Louise will be back soon. I know a home-cooked meal is an ultimate luxury to a traveling man. Can you stay for dinner?"

"Ah, Louise is an excellent cook."

A compliment was not an answer. Was he upset with Uncle? Or bringing unwelcome news?

"May I get you a coffee? We have Brazilian grown." Uncle Hamilton said. There was a hint of tension in his voice.

Uncle Hamilton preferred the burgundy colored leather wing-back chair in the sitting area beside a wall of floor-to-ceiling bookshelves. This inner wall of the house had doorways at either end, one that led to the hallway to the back door and another that led into the formal sitting room toward the front of the house. The Ambassador sounded farther away as if he was standing by the large picture window overlooking the backyard oaks. Perhaps he paced in front of Uncle's long L-shaped computer desk. Though the bend of the desk fit in the room's corner, one part of the desk overlapped the window. The room's thick Oriental rug covered the center of the floor and tended to silence the sound of footfalls.

"How are things at home?" Uncle asked.

"When I told mother I was coming here, she warned me that we're too old and too well known to get drunk in public." The Ambassador's voice grew louder. Squeaking leather told Nefi that the Ambassador had settled into the other chair by her uncle.

"She's never going to let that go, is she?"

"Mother declares disorderly conduct unsuitable for gentlemen."

Both men laughed.

Uncle Hamilton's hands slapped on leather. "Whose idea was it to drink at every bar in Cambridge?"

"Herman's."

Nefi flinched at the mention of her father. She had never seen him drink alcohol, even in Manaus.

The Ambassador said softly, "To celebrate his twenty-first birthday."

Somber silence fell between the men while Nefi tried to imagine her father young and drinking.

"We could have a drink here in private," Uncle Hamilton said. It sounded partly like an invitation, mostly like a dare.

"First," the Ambassador said, "I need to ask you a few questions."

"Whatever weighs on you, please, let's discuss it."

Nefi closed her eyes to concentrate.

"When you learned that Herman and Marta had a child, you hired three men to search for her," the Ambassador said.

"Yes."

"And what date was that?"

"The day after you called me, I called Admiral Ramos for advice. He recommended his son Ruis and two Marines."

The Ambassador jotted on his notepad. "And how soon after that did they go to Brazil?"

"The next day they flew into *Cruzeiro do Sul*."

"Yes, and they met with IBAMA officers," he said checking his notes, "Raposo and Machado."

Hamilton stood and disappeared. His desk drawer *thunked* then his chair squeaked. "The men gave me these reports when they delivered Nefi."

"May I have copies?"

Nefi sat upright to breathe. She had forgotten about the reports. Her pulse accelerated. What had Vincent written about her?

"Of course," Uncle Hamilton said. "Al, is there news about the investigation?"

"It's still an open case."

"I see."

"Forgive me," Ambassador Morales said. "There's a second investigation. The bodies of two Brazilian nationals were found near the settlement where Herman and Marta lived."

"More victims?"

"The dead men were known criminals. Petty thieves and drug runners. They had been shot."

Nefi opened her eyes. She remembered the flash of the rifles temporarily blinding her. That sound cracked open the night like lightning splitting a tree.

"Drug runners? You don't think Herman was involved in that sort of thing, do you?"

How could Uncle Hamilton ask such a thing? Nefi kept silent by biting her lip.

"Not at all."

"Then what does the one investigation have to do with the other?"

"Machine guns were found by the bodies of the drug runners. Ballistics technicians matched the bullets from one of these weapons to the bullets recovered from the two nationals. The bullets also matched the ones recovered from Herman and Marta."

Uncle's voice crept higher. "Are you saying the men shot Herman and Marta and then shot each other?"

"You see the puzzle," Ambassador Morales said, "The villagers identified the nationals as two of three men who came to the village the day Herman and Marta died. They say the man who did the killing was not one of the bodies."

The room swayed, so Nefi silently braced her hands on the doorjamb of the closet and the dresser. No. The Pirarucu Man must be dead.

"And who is he?" Uncle Hamilton asked the question on Nefi's mind.

"The killer was a fish buyer known as the Pirarucu Man." The Ambassador sighed. "It seems unlikely the killer would shoot his own men."

An unease seeped into Uncle Hamilton's voice. "Would the villagers?"

"None of them owns guns."

"You aren't suggesting my men did this, because—"

"The dates on their passports clear your men. Besides, the nationals died within days of Herman and Marta."

Uncle Hamilton said, "Do you think the villagers could have ambushed these killers, making them panic and shoot one another?"

"Possibly, but there is one more puzzle piece that defies explanation. There was a human hand found near the bodies. It didn't belong to the nationals. Investigators checked the villagers and no one was missing a hand, so the assumption is that the hand belonged to the Pirarucu Man. Forensics says the hand was probably cut off with a machete."

Uncle Hamilton cleared his throat. "I remember that gory detail from the reports. Wouldn't he bleed to death?"

"I don't know. The investigators also found one set of fingerprints on the guns that didn't match the villagers or the dead men or even the hand." Ambassador Morales cleared his throat. "Would you allow me to get Nefi's fingerprints?"

"You can't be serious."

"To rule her out."

Her? Who? Me? Nefi leaned back against the wall and her satchel.

The back door squeaked and shut. *Aunt Louise!* Nefi pulled the strap of her satchel until the satchel was centered on her back, then dropping to her hands and knees, she crawled from the master bedroom, across the open floor space that was framed by three doors and the upper railing of the staircase to her own room. Voices echoed in the foyer as Aunt Louise greeted the Ambassador.

Her heart racing, Nefi paced her room like a caged jaguar. *The Ambassador wants my fingerprints?* Staring at her hands, she balled them into fists.

"Nefi," Aunt Louise called. "Come down dear. We have company."

Nefi took a few deep breaths, composed herself and strode from her room to the top of the spiral staircase. In blue jeans, a white Oxford shirt, and brown leather sandals, she straightened her back and grabbed the smooth wooden banister.

The Ambassador tucked a white card inside his jacket.

Nefi trudged down the stairs as a suspect. On her way down the stairs, the smell of roasted meat and vegetables grew stronger, awakening her appetite. In the foyer, she hugged Uncle Hamilton, then Aunt Louise and then faced the stranger. The man's face transformed from seriousness to charm.

"This is His Excellency, Ambassador Alfonso Morales from Brazil," Uncle said.

She remembered his name from the thank-you card she had mailed to him for the camera. His thick dark brown hair reflected an almost blue shine, and his keen brown eyes seemed to take in everything quickly. He probably had servants for labor while he negotiated for the country. A subtle scent of spices—aftershave or cologne—wafted from him.

Nefi found her voice. "Thank you for the camera."

"I'm so pleased you like it."

The Ambassador offered his right hand. His hand was warm and soft like Aunt Louise's. Nefi shook his hand, then clasped her hands behind her.

"She carries it everywhere," Aunt Louise said. She glanced at the satchel as if to remind Nefi that she did not need to wear it all the time.

Though Nefi understood she didn't need to wear it all the time, she wanted to nonetheless. Uncle Hamilton called it a security blanket, whatever that meant. Wearing the satchel came more naturally than wearing shoes. Besides, Aunt Louise carried a purse, as did grandma. Was it such a strange thing here to carry a satchel? Aunt treated the satchel as an unacceptable habit, but she had been simply horrified at the photos the cabbie in Manaus had taken of her with Blake, Ruis, and Vincent. She pointed to the hunting knife strapped to Nefi's leg as if it was a poisonous snake.

If only Aunt understood life in the jungle, she would accept the satchel and the knife as common-sense necessities. Nefi sighed.

Ambassador Morales studied Nefi's face. "You have your father's height and your mother's beauty." He smiled.

Nefi examined his face for deception and found no signs. Suddenly she recognized his smile. She dashed to the study, searching each shelf on the bookcase set in the wall until she snatched a framed photo from a shoulder-level shelf and rushed with it back into the foyer. There she shoved the picture frame into the Ambassador's hands.

Smiling, he looked at her face while he held the frame. He glanced down. "I'm surprised you recognize me from this." He held it toward Uncle. The photo, dated decades ago, showed Uncle Hamilton, Nefi's parents—Marta and Herman—and Alfonso Morales wedged side by side in a circular wooden booth.

"Those were happy days," Uncle Hamilton announced. "I told Nefi this was taken near Harvard."

"Please stay for dinner," Aunt Louise said, "and if it isn't a complete breach of protocol, your driver is welcome to come inside and eat."

The Ambassador kissed Aunt Louise on the cheek. "You are so kind. He's my nephew. Let me get him." He passed the framed photo back to Nefi.

"I'll put it back," Uncle Hamilton said.

"I'm going to check the roast," Aunt Louise said on her way to the kitchen.

Nefi followed her uncle as far as the sitting room. There he picked up the file and placed it back in his desk. Before he turned around, Nefi ducked back into the foyer. She hoped the file would stay there for her to read later in secret. She had to know what Vincent wrote about her.

The Ambassador reentered the foyer with a young man who resembled him in coloring, body type, and handsomeness. "Nefi Jenkins, allow me to introduce my nephew, Antonio Morales."

Nefi nodded at him. Without her aunt and uncle, she felt unsure of what to do next. She thrust out her hand.

"I'm pleased to meet you," Antonio said shaking her hand. "I'm so sorry to hear about your parents. I hope you have many *good* memories of Brazil." The young man's English was far better than hers. He held his chauffeur's hat in his left hand. He continued to hold Nefi's right hand in his own.

Aunt Louise stepped into the foyer and raised an approving eyebrow at Antonio. Nefi rummaged in her messenger bag and pulled out her camera. She directed everyone to stand side by side together on the staircase for a few photos. Soon all were blinking like bats forced into daylight.

Hours later after dinner, Nefi went out for a walk with Antonio while Louise cleaned up in the kitchen, so Senator Hamilton and Ambassador Alfonso retired to the study for brandy, cigars and to continue their conversation in privacy. They spoke with the casual familiarity of long-time friends as if only days instead of years had passed since their visit.

Hamilton did all he could to persuade his old friend that Nefi was a sweet girl who was overcoming great tragedy. He explained how, weeks earlier Nefi had arrived with all her belongings in a small suitcase, and although she owned so little, she filled the home. Just as effortlessly as Nefi brought life and energy to the home, she had changed the mood of the evening from darkness to light. She had charmed Alfonso and Antonio seemed smitten by her.

Alfonso must have backed down on the idea of fingerprinting Nefi, because he did not mention it again.

Hamilton told Alfonso all about his plans to submit a bill on raising the punishment for certain drug-related crimes to capital punishment. Alfonso draped his jacket over the back of his chair. In the lamplight, Hamilton spotted a touch of gray at Alfonso's temples. Hamilton briefly outlined the bill itself and his plans to promote it. He finished up by giving his reasons for sponsoring the bill.

"If my brother died as a casualty of the war on drugs, then that gives me another personal stake in establishing stronger laws here." Hamilton watched Alfonso's expression soften. Alfonso had attended Jason's funeral, but he had never asked how he had died.

"Jason, too?" Alfonso asked in a whisper.

"An overdose. As much as I would like to believe it was accidental, I'll never know for sure." Denial was a powerful temptation and a balm to self-blame.

Alfonso loosened his tie and unbuttoned the top of his dress shirt before he stared into his Brandy and spoke. "How do you plan to share your losses with the public without giving the impression of exploiting their deaths?"

Though it stung to hear it, Hamilton understood Alfonso meant to be helpful. "I will emphasize that my personal tragedies are the reasons I drafted the bill. I intend to show no one is immune from the violence of the drug trade. It's everyone's problem. The poor already understand the dangers, but I suspect people with wealth, position, and political influence have a tendency to feel immune. I want to destroy that illusion by example."

At that, Alfonso raised his glass toward Hamilton, who also raised his glass.

Hamilton took a swallow of brandy, set down his goblet and leaned forward in his leather wingback chair. "I've been meaning to ask you something. Where did the newspapers get the absurd idea that my brother was a missionary?"

"Not from me. He was registered as a foreigner doing social work, teaching Portuguese to the indigenous Indians, that sort of thing. I've been trying to figure out why he overstayed his VISA."

. 8 .

March 31, 2006

Having been summoned, Damiano Guerra waited on a plush black leather sectional sofa for his boss. It was the last day of March. Sometimes he had to sit for hours until the great Victor Alexandre 'Xano' Rodrigo Cortes dragged himself from bed. Such was the privilege of power—to make others wait. The view of Rio de Janeiro from this room inspired Damiano because from here he looked down on the city that once looked down on him.

Alexandre, long before he became one of the most powerful drug cartel leaders in South America, was Damiano's only friend. Alexandre was known as Xano back then. In his childhood, Damiano used to fend for himself, and although he was quick and smart, it wasn't until he met Xano that he learned his three most valuable survival skills: lying, stealing and bullying. Their band of boys represented a small part of the *meninos da rua*, the children of the street, who at one time numbered in the tens of thousands.

Rather than being ashamed of homelessness, Xano called it the ultimate freedom. He had a grand plan to unite the homeless population into one huge family that would work together and grow into its own powerful force in the city. He had formed a coalition with two large packs, whose territories overlapped at the

104

Candelaria Church, but disaster struck. Since then, Xano called Damiano his lucky charm.

Xano had called for a meeting at the church for the leaders of the two other rival packs at midnight on July 23, 1993. On their way to the meeting, Xano gave Damiano his first cigarette, daring him to smoke it without coughing. Damiano took the dare. Halfway through the cigarette, he puked. Another boy mocked him, so Damiano punched him. Their fight escalated into a bloody match that Xano had to break up. This delayed Xano from reaching the meeting on time.

When another boy told Xano the time, he grabbed Damiano by the collar. "I have to take you with me so the others know why I am late," Xano told him. "Don't wipe off the blood."

One block from the Candelaria Church, a car passed with three men inside it holding rifles. Xano recognized them as policemen, but they were not in uniform. He pulled Damiano into an alley. The car rounded the corner at the church. Xano climbed the fire escape of a building that overlooked the square where the church stood. Damiano followed. The police openly despised the street children.

Xano reached the roof's edge at the same moment all the doors of the unmarked police car swung open. Four men climbed out of the car and ran to the church. Bullets flashed as their guns cut down eight boys. Damiano saw the boys' faces lit up by the rifle flashes. The men kicked the bodies. Muttering, the officers climbed back into their car and sped away from the carnage. It was the last time Damiano cried.

Since that night, he pledged to help take revenge on authorities. The boys agreed to trust only each other though he suspected that Xano thought of him more as a good luck charm than a friend. Damiano stopped feeling twinges of guilt for stealing.

The only kind adult they found was a sculptor named Yvonne Bezerra de Mello, who held a vigil at the church in honor of the boys the police killed. She harassed the police and the newspapers to find and convict the boys' murderers. In the evenings, she met homeless children at the church to teach them to read. She fed them. She made public what the street children already knew — that over a thousand children had been shot to death the previous year at the rate of four a day. When it became public news that the killers were off-duty military policemen, public opinion polls showed sixteen percent of Rio de Janeiro's citizens *still* approved the shooting of the homeless children.

Xano and Damiano vowed that if society treated them like vermin, then they would treat society in kind. In almost twenty years, they raised themselves from poverty to power through drugs, guns, and blood. They embraced the beliefs that 'might makes right' and the strongest deserve to survive. As Xano's money and influence grew, he told Damiano to call him Mr. Cortes, like the other employees as a sign of respect. Damiano respected his wish and called him Mr. Cortes from that day since.

While waiting for Mr. Cortes, Damiano picked up the television remote control with his good hand from the black lacquer coffee table. He aimed it at the sixty-inch plasma screen on the opposite wall. The screen glowed in dense colors and high-definition precise images, sharp and clear like being in person only bigger. A giant face came into sharp focus above a running banner of numbers. The stock exchange reported lower earnings in car manufacturing with layoffs expected. Watching the Cable News Network helped him learn English. Cortes had said he had plans for expanding his trade in the northeast United States.

Learning English would be easier if the gringos spoke slower. Damiano listened to the news as fast as he could. He struggled to understand the news from the United States about a woman in a coma who died. The newsman said she had been unconscious for years, living on a feeding tube. Terri Schiavo. Why was one death news? Had anyone expected her to wake up and walk from the hospital? He shook his head and listened harder as the next news item played.

"Congressional leaders press hard to present bills before the holiday recess. The most controversial bill scheduled for a vote is an anti-drug bill drawn up by Senator Hamilton Jenkins of Alabama. This bill proposes, in part, to change the penalty for illegal drug distribution from a maximum of fifteen years to a possible death penalty by tying the crime of distribution to the Rico Act. The Rico Act involves criminal organizations, like the Mafia and other organized criminal groups."

Senator Jenkins appeared on screen in a video clip, shocking Damiano. The man looked exactly like the missionary he killed four years ago, just before he lost his hand. *Twins?* The senator held up a photo of the missionary couple. Damiano compared the photo with his last bloody memory of them and smiled. *Jenkins. Yes. The same name.*

"I ask you to call your congressman to demand passage of this bill so that you will not lose any of your family to this deadly industry," Senator Jenkins said. "Those who perpetuate the drug trade, and those who profit from it kill anyone who gets in their way. Like my brother and sister-in-law who served the indigenous Indians in South America. Brazilian authorities say they were shot to death by drug runners. My brother left behind a daughter, who was rescued with the help of the Brazilian Federal Police." His face was hard, but his eyes gave away the depth of his loss.

The camera zoomed in on an old newspaper photo of a teenager looking over her shoulder from the steps of the U.S. Consulate in Manaus. The girl's face was painted red and black as an Indian's. The girl's long brown hair was too light to be an Indian's. Then he saw her yellow eyes staring back at him.

He stood, dropping the remote control. She must have seen her parents die. Cortes warned him, never leave a witness. But the Indians did not count. They knew better than to challenge men with guns. They would *never* travel to any Brazilian court. They settled things their own way, right away. He admired them for taking his hand instead of seeking the help of the IBAMA or the Federals. But the girl was a different matter. She wasn't part of the tribe. She might talk to police. What did the girl look like without the paint? How could he find her? *Where was she?*

His breath and heartbeat quickened. The voice on the television recaptured his attention.

Senator Jenkins held up another picture. "...like my son, who became addicted to drugs and poisoned himself. Don't believe anyone is safe from the illegal drug trade. Help me toughen the laws so we can win this battle."

Cortes plopped down on the sofa beside Damiano, startling him.

"What," Cortes asked in English, "are the Americans whining about now?" He plucked the remote off the floor.

Damiano considered telling his boss about the girl, but Cortes might blame him for leaving a witness. "They don't like us."

Cortes laughed. "They looooove our cocaine." He held a thumb to his nose and sniffed.

Keyed up at a potential opportunity for revenge, Damiano pointed to the screen. "That Senator named Jenkins wants to make a law that drug dealers can be put to death."

"Let him make his laws. It is only when the Americans want to enforce their laws that we have to worry. Do you want a drink?" This was Cortes's way of telling Damiano to get him one.

"What would be good for this time of day?" Damiano did not want to guess the kind of drink Cortes wanted.

"Rum and cola, the breakfast of predators." Cortes changed the channel to an exercise program featuring shapely women in leotards. He muted the instructor's voice.

Damiano rose off the deep cushioned sofa by leaning on his good hand, his left hand, causing him to lean toward Cortes, who planted a hand on his back and shoved him.

"Are you left-handed or right-handed?" Cortes's mind jumped in unexpected directions at times.

"Left," he answered. He did not take offense because showing hurt or anger invited mocking. Only the weak showed their feelings.

"That's good." Cortes stared at Damiano's prosthetic right hand. His serious expression switched into a wicked smile. "It would be a shame to lose your backup lover."

He forced a laugh. "A casualty of business." He said it to remind Cortes of the story about losing his hand. Cortes valued loyalty above all.

"How is the new one working?" Cortes had paid for the new hand. He bought it from the finest prosthetic specialist in Brazil. Cortes rewarded loyalty with money.

"Good."

It looked real enough. The specialist offered another type of replacement hand that moved when stimulated by muscle twitches. It looked like shiny plastic, but it made noise when the fingers moved. There were situations in which such a small noise would be fatal, so he chose the immovable hand. Cortes had argued that with a little extra engineering, the powered hand could produce a death grip. He fantasized about having one hand with super power. The moving hand would never fire a gun or count money. These were the things his old hand did.

He prepared two rum and colas with his left hand, using the prosthesis to push the glasses together. He managed slowly without spilling. He loaded the drinks on a small gold tray and carried it to the coffee table. He knew Cortes was watching him, judging him.

"To expanding our territory." Cortes raised his glass.

Damiano lifted his glass and held it still while Cortes clinked his glass against it. Both men drank a hearty first gulp. The rum warmed. The cola cooled. The opposites balanced one another.

"I have been watching American television," Cortes said, "and

I got an idea from one of their shows about how to set you up to travel freely in the United States without fear of the police."

Now that he knew a witness was alive and who she was, Damiano longed to go finish his business with the Jenkins family. If Cortes could get him near Washington D.C., it would be worth the risk. He paid attention.

"It may take a few years to reach my distribution goals, but once everything is set up you will be untouchable. I depend on you to bring me luck as always." The prospect of greater wealth and power animated Cortes. He was a predator with a plan.

Damiano carried rage like a loaded gun, always ready to kill once given a target. Eliminating the American couple had been easy, but it had cost him his hand. Killing the American girl would be the best way to avenge his hand and silence a potential witness.

The secretary at the office of Psychiatrist Ethan Sloan in McLean, Virginia, pressed the intercom button. "Miss Jenkins is here."

"Send her in."

Sloan nodded at her as she entered. Nefi at age eighteen was tall with waist-length brown hair. She had an athletic figure. Fresh from track practice, she had changed into the popular preppie look, a short khaki skirt, and a striped polo top. She felt at ease in clothes one size larger than necessary to allow full, free movement. Unlike most girls her age, she had not pierced her ears but left them bare as a newborn's. Her makeup was minimal lip gloss and eyeliner, playing up her amber irises, which the boys seemed to stare at. She strolled in low-heeled Mary Janes to the rack where she hung her coat. Taking her usual seat on the soft brown recliner, she shed her backpack on the floor. She cranked the lever on the side to raise the foot rest. Pushing on the chair arms, she arched her back slightly until the chair fully reclined.

Doctor Sloan dictated, "March thirty-one, two-thousand-six, session with Nefi Jenkins. The subject is adjusting very well in her senior year at Langley High School. She has passed successfully through the stages of grief so we will focus on her personal life, namely her relationships." He checked his notes.

Nefi raised her eyebrows at the tall, middle-aged black man she had grown to trust. Doctor Ethan Sloan, keeper of secrets. He kept his black and gray hair trimmed close to his scalp and jawline. At a glance, he looked like a college professor in tweed and khakis.

He continued dictation. "Last session she reported that boys have ridiculed her for her height and for her excellent grades. She said she's anxious about being accepted at a top college. I will again attempt to discuss her obsession with one of her rescuers."

Not that again.

He closed Nefi's file. Doctor Sloan took his usual place sitting upright on the other recliner. "Good afternoon, Nefi."

"Good afternoon, Doctor."

He looked over the top rim of his frameless glasses at her. "What are you getting from our sessions?"

"Time away from homework."

He smirked. "Then why are we meeting?"

"For Uncle Ham and Aunt Louise."

"We're meeting for their benefit?"

"As long as you counsel me, they worry less that I will make terrible decisions like Jason."

Doctor Sloan nodded. "How much have they told you about his death?"

"They say they think his overdose was accidental since he didn't leave a note."

"And how do you feel about that?"

The man is obsessed with feelings. "His death haunts them. I don't want them to worry about me. I don't take drugs, and I don't like the taste of alcohol."

Doctor Sloan jotted a note on his pad. He held out his hand.

Nefi dug her journal from her backpack and set it on his open hand. The flowery cloth cover, worn at the spine, had been her safe place to reveal her thoughts, feelings, observations and decisions over the last four years. She had written things in this small lined book she could never discuss with Aunt Louise and Uncle Hamilton. Perhaps they were curious about the contents of the book, but they had never asked to read it. They trusted Doctor Sloan as much as she did. He had counseled them after Jason's death.

While he reviewed the latest entries, she spoke. "Will you promise me something?"

"That depends on what that something is."

Fair enough. She knew he'd tattle on her in an instant if he suspected she was a danger to herself or others. "Promise me that if…something happens to me you'll give my journal to Uncle Hamilton."

Alarm had flashed on his face before he composed himself. "I can promise that. Just write that permission on the inside cover. Do you think something is going to happen?"

"No."

"Then why—?"

"A boy at school died in a car crash. I heard his sister say that she never told her brother she loved him."

Doctor Sloan swallowed. "You want to give your aunt and uncle closure."

"Yes." The journal could answer so many questions they were afraid to ask; everything she was afraid to admit.

"Do you tell them you love them?"

"Yes, but they might need to read it one day when they are sad."

Sloan held out the flowered journal.

"You can keep it." Nefi clasped her hands in her lap.

"Congratulations. Does this mean you won't be meeting with me anymore?"

"I'm done writing in it."

"Ah," Dr. Sloan said. He set it on the small round table beside his chair.

"I have been accepted at Brown, so the pressure is off. Still waiting to hear from Harvard."

"And have you decided on a major?"

"Psychology or criminology."

"Tell me your reasons."

"I want to make a difference." She rubbed her right thumb on her left palm. Such a gesture in other patients looked like shyness or hesitation, but she did it when considering whether or not to speak about a sensitive subject.

The doctor waited. The phone rang outside the masculine wood-paneled room. His secretary's muffled voice sounded muted and distorted, as if underwater.

"I want to prevent crimes."

"Prevent them? How?"

Nefi sighed. "I'll tell you if you promise to test me."

The corner of his mouth flinched in an almost-grin. "I don't know what to test for until you tell me."

"I know there are tests for this."

"For a way you can prevent crimes?" Sarcasm oozed from him.

"Tests for what I can do."

"What do you mean?"

"Think of an object, a specific object that only you would know."

He opened his mouth.

She raised her hand. "Just think of it. The more obscure, the better."

Scientists and doctors like Sloan learned that perception was reality, and although he could guide patients to challenge their perceptions, he could not make them believe any truth, no matter how obvious that truth was. She believed he would take her unusual ability in stride, but he might consider it a delusion.

He put on his game face and played along. He glanced around his office, which gave Nefi the clue she needed. She knew exactly what he would label as obscure.

"Hockey skates," Nefi said.

He recoiled as if slapped. His mouth dropped open. "How did you do that?"

Nefi shrugged. "If it's someone I know it's easy. Like recognizing a voice. And I did ask for something obscure."

"Hmm. Is this a parlor trick or are you suggesting you have extra-sensory perception?"

"No trick."

His face clouded as if he'd been betrayed. "After four years you share this with me? Why did you wait so long to tell me?"

"My parents warned me that people treat us differently once they know, so they made me promise to keep it secret. One time," she said leaning forward in her chair, "this naked tribal chief asked me to be his shaman. In his tribe, the shaman is traditionally the chief's wife. Ewww." A shudder ran through her body at the memory of the small, smelly, pot-bellied chief.

"Is this an early April Fool's Day prank?"

"No, sir."

"Sorry. It's just that your announcement surprises me." He did not like it when sessions veered off in wild directions. Clearly, he needed time to 'process' this surprise. Stroking his trim beard, he asked, "Did your parents have this gift?"

"Yes, sir. Father could only see things once in a while in his dreams." Nefi crossed her ankles. "Mother sometimes heard what people didn't say, but she always knew when they were lying."

"So you trust me enough to tell me." He leaned forward in his seat. "Why have you kept *this* a secret?"

"It isn't accepted in this culture to be...different." Nefi flipped the foot rest down with her feet. "So I need your help."

"I thought I was helping you." He peered over the rim of his glasses.

"Test me." Nefi sat on the recliner's edge with her hands folded neatly in her lap in proper prep school fashion. She understood she was different from her classmates, from her neighbors, and frankly, from everyone she knew. The Indians recognized her difference and treated it with fear and awe. She missed being respected that way. If she had to be the odd one, at least she could have recognition for it in this society. Her gift had a value that could grant her opportunities others could not reach.

"I would need to determine which tests would be appropriate." He tapped his pen tip on his pad and spoke almost to himself. "The tests must be above reproach. They must be conducted by experts. Only two researchers in the northeast were worth calling. Why is *proving* such an ability important to you?"

"I need proof. I want to use my ability to prevent crime, but first, I have to demonstrate I have it with objective testing." Nefi stood and paced the room. "I think about this all the time. Like boys think about sex."

"So you believe you can hear other people's thoughts?"

"Yes, sir."

"Does this apply to everyone?"

At this, Nefi froze in place. "Everyone but one."

"And who is that?"

Nefi rubbed her elbows with her hands as if hugging herself. Her pacing led her to the window, and she looked outside. Bowing her head, she said, "If I tell you, you'll say it's part of my obsession with one of my rescuers."

He flinched. "So do you believe you can hear everyone's mind but Vincent's? Why is that?"

She leaned on the window sill. Her hand toyed with the shot bead chain of Vincent's dog tags tucked under her collar. "His beauty distracts me."

"What would you like to hear from Vincent's mind?"

She glowed with hope. "That he loves me. That I'm the one he waited for."

"Because you're waiting for him?"

She felt stabbed by his directness. Sloan, Aunt, and Uncle, everyone it seemed was upset that she wasn't dating. Like it was unnatural to refuse dates from all the sex-hungry boys at school. Why couldn't they see that the boys at school did not, could not, and possibly never would measure up to Vincent? Even her best friend Martina privately mocked her. She crossed her arms. "Because I'm the person God wants him to marry."

Sloan blinked rapidly as if trying to accept her bold statement without laughing. "Has God told you this?"

She envisioned the agnostic doctor strapping her into a straitjacket. She chewed her bottom lip, then said, "He put it in my heart."

"How will you know if God put this same sentiment in Vincent's heart?" He scratched the tip of his nose. No doubt he thought of God with a small g, one of many pagan idols that small minds trusted at their peril.

"I'll know when I see Vincent again, but it's too soon." Nefi sighed. "You don't believe me."

"You say you can hear other people's thoughts." As if by habit or training, the doctor switched topics when he sensed resistance. "What disorder is it when people hear voices that aren't heard by others?"

Nefi scowled. "Then test me for schizophrenia." She planted a hand on her hip. "But test me for psychic stuff, too."

He sighed. "At least you have the terminology correct. Let's assume for the sake of argument that you can read other people's minds. My concern is how you interpret your ability. If a boy looks at you and his thoughts are impure, do you feel justified to slap him?"

Nefi tilted her head as if weary of holding it up. "I would have been expelled by now if I reacted every time a boy imagined me naked. We learned in sex education class that the male teenager thinks about sex every few *minutes*."

Doctor Sloan crossed his arms and propped his chin on one hand.

Nefi knew he was holding back another long sigh. "I haven't had any incidents with boys since my first week of school. I told you about that boy who flipped up the back of my skirt to see what kind of underwear I had, right?"

Sloan nodded.

The other boys had laughed like monkeys. Martina explained it was a game the upperclassmen play on the freshmen. Thong or granny panties, Martina had called it.

"You reacted to his actions, not his thoughts. And if I recall, you were suspended for your actions."

She had set down her lunch tray, marched back to the boy's table, reached into the back of his pants, and lifted him out of his chair by the waistband of his underwear. She grinned at the memory of the boy's utter shock when she declared, "Boxers."

Sloan plucked off his glasses and rubbed his eyes. "Have you spoken to Hamilton about your ability to hear other people's thoughts?"

"No."

"Perhaps it's time to bring your uncle into a session."

Nefi nodded. "He can sense things, too, but it scares him."

"Then let's run the tests *before* we bring him in." Sloan moved to his desk calendar on his computer screen. "Then we'll have something to present him."

"Psychic or schizo," she said. She spoke the words his mind was forming.

He shuddered. "You said it's easy for you when you know a person. What if you don't know a person well?"

"I can judge strangers' thoughts when they're in an extreme emotional state—something primal, like fear, or ecstasy, or stress, or hate, or deep love or when they think of something intensely personal, like a secret. Or something they cherish deeply." She grinned. "Maybe I'm not psychic, but you have to admit you were shocked when I named your hockey skates."

He chuckled. "I was. If I had been a better athlete, I might have pursued hockey instead of psychiatry. Such an aggressive, fast-paced sport, it appeals to my inner child." After clicking his desk mouse, he looked up again. "Not everyone who lives in snow country plays hockey, and there aren't many African-American hockey players. How did you know I played?"

Nefi strode to his wall of awards, diplomas, and certificates and pointed to a high school team photo. A younger version of him knelt in the front row of padded, smiling boys in uniform who encircled a three-foot trophy. "Your 'love me' wall says you played."

He scowled at her. "There is a huge difference between being observant and reading minds."

"Thus the need for testing." She emphasized her point by extending her hands.

After a few phone calls, and calling in a favor, Sloan scheduled paranormal testing for the following Monday with a specialist at the FBI Behavioral Sciences department in Quantico. Nefi entered the date, time and address of the appointment in her smart phone on her electronic calendar. *Quantico!* A rush of joy flooded her at the idea she would get to go inside a real FBI building.

"Since your uncle is a busy man, let's meet with him for your next appointment." He flipped through his card file. He dialed a number.

"Uncle's secretary is Betsy," Nefi said.

"Really?" he asked absently. After a moment, he checked the card file.

Nefi, thoroughly pleased to catch him off guard, grinned at him.

He pressed a button on his desktop phone. Ringing sounded. Speakerphone. A woman answered the call, identifying the Senate office.

"This is Doctor Ethan Sloan. I'd like to set up an appointment with Senator Jenkins to discuss his niece. I'm looking at times late next week at his home, or my office, or even after hours at his convenience."

Betsy found an opening on April fourteenth, in the evening at the senator's home. Sloan held out his hand to confirm the date with Nefi.

Nefi nodded. Their session time was spent, so she donned her coat and shouldered her backpack.

"Thank you." Doctor Sloan checked his watch. "And by the way, is your name Betty or Betsy?"

"Betsy, but everyone gets it wrong so I answer to Betty, too."

"Thank you, Betsy." He clunked the phone back in the cradle and jabbed the speakerphone button. Sloan corrected his index card.

Nefi smirked at him.

"That's still not mind reading."

She plucked her cell phone from her backpack and typed the appointment with her uncle on her electronic calendar with her thumbs for Friday, April 14, 2006. *We'll see, doc. We'll see.*

Sloan waved her back to the chair.

Nefi touched her fingertips to her forehead. "And now you want to discuss my dating life or lack of it."

Doctor Sloan eased into his recliner and picked up his pen and paper. "Let's call it avoidance behavior. You take no risk of rejection, or loss, by avoiding relationships with half the population."

"I'm not avoiding males. But I am avoiding relationships with them because their concept of a relationship seems entirely based on having sex. They want it, and I don't. If I don't go out with a guy, then I'm called frigid or homosexual. If I go out with a guy, he asks for sex, I say no and then I get labeled a tease. It's a no-win situation."

Doctor Sloan raked his fingertips through his trim hair from forehead to neck. "So how do you plan to establish a relationship on your terms?"

"I will wait for the right man." She held her hands in her lap to prevent pressing the dog tags under her shirt.

"Isn't it sabotaging your future happiness to presume only one person can be right for you?"

Near midnight, Vincent and Blake stood in Oscar's dormitory room at Columbia University surveying their work. Vincent's younger brother, Oscar, and his roommate Chase were asleep on their backs with their legs hanging over the side of their beds. Their feet were set in large plastic tubs filled with a layer of warm water followed by a layer of Styrofoam peanuts capped off with plastic sheeting taped to the sides of the tubs and legs to create a watertight seal. Blake finished mixing the plaster in a two-gallon bucket and poured a thick layer of it on top of the plastic sheeting. The final result gave the illusion of having feet secured in cement. Vincent felt a twinge of guilt.

"Chase wet himself," Vincent whispered. "I told you the water was too warm."

"How do you think they could get to the toilet?" Blake poured cement plaster into the second tub. "This is perfect timing. They'll wake up on April Fool's Day."

"You really enjoy April Fool's Day, don't you?"

"My brothers and I consider it a family holiday."

Oscar snored open mouthed. Four hours earlier he had been

celebrating his twenty-first birthday with a few drinks until he slid off his barstool at the Hogs & Heifers Saloon. Vincent had warned Oscar and Chase to pace themselves with the Captain Morgan mixers, but like college boys, they shrugged off sound advice to earn their first legal hangovers. Vincent had been watching women dance on the bar, so he didn't notice Oscar on the floor until one dancer pointed to the empty stool. Two drinks later the roommate toppled.

Looking at his snoring brother, Vincent was proud. Years ago Vincent managed to graduate from high school at seventeen, and although he had the grades and the drive to succeed in college, his father's sudden death required the family to draw on savings. Vincent relieved his mother of the burden of having to choose which son to send to college. He enlisted. So here he was at twenty-three, finally attending college.

"Are you jealous Oscar will graduate before you do?" Blake asked.

"I'm jealous of his looks and his popularity, and the fortune he'll earn in engineering, but graduation? Nah."

"My brothers are already making more than I probably ever will, but I wouldn't trade places with them. I'm doing what I really want this time around."

A good Baptist wouldn't believe in reincarnation. "What do you mean this time?"

Blake's smile faded away. "I attended Auburn with delusions of becoming a lawyer. That lasted six months." He scuffed his cowboy boot against the leg of Oscar's desk. "Dad showed up on campus with an ultimatum. Join the Marines or be disinherited. I suppose he believed my behavior was damaging the family name. I think he feared I was producing litters of bastard Claytons."

"How did he know what you were doing?"

"Oh, Auburn sent him a letter, telling him in shameful detail how my performance wasn't up to their academic standard."

Vincent had always suspected Blake had a wild streak.

"Dad was flat-out dumbfounded when I told him I got into another college." Blake set his bucket by the trash at the door. "He might just keel over in shock when I graduate."

"With high honors."

"For pity's sake don't tell him that."

Vincent placed Oscar's cell phone within reach on his bed. Satisfied he had taught a memorable lesson about drinking, he picked up half of the trash from their supplies at the door. Blake held up his cell phone and took photos of the boys. Two flashes later, he took up an armload of trash and followed Vincent out the door.

"Speaking of graduation," Blake said gently closing the door, "When does Miss Nefi Jenkins graduate?"

"In June," Vincent strode to the elevator where he pressed the down button.

"Uh, huh." Blake's voice had a twinge of challenge in it.

"What?"

"Nothing."

A gaggle of co-eds emerged from the elevator. They flirted and gawked at Blake. Vincent entered the elevator and held the door open for Blake, who summarized his opinion of the girls with a sigh. Blake stepped into the elevator.

"Say what's on your mind," Vincent said. He pushed the button for the ground floor.

"Nefi's the reason you took Spanish." Blake grinned.

"What if it is?"

"Are you two *pen pals*?"

"No."

"Talk on the phone?"

"No."

"Emails?" Blake's tone changed to seriousness.

"No."

He pulled his head back so far his neck fattened under his chin. "Are you following her on one of those online social networks?"

"No." Vincent watched the floor numbers count down.

"So you're stalking her."

"Don't make me thrash you," Vincent said.

"Then how do you know when she graduates?" Blake adjusted the trash tucked under his arm.

"Simple math. She started high school in the fall of two-thousand-two, so she should graduate in two-thousand-six."

"You said *June*. How do you know which month she graduates?"

Vincent sighed. The elevators were so slow. "Ruis told me. His sister Martina and Nefi are best friends."

"Yeah, right."

"Ruis's sister and Nefi go to Langley High School." Vincent adjusted the trash under his arm.

"Humph. Wonder what she looks like without war paint?" Blake asked.

Vincent had tried to imagine. After four years, would he recognize her? He decided to check online for her name and Martina's on that social networking site that Oscar used. Was it only for college kids? Was Nefi planning to go to college? Was she happy?

"I wouldn't count on getting an invite to a girl's high school graduation," Blake said.

"You shouldn't. She asked for *my* dog tags."

Blake shook his head, barely hiding a grin. The elevators opened, and the men crossed the lobby in the quiet of a Saturday morning. They stuffed the evidence of their prank—empty bags of plaster mix, half a roll of plastic sheeting, the box that held the Styrofoam peanuts, a four-gallon plastic bucket and paint stirring sticks—into the dumpster. They hailed a cab near the Columbia School of Engineering and rode it six and a half miles South on Broadway to their apartment building near Berkeley College. They parted on the second floor. Blake was two doors down the hallway when he spoke.

"Oscar will learn who his friends are when he calls for help." Blake unlocked his door.

"If he calls us," Vincent said, "let's act surprised."

Blake stepped into his apartment. His laugh carried into the hallway.

Vincent entered his own modest apartment and tossed his keys onto the kitchen counter. Musing about what Nefi might look like without war paint, he slouched into his sofa and pried off his shoes. *It wouldn't do any harm to check up on her, just to make sure she's adjusting.* After all, he held some responsibility for bringing her to her new life in the states. He would ask Ruis to keep him updated on how Nefi was doing. Ruis would understand.

. 9 .

On Friday, April 14th, Nefi paced from the kitchen to the foyer to the sitting room to the study, waiting for Doctor Sloan to arrive with her test results. Aunt Louise's roast beef filled the kitchen with the scent of meat, carrots, and potatoes. On her second pass through the study, she noticed Uncle Hamilton slouching in his desk chair, staring through the large window at the backyard.

"Uncle, what's wrong?"

He spun in his chair to face her. With his tie hanging undone and his collar unbuttoned he appeared...unkempt and weary. "I'm monumentally disappointed about my drug-crime bill. My colleagues had gently warned me to let it go until the next session. After the vote, they suggested I could probably muster more support next time. *Next time.*" He raked his fingers through his wavy gray hair. "My bill was already burdened with more pork than grandfather's farm ever produced. I feel as if I've let everyone down."

"I'm sorry they didn't pass it." She stepped behind the desk and held out her arms to hug him. "You haven't let me down."

"Thank you, my dear." He stood and patted her back.

A hug was a small thing, but it always lifted his mood. At times, she felt he was less like an uncle and more like a father.

He then swayed and shook his head.

"Are you ill?" Nefi's hug tightened, holding him on his feet.

"Too much coffee, I think." He reached out for the chair back and grabbed hold.

Nefi helped him back into his chair then dashed out the back door of the study toward the kitchen. She tiptoed in balancing a water glass filled to the very brim.

"My dear girl," he said by way of thanks. He drank carefully to avoid spilling on his suit. He protected his tie with his other hand. Aunt Louise fussed about tie stains far beyond their worth. "I'll live."

The doorbell chimed, sending Nefi dashing to the door. She opened it and grabbed Doctor Sloan by the arm. "Uncle is ill. He's in the study."

They fast-walked through the sitting room to the study.

"Hamilton, how do you feel?" Doctor Sloan asked. He tossed his briefcase on a leather wing-back chair on his way to Uncle Hamilton.

"Are you asking as a physician or as a psychiatrist?" Uncle smiled warmly at Doctor Sloan and shook his hand.

"Whichever you need."

"I seek an antidote for coffee."

"Ah. Read congressional bills." Sloan tugged his sleeve away from his watch and checked Uncle Hamilton's pulse at the wrist against his own watch. After a nod, he released Hamilton's wrist.

Hamilton stood slowly and paced the room. "I'm fine. I had a checkup last week, complete with a stress test."

Doctor Sloan pursed his lips as if holding back from speaking.

Nefi rolled the desk chair toward the two wing-back chairs and a small table on the other side of the study from the desk. She then hooked an arm around Hamilton's waist and led him to his desk chair by the table.

After settling into his comfortable desk chair, he said, "Now, tell me. Which of you called this meeting?"

Doctor Sloan put his hands together as if to pray, even though everyone knew he was an agnostic. He took a seat to Hamilton's right. "Nefi has made impressive progress despite the language barrier, the cultural differences and a host of other obstacles. She has worked hard to achieve and adapt."

Nefi took the empty seat on her uncle's left.

"We're very proud of her. We're also grateful for your dedication to helping us adjust to our new life as a family." Hamilton reached to his left and squeezed Nefi's forearm.

Pride welled up in her. She smiled.

"In the course of our sessions," Sloan said, "it has come to my attention that Nefi has a rare ability."

Hamilton paled.

Nefi feared he might pitch forward in a faint.

Doctor Sloan stepped over to his briefcase and drew out a small stack of papers that he unfolded on his way back to his seat. Charts and numbers covered the first page of the papers that he set on the table. Nefi scooted her chair beside her uncle to read them.

She scanned the titles: Neuroscan results, Bioscan, and Cognitive Symbol Card Test. Flipping through the stack, her uncle shuffled through test result after test result. All related to brain activity. Though written in English, in detailed medical specifics, all that Nefi could decipher was that the data measured her readings against the normal range, which meant that although Doctor Sloan had declared her progress impressive, something was seriously odd. Her readings tracked far outside of the indicated normal range. *Abnormal.* It had to mean the kind of news that deserved to be delivered face to face. But how bad was it?

"Because Nefi is under twenty-one, I had the tests conducted listing her as Jane Doe." Sloan had his hands on his knees.

"What kind of ability?" Hamilton dropped the papers on the table.

"She believes she is psychic."

"Psychic?"

The room temperature dropped ten degrees. Hamilton held

the chair's armrests as if they could anchor him. A tingling panic zipped through Nefi.

"Whose idea was this?" Uncle Hamilton's tone reminded Nefi of her father when she had captured a monkey and asked to keep it.

"Nefi asked to be tested," Sloan said, "and her results are above average, but—"

"Who conducted these tests?" Hamilton demanded.

"Doctor Spinnaker is the leading authority on psychic ability in the northeast. His research is used by—"

"And this doctor knows my niece as Jane Doe?" Hamilton glowered at Dr. Sloan.

Nefi's stomach clenched.

"Yes." Doctor Sloan's tone attempted to soothe.

"You shouldn't have done this without my knowledge."

"I conducted the tests to *disprove* her. She made it clear that this was important to her."

"I'm sure it is." Hamilton glanced at Nefi.

Stricken on the verge of tears, Nefi took deep breaths.

"I'm not upset with you, dear," Hamilton said. "I just know how this kind of thing can take on a life of its own." He addressed Dr. Sloan. "Perhaps you haven't watched the news lately, but it wouldn't take much effort to link her identity to mine. No doubt Doctor Spinnaker is the kind of person who watches CNN or congressional hearings. Even scientists pay attention to the bills and budget issues debated in congress. Where do you think grant money comes from?"

Sloan's jaw clenched. "There's a reason she confided in me about her ability. It's the same reason she wanted to trust you with this knowledge."

"All right. Tell me why," Uncle's voice rang like a challenge.

Nefi's voice quavered as she joined the argument, "I wanted to know how I knew things that other people didn't."

"So you thought you were psychic?" Hamilton cringed. "And what is your evidence?"

Nefi shook though her voice was forceful. "Everyone jokes that I'm psychic. I wanted to know if I was."

"Did your parents encourage this belief?" Hamilton could not very well call her parents idiots without breaking her heart, but still, Nefi sensed he was on the verge of it.

Nefi nodded, blinking free tears that fell on her lap.

"Nefi, listen to me." Hamilton softened his voice to a whisper. "You don't want people to call you a psychic because it will set you apart from others. It invites ridicule and mocking. You know what the *Bible* says about speaking with the dead and sorcery."

"I don't talk to the dead, and I'm not a witch," Nefi rubbed her hand across her eyes.

Uncle Hamilton's startled expression led Nefi to check her reflection in the glass of the bookcase. Her smudged makeup created a black streak from her eye to her hairline. It looked in part like her tribal markings.

"Of course you're not a witch." Hamilton pinched the bridge of his nose.

Too late, Nefi realized that her uncle equated being different as code for mental instability. Did he fear she was unbalanced or delusional? That she might get suicidal like Jason?

Doctor Sloan clamped a hand on Hamilton's forearm. "Listen to me. Nefi doesn't hear voices. She's not dabbling in witchcraft or telling fortunes. While she isn't psychic, she has an extremely refined ability to read people. This is a *rare* natural talent. Agents in the CIA and the Mossad train for years to read the micro-expressions and nuances of gesture that Nefi can do as easily as telling the color of a person's eyes."

Surprised to learn that her gift was visual and not psychic, she blurted, "So I'm not a freak any more than someone with perfect pitch?" She straightened her posture.

"That's right," the doctor said. "You're more observant than others."

Hamilton patted her shoulder. "I'm sorry. I reacted badly. I need time with Doctor Sloan to discuss this news."

Nefi stood and hugged uncle. She left. Her footfalls echoed through the foyer. She wasn't stomping her feet, but she wasn't light on them either as if carrying her disillusionment like a massive weight. At the top of the stairs she remembered that Aunt Louise was at Bridge with Mrs. Ramos, so she veered into the master bedroom in the dark and eased herself to the floor over the vent. Over the years, she had kept the vent control wheel oiled for just such an occasion. Gently, slowly, she thumbed the wheel until she could eavesdrop through a slit in the blades. Their voices carried easily up through the vent.

"It's vital that Nefi gets through her last few months of school without...problems. She's been accepted at Brown. I expect you to abide by patient-doctor confidentiality and take these test results to the nearest shredder." Hamilton emphasized his statement by tapping the papers.

Sloan leaned back in his chair. One hand tugged on his trimmed gray beard stubble. "You don't have to believe in her ability to believe the test results. I assure you the science of these tests is impeccable. Nefi is like a human lie-detector. She wants to work in law enforcement, and her skill is highly valuable whether you believe in it or not."

"The problem is that I do believe in her ability." Hamilton leaned forward, resting his elbows on his thighs. "I've suspected it from the day she arrived. It could be inherited. It's the reason I didn't speak to my brother after college. Now I see that it's the reason he kept Nefi in the jungle, away from the influences of civilization."

"I don't understand."

Hamilton sighed heavily. "Imagine growing up in a small Southern town where your mother and grandmother are known as the local psychics. They could read people as if everyone's wishes, fears, and desires were printed on their foreheads. They never admitted they used keen observation. Instead, they used props like Tarot cards, tea leaf readings, palm readings, you name it. My childhood home was a gathering place for the weak-minded, the superstitious, and the confused."

"Aren't most teenagers embarrassed by their family?" Sloan asked.

"Let me help you understand. After a few drinks, my brother would show off his ability. In our senior year of high school, we went to a party. The pitcher on the baseball team teased him about being the son of a witch, so Herman decided to get him back. He announced that the pitcher's girlfriend was pregnant. Right there at the party, the boy confronted his girlfriend, and she denied it. Three days later the girl tried to kill herself."

Nefi covered her mouth with both hands. Forcing herself to breathe slowly and deeply, she calmed herself the way she learned to do as a child when a snake crossed over her feet.

"Do you blame your brother for the girl's suicide attempt?"

Uncle's voice dropped to a whisper. "We both violated that girl's privacy."

"Both of you? How?"

"I noticed changes in her, weight gain, appetite and such. Then she got weepy and withdrawn and lost weight. Then to make the matter worse, I mentioned it to my brother, which gave him the means to conclude the truth and publicly humiliate her." Uncle shifted in his chair. "After that, I refused to pay such close attention. At first, it was challenging to tamp it down, but in time,

I learned to ignore it the way people who live near railroad tracks stop hearing trains."

"And then what happened?"

"Herman fled to the church in search of redemption. Later he visited the girl in the hospital to beg for her forgiveness."

Papa sought redemption in the church, Nefi concluded.

"And you?" Sloan asked.

"I started respecting people's right to privacy."

"So why alienate yourself from your brother?"

"After he married the girl, we all went to college together."

Nefi gasped and rolled away from the vent. Truth cut like broken glass, but she had to grasp it. *Mother had tried to kill herself?* Then another horrible thought struck her.

In the painful darkness, Doctor Sloan's voice slipped through the vents. "Is Nefi—?"

Nefi held her breath, fists against her mouth.

"What? No. Marta miscarried that child in her first trimester."

Breath escaped from Nefi like an untied balloon, deflating her. Though grateful she was really her father's child, she mourned the loss of an almost half-brother or sister. *Poor mama.*

"And then Marta discovered *she* could tell when someone was lying. After college, they both went off to Brazil, like hippies. They were going to teach the poor Brazilian Indians how to harvest rare plants for medicine. They wanted to teach them Portuguese because a friend of ours told them a few tribes wanted to learn it. Herman and Marta didn't even speak Portuguese, so they took a year of classes before they left the states. They also told me they were going to use their gifts for God."

"I thought they were missionaries," Sloan said.

"No."

That word cut Nefi to the core. *Surely Uncle was mistaken. Everyone knew they were missionaries.* Nefi could no more accept this denial than she could believe the sun rose in the west.

"But Nefi believes they were missionaries."

"Because everyone called them that." Uncle Hamilton sighed heavily. "The truth is they used free children's *Bibles* to teach the natives how to read."

Truth cut through her.

"Why haven't you told her?"

"And how exactly would I go about changing her life-long perception of her parents? What good would it do?"

Stunned, Nefi rolled back to the air vent.

"Since your brother moved away, why alienate yourself from him?"

"The last time we spoke, I argued with him. I told him I don't see this gift as coming from God."

Nefi darted from the master bedroom to her room to distance herself from the conversation. *How can this be? My whole life...everyone hid the truth from me.* She flung open her closet door and jerked her heavy coat from its hanger. On her way back to the master bedroom, she jammed her arms through the sleeves. *Mother lost a baby?* Marching through the master bedroom, she stopped at the French doors to the balcony overlooking the backyard. *Not missionaries.* It always upset Aunt Louise the way Nefi brooded in the high branches of the biggest oak tree on the property. *Normal* girls, it seemed, slammed doors, screamed and stomped their feet when upset, but she wasn't like other girls. Accepting her differences, she opened the balcony doors and closed them quietly behind her. *Missionaries. Not missionaries. They taught me about God. Was it all a lie?* In the dark, she found the straight handle to the zip line Martina gave her for her fifteenth birthday. *I am not psychic.* The zip line ran one hundred feet from the upstairs balcony to the trunk of the largest oak in the acre size back yard. Trees comforted her. She clipped the handlebar to the cable trolley attached to the galvanized aircraft cable that ran down to the great oak. Stepping onto the railing, she gripped the handlebar with both hands and pushed herself off the railing into the night air.

Spring air blasted her coat open, chilling her on her descent. The cable trolley whirred as Nefi held up her feet toward the tree trunk. Two long metal springs at the far end of the cable caught the trolley to slow her just enough to reduce the impact of her shoe soles striking the bark. The springs bounced, pushing her away from the trunk for a moment, then she swung her feet to the thick branch to her right. Sniffling, she climbed branch to branch to her brooding place, which was the highest intersection of branches able to support her weight. Traffic sounded in the distance. Next door the old neighbor practiced scales on his cello. Leafless, the tree gave an unobstructed view of the starry night sky, of the distant lights along the river, and of lights from windows of neighboring homes. She settled into the crook of two branches, a flat area the width of her hips, with her back to the wide trunk. There, she wrapped a coat around herself and wept. The tree welcomed her without judgment, cradling her in its great branches, whispering songs through the leaves, and rocking her to sleep.

Meanwhile, that same day, Damiano waited in a holding cell at the FBI building in New York City while the agents who had interviewed him verified his tip. They had threatened that if the tip didn't pay off, he would be charged with felonies and spend years in prison. They took his two kilos of cocaine as evidence. They also took his fake passport, the one Cortes had made for him under the most common surname in Brazil—Silva. In America for a full year, he had learned to answer to the name Juan Silva. *Cortes' plan had to work. It just had to.* So he waited and chewed his fingernails, spitting them on the floor. He also calculated the street value of the cocaine to pass the time. It was a pricey gamble. He had not learned English just to use it in prison.

FBI agent Lenny finally returned to the holding cell.

"Congratulations, Mr. Silva. We caught the dealer with his goods."

"I can go?" Damiano asked.

"Since this is the first time you've been arrested, I could have the charges dropped. We are more interested in finding out who is in charge of getting all this cocaine into the country."

It had been as easy as Cortes promised. Damiano remembered what he was supposed to do when they asked him to give up the name of his dealer. "So I give you a name, and you let me go?"

"Not exactly." Lenny nodded to the officer with the key to the cell.

When the door opened, Damiano stepped out and obediently followed Lenny, passing two men in business suits in the corridor, to an interrogation room. It looked just as he expected it would with the large one-way mirror window on the wall, a plain table, and five chairs. The drab gray walls matched his mood.

"Have a seat. I'll be right back."

Lenny stepped out of the interrogation room into the observation booth.

Director Flanagan stood behind the recording equipment operator.

"That's the guy I told you about," Lenny said. "He's a Brazilian national with a handful of arrests, but no convictions."

"You can sign him up, but never, never trust him without verification and backup," Flanagan said. "A man who will sell out his colleagues thinks only of himself."

Lenny nodded and headed back to the interrogation room.

Damiano sat facing the one-way mirror on the wall. After a

few moments, Lenny came back with two papers in his hands. The men from the corridor entered the room as well. Lenny and the others sat across the table from him.

Damiano sized up the men in business suits. *Who are these men?* "What is going on?"

"I would like to propose an arrangement that will keep you out of jail, by helping us find the people who profit the most. You see, you are expendable, and your boss knows it. He uses people like you to do the real work of moving and selling drugs and if you get caught, you pay the price. Your boss doesn't even suffer a minute because you go to prison for years. I would like to put you in the position of power. I would like you to work with us, just to give us information from time to time."

"And you will let me go?"

"Provided you follow our rules," Lenny said.

"Can I get my cocaine back?"

"No."

"Same as in my country."

"What do you mean?"

"Nothing." Damiano remembered that Cortes had told him the cocaine was bait. *Let the big fish keep the bait; the hook was set.* Evidence or bribe, it was always the same. The authorities kept what they caught.

Lenny slid two papers across the table toward Damiano. "We need you to sign a contract."

"I can't read English."

Lenny introduced the other men as a translator and a lawyer. The translator gave Damiano a second set of papers and his Brazilian Juan Silva passport.

The translator said in Portuguese that he had copies of the contract in Spanish and in Portuguese." He held one in each hand.

Damiano answered in Portuguese, "I don't read."

The translator read the contract aloud in Portuguese.

Damiano nodded and pretended to listen. After reading the pages placed in front of him, he said, "Where do I sign?"

Lenny pointed to the bottom of the second page and handed over a pen.

After scrawling his mark on the page, he tossed the pen onto the table and sat back. "You want information on drugs? What about smuggling?"

"We'll take any information you give us." Lenny took back the papers. "Until further notice, Mr. Silva, you contact me directly. If I get pulled out of town for another case, I'll call you and give you the names of other agents to take your information."

Damiano nodded.

Lenny gave him a black cell phone and an electrical charger. "My number is preprogrammed under my name." He demonstrated how to find the number on speed dial. He pressed it. Moments later Lenny's cell phone rang in his pocket. Lenny held up his own blue cell phone, disconnected the call, and pocketed it.

The meeting ended at dawn, so Lenny took him, in an unmarked car, close to the neighborhood where he had been arrested. The whole ride he had to suppress the urge to smile that he was supernaturally lucky. Later, when Damiano called his boss to tell him the good news, his first words to Cortes were, "Just like you said, the *Americanos* are *imbecils*."

. 10 .

June 17, 2006

Months later on a sunny Saturday, forty people arrived at the Jenkins' home in McLean, Virginia, to celebrate Nefi and Martina's high school graduation with more guests on the way. Nefi marveled at her aunt's party-planning skills. The catering truck arrived on time to set up the tables and chairs in the back yard. The caterer took over the kitchen with a crew of five, so Nefi stayed out of everyone's way. She considered today a significant milestone in her journey to prove herself to Vincent.

I am officially no longer a high schooler. Hence, one step closer to being an equal, an adult, and a grown-up woman in the eyes of the world and especially in the eyes of Vincent. Everything had a purpose. High school had served its purpose by preparing her for college. Nefi tied her sneakers. Though sorely tempted to slide down the great circular banister, she reminded herself of her adult status. She *glided* down in gentle, ladylike steps, the way Aunt Louise taught her. In her mind, she vowed to stun Vincent with her sophistication and grace and regal bearing. College graduation, perhaps, in high heels and a designer dress. The way it played out in her imagination, he wouldn't recognize her from memories of a blood-stained, exhausted savage in face paint. She

138

would have to introduce herself and wait for the shock of recognition to rock him to the core. She might even have to help him overcome doubt by showing him his dog tags.

"Nefi!" Aunt Louise's voice broke Nefi from her reverie at the bottom of the stairs. Aunt Louise's furrowed brow and fixed stare revealed concern.

Nefi stepped toward her and mid-hug she said, "Thank you for hosting the party."

"I hope you enjoy a couple of surprises today." Aunt Louise broke the hug and wrapped her soft hands gently around Nefi's wrists. "You might want to change into something more...feminine and put on a touch of makeup."

"Why?"

"I invited two special gentlemen." Aunt Louise's voice turned sing-song. She gave Nefi's wrists a squeeze then released them.

Excitement and confusion swirled through Nefi. More relatives?

Aunt Louise's gaze dropped to Nefi's neck, the only place where the shot bead chain to Vincent's dog tags showed.

What? No! She was dressed to play volleyball in the backyard with her friends. She wasn't ready to see Vincent. Not yet. Not like *this*. The invitations had said sports casual. She had *not* put Vincent and Blake on her invitation list. "Vincent and Blake?"

Aunt Louise nodded.

Uncharitable thoughts toward her sweet aunt raced across her mind, followed by denial, then a surge of panic rose from her chest to her neck, choking her and bringing her brain to a complete stop.

Aunt Louise whispered, "If you don't want to freshen up, then at least stand straighter." She nudged Nefi from the foyer toward the entrance to the sitting room.

Fear and curiosity battled in Nefi. Her heart raced when she heard a familiar deep voice. With her aunt's hands pushing against the middle of her back, Nefi stumbled into the doorway of the sitting room. Cornered with his back to the wall, Blake asked four tall girls from the volleyball team to direct him to Nefi. The girls touched his chest and squeezed his biceps as they inquired if he ever played football, if he worked out every day, if he had a girlfriend, and if he wanted one. He looked handsome with his hair longer. He wore a deep green polo shirt and khaki pants. Nefi peered through the threshold into the rest of the room. Surely, if Blake was here, Vincent would be. But where?

Aunt Louise's voice came softly from behind. "Go rescue Mr. Clayton before your friends tear his clothes off."

Nefi giggled while images danced into her head. She suspected that Blake would not resist in another time and place. Vincent was not in sight. Maybe she had time to put on makeup, or change before he arrived. Until then, she should rescue Blake. She strolled to a tan wall of muscled backs and ponytails to make eye contact with him over the shoulders of the middle two girls. Perfume vaporized off her teammates like a cloud of pheromones.

"Nefi!" he called out with a hint of desperation in his voice.

The group divided, opening a path between Nefi and Blake. Four disappointed expressions greeted Nefi. Blake stepped through the divide and gave Nefi half a hug. He juggled four packages under his other arm.

The doorbell rang, so the girls dispersed toward the foyer.

Blake whispered. "Look who's all grown up." He broke off the embrace. Examining her at arm's length, he shook his head. "Tall like a model, but without the anorexic look."

Did he mean she looked skinny or flat-chested? "Yeah, I gained a little weight after volleyball season ended." Nefi tugged the hem of her cotton top.

Blake's pupils dilated slightly. He took a gentlemanly step back as his attention darted up to her eyes. "You wear it well."

The boys' track team flowed into the foyer. The girls' voices grew louder as they greeted the boys and escorted them to the back yard. The captain of the boys' track team had waved at Nefi before he was towed out of view. He had asked Nefi to prom, but she declined, so he had taken Jenny, captain of the girls' varsity volleyball team, instead.

Blake set two of four packages on the coffee table. "Those are for Martina." He held out a third gift wrapped in bright red paper tied with a white bow.

She read the card aloud, "from Blake with love." She kissed his cheek and caught a whiff of spicy-clean aftershave "Thank you."

"You don't know what it is yet."

"Thank you for being here today, too." She tore off the wrapping letting it fall to the coffee table. Was Vincent late? Not wanting to hurt Blake's feelings, she delayed asking about him. She opened the box, tossed the lid, and lifted out a thin leather-sheathed hunting knife with a textured black grip handle.

In unison, Nefi and Blake declared it "a good snake knife."

Nefi unsheathed the knife and flipped it, catching the handle in her palm.

His expression showed how shocked he was that she handled the knife so confidently. "You didn't learn *that* in prep school." He sounded impressed.

Nefi sheathed the well-balanced knife. She could have told him about the martial arts classes she and Martina took, but instead, she decided to be mysterious. Men liked mysterious women. She replied with a shrug.

Blake maintained eye contact while he held out the fourth package wrapped with green and gold paper, matching Nefi's school colors. His mouth smiled, yet his eyes did not. "Vincent sends his apologies. He really wanted to be here."

Nefi nodded. Her excitement dampened as the might-have-been surprise of seeing Vincent fizzled. A second thought crept in. Was Blake being polite? Was he covering for Vincent because Vincent didn't *want* to come?

Blake planted his hand like a warm baseball mitt on Nefi's

shoulder. "His mother is losing her battle with cancer. She's in hospice care."

"Oh, that's awful." *Poor Vincent.* Her uncle had told her how Vincent's father died on the job. Nefi set her sheathed knife on the coffee table. She cradled the gift from Vincent for a moment before setting it on the table. Her heart rose from the rubble of sorrow for Vincent. Vincent had wanted to come. Aunt Louise said one could judge a man's character by how he treats his mother. If Aunt knew this, she would approve of Vincent even more. What a fine man.

"He's going to ask me about your reaction."

"What?" Nefi asked Blake.

"To his gift."

Oh. Nefi plucked the small white envelope from under the green bow. She tore it open and read the hand-written inscription aloud. "From Vincent, to keep worthless boys away." She ripped through the paper and opened the box. A small pink device sat in a pre-formed velvet cradle. *What? Oh!* She blanched at her first guess of what the device was and silently blamed Martina for polluting her mind. Did this thing keep the *need* for boys away? She snapped box shut. Heat rose from her neck to her face. *It isn't fair to blame Martina,* Nefi thought, *just because I associate sexual thoughts with Vincent.*

"Okaaaaay," Blake said, his head tilted like a dog's. "I don't know what to make of your reaction."

On the spot, Nefi bit her bottom lip. Vincent wouldn't give her something like that. Would he?

"You don't like it?" Blake practically squirmed.

"I...don't know." Nefi held the box, unsure of what to do with it, afraid to examine it closer. Martina would know.

"Hmm." Blake scratched his jaw. It sounded like he was filing his nails on his beard stubble. "This should make one interesting thank you note."

She had once trusted him with her life, so maybe she could ask him. Maybe this kind of gift was common among sexually-active

NORTH OF THE KILLING HAND

adults. Impatient and curious, she whispered, "What is it?" She pried open the box and held it out to him.

Blake peered into the box. "Why it's a Taser. A *pink* Taser."

Thrilled, Nefi gasped, closed the box, and held it against her breastbone. "I can't wait to try it."

"Whoa, there. No." Blake clamped his hands around Nefi's and the gift box as if to restrain her.

"I better put these away," Nefi said.

Blake released her hands.

Picking up the knife, Nefi added, "Aunt Louise would faint."

"That plan works for me."

"Martina's upstairs at the zip line."

"You have a zip line?" Blake picked up the gifts for Martina and followed Nefi to the foyer. "Of course you have a zip line. If I was your age, I'd probably have one."

Why was he nervous and babbling? Had the other girls overwhelmed him? *Calm yourself, Blake.* She pivoted toward the circular staircase. "Ruis told me you and Vincent are studying at Berkeley."

"Yeah, we both want to work for the FBI, but to be a field agent, you need a degree. A master's degree isn't as tough as I thought it might be."

Halfway up the stairs, Nefi said, "I'd like to work for the FBI or the CIA."

"What does your uncle say about that?"

"I haven't told him." At the top of the stairs, Nefi banged her fist on the master bedroom door. "Why is this door shut?"

Martina opened the door enough to reveal her face. "You can't come in, Nef."

"Martina, meet Blake Clayton. And he's bearing gifts."

"*The* Blake Clayton?" Martina eyed him and gave a smile of approval.

Blake raised his eyebrows at Nefi as if to ask what made him famous.

"Ooo. Semper Fi," Martina grabbed Blake's wrist, "You're just what I need."

While being pulled into the master bedroom, Blake glanced at Nefi with wide-eyed panic. The door closed. "In here?" His voice sounded higher than normal.

Nefi stepped into her own room and placed her new weapons inside her top dresser drawer between her panties and sports bras. As if seeing them for the first time, she realized serviceable underwear would not serve her future underwear needs. She closed her door on her way out and leaned against it for a moment. Vincent had thought enough of her to send a gift. It was something to cling to in his absence. This tiny brilliant hope that he cared for her kindled her first memory of him in the jungle, magnificent and shirtless. That image fed her fantasies at age fourteen and sparked sensations far more physical in her at age eighteen. *One day my Vincent. One day...when I have lacy underwear.*

Sunlight flooded the foyer.

Uncle Hamilton's deep voice boomed, "Welcome. Good to see you."

"Thank you, sir. Has Martina arrived?"

Nefi recognized that guest's voice in three languages.

"She's upstairs doing something on the balcony," Uncle Hamilton said.

"Ah, yes."

Quieter, her Uncle said, "Beware, you're entering an estrogen storm."

"Fujita Scale?"

"F2, F3." Uncle wagged his open hand.

Ruis nodded.

"Nefi's varsity volleyball team is here. And then there are the cheerleaders. And the track team. They won the state championship. Amazons all."

Nefi grinned. She was the one true Amazon on the team. Descending the stairs gracefully, slowly, she stepped around a couple necking on the fifth stair from the bottom and called out to her guest.

"Ruis!"

"There's the graduate." When he hugged her, his body felt like marble statue warmed by sunlight. Fit did not begin to describe his physical condition, mostly disguised by loose-fitting clothes. In a white polo shirt and navy chinos, he could have passed for a model in a fashion magazine. Ruis was so handsome that Martina questioned the loyalty of some of her friends, especially when they insisted on meeting at her house. Martina trusted Nefi's loyalty because of two unshakable truths. One, Nefi treated Ruis like a brother. And two, Nefi loved Vincent.

"Excuse me, I'll check on things upstairs." Uncle Hamilton headed up the stairway.

What is Uncle up to?

Three tall girls dashed from the dining room into the foyer, taking formation around Ruis. The shortest of the girls was his height.

"This," Nefi said, "is Martina's oldest brother, Ruis."

The girls *oooooed* and *aaaaahed* and introduced themselves by first names and flirtatious smiles. Jenny blurted out he wasn't wearing a wedding ring. Tanya, a dark-skinned runner from the track team, elbowed Jenny. A few bars of a rap song played. Angie from the volleyball team reached into her sports bra and pulled out a cell phone. She read it and tucked it back into her bra.

Ruis observed the cell phone's journey up to its abrupt disappearance.

"The big guy is on the balcony with Martina," Angie announced. "She says to go out back."

"Nice to meet you, Martina's brother." The girls bounded from the room toward the back of the house, leaving Ruis and Nefi in the foyer.

No doubt they hoped 'the big guy' would take off his shirt. Nefi smirked.

The skin between Ruis's eyebrows bunched. "Who's the big guy?" His protective tone amused Nefi. Even in heels, makeup, and a push-up bra, Martina would always be the baby sister.

"Blake."

"Ah." This news calmed Ruis. He handed Nefi a small Tiffany-blue box wrapped with a white satin bow. She recognized Tiffany's wrapping from her birthday gift from Aunt Louise that had contained gold heart design pierced earrings. It was Aunt Louise's way of suggesting pierced ears. "Congratulations on graduating without sending anyone to the hospital."

So he'd heard about the incidents. Ruis was comfortable with secrets, so it was understandable that Martina would trust him, but still. Had she volunteered information? Ruis was almost as observant as Nefi when it came to people and situations. He had earned his skill the hard way, through training and experience. It seemed to Nefi that he sensed and respected her ability. Poor Martina couldn't lie to either one of them. Perhaps Martina blurted out everything that crossed her mind to her big brother to avoid being interrogated over things he perceived as secrets. It was pointless to keep secrets from Ruis. Like God, he'd find out.

She hugged him to thank him for the gift. She peeled off the white ribbon and sky blue paper, letting them fall on the floor. Inside, a small jewelry case contained a pair of diamond stud earrings that sparkled like Aunt Louise's chandelier in sunlight. *Fine.* It was time to pierce her ears. "Wow. I'll wear them on my first day at Harvard."

"Congratulations!"

"Uncle insists Harvard is a family tradition."

Blake bounded down the stairway, deftly dodging the kissing couple by the banister. For a big guy, he had an unexpected lightness on his feet. "Hey, Ruis!"

Ruis nodded as Blake dashed by to the back door. "What do you plan to study?"

"Sociology or psychology with an emphasis on criminology."

Aunt Louise leaned out into the hallway from the kitchen. "There you are come out back. Hello, Ruis. You come too. I'm sure a Navy man knows first aid."

Ruis and Nefi followed Louise under the stairway through a short corridor connecting three doorways: the kitchen on the left, the back porch through the center, and the study on the right. They took the doorway to the back porch.

"Who's hurt?" Ruis asked.

"No one yet," Louise said. "I believe a promise is about to be kept."

Nefi pulled Ruis by the hand through the kitchen to the backyard.

Aunt Louise nodded to Blake, who stood in the shade of the giant oak in the back yard.

"Here we go," Aunt Louise said. She was looking up toward the balcony.

The girls in the backyard chanted. "Go for it. Go for it. Go for it."

Martina appeared beside Nefi, and the two of them linked arms.

Uncle Hamilton leaned over the edge of the balcony. He was harnessed to the cable trolley. Adjusting his helmet strap, he smiled down at Nefi and Martina. He quieted the crowd by raising his hands. "When Nefi and Martina installed this zip line, I promised them I would ride it if they both graduated with honors."

A cheer rose from the students and adults scattered in the backyard shade. Admiral Ramos, Martina and Ruis's father, shook his head. He didn't even have to say the word for Nefi to hear the word he often used. Foolishness.

"Congratulations, ladies," Uncle Hamilton said, bowing. "Are you going to make me be a man of my word?"

Nefi and Martina shouted in unison, "Yes!"

After a test tug on the harness, sixty-year-old Senator

Hamilton Jenkins stepped up on the balcony railing. He grabbed the bar that hung from the cable trolley and stepped off. He whooshed overhead along the buzzing wire toward the great oak. The cable sagged under his weight as he zipped down the long cable. Blake held his hands up toward Hamilton.

The double springs at the end of the cable caught the trolley and stopped the Senator two feet from the tree. The springs bounced him back, so he swung a few times before his motion stopped. Blake and Ruis secured a ladder, one end under Hamilton's feet, the other anchored to the lawn with their feet bracing the bottom. Hamilton spun slowly in the harness to the applause of the crowd. Louise patted her heart.

"Thank you." He stood on the top step of the ladder where he unfastened the harness.

Louise sidled up to him when he touched the ground. "Are we having fun?"

"Your turn." He hugged her and spun around with her.

Aunt Louise squealed in mock protest. The graduates applauded and whistled.

"He really did it!" Martina laughed. "Your uncle is brave for a man his age."

Nefi nudged her best friend with her shoulder. "And how did your dad become an Admiral?"

"Point taken."

Girls herded into the house while shouting over who would have the next ride. They clamored past Nefi and Martina and startled the catering crew who stepped aside from the stampede.

Martina spotted Ruis and headed toward him. Nefi strolled onto the back porch where the caterers carried loaded trays from the kitchen. Caterers filed past her, elbowing the back door open. Nefi plucked a fried chicken leg off a passing tray. The view from the porch revealed the whole yard. At a table in the shade, Admiral Ramos bounced his first grandbaby on his knee while Mrs. Ramos took pictures. Tablecloths flapped in the breeze.

Students huddled in animated conversations. Nefi watched her aunt and uncle flirt like newlyweds. Aunt Louise untied him from the harness which she handed off to Ruis.

Despite the joyful celebration all around, melancholy settled on Nefi like a robe she couldn't shrug off.

She had lived in two worlds so far in her life. The first world of her childhood included her parents, the jungle, and tribal ways. The second world in her high school years provided comfort, safety, and educational opportunities in a so-called civilized culture with her extended family. She would miss her friends and her privileged life in McLean, Virginia. Her friends planned to disperse across the country. Martina won a scholarship to Oxford in England.

Graduation marked a great transition into a third world—the world of her future, adulthood, college, and independence. She longed for that future. For Nefi, moving away to Harvard meant starting over again with strangers in a strange place. This time, this change, she was prepared. She had mastered the language of the new place well enough to dream in English instead of Portuguese. She had specific goals and desires to fulfill, and all of them pointed to Vincent. She longed to launch herself into her future, but she had grown comfortable as part of a family. She almost felt like she belonged. The present and the future played tug-of-war with her.

She sensed a presence behind her.

"There you are," said Grandmother Wright.

Nefi spun around and hugged Grandmother Wright, who wore her silver hair in loose waves framing her face. At five-feet-four-inches tall, she had a look Martina summed up as "never too rich, never too thin." She had the softest, palest skin Nefi ever touched. Grandmother had an opinion on everything and everyone that she shared unrequested. She also tried to relate to Nefi as an equal, an absurdity that became especially amusing when she tried to use teen slang. She came up beside Nefi and looked over the railing at the crowded back yard. They leaned their elbows on the railing so that she and her grandmother, shoulder to shoulder, watched Blake standing on the ladder while he unfastened the harness from the line. Ruis shouted instructions up to his sister on the balcony. They hand-carrying one harness while another was being prepared for use.

"Is that your Vincent?" Grandmother asked.

"That's Blake Clayton, his friend. He's working on his masters at Berkeley College same as Vincent."

"Where is Vincent?"

"He couldn't be here, but he sent a gift."

"May I ask what it was?" She asked if she could ask. That kind of question confused Nefi because it had no real answer. To say 'yes' meant that she had permission to do what she had already done; to say 'no' was pointless because the question had been asked. Rather than irritate her grandmother by pointing out her illogical question, Nefi answered her.

"A Taser."

Grandmother Wright's mouth dropped open, elongating her wrinkles from her nose to her chin. "He did no such thing."

"In pink," Nefi added to soften the news of being given a weapon.

Grandmother Wright's mouth snapped shut. She crossed her arms and squinted at Nefi as if deciding whether or not she was being teased. "How romantic."

"Isn't it?" Nefi re-read Grandmother's body language. "Oh. You're being sarcastic."

"And what's wrong with those two handsome gentlemen?" Grandmother Wright aimed an arthritis-gnarled hand, jingling a collection of silver and gold bracelets, at Blake and Ruis even though she repeatedly told Nefi that pointing was rude.

"Ruis has a serious girlfriend, and he's too old for me," Nefi said, "and I'm not the type Blake is looking for."

"He's gay?" she sounded doubtful.

"Of course not. He's a Southern Baptist."

Grandmother Wright shook her head.

"What's wrong with being a Southern Baptist?" Nefi wondered how Grandmother developed such rock-solid opinions about things. Aunt Louise called it a hardening of the attitudes.

"My dear girl, you shouldn't assume that being a Baptist and being gay are mutually exclusive." Grandmother acted like it was her duty to dispel the beliefs of others.

She always treated mother's life in the jungle like a prank. Every year when Nefi and her mother traveled to Manaus for doctor's appointments, her mother would call home, and they would conduct the same argument. Grandmother would tell her to stop wasting her life and come back to civilization. Mother would tell grandmother that God loves all his children. Though she never dared say it in Nefi's presence, Nefi suspected that Grandmother secretly believed her fears for her daughter were vindicated four years ago. Did it lessen her grief to believe she was right?

"And you shouldn't assume," Nefi said, in what Grandmother called her impertinent tone, "that being a gentleman and being heterosexual are mutually exclusive. Blake demonstrates all the fruits of the spirit: love, peace, joy, kindness, goodness, gentleness, faithfulness *and* self-control. He's handsome, athletic and funny. There's nothing wrong with Blake. He's just not—"

"You really must stop judging all men on the Vincent Scale."

Nefi opened her mouth to object and froze. *It was true.* She did judge all men against Vincent. It wasn't her fault they all fell below a perfect Vincent score. It was what it was.

Jenny squealed down the zip line. She came to a soft stop at the oak tree. Unfastening herself from the harness, she looked down at Blake. He steadied the ladder for her so she climbed down tenuously, watching her own feet touch the rungs as if she'd never been on a ladder before. At the bottom of the stairs, she flung her long blonde ponytail over her shoulder, swatting

Blake's face with it. A total flirt, Jenny drank in the attention of men. Having secured volleyball scholarships at multiple colleges, she once told Nefi that she selected her college based on the ratio of men to women. She said she wanted to find an equal in height and athletic interests. If she was even half as sexually experienced as her reputation suggested...Olympian would sum it up.

"Do you plan to date in college?" Grandmother said.

"Yes."

"Good. I was afraid you were going to wait another four years for Vincent to pay attention to you."

He's *seven years* older. *Honestly, does she ever listen?* "He couldn't date me while I was in high school."

"Older men date younger women all the time." Grandmother's dismissal of such behavior irritated Nefi to the core. Once over Easter dinner, Grandmother had declared that the marriage between a famous movie director and his ex-lover's adopted daughter was an epic romance that deserved to be made into a movie. When Uncle Hamilton pointed out that the thirty-five-year age difference between the director and his child bride sounded more criminal than romantic, Grandmother accused him of being a typical small-minded Christian. Aunt Louise suddenly left the room on the pretext of 'fetching' dessert even though no one had finished the main course. Having said nothing during that debate, Nefi felt compelled to voice her opinion this time.

"Honorable adult men don't date minors," Nefi said louder than she had intended.

A male caterer passing by flinched, glanced at Nefi, then continued carrying a tray of drinks to a table on the lawn.

Nefi unclenched her fists. Grandmother! What a contrary woman. No wonder Uncle Hamilton and Aunt Louise avoided her. She fled the kitchen to the farthest part of the back yard where she internally continued her argument in defense of Vincent.

Martina followed her to the back fence. "You have that look."

"What look?" Nefi pivoted away from her grandmother to calm herself.

"Like you're going to hurt someone." Martina eyed the crowd. "Like the time you tackled the track coach."

Blake's voice sounded from behind Nefi, "Why did you tackle the track coach?"

Nefi emitted a nervous laugh. Her first weeks in high school had been so much worse than awkward. She nearly got expelled twice.

Martina, clearly flirting with Blake, propped a hand on her hip. "Nefi tried to assimilate that first week of school, but she's a force of nature, like a storm cloud, unstoppable. One of a kind. All she had to do was wait for me to finish cheerleading practice. But no."

Nefi leaned against the tree. Blake would tell Vincent about this, but Martina, like fire, was equally unstoppable.

"The cheerleaders had the infield while the track team gathered at the starting blocks for practice before their first meet. Nefi sat in the bleachers." Martina had told the story often. "All was going well until the track coach lined up the boys and fired his starter pistol. That's when Nefi leaped down from the bleachers. Head down, she ran like a blur along the outside of the track. The coach lowered the starter pistol to his side while he watched the runners. He turned toward Nefi a second before WHAM." Martina clapped her hands. "She tackled him right off his feet."

Nefi squirmed at the realization Blake had seen her do the same to Vincent. "It's not a habit. Really."

Blake nodded, his face impassive. "So you say."

"So I run over to Nefi and yell at her to let go of the coach, first in English, then in Spanish. She hands me the starter pistol. Raised in a military family, I know to hold it by the handle with the barrel aimed at the ground. About that time the assistant track coach lifts Nefi to her feet. Everyone is shouting about it, so I plead her case by emphasizing the extenuating circumstances. About possible PTSD because of her parents and so on. Nef said she thought the coach was shooting *at* the boys, so she didn't get expelled."

"You ran at an armed man to protect other people?" Blake's voice rasped.

Nefi nodded.

Martina touched her fingertips to Blake's chest. "Are you listening?"

Blake nodded.

"The coach she took down was old. Had to be in his forties, at least, but he was heavyset."

Martina didn't notice that Blake winced at the mention of age. Nefi did.

"It's like my dad says—it isn't the size of the dog in the fight, but the size of the fight in the dog that matters. No offense, Nef."

"Woof."

Blake chuckled.

"So then the assistant coach mentions how fast Nefi ran and the next thing you know, she's asked to race the boys' track team just once around the track. The boys! I translate for her and remind her to lace up her shoes, she still wasn't used to wearing them, you know. Looked like a kindergartener struggling with them. Honestly."

"She lied to me," Nefi said.

Martina smirked. "Yeah. Yeah. I told her she wouldn't get suspended if she beat the boys in the race. I was motivating you. The coach put her in the outside lane. Of course, didn't use the starter gun, so he counted down from three."

A slow grin formed on Blake's face.

"The race started clean with Nefi on the outside." Martina gestured as if watching the event again. "By the first turn two boys outpaced the others, but by the middle of the straightaway, she led the fastest boy by ten feet. The cheerleaders were shouting, the boys were sweating it full speed. When the fastest boy catches up with Nef, she lowers her head and charges faster, crossing the finish line two strides ahead of him. Then she jogs back like she just *walked* the track and the boys are panting like greyhounds. The next day the girls' track coach invites her to try out."

"Martina's been keeping me out of serious trouble for four years," Nefi told Blake.

Martina continued to flirt with Blake with another story involving underwear.

Nefi tuned out the sounds and observed Martina's flirting body language, or mating behavior if she ever carried it out. The hair flip, the hand to her chest gesture, and leaning in close to whisper—these were the skills her friend had mastered that Nefi needed to learn. Too bad they were headed to colleges an ocean apart. She would miss having Martina teach her the ways of femininity in this culture, like grooming and makeup and wearing pink. She would also miss having Martina around to remind her to keep her emotions under control.

If not for Martina and Psychiatrist Ethan Sloan, Nefi would have remained a dangerously angry person. Between her psychiatrist and best friend, neither understood the full scope of the fury restrained inside her.

Later that afternoon as the crowd thinned, Louise Jenkins had a private chat with Blake at a table under the elm.

"I must confess, I've done something awful," Louise said. She toyed with her sweating glass of sweet tea. "I never discouraged Nefi from her infatuation with Vincent. She has worn his dog tags since the day she arrived."

"So why's that so awful?"

"I did it for selfish reasons. I thought that if she had her heart set on him, she would be less likely to get in trouble with high school boys."

"That doesn't sound awful to me."

Louise pursed her lips. After a sigh, she said, "She hasn't dated *at all*."

"Oh."

"Precisely." Louise wrung her hands. "Now with her heading off to college, she might try to contact him. Do you think Vincent has any feelings for her?"

"We've talked about her—"

"I'm sorry. I shouldn't trouble you with this." Louise sighed and dropped a hand on Blake's forearm. "I just don't want him to be unprepared or caught off guard. May I have his phone number?"

Blake patted Louise's hand. "Leave it to me. I'll bring Vincent up to speed on the situation."

Louise brightened. "That would be so gracious of you. Do please let him know how sorry I am for putting him in an awkward place."

Blake said, "To be worshiped by Nefi...I would consider myself lucky to be in such an awkward place."

Louise swatted his shoulder.

. 11 .

The Gunnerson house had not been this crowded since his father's funeral reception. The ancient air-conditioner strained to cool the house in July's New York City heat. The same officers who had served with Vincent's father had come to pay their respects for Vincent's mother. He mourned that his mother didn't live to see him graduate from college. He knew she was proud of him. But still. As it was, she got to see Oscar receive his diploma. A photo of the three of them around Oscar's diploma hung proudly over the sofa beside his parent's wedding photo. Just one more year and Mom could have attended his graduation, and his graduation photo would have hung on the family's treasure wall. He sighed.

Vincent admired the way his brother Oscar fielded questions for the umpteenth time about why he had chosen a career in engineering instead of law enforcement.

"I'm honoring my father's wishes," Oscar said, stealing a glance at Vincent. "Not all of us have the skills to serve and protect. I'm more of the design-and-build kind of guy."

A circle of uniformed officers nodded in unison. They parted to welcome the chief of police into their conversation. A burly man with salt and pepper hair, the chief nodded at Vincent and spoke in a deep, gravelly voice that reeked of smoke.

"I hear you're earning a master's degree in law enforcement," the chief said.

"Yes, sir." Impressed that the chief knew, Vincent respected him all the more.

"Are you aiming for a law degree down the line?" One cocked eyebrow hinted at the chief's low opinion of lawyers, in general, and defense attorneys in particular.

"FBI."

A chorus of rising and falling voices responded.

"Well, then perhaps we will get that inter-agency cooperation we've been promised all these years." The chief smiled.

The doorbell chimed. Oscar excused himself from the group and moved through the soft speaking clusters of people in the living room to the door. He opened it and immediately shut it with a resounding *thud*.

Vincent excused himself from the group and stood beside Oscar. "Jehovah's Witnesses?"

"Worse."

Vincent opened the door. Blake Clayton, dressed in a black suit, white shirt, and deep green tie, leaned on a dolly laden with cases of liquor. Who knew he owned a suit? Blake wheeled the dolly over the threshold toward Oscar's foot, but Oscar hopped out of the way. Blake paused in the center of the living room. Conversations stopped. Heads turned toward the large red-haired man and the cases of liquor.

"Pardon me. I heard there was a wake in the neighborhood. Came to pay my respects."

Vincent gave Blake a back-slapping hug. To the guests, he said, "Blake's Irish."

Conversations resumed with renewed energy.

Vincent had not seen Blake since the end of the spring semester when he went home to visit his family in North Carolina to help on the ranch or farm. Whatever it was, Vincent believed Blake knew how to handle animals. He wondered how common it was for rural Southern families to own livestock. He pictured a wood-frame farmhouse with chickens scampering in the yard. Though he had not expected Blake to travel five-hundred miles to the funeral, he was grateful he did.

Vincent led Blake to the kitchen. Oscar followed them into the kitchen. Blake tore open a case of Johnny Walker Blue Label whiskey and lined up bottles on the Formica counter near the refrigerator. He tossed the empty box against the back door of the kitchen.

"And for the ladies and lightweights," Blake said opening a case labeled *Chateau Ste Michelle* Cabernet-Sauvignon. He handed a bottle to Oscar.

Oscar set the wine bottle on the counter. "I don't think we have enough glasses." He lifted a sleeve of plastic glasses from the counter.

Blake handed his car keys to Oscar. "I picked up two racks of real glasses from a caterer. They're in the back seat of the red pickup across the street."

Oscar took the keys, grabbed the handle of the dolly, and smirked at Blake before he left. Who else but Blake would drive a red pickup to a funeral reception? He concerned himself more with substance than style. How many from the police department had come to the reception just to see who else had shown up? Blake did not care what people thought of him. With Blake, even death was a come-as-you-are party opportunity.

"I'm glad you're here," Vincent said.

"I want to get your friends drunk so they'll tell me stories about you when you were young and dumb like Oscar."

Vincent smiled. It had been an agonizing two months at hospice watching his mother die in stages as cancer chewed away at her body, then her brain. While still lucid, she had admonished both her sons to marry for love and to marry girls of faith. She warned them that they had to love a woman as is and to find a woman who loved them as is. She had witnessed too many of her friends suffer through relationships in which they believed they could fix the men they married. Vincent and Oscar promised her they would marry for love or not at all. Neither of them could name any candidates, but Vincent had thought, *someone like Nefi.* They had kept a bedside vigil so mom wouldn't die alone. As it happened, Oscar had been on watch the morning she gasped her last breath. She was, at last, out of pain. That day Vincent decided there were many things worse than death.

"Like cow tipping," Blake said.

"What?" Blake's comment shook Vincent from his sorrow.

"The dumb things you did in your youth. Among other things, I got in trouble for cow tipping."

Raising a hand toward Blake, Vincent said, "I don't even want to know what that is."

"In case the situation ever presents itself," Blake said, "don't try it on a bull. I'm just saying."

Oscar plunked a crate of tumblers and wine glasses on the counter beside the liquor bottles. Having heard Blake's last comment, Oscar raised his eyebrows at Vincent as if to ask for an explanation. Vincent shook his head. Oscar picked up a bottle of Johnny Walker from the counter.

"You broke into your redneck piggy bank for us," Oscar said. "I'm touched."

"Pace yourself, junior," Blake said. He took the whiskey from Oscar and set it back on the counter. He nabbed a can of Coca-Cola from the counter and handed it to Oscar.

"Yeah, right," Oscar said, "got any rum to go with this?"

Blake slapped the edge of the counter. "Don't tell me you want a little paper umbrella in your drink. I'll worry about your orientation."

Two women from mother's bridge club entered the kitchen. They carried empty food trays. Dressed in black, they rolled up their sleeves and approached Vincent.

"Before my career in nursing," Mrs. Henderson said, peering over her spectacles, "I was a bartender."

Dear Mrs. Parsons piped in, "And I was a waitress. Can we help?"

Blake tore open the third box to reveal assorted bottles of syrup, bitters, a bag of oranges, two jars of cherries, a pint of whipping cream, and two bottles of rum. All the others leaned over the box to peer into its contents.

"Please, take over, ladies" Vincent hugged them both at once. "Oscar, get more ice from the freezer," he said pointing to the garage.

To his credit, Oscar wheeled around and marched toward the garage.

The ladies shooed the men from the kitchen.

Vincent strode to the back porch and Blake followed. They sat on sturdy wrought iron outdoor chairs facing the garden. Once his mother's small flowering sanctuary, it remained colorful despite the desperate need for weeding. It looked so much smaller than Vincent remembered. The house, too, had shrunk and faded since his last visit. Without his mother in it, the place was just old plumbing, brick, wood, memories, and drywall.

"Saw Nefi last month," Blake said. He loosened his tie and opened the top button of his shirt.

"How is she?"

Blake's green eyes shone with mischief. "I think she wanted to try out your gift on me."

Vincent chuckled. He instantly imagined Blake thrashing involuntarily on the Oriental rug in the entranceway of the Jenkins' McLean, Virginia home. Mrs. Jenkins would have grounded Nefi for life for torturing a good-old Southern Baptist.

"Nefi still wears your dog tags."

Vincent's lungs clenched. *No way.* "Aren't you a comedian?"

Blake pointed to himself. "This is my serious face."

A small fire lit in Vincent's heart for being remembered. He was proud of his part in finding her and bringing her safely to her relatives. So what if she had a touch of hero worship toward them? It was sweet.

"Who's Nefi?" Back from hauling ice, Oscar stepped out onto the porch.

"Senator's niece," Blake said, keeping it simple.

"And she likes Vince? Way to go, brother. How come I haven't met her?"

Vincent cringed at Oscar's eagerness to learn more. "She lives near Washington D.C. Her family sent that large arrangement of orchids." He had pocketed the handwritten note from Nefi that arrived with the flowers. She had written how sorry she was that he, too, had become an orphan. Her note encouraged him to remember that he would see his mother again one day in heaven. That hope had sustained him through hospice care.

"So how long have you been dating?" Oscar dragged his chair up to Vincent. Oscar's question dropped like a time-bomb between them.

Blake leaned his elbow on the arm of his chair and rested his chin in his hand. The smirk he gave Vincent was as clear as saying—*I can't wait to hear you explain this.*

"It's not like that." Vincent sensed the questions to follow were inevitably explosive. The same curiosity that drove Oscar to take apart a clock when he was six drove him into engineering. Stubborn curiosity was hard-wired into his personality.

"You haven't asked her out?" Oscar leaned back in his chair. After a quick glance from Blake to Vincent, he grinned. "Wow. My big brother the marine is afraid to ask a girl out?"

Tick. Tick. Tick.

"Something like that," Vincent said. He hoped his brother would lose interest if he agreed with him. It was better to be thought of as shy than to explain Nefi.

"How tough can it be?" Oscar leaned over to address Blake. "What's her deal?"

Tick. Tick.

Blake tossed a question back to Oscar. "You got a girlfriend?"

"Don't change the subject," Oscar said to Blake. To Vincent, he said, "Either you like her, or you don't. Which is it?"

Vincent blurted, "I haven't seen her in four years."

"Nice dodge," Blake said.

"So?" Oscar said. "She's not married or engaged is she?"

Blake answered by shaking his head.

With a sigh, Vincent sat back in his chair. Oscar would not let up until he had something solid. He dreaded the direction of the conversation, but the truth was the truth. "The girl we're talking about is seven years younger than me."

Oscar's eyes widened. "How long ago did you meet her?"

Tick tick tick tick tick.

"Four years ago."

It took a nanosecond for Oscar to calculate, another nanosecond to stand. "When she was fourteen?"

Kaboom.

The way Oscar looked at Vincent cut like shrapnel. It sounded positively criminal phrased like that.

Blake stood and cornered Oscar on the porch. "Hold up a minute. Don't go leaping to low-minded conclusions. We found the girl just after her parents were murdered. We escorted her to safety, that's all. She happened to develop a crush on Vincent, and he gave her his dog tags. End of story."

Oscar's attention darted from Vincent to Blake. He muttered, "She's younger than me." He elbowed his way past Blake and tromped into the house.

Blake dropped his arms to his sides and hung his head. "I am so sorry."

"It's not your fault," Vincent said. He felt his pulse in his ears.

"Maybe Nefi's parents had the right idea about raising her outside the U.S. Our society fosters a culture of assume-the-worst." Blake slumped in his chair. "He may be smart in lots of ways, but your brother can be stupid when it comes to people."

Vincent reassessed his interest in Nefi. Was he intrigued by her because of their common losses? If so, that was not a solid foundation for a relationship. While their age difference seemed vast today, he believed it would matter less over time, but what about their other differences? She was the relative of a senator and a prep school graduate. He was the son of a cop and graduated from public school. Surrounded by Harvard students, she would outgrow her crush. *She needs to date guys her own age, her own class.*

Blake held a frosty bottle of Coors in front of Vincent. Holding up his own bottle, he said, "May you find the kind of love your parents had."

Vincent took the bottle. "Same to you." 'Til death.

Meanwhile in McLean, Virginia, Nefi sorted through clothes to decide which to pack for school and which to store in the attic. The future demanded her to sort through her past and present. Boxing her letterman's jacket was an easy call. The volleyball team uniforms and track uniforms were to be donated back to the school. She wanted to present herself to college as a college student, not as a high school student visiting campus, so she lugged the box of uniforms to the hallway. She then carried the box with her letterman's jacket and yearbooks to the attic. The black permanent marker squeaked and emitted a strong, pungent odor as she labeled the box. Snorting, she leaned away from the noxious odor.

"Nefi?" Hamilton called up the narrow stairway.

"Up here, uncle!"

Thudding footfalls preceded his appearance at the top of the attic entrance. He ambled to the box, creating a wake of dust with each step. He tilted his head to read the top of the box.

"You should tape that shut so insects don't get in."

"It is awfully dirty up here."

He looked around until his attention fell on a locked black trunk trimmed in dull brass. Nefi remembered seeing the trunk every time she and Aunt Louise came up to retrieve holiday decorations. She read his expressions as they ebbed from sorrow to relief and swelled into a decision. He dug into his pants pocket and drew out a small brass key.

"I believe you're mature enough to take possession of the trunk." He handed her the key.

Nefi stood. The trunk, a large black and brass behemoth parked at the back of the attic between Christmas decorations and a filing cabinet, had attracted her curiosity over the years. She had assumed it contained Jason's belongings because no one disturbed it or discussed it.

Nefi took the small warm key with trepidation.

"It arrived while you were missing in the jungle." Hamilton hugged Nefi.

That keened her attention. "What's in it?"

Hamilton eased away from her hug. "After I found out about you, I couldn't bring myself to open it."

"Why not?"

"Guilt mostly. It's my fault I didn't stay in contact with your parents. It's my fault I didn't even know you were alive until..." He looked away as his eyes welled.

"Please don't carry that guilt anymore. Where would I be without you?"

"Living with your grandparents."

"See? You rescued me."

Hamilton laughed and shook his head. "Let me help you carry it downstairs."

Together they wrestled the heavy trunk down the narrow

stairway. When they reached the corridor between the master bedroom and Nefi's room, Nefi adjusted her grip on the trunk handle to stop the way it pinched her little finger.

"You know your grandparents love you very much."

"I would have been a huge disappointment to them."

Hamilton shouldered open the door to Nefi's room. "Why would you think that?"

She searched her memory for proof to back up her statement. It came to her the moment they set the trunk in the middle of the room on her fluffy pink and purple rug. Though her proof would stir up another sensitive topic, she had to say the one thing that would dispel her uncle's guilt. "I believe Grandma Wright would have taken me in as a replacement. Like me, Mom was an only child." Having an only child was another sore topic with Hamilton and Louise, especially since they lost theirs. "How could I ever be enough like my mother to satisfy grandmother?"

At this, Hamilton's countenance slackened. "I suppose you're right. It's impossible to live up to people's expectations."

She suspected her uncle was thinking about his lost son, and his fears about whether or not he contributed to his son's desperation and, ultimately, to his suicide. She ventured out on a ledge, toward the unspoken, to draw him back from deep grief. "Thank you for setting low expectations of me."

"I did no such thing."

"I heard you on the phone once with Doctor Sloan." Nefi grinned. "You said all you wanted was for me to graduate without getting addicted, pregnant or arrested."

He hugged her. "Keep up the good work." After kissing the top of her head, he quietly left and shut the door.

Nefi unlocked the brass lock and set it aside on the floor with the key still in it. She placed her hands on the dusty brass corners of the lid and took a deep breath before facing her past. She raised the creaking lid and locked the braces to prop the lid open. Faded flowery paper lined the inside. A musty fungus scent triggered memories. This trunk had been at the foot of her parent's bed in the jungle. Mali, the family cook, kept it covered with a quilt so it would be soft enough to sit on. The smell of mud and the scent of her mother's perfume emerged from the mass of colorful clothing, blankets, and books. Nefi lifted the blanket to her face and inhaled — mother's perfume, sweat, mold, sweet memories. The bottom section of the blanket was stained. Underneath the blanket sat a broken perfume bottle. Surrounding the bottle, a golden brown stain spread to hats, scarves, shoes and books nearby. She found a children's *Bible* in Portuguese. She recognized mother's perfume and that recognition triggered a profound sense of loss. As her tears landed on her legs, she could almost hear the distant beating of her hollowed-out heart. Losing her parents had torn away part of her heart. Activity and friends could not fill that particular void.

So giving, so kind, her mother never harmed a soul. She didn't deserve her death. God knows. God sees all. All her mother's kindness and love and life were shot down by a mad man, by that frog-faced, ugly fish buyer. *No, no, no. Let it go. Can't let hate win. Mama and Papa are in God's care now.*

She gripped the edge of the trunk to calm herself before plunging back into her past. The clothes ruined, the shoes stiff with dried mold, Nefi plucked out the damaged belongings to pile them to her left. The books, though stained, remained usable, so she stacked them on the floor to her right. Primers on Spanish, English and Portuguese, picture books, children's stories, science and math books, National Geographic handbooks on flora and fauna of the rainforest, and workbooks formed an unsteady tower to her right. Perhaps, one day she might have children of her own to teach. The blanket ended up draped on the bed post.

In a wooden cigar box, she found a few silver and gold rings, various simple earrings made of pearl and aquamarine, a gold chain and a crude handmade string of colored wooden beads that Nefi made when she was ten.

A rapping on the door pulled her attention from the trunk.
"Come in."

"One more thing. This arrived with...the choker your father
wore," Hamilton said. He handed her a small, hinged, velvet box.
He quietly left the room and closed the door.

Her father had been wearing the choker when he died.
Somehow it had reached Uncle Hamilton, who gave it to Ruis,
who gave it to Vincent. If the choker arrived separately from this
trunk, then...*oh*. It came with his body.

Nefi stared down at the unopened the box. After a few ragged
breaths, she pried open the dark blue velvet-covered box. Tucked
inside were a diamond solitaire wedding ring and a larger
matching gold band. Inscribed on the inner band of each ring
were the words— *TIL DEATH*.

These words stung her eyes. She tried on her mother's ring on
her right hand. It fit.

"You kept your vows."

Tears plopped on her t-shirt while she reset the rings in the
box. Snapping it shut, she shoved it into the wooden cigar box
then she tucked it out of view along the outside of the trunk. She
sorted through papers that rendered drawings and characteristics
of medicinal plants made by her father. At the bottom of the trunk
sat three untitled cloth-bound books. The first, a red one, began
with a handwritten entry.

*1-24-92 Nefi spoke her first words today, and Marta cried at the
sound of them. Nefi told us she did not want to wear clothes.*

Nefi calculated the date—her fifth birthday. First words at age
five? Did he mean the first words in English or first words of any
kind? She read on.

*We were so worried that she might be autistic or perhaps retarded in
some way, but this confirms our highest hope that she is mentally
normal. I asked her why she had not spoken until now, and she just
laughed. The Indians have a saying, that silence makes words
meaningful. Nefi has proven that true. Maybe she has discovered it is*

more important to watch what people do than to listen to their words.

After dinner and through the night she read the second of the cloth-bound journals and most of the third. It became evident through the journal entries spanning her childhood that her parents deliberately kept her in the jungle to protect and nurture her. Father detailed his disparaging opinion of 'civilized culture' in America as sin-loving, violent, and self-absorbed. He was particularly disturbed by television as a destroyer of children's minds. His idyllic view of tribal culture ignored the violence, sin, and selfishness Nefi remembered. People were people no matter whether they lived with few possessions or many, high technology or no electricity, in the city or in the jungle.

It was true she had a vastly different childhood experience than her mother or father had, but her father's focus on the differences seemed naive. Of course, she probably read more books than other children, because she did not have the distractions of cable television, video games, organized team sports, or children her age to play with. But she also had a more limited education because she did not have peers and teachers to learn from. An odd thought crept into her consciousness that she was seeing her parents in a new way—like Uncle did.

In the solitude of her bedroom, the bedroom Jason had died in, Nefi took a hard examination of herself.

Who am I?

She was not a part of the tribe despite living among them for fourteen years. Though it crushed her when they told her she had to go to her relatives in the United States, the tribe was right. She didn't really belong there no matter how comfortable she had become living among them. She wasn't psychic even though the Indians feared her second sight and her classmates labeled her a mind reader. She certainly didn't want to destroy people with her gift the way her father almost did. As much as she wanted to deny the truth, Doctor Sloan was right to demand that she accept the test evidence. It also became increasingly clear that her parents were not missionaries. With no mention of the church, or fund-raising, or worship services, they could not have been working for a church. They believed in God and prayed. This she remembered. Ultimately, she was not the child of missionaries, but teachers. Maybe her uncle was correct to label her parents misguided for taking up the task of teaching Indians Portuguese.

Her childhood self-image crumbled like her rotted baby shoes in the trunk. Ashes to ashes, dust to dust.

She remembered her history teacher's saying that those who don't learn from the past are destined to repeat it. He was referring to governments and nations, but the saying held true for individuals as well. Nefi did not want to repeat her parents' mistakes, nor the mistakes of her other family members or friends. There were so many lessons to learn in life and a few could have fatal consequences. Learning everything by experience was unwise. Better to learn by observation and the example of others. She picked up her father's final journal to learn more about her history.

Near the end of the third journal, she found one entry that mentioned the Pirarucu Man. It was dated two months before he murdered her parents. Her father wrote:

A man in a fast, sleek boat came by to ask the villagers how much Pirarucu they could catch for him. I asked him if he knew how dangerous it was to catch them and he said he'd pay double the usual price. I suppose one of the many adventure tour groups wants to recreate a ceremony using this fish, but I'll ask the Federal Police in Manaus about it on the next trip. I don't trust this man.

In the last journal entry, dated a week before his death, he wrote:

We promised Nefi a trip to the States on her sixteenth birthday, but how shall we teach her to distrust strangers after raising her to reach out to them? How shall we teach her that the outside world is a dangerous place after she has mastered the dangers of the jungle? How can we warn her to hide the very rare gift that God has enriched in her beyond our wildest hopes? We must. For her sake, we must. Once she visits America, she will want to stay. Our most painful responsibility is to raise her to become independent, to let her go.

Nefi hugged the last journal.

She understood her gift for reading people had value when she trusted it. So what if others didn't believe it? So what if others mocked it or feared it or misunderstood it? Let them. *I am responsible for my thoughts and my behavior. I believe in myself. I did not ask for it, but I believe God gave me this gift for a reason.* Her mother and father believed in their gift, but they did not fully understand it. *I can learn from scientists about it.*

Her psychiatrist always wanted to know how she felt about things, but feelings don't matter as much in life as what a person does. *I can be scared and still fight evil. I can be shy and still seek love.*

She piled up the items she would throw away. Silently, she promised her father she would use her gift against the evil ones in the world to detect them, to hunt them, and to help convict them. She repacked the trunk and left the key in the lock. She promised her mother she would be brave and kind. Finally, she set aside all the clothes, shoes and other things she planned to take to Harvard, packing the rest in boxes.

That night before bed, she promised to find someone with whom to share an exciting life, someone she would gladly accompany to the ends of the earth, someone worth promising to love until death stopped her. She fell asleep holding Vincent's dog tags.

. 12 .

It was a year after his mother's funeral, on June 29, 2007, when Vincent stood in the living room of his mother's house with a life-changing letter in hand. The letter made it official. He muted the television news which was blaring something about two car bombs found in Picadilly Circus in the heart of London. *Bombers are the worst kind of cowards*. He called his brother first.

A groggy voice answered, "Hello?"

"Oscar?"

"Vince, is that you?"

Was Oscar *sleeping* in the middle of the day? "How are the job interviews going?" Vincent glanced at his phone in disbelief.

"I think I passed. Hard to tell. The Japanese are so polite. They might think I'm an idiot, but they treated me well in the interview. They took me out for sushi."

"Where are you?"

"Nagoya, Japan. It's the third largest city. They call it *monozukur*, which — as far as I can tell — means we make stuff."

"Sorry about the time difference." Vincent sat on the frayed green sofa in the family room. He glanced out the wide picture window at the street. He had given Rose clear directions to the house. She was late. Was she lost?

"I'm so jetlagged I don't know whether to eat breakfast or lie down. Did you know *sake* is served warm?"

"Hungover?"

"A little," Oscar said.

"I report to Quantico at the end of September," Vincent said. Saying it aloud felt good.

"Oh, hey, congratulations. My brother the Fed."

"They haven't actually hired me. I have to pass training."

"Like you wouldn't?" Oscar made a hissing sound.

"I have to pass exams on law, ethics, investigation techniques, interrogation, and forensics." Vincent believed his brother got the looks and the brains in the family.

"You can do it."

"Thanks for the vote of confidence." Vincent gazed at photos on the upright piano of his parents together on the beach in Panama City. They used to call it the redneck Riviera. They were in love all those years, through good and bad times. Atop the television, a large box frame held a professional photo of his father in his NYPD uniform and a folded flag. *In love until the very end.* Vincent longed for the kind of love that lasted a lifetime through the great and miserable times.

"Has anyone looked at the house?" Oscar asked.

"The realtor brought by a couple last week."

The plan they had agreed on, to sell the house and divide the assets, would take time in the crummy housing market according to the realtor. Vincent and Oscar had granted the realtor a little bargaining room. They weren't in a rush to sell. Neither brother had urgent debts to cover.

"I suppose I should come home and pack up my stuff."

Vincent grinned. "I'm sure you'll need your Batman sheets for your new place."

"Like you'll need your life-size Star Trek cut out of what's her name."

"Seven of Nine." Vincent smirked at the thought of the science fiction character. The combination of form and fearlessness made her memorable.

"Looked like a perfect ten to me, but whatever." Oscar cleared his throat and yawned.

The doorbell rang, so Vincent rose from the sofa to go to the front door. He opened it and greeted Rose with a quick kiss.

"Sorry I'm late," said Rose. She dropped her red leather purse on the coffee table and planted a hand on the middle of her hourglass shape. Her perfume invaded the room.

"Hey, call me when you get back in town. Oscar, I gotta go."

"Who's there?"

"I have a date," Vincent said.

"Just tell me she's of legal age."

Stung, Vincent said, "I'll introduce you to Rose when you get back. She graduated in my class."

"That's a relief."

Vincent hung up and headed to the front door. He grabbed his keys off the table in the hallway.

"Who was that on the phone?" she asked, following. Her heels clicked on the tile of the entranceway.

"My brother. I'll introduce you to him when he gets back from Japan." Vincent opened the door for her.

"Nice."

Hours later, after his dinner date with Rose, Vincent made his second call and woke up Blake.

"Make it good," Blake mumbled. "I have to clean stalls at dawn."

"You got a summer job cleaning bathrooms?"

"Horse stalls."

How broke was Blake? Vincent wouldn't do that job for less than a hundred dollars an hour. "Did you get a letter yet?"

"No. Did you?"

NORTH OF THE KILLING HAND

"Yeah."

"And?"

"I report the last week of September to Quantico."

"Congratulations. That makes me want to shake down my mailman."

"Go back to sleep." Vincent pitied his friend. "Call me when you hear."

"You betcha."

Vincent waited until morning to make his third call. Ruis congratulated him.

"Thank you for your recommendation. Yours and Senator Jenkins' probably grabbed someone's attention." Vincent gazed out the back yard with his coffee in one hand, phone in the other. The sprinkler system he had installed was spraying the flowers.

"No problem. So has Blake heard yet?"

"No."

"Did he apply under affirmative action?" Ruis asked.

"Ha! Maybe he should have. I bet his argument about being a white Southern gentleman would get all kinds of attention."

"If he doesn't get accepted this time, tell him to learn Farsi. Or Chinese. I hear they're in big demand." Ruis spoke over the whine of helicopter rotors winding up.

"I doubt there is a Chinese equivalent for y'all."

Ruis laughed. After a rustling sound and a *thump* like a vehicle door closing, the engine sounds of the helicopter muted.

"Say, how are the girls doing?" Vincent tried to sound casual.

"Martina's at Oxford. Nefi's at Harvard. They communicate by text and email and one of those online social network websites."

Vincent had seen Oscar's page on a social network. It had

photos, comments from friends, daily trivia, and personal information on it. According to Oscar's page, he had two-hundred and ninety-eight friends. Each had a page like Oscar's. Was it an electronic popularity contest of sorts? "I don't understand online social networks," Vincent admitted. "Or texting. My brother asked a girl out by text message."

"He's an engineer. What do you expect?"

"He does love technology."

"Did the girl go out with him?"

"I don't know," Vincent said. "Maybe they cyber-dated. Maybe the whole relationship is electronic."

"I suppose that's the natural progression for a generation raised on video games and television." The distinct metal-on-metal click of a magazine being loaded or unloaded sounded in Vincent's ear. Ruis was at work.

"Speaking of dysfunctional people, I was talking with Blake recently, and he said Nefi wore my dog tags through high school. Is he kidding me?"

Ruis sighed. "I think she needed a security blanket. But don't worry about her. She'll do well at Harvard. She's beautiful, smart, and she knows what she wants."

"Oh, what's that?"

"She's studying psychology with a focus on criminology." The helicopter sound grew louder. "My ride's waiting. I'll catch you later."

Sure enough, the call disconnected. Vincent smiled. "Good for her." Law enforcement made sense. He worried about the psychology focus. Every psych major he knew was crazier than a crack addict. Every one of them obsessed with personal traumas from childhood.

. 13 .

Nefi flew into Rio de Janeiro on February 1, 2008, arriving mid-morning, excited to see Ambassador Alfonso Morales and his nephew, Antonio. She had often heard that Brazilian women were sexy, so in her campaign to win Vincent's heart, she planned to study Brazilian women. Having just received news of Ruis's wedding, she had until September to prepare to see Vincent again. Martina had verified Vincent was on the invitation list. Nefi had seven months to reinvent her image before Ruis's wedding.

Ambassador Morales had told her to use her Brazilian passport to go through the shorter line at customs and to avoid having to obtain a tourist visa. He was right. The customs officer's gaze bounced from Nefi's passport, picturing her in tribal face paint, to her bare face and back before he slowly addressed her in slow Portuguese. He asked if she had been in the United States of America since two-thousand-two and if she had traveled to any other countries since then.

"*Nao, senhor,*" Nefi said. She did not remember getting the passport stamped when she had arrived long ago in the U.S., and yet the only U.S. Customs stamp was dated August 2002. Six years. It seemed a lifetime ago.

"*Boas vindas, senhorita,*" he said, welcoming her back home. He stamped the passport and handed it to her.

Hearing Portuguese stirred her heart. According to her

father's journal, her first words had been in Portuguese. She had told her mother she didn't want to wear clothes. Oh, to have been able to tell her anything again. But no. She reminded herself to dwell on the good and to embrace the spirit of carnival. Martina had tried to explain the connection between Catholic observance of lent and its relationship with the carnival, but it struck Nefi as peculiar to overindulge in the things one pledged to give up for lent. She suspected God would not approve.

Antonio met her outside the customs area. He wore a short-sleeved pale blue silk shirt and long navy pants. He had grown slightly taller since she first met him when he was his uncle's driver. She congratulated herself on remembering to wear flat shoes so she wouldn't tower over him. He was almost her height. He greeted her with a kiss on each cheekbone followed by a hug. Nefi inhaled his scents, aftershave, hair gel and musky cologne. He smelled of well-groomed masculinity.

"Thank you so much for coming," he said holding her at arm's length. He eased his warm hand under hers on the suitcase handle.

"Thank you for inviting me, Antonio."

His face brightened at the mention of his name. He pivoted the wheeled suitcase toward the exit and grabbed Nefi by the hand as if they held hands out of habit. She gently squeezed his warm hand and allowed him to lead her into whatever vacation plans he and his uncle had prepared. Uncle had promised the Ambassador would show her the finer side of Rio.

Antonio wheeled her suitcase to a diplomatic limousine waiting at the curb, where he handed off her suitcase to the driver. Antonio opened the back door and tugged her by the hand to climb in. Nefi stepped inside to the back seat. Facing her with his back to the driver was Ambassador Alfonso Morales. He told someone on his cell phone that he had to go, and he promptly hung up.

Antonio climbed in beside Nefi and the driver shut the door for him.

"Nefi Jenkins," Ambassador Morales said, dropping to a knee in front of her. He kissed her on both sides of her face and gave her a quick hug before returning to his seat.

"Thank you, Ambassador, for inviting me to my first carnival."

"How could we not show you the world's greatest party?" He addressed Antonio. "See? I told you she would grow more beautiful every year." His English shamed her Portuguese. He rapped his knuckles on the glass partition between the driver and the passenger section of the limousine.

The car rolled into traffic.

Sadness settled around Ambassador Morales's eyes, in contrast to his smile, when he added, "You look like your mother did in college."

"I'm so glad."

Ambassador Morales planted his right hand over his heart. "If it would not distress you, I can show you an album from my college days. My mother loved what you call scrapbooking. She collected all the photographs I sent home. Herman, Marta and Ham were my closest friends in school."

"I would love to see your album." Nefi bubbled with joy. "I have so few photographs of them."

Ambassador Morales nodded. Nefi had been working with Dr. Sloan and a specialist to hone her behavior-reading skills. If she had to translate the Ambassador's expressions, she would have said he was forming a plan to copy the album for her. Time would tell if she was correct.

"How is Hamilton?" Ambassador Morales asked.

Her uncle's parting words rang in her head. "He told me, 'Have fun, but don't make me send bail money.'"

Ambassador Morales laughed from the bottom of his lungs. "What happens here stays here, unless you choose to tell."

Antonio eyed his uncle with mixed expressions of amusement and confusion. "Don't be concerned about the violence from last year's carnival. Those deaths were drug-related. They did not occur at the parades."

Nefi had heard about the deaths through the news. Her uncle had warned her to keep close to the Ambassador and Antonio at all times. Ambassador Morales scowled at Antonio.

Backpedaling, Antonio said, "Just don't buy anything from strangers at the parade. Some dealers sell cocaine at the Sambadrome. I'm afraid even the police look away during carnival."

"Antonio," Ambassador Morales said, "how about if you tell Nefi what we have planned?"

"We will see carnival from a *camarote*." Antonio glanced at his uncle.

"Box seats," Ambassador Morales said.

"From box seats on the second level of the Sambadrome. From there we can see the parade for blocks," Antonio said. He extended his hand as if the parade played in front of him then and there. "All the Samba schools compete. Four days and nights hundreds and hundreds of dancers parade by in fantastic costumes." He raised his hands over his head. "Enormous headdresses. You won't believe it. Your eyes will feast; your ears will burn on Samba, Samba, Samba. This is my third carnival."

Nefi found his enthusiasm irresistible. He was a full-grown man excited about a parade. The more he described the non-stop parade, the more she believed it could well be the world's biggest party. It was worth the extra homework from missing a week of classes to tour the great city of Rio de Janeiro with people she knew. She was tired of having people ask her about carnival whenever they learned she had grown up in Brazil. How could they understand that she had never been to a carnival? How could they imagine growing up in a place where the rivers were roads and where no one had telephones, or televisions, or computers, or the kind of technology that children in the U.S. took for granted? Even her best friend Martina did not appreciate that Nefi knew the real Brazil, the largest part of Brazil, the genuinely wild Brazil, as the Indians did. Foreigners flooded in for carnival, but few traveled into the rainforest.

Antonio's hand fell into Nefi's while he told her they would go to Ipanema Beach and Copacabana beach, beaches that have songs about them. His aunt and mother wanted to take her shopping. His words poured out like rain in the heat. His hand felt natural in hers. Was he usually this familiar by culture or was he nurturing a relationship? Flirting? Martina would have melted like butter in the heat of his presence. His broad shoulders tapered to narrow hips and muscular legs. He had been the captain of his college soccer team. Perhaps he still played. Nefi fingered the shot bead chain that held Vincent's dog tags.

Antonio noticed it. "What is this?" he said pointing to the chain.

Nefi lifted the dog tags from inside the front of her shirt.

Antonio's eyes widened. "You joined the military?"

"A friend gave it to me."

Antonio leaned close and read the dog tags. He released them and glanced at the Ambassador, who was again on his cell phone. He whispered to Nefi, "Your boyfriend?"

"No." *Not yet.*

"Ah, good." The hungry look in his eyes was unmistakable.

That same day, Vincent stood in a gym at Quantico, nearing the end of his twenty-week FBI training. The town of Quantico, with a population under 500, was forty miles south of Washington D.C., and west of the coastal plain of Delaware. The exercise of the day, known as the Bull-in-the-Ring, toughens up trainees for hand-to-hand fighting. Agents in the field have to become familiar with the experience of being assaulted so that they can overcome the shock and pain quickly enough to fight back. Their lives and the lives of others depend on field agents' ability to control their emotions and to regain control of a violent suspect or situation.

The exercise places one trainee in safety gear in the middle of a circle of others who are instructed to punch the trainee standing in the middle. Shouting commands outside the ring, the instructor prompted them to hit hard. Vincent dreaded his turn. He had gotten to know the twenty-six-year-old woman in the middle as a friendly, computer genius. While most of the trainees had come from law enforcement or military backgrounds, the petite computer genius had come from Columbia. She had been a classmate of Oscar, Vincent's brother. Vincent would have rather taken another turn in the middle than hit sweet little Jo Cho. It felt wrong, even dishonorable to hit a woman, but everyone had to because Cho's life might one day depend on her quick recovery from a punch.

Cho reeled from a head shot that spun her around to face Vincent. She blinked rapidly, huffed and tried to pull herself up to her full five feet two inches. Looking up at Vincent, her eyes widened.

"Hit her!" the instructor ordered.

Vincent stepped forward and looked way down at the top of her padded helmet. He didn't want to hit her in the helmet because she was hired for her brain, and he couldn't bring himself to hit her in the chest, so he swatted her shoulder with his boxing glove. The blow shoved Cho hard enough to force her sideways. She stepped back in place quickly.

She took another punch to the shoulder from a woman.

The instructor stepped into Vincent's peripheral vision. "Hit her like you mean it. Love pats won't toughen her up for fieldwork."

Cho bit down on her mouth guard. Shifting her weight from foot to foot, she looked around at the others. She glanced at Vincent and gave the slightest nod as if encouraging him to do what had to be done. Cho raised her hands to cover her face.

Vincent jabbed her forearms. Even if he hadn't heard the unmistakable snap, he felt the bone give when he made contact. He stepped back immediately and dropped his hands to his sides.

Cho yelped. Using her uninjured arm, she took two steps toward Vincent and punched him hard in the chest. Vincent grunted. Cho, at least, hit like she meant it. The instructor stepped between them.

"Time out." The instructor pulled Cho from the ring and ordered another female trainee in the middle.

"Sorry," Vincent said. The implications of Cho's broken arm crashed down on him, crushing him with guilt. She would fall behind the class.

Cho spat out her mouth guard and spoke over her shoulder while the instructor led her to the sidelines, "I can still out hack you." She winked.

That was the last he saw of Jo Cho that day. Why on earth had she winked?

Damiano received a call from Cortes to fly to Rio de Janeiro for two reasons. Cortes said he wanted an update on the status of the drug business, and he had a surprise. That same day Damiano boarded a TAM airlines flight from New York to Rio with dread and a light carry-on suitcase. He feared he was in trouble. Even though he had eliminated much of the competition by informing on them to the FBI, had the business grown quickly enough to please Cortes? The Brazilians he had recruited worked for a Greek-owned plumbing company, which gave them access to any neighborhood in the city, day or night, without attracting attention. They had developed many profitable contacts.

When Cortes greeted him at the Antonio Carlos Jobim

International Airport in Rio, Damiano's heart pounded in full-fledged anxiety. Sweat ran down his back. They walked out of the terminal into the balmy beginning of summer. The heat disoriented him. The familiar stench of Guanabara Bay reminded him of the time a pipeline broke years earlier dumping over a million liters of fuel oil into the bay, leaving a strong, acrid chemical smell. He coughed at the fierce aroma of dead fish. The bay had not improved.

Cortes laughed. "Why are you wearing a coat?"

Damiano peeled off his heavy jacket. "It was snowing in New York City."

"Snowing? You tease me, Damiano."

"No, no. It's true. In the north, their seasons are opposite."

"How crazy is that?" Cortes stepped to the curb, and his car arrived in front of him within seconds.

The driver, a thin, twitchy man in his twenties, leaped from the limousine and opened the back door for Cortes. He took the suitcase to the trunk and gently tucked it in. He nodded at Damiano and dashed back to the door. Damiano climbed in, and the driver shut the door for him. While the young man strode around to the driver's side of the car, Cortes spoke.

"The driver wants a raise."

Damiano nodded. Who didn't want to make more money? The driver watched him in the rear-view mirror. Was the driver nervous because he knew something? Cortes was generally suspicious and distrustful of people. When his suspicions grew wild, anything could trigger his rage. Damiano regretted having to leave his gun in New York City, but it would have been stupid to bring it on the plane. He hated the security measures at airports. He preferred to travel by boat because dock security officers seemed more interested in collecting fees than inspecting cargo or passengers. Cortes had insisted on a flight. What was so urgent?

On the drive from Governor's Island to Cortes' home up on

the hillside, Cortes spoke in English, "Remind me how much money you deposited this year?"

Damiano pulled out his notepad and read the total in U.S. dollars he had scribbled under the date 2007/12/31. He had followed Cortes's instructions carefully. No deposit could be larger than eight thousand dollars. He could make deposits but not withdrawals from this account. The account had to be in the name of Damiano Guerra so it could not be traced back to Cortes. Only Cortes could make withdrawals because he had the checks. He studied Cortes' expression. It was a terrible thing not to be able to read, but Damiano could calculate and write numbers easily. Numbers were real; letters were nothing more than ink on paper made to imitate noises. Numbers mattered because they could be counted, like money.

Cortes's lips moved as he muttered. Was he converting the exchange rate of the dollar to the Brazilian Real? Cortes finally nodded. He reached into a black cooler on the floor between the front seats of the car. He plucked two bottles of Ambev beer from the cooler and handed one to Damiano.

"Oh, let me," Cortes twisted off the top of Damiano's bottle then his own. "We must toast to our success in the New York City market." He clinked the top of his bottle to Damiano's.

He gaped at his boss. *Cortes was pleased.* Both men took a long swig of cold, tangy beer. Damiano relaxed into the seat cushions.

"Our next step is to flood the market with a giant shipment. I saw this strategy on a television show. Other businesses use this and so can we." Cortes continued in English.

Was Cortes speaking English to impress the driver or to keep him from understanding what they said? Damiano nodded. "When?"

"It will take a year to buy up all we can get. This will make the product scarce and drive up the prices in the U.S. Then we ship in so much that the competition cannot keep up."

"With so much, won't the prices fall?"

"Yes."

"How will this help us?"

"Because we will have the biggest supply. The other dealers will run out, and all their customers will come to us."

Damiano gulped his beer. He did not want to voice his questions because questions would be treated as challenging his authority. How long would the supply last? What happened when they ran out? Why not keep the prices high and ration the supply?

"You think it sounds *loco*. That is exactly why it will work. You will see." Cortes swallowed his beer quickly, following it with a hearty belch.

"It sounded *loco* when you sent me to the United States to get arrested." Damiano took another swig of beer. If the plan had failed, he would have gone to prison. How did Cortes know it would work?

Cortes laughed. "Genius, they say, is often misunderstood."

Damiano shrugged. He rarely understood his boss's mind. "What do you want me to do?"

"We can discuss business in detail another day. I told you I had a surprise."

Prostitutes again? Damiano lowered his beer to his lap. Condensation on the cold bottle seeped through his pants, chilling his skin. No matter how much the bitches earned, they always looked at him with grim determination as if the money wasn't enough. Never with lust. Never with eagerness.

"Tonight is the start of Carnival."

Damiano gasped. "Are we going to *Banda de Ipanema*?"

Cortes dismissed the street parade with a wave. "We are no longer pickpockets." He leaned into the leather seat and dropped his empty hand to his thigh. "We're going to the Sambadrome."

Damiano's mouth fell open. Such a dream to see the Samba competition parade up close! It stunned him to imagine being part of it. Seeing four days and nights of parade after parade of Samba school women dancing in nothing but strings and feathers and high heels had been his fantasy since his voice changed. Brazilian women were the sexiest women in the world. Everyone knew it. Memories of the rhythm of the Samba pulsed through him.

"Is it true the women are topless?" Damiano asked. He had heard so many stories over the years he did not know which ones to trust.

"Most of them." Cortes smiled. "We will watch from a *camarote*, up close enough to see the dancers' nipples."

Damiano marveled at his boss's generosity. A viewing box like that cost fifteen hundred dollars. Soccer stars, politicians, actors and diplomats bought *camarotes*.

"It seats twelve people, and you will sit in front with me and a few ladies."

"I never thought I would get to see carnival from the Sambadrome."

The car arrived at Cortes's mansion, and the driver scurried out. The door by Cortes flung open. Cortes stepped out and handed his empty bottle to the driver. Damiano stepped from the limousine like a rich man, a very lucky man, a whole man, a man about to live a dream.

After dinner, Vincent braved the cold at Quantico for an extra-curricular jog to avoid facing the other trainees. The threat of an ice storm kept the others indoors. Puffs of hot moist air from his lungs clouded up in front of him. Sweating under his thermal layer, he took stock of his body parts that ached, the parts that stung from the winter chill, and the parts that were damp. Aches outnumbered all other sensations.

A bundled figure ahead on the trail was bent over with hands on knees, wheezing. As Vincent jogged closer, he spotted a shock of red hair sticking from the back of a wool cap.

"Are you okay, redneck?"

Blake coughed. Or was that a laugh? He seized deep breaths. Steam rose from his bare freckled neck. A gloved hand rose as if to signal he needed another breath before answering. "I didn't realize," Blake said, "how out of shape I was." He groaned as he straightened.

Great globs of snowflakes plopped around them. Vincent looked up and caught one in his mouth. Wind gusts blasted from the direction of the Potomac River, swirling snow in patterns and ankle-high tornados.

"Did ya ever wonder what happens to the stuff that gets flushed out of airplanes in flight?" Blake asked.

Vincent spat out the melted snow.

"I'm just saying, pure as the driven snow is an oxymoron."

"Getting peed on would fit with the rest of my day."

"I heard." Blake headed back toward the barracks. "I signed Cho's cast. For what it's worth, she didn't seem mad at you."

"She won't be able to shoot with a cast on." He had knocked her out of the running for this graduating group.

"Oh, she knows it." Blake paused on the pathway. "She confided in me she was really afraid of getting walloped by the other female trainees."

Vincent stopped and acknowledged Cho's fear with a "Huh." Cho's wink suddenly made sense. He suspected the women who had come from the military or law enforcement felt the need to prove themselves. Everyone had to prove worthy, yet the women seemed more intense about it, more competitive against the men and each other.

"She didn't cry did she?" Blake's group of trainees had been performing a different challenge, so he had not witnessed Cho's injury.

"She punched me back." He rubbed his bruised sternum.

"Good for her."

"And you call yourself my friend." Vincent resumed walking.

"I mean, it beats carrying a grudge," Blake said. He caught up with Vincent. "Do you really want a computer expert mad at you?"

Vincent shook his head.

"I'm just saying as your friend," Blake said, keeping pace as Vincent fast-walked. "You need to work on your people skills."

The snow clumped, heavy and wet, falling thicker and faster on the verge of becoming sleet. No point in jogging in sleet. He didn't want to be sidelined by an injury in the last two weeks of training. Tough break for Cho. He had apologized, but he still felt guilty. Perhaps a goodwill gesture would cheer her. Cho knew he had not meant to hurt her, didn't she? "I should send Cho flowers."

Blake shrugged. "The other women would punch you for it and call you sexist. But Cho doesn't seem to have a feminist chip on her shoulder. It's Rose you have to worry about."

Rose, Vincent's girlfriend, had graduated from Berkeley College in Manhattan with Blake and Vincent. With her degree in fashion marketing, Rose moved straight from school to an internship at what she called 'her dream job' as a buyer for Sak's Fifth Avenue. She was a woman driven by ambition. Vincent found her confidence and style sexy.

"If she finds out, I'll explain the circumstances," Vincent said. He doubted Rose's vast social connections reached into Quantico.

"Just to be safe, you could call Rose and ask for her advice." Blake had a point. He had amazing people skills with women, who automatically trusted him.

"Good idea." Vincent doubted he could ask any florist for advice on the kind of flowers to send to apologize for breaking a woman's arm. Rose would know the kind of flowers to suit the situation.

Snow stuck to Blake's eyebrows making him look like a large, prematurely graying, green-eyed leprechaun.

"What?" Blake asked, peeling off his knit cap.

"Nothing."

After entering the barracks, they went their separate ways. Vincent's mind drifted from Cho to Rose to Nefi. Their similarities few; their differences vast. Cho's brilliant mind intimidated her colleagues and impressed her instructors, yet she was physically fragile. Rose exuded sensuality and confidence in everything she said and did, but she tended to think emotionally rather than logically. If faced with violence, she'd probably just scream and expect men to run to her aid. *But Nefi?*

In his room, he peeled off his damp coat, hat, and scarf. *Why couldn't more women be like Nefi?* He hung up his coat. At fourteen she kept pace in the jungle with adult men. He stomped the snow off his boots. Nefi was tough but vulnerable at the same time. She spoke Portuguese, Spanish, English, and two tribal dialects that he knew of. In her second semester at Harvard, she would make connections with influential people to add to her powerful family connections. She would have managed just fine in the Bull-in-the-Ring exercise at receiving and delivering punches. She understood that the world was a dangerous place. It figured that when he moved from New York City to Quantico, she would be at school five-hundred miles away in Boston, leaving no chance to run into her. He hoped she was happy.

He sighed and called Rose.

. 14 .

On the second day of carnival in Rio, Nefi strained to stay awake despite having stolen a few hours' sleep with earplugs. The Ambassador had introduced her to the high society of Brazil. The relentless Samba music was as loud as the cheerleading competition Martina had once dragged her to. Her ears were ringing. He woke her to meet the President in a nearby *camarote*. She had read about President Luiz Inacio da Silva as a man of the people. Nefi brushed her hair, put on lip gloss and grabbed her camera from her satchel.

"You look lovely," Ambassador Morales shouted over the music. He pulled her right hand into the crook of his left arm and patted her hand. He spoke to Antonio, who was groggy from his third drink. "Doesn't she?"

Antonio briefly kissed Nefi on the mouth. "And she tastes sweet."

Nefi's face heated up. She playfully shoved him back into his chair. "You taste like rum."

The Ambassador clicked his tongue at Antonio. He then led Nefi up to the third level of the Sambadrome with two security guards following. On the stairway, four other security guards stopped them.

"*Boa-noite*, Ambassador Morales," the oldest guard said, shouting over the parade music. He removed his hat and smiled at Nefi. "*Quem e esta bonita jovem mulher?*"

Nefi smiled at being called a lovely young woman. Amid a parade of predominantly naked women dancing the Samba, did he really consider her lovely or was he being polite?

"Nefi Jenkins *os Estados Unidos*," Ambassador Morales said.

"Yes, yes. The President is expecting you. Welcome to Brazil, Miss Jenkins." He stuck out his hand. Was he showing off his English or did he assume she didn't understand Portuguese?

Nefi shook his hand. "*Muito obrigado, senhor.*"

The guard beamed and gave her a smart bow of the head. The other guards smiled and flattened against the wall to open more room for the Ambassador and Nefi. They, too, removed their hats. Nefi sensed their stares at her backside all the way up the flight of stairs.

President Luiz Inacio da Silva rose from his chair and greeted Ambassador Morales with a kiss on each side of his face before he faced Nefi. He looked at her eye to eye and glanced down at her feet as if to figure out what made her so tall. Nefi remembered to wear flat shoes for comfort, but they also kept her from towering over people. It would have been awkward to look down at the President. His black and gray hair transitioned to all gray on his trim beard. Solidly built, his experience as a steel worker showed in his shoulders. It was his second term as President, elected this time on a platform to reduce crime and improve education. He was stockier and stronger than Nefi expected.

"May I present Miss Nefi Jenkins?" Ambassador Morales said.

"You may indeed," President da Silva said, sandwiching her hand gently between his calloused, strong hands. "Miss Jenkins, please know that we have not stopped investigating the murder of your parents. In time, evil ones always face justice. If not here," he shrugged, "then at God's hand."

"Thank you, sir. I am honored you remember my family." She was also honored that he spoke to her in English. It was a challenging language to learn. Nefi held up her camera. "May I have a picture taken with you?"

"Of course," President da Silva raised his hand as he smiled.

A muscular male assistant appeared at his side.

"Take our pictures." The President plucked Nefi's camera from her and handed it to the assistant. He put Nefi between himself and Ambassador Morales.

When the assistant raised the camera, both men straightened their backs and sucked in their bellies. The first flash caught Nefi smiling. The second captured all three laughing.

"Who doesn't want to look good for the camera?" The President asked. "Alfonso, I see you eat well, too." He patted his own rounded belly.

"A vice I confess."

The male assistant handed the camera to Nefi. A second assistant appeared beside the President, who raised his eyebrows as if to ask why he was being interrupted. The second male assistant shouted over the parade noise in Portuguese that the entire parade had stopped. A Samba school was waving and looking for their President.

The President chuckled.

Ambassador Morales placed his hand on Nefi's back to gently nudge her toward the exit. "Thank you, Lula. We need to go."

The President smiled at them then bounded toward the viewing area. When he stepped up to the edge of the *camarote* and waved, a roar of cheers rose.

After returning to the Ambassador's *camarote*, Nefi giggled and tugged on the Ambassador's sleeve.

"Why did you call the President a squid?"

"I did no such thing."

"In Tupi, *Lula* means squid."

"Ha! In Portuguese, Lula is also a nickname for Luiz."

Hours later when Ambassador Morales, Antonio, Nefi and two guards walked from the Sambadrome to the limousine, they passed a pair of men swearing in Portuguese. The taller one, wearing more jewelry than Nefi considered masculine, told the shorter one to stop insulting the whores. Antonio glared at the men and placed his hand on the small of Nefi's back.

"How good is your Portuguese?" he whispered to Nefi. He cringed as the two men argued in vulgarities.

"Better than his," she whispered.

She stole a glance at the men. The shorter man crossed his arms over his chest. One hand held a cigarette; the other gleamed like plastic. It was artificial. Nefi flinched.

"Never mind them," Antonio said. He nudged her sideways toward the open door of the limousine. "Don't stare. It might provoke them."

Nefi followed Ambassador Morales into the limousine, taking the window seat near the door so that Antonio had to step over her legs to sit on the far side of the seat. The guards shut the doors. At last, the riot of Samba music dulled, replaced by the *whoosh* of the limousine's air conditioning system cranked to full power. One guard tapped on the hood to signal the driver to leave. As the car rolled away, Nefi looked back at the man with the artificial hand to see his face. His flattened nose and wide face resembled a frog's. Cold air condensed the sweat on Nefi's arms and legs. Chills shot through her from the inside out. Could that have been the Pirarucu Man? *Could he be alive?* She regretted she had not snapped a photograph of him. She also regretted that she had not heard either of the foul-mouthed men use their names.

"Tomorrow is the last day of carnival. If you would like to attend tomorrow, we can, or we could have a quiet dinner overlooking the ocean." Ambassador Morales waited for Nefi's reply.

Her head rang with a Samba beat. The gracious man had gone to such generous effort and expense to win her affection for Brazil. A quiet evening appealed to her. Three days of carnival had begun to blend together. What if that one-handed man was at the Sambadrome tomorrow? How could she stop herself from staring? Or from confronting him or attacking him if he too closely matched the ugliness of the Pirarucu Man? It wasn't a crime to be ugly or to have an artificial hand. It was not enough to confront him, yet too much to bear thinking about. If that was the Pirarucu Man, then it proved the adage that only the good die young. Nothing could kill him.

"Would you be disappointed to miss the last day?" she asked.

"Not at all. I fear for my hearing as it is."

"What about you, Antonio?" Nefi asked.

Antonio clapped his hands together as if in prayer. "I vote for peace and quiet with a view."

The limousine eased through dark, empty streets while Nefi tried to shake off thoughts of the ugly, whore-insulting, one-handed man.

. 15 .

The next morning at breakfast, Nefi brooded. With a spectacular view of the beach from the suite balcony, she chewed through sweet mango, crisp bacon, and thick toast while her mind digested her choices about what to do. She was scheduled to spend the morning shopping with Ambassador Morales's wife and Alfonso's mother. The sisters, it seemed, had dedicated the morning to transforming Nefi from the crown of her head to the soles of her feet from her functional college style dress into a junior *fashionista*. The women had covered their mouths and shaken their heads at her when she arrived at breakfast in a green short-sleeved Oxford shirt, jeans, and sandals, with her hair in a ponytail.

As dearly as Nefi longed for help with her image, she also felt compelled to learn more about the ongoing murder investigation. She waited until the others had finished eating to pose a question to the Ambassador.

"Would we have time for me to go to the police department to look at photos?"

Ambassador Morales set his coffee cup on its china saucer. "It has been what? Six years? How would you recognize him?"

"Uncle said a right hand was found with the bodies of the men who attacked the village. Such a fact should narrow the list of suspects."

"It does. However, the Federal Police are investigating the

196

murders, not the city police." His discomfort on the topic showed in his quiet, controlled demeanor and in his strained smile to his wife.

In the past few days, his wife had admonished him to set aside his work and all unpleasantness to live in the moment, to enjoy his vacation. The impression Nefi gleaned from their conversation was that vacations were rare events. She regretted disturbing the vacation, yet she saw the opportunity to identify the man with the artificial hand as an especially rare event.

"Could we stop by their office?" Nefi asked.

Ambassador Morales leaned toward Nefi and placed his hand on her forearm. "During the carnival, all our law enforcement agencies stay very busy. I'm afraid the effort would be in vain at this time. Let me make inquiries. Perhaps the Federal Police will issue you a report on the status of the investigation."

His answer was a polite, firm no. He was right to question her memory. How would she recognize the face of a killer she had seen in the dark six years earlier? The temptation to point to a photo in hopes of solving the crime might lead her into the sin of bearing false witness. Breaking one commandment to resolve another broken commandment would not please God. She had to be certain. She had to remember. *But how?*

"I am sorry if I've upset you," Ambassador Morales said. He squeezed Nefi's forearm. "I shouldn't have shared the photo albums with you."

Nefi planted her hand on his. "I enjoyed the albums very much. Please, forgive me for disrupting your vacation."

"Of course. You have two forces driving you to think about solving this terrible crime: your personal stake in the matter, and your future career in law enforcement. I ask you to set aside your past and future for a few days. Enjoy the present. Live for today."

Nefi sighed. Perhaps it was arrogant of her to imagine she could solve the crime that professional investigators had worked on for years. She did not surrender her hope to identify the

Pirarucu Man. She merely delayed it until she had a solid, workable plan. "My friend Martina made me promise to buy all new clothes and to learn how to wear makeup. She says Brazilian women understand style and sex appeal."

Ambassador Morales nodded to his wife. "Then I leave you in the skilled hands of two stylish, beautiful women." He tossed his linen napkin beside his plate, and he pushed back his chair. His gleaming white and navy tennis outfit fit him handsomely. "Antonio. Are you ready?"

Antonio called from his room in the spacious suite. "I can't find my shoes."

Nefi bolted from the table and dashed to her room. She found her tennis shoes in the closet. She took them to Antonio's room and held them up in the doorway. They were clean, multi-purpose cross-trainers, size nine.

Antonio plucked them from Nefi's grasp. "Thank you."

"Antonio!" Ambassador Morales said. "I would like a word with you."

Antonio followed his uncle to another bedroom. After a hushed exchange, Antonio reentered the living room area of the suite and held up the shoes.

"Nefi," Antonio asked, "whose shoes are these?"

"Mine." Nefi did not immediately understand the problem of loaning of her shoes. They would fit him.

"See?" Antonio said.

"But they look like yours," Antonio's mother said, rising from the table. Her pale, manicured hands poked the shoes.

"Mine are like these." Antonio shrugged. "Same size, too."

Nefi suddenly realized that if the shoes *had* been Antonio's the next question would have been why they were in her room. The hint of impropriety between Antonio and Nefi had alarmed the ambassador and his wife.

Mrs. Morales chuckled. Her gold and diamond bracelet sparkled in the morning sunlight as she clutched her hands together. "My sweet girl, if you have shoes a man can wear, you must change your ways."

The Ambassador let out a long sigh then he and Antonio left for tennis. The women were granted full use of the chauffeur and limousine for the day. The chauffeur could drive well enough, but Nefi believed by his watchfulness his true skills were as a bodyguard.

Nefi surrendered to the will of Mrs. Morales and her sister on every purchase that day. Whereas shopping with Martina had always frustrated Nefi, shopping with these two wise women had been a joy. By following their advice, Nefi discovered how to draw attention to her best features and how to diminish her less attractive ones. For example, in three-inch heels, her feet transformed from duck like to shapely, while also elongating the line of her athletic legs. The greatest change came from buying bras that fit properly. She marveled at her reflection in the dressing room mirror, shocked to have cleavage. *At last.*

With every purchase, she became more confident about re-introducing herself to Vincent. Surely, her adult, stylish appearance would erase all thoughts of her as that scared, machete-armed wild thing that attacked him six years ago. She was eager to impress him as soon as the opportunity presented itself. Could she wait until September for Ruis's wedding? According to Martina, both Blake and Vincent had been asked to serve as ushers. They *had* to accept. Who could say no to Ruis? How could she bear to wait seven more months?

Mrs. Morales handed an armload of purchases to the long-suffering driver. She then pulled Nefi toward a perfume counter and handed her a tester bottle labeled Hypnotic.

"That's it," Nefi whispered.

"You haven't tried it on," Mrs. Morales said. "You must try it on your skin."

"Hypnosis," Nefi touched Mrs. Morales's wrist. "I can ask to be hypnotized so I can remember exactly what the killer looks like."

"How very clever," Mrs. Morales said. She consumed crime novels. "You will also need a sketch artist."

Her sister, also an avid reader, nodded. "Do you know anyone at the American FBI?"

"My," Nefi avoided calling him a psychiatrist, "doctor works with the FBI on special cases."

Mrs. Morales added, "Alfonso can get the case number so you can send the artist's drawing directly to our investigators."

The ladies eagerly conspired over lunch.

Within a week after Nefi resumed classes at Harvard, she had arranged for Dr. Sloan and an FBI sketch artist to render a drawing of the Pirarucu Man. The session, conducted by the FBI's Behavioral Sciences Department, took three hours. Dr. Sloan counted down, drawing Nefi back to full consciousness. Later, when the artist handed the sketch to Nefi, the face of a killer stared back from the page. His appearance was not particularly menacing, just ugly. The accuracy of it drove a chill up Nefi's back. She handed the pad back to the artist.

"I am surprised you remember so much detail," Doctor Sloan said, "from seeing him through binoculars."

Her stomach tightened. What had she said under hypnosis? She read his expressions and body language. He was not challenging her. He seemed genuinely surprised.

"He came to the village twice to buy fish," she said, "before—"

"It's all right. You're safe now," Doctor Sloan said.

Nefi gave the sketch artist the information on where to send a copy of the sketch so it would reach the Brazilian investigator assigned to the case. *One big step closer to identifying him.* Maybe the investigator could match the image of the Pirarucu Man with a name. Maybe even to a corpse.

. 16 .

At long last, after seven months of waiting, Nefi was ready to ignite Vincent with the new and improved, adult version of herself. She had a year to go before college graduation. She knew that Vincent was working at the New York City office of the FBI and that he was an usher at Ruis's wedding ceremony. She had spied him from the back row of the church, but he had not spotted her. It was blustery outside as she strode from the cab into the Crowne Plaza Times Square Hotel. Her invitation announced the date—September 17, 2008—a day she claimed to re-introduce herself to Vincent.

For the moment, she sat alone at a six-seat table in the reception hall, once again skipping classes to enjoy a special occasion. Like the other wedding guests, she waited for the bridal party to finish their photo session at the church. Tables laden with fruit and cheese and crackers had lured Aunt Louise away. Uncle Hamilton stood in line at the bar with a group of Navy officers and Admiral Ramos. Nefi examined the small screen of her digital camera photo by photo.

The reception hall had been dimmed so much the camera screen glowed with images—all taken without the flash so as not to disrupt the ceremony—Ruis at the altar with Sofia saying their vows, Martina and the other bridesmaids in pale blue dresses lined up like exquisite dolls, the groomsmen looked like an optical illusion because Ruis's brothers resembled him so closely, and Blake and Vincent as ushers, who, even from a distance, loomed head and shoulders taller than the groomsmen. How magnificent Vincent looked in a tuxedo, so tall and broad-shouldered, that Nefi sighed at the camera screen. She longed to see him up close, to show him a grown up woman had replaced the face-painted feral child he had hauled out of the rainforest. The last photo showed Uncle Hamilton and Aunt Louise in the lobby. Nefi was smiling at this photo when a warm male voice with a Southern accent sounded behind her.

"It's a crying shame to see a lovely woman sit all alone."

In the dimly lit ballroom, Blake appeared as a giant silhouette bearing a flute of champagne in each hand. Nefi stood and hugged him. He looked perfectly handsome in a tuxedo. A hint of aftershave lingered from the hug. Over the last few years, he had grown his hair slightly longer and had gained a few pounds in the middle. When she released him from the hug, he also assessed her with a quick look over.

"I'll take that as an invitation." He sat in the chair to Nefi's left. His teeth reflected like white tiles in the light of the table's candles.

Out of habit, Nefi read his face for the unspoken. She realized that Blake, trying to guess her age, hoped for older than she looked. Though they had exchanged a few emails since she graduated from high school, they had not exchanged photos. *He didn't recognize her.*

Blake's lack of recognition prompted Nefi to measure the changes in her own appearance. Since her high school graduation she had, as Aunt Louise said, 'filled out' to a C cup bra. Her brown hair hung in curls to her waist instead of being pulled up into her usual ponytail. She had learned to walk comfortably in three-inch heels, and she wore makeup.

"Are you family, a friend of the bride, or friend of the groom?" Blake asked.

"Friend of the groom." *Was it really that dark in here?*

"Me, too. Are you here alone?"

The situation was deliciously awkward. "My aunt and uncle came with me," Nefi said, nodding toward the empty chairs to her right. Aunt Louise's beaded clutch sparkled in the candlelight.

"So make my day." Blake's green eyes glinted with mischief.

This probably wasn't his first drink of the evening. So did he think she was attractive because he had been drinking? *Hmm.* Martina called that looking through beer goggles.

"Tell me you're over twenty-one."

Blake! "Next month."

Blake set one flute of champagne out of her reach. He took a sip from the other glass in his left hand. He seemed disappointed, but not dissuaded. Nefi was equally surprised and pleased that he found her attractive enough to flirt with. She wondered how long it would take for him to recognize her.

Maybe his memory just needed a push. "Congratulations on joining the FBI."

"Ah, thank you." He leaned back in his chair. He looked amused and confused. He leaned close, squinted and then his eyes widened and his mouth fell open. "Oh, man." He slapped his free hand on his face.

Nefi giggled. Her golden irises usually set her apart. "Did they teach you those keen observations skills at Quantico?"

Uncle Hamilton and Aunt Louise approached the table. Blushing furiously, Blake set down his glass and stood. He stepped around the table to greet Uncle Hamilton with a handshake and Aunt Louise with a hug. Southern gentlemen, Aunt Louise always said, recognized a Southern lady. Blake pulled out Aunt Louise's chair. Her smile thanked him. He fidgeted as he stood between Aunt Louise and Nefi as if deciding what to do with his hands or whether or not to run.

"Good to see you again," Uncle Hamilton said. "What's it been—two years?"

"And what a difference," Blake said, "a couple years makes." He tucked a finger under his collar and tugged at it.

"Please," Aunt Louise said, "sit with us for a spell and tell us about your work."

Blake sat in the empty chair beside Nefi. Stealing a glance at Nefi, he took a gulp of champagne. Directing his answer to Aunt Louise, he said, "Don't believe what you see on television. It's far more paperwork than car chases. And what have you been up to?"

Aunt Louise told him about the fundraisers she supported and her travel overseas. She was well into her story about seeing a whale fully breach the water at Maui when applause attracted everyone's attention to the main door of the reception hall. Everyone stood. Ruis and Sofia drifted through the crowd and took their seats at a small ornately decorated table facing the dance floor. The tables on either side of them quickly filled with the parents and grandparents of the bride and groom.

"One usually sees the wedding party seated by the bride and groom," Louise said.

"I'm just an usher. We've been ordered to mingle," Blake said.

Aunt Louise smiled at Nefi to signal her approval of Blake. Aunt Louise adored introducing Nefi to the sons of her society friends. None of those fine young men in the flesh compared to the hope of Vincent. *Magnificent Vincent.* If she had never met Vincent, she might have let charming Blake capture her heart. He had the right combination of impeccable manners and raw animal attraction. He also gave Nefi the impression that he would never start a fight, but he would, if challenged, end it the victor. Predominantly, she thought of him as Vincent's loyal friend.

As if summoned, Vincent entered the reception hall and towered over the largely Hispanic crowd. Clean-shaven, he looked more handsome than she remembered with short-cropped brown wavy hair instead of the high-and-tight Marine cut. Nefi stood for a better view of him. Then the crowd shifted. Hanging onto Vincent's arm was a short bosomy woman in a red designer dress straining at the seams. The woman pointed to a table near the bar. Nefi's heartbeat syncopated, rushing, then faltering like a wounded animal. Vincent guided the woman in red toward a table at the edge of the dance floor. Nefi's throat tightened. Vincent tapped Ruis's sister Martina on the shoulder and talked to her. The room throbbed with noise as the band saluted the bride and groom. Nefi wanted to tunnel into a dark hole and die. Across the room, Martina's mouth dropped open and then she turned toward Nefi. She looked almost as stricken as Nefi felt.

Oh, no! No. No.

Nefi bolted for the nearest door.

Rose had insisted on being introduced to Admiral Ramos, so Vincent complied. Next, she pleaded to meet Senator Jenkins, so he escorted Rose toward the Senator's table, following close enough behind her to catch her in case she toppled off her spiked heels. In that tight dress, she didn't stand a chance of bracing for a fall or climbing back to her feet. He wanted to see Nefi more than he'd admit. When they reached Senator Jenkins' table, the Senator stood. Reluctantly it seemed, Blake stood. Vincent introduced Rose, who shook hands with Senator Jenkins and Mrs. Jenkins then she gave Blake a cool nod. He wasn't sure why Blake didn't like Rose, but the dislike was mutual. She exuded a strong musky perfume as if she'd been dipped in it.

"You just missed Nefi," Blake told Vincent.

Vincent's pulse quickened at the mention of her name. He peered over the crowd. "She's here?" His interest drew a scowl from Rose.

Rose then glowered at Blake. "Your date?"

"A friend."

"And how would Vincent know your friend?" Rose asked Blake. A tight, plastic smile formed on her face.

"She's a mutual friend," Blake said as if to taunt her.

Vincent was tempted to tell them both to knock it off and play nice.

"It's a pleasure to meet you, Senator and Mrs. Jenkins," Rose said while clinging to Vincent's arm.

Between her tugging on his arm and her tone, he understood she wanted to go. "Please, tell Nefi I'm sorry I missed her," Vincent said to Senator Jenkins. He then went in the direction Rose pulled him, past the bar near the dance floor toward their remote table.

Blake was not sorry to see Rose go. Her back was her best feature because it meant she was leaving. He believed women like Rose should wear warning signs, like *Dangerous Curves* or *Dead End*. Rose showed signs all right, but Vincent ignored them. In the months that Vincent dated Rose, she had changed from charming to demanding which signaled to Blake that Rose was the kind of woman who treated men like rungs on a ladder, the kind whose interest perked up at the chance to discover a man's financial situation. Once he had caught her scanning through the directory on Vincent's cell phone. Blake told her that relationships are built on trust. She told him to mind his own relationships. Blake had ventured as far as asking Vincent what he would do if he found his girlfriend searching his cell phone directory. Vincent had laughed. Blake dismissed the behavior as a big-city thing though it bothered him more than it bothered Vincent.

Blake realized he was still standing when Senator and Mrs. Jenkins looked up at him.

"What's with Nefi?" Blake asked Mrs. Jenkins.

Louise said, wincing, "She still wears his dog tags."

Sobering, Blake shook his head. Seven years ago she favored Vincent with teenage infatuation. Shocked that Nefi still nursed her feelings through high school and now college, Blake set aside his pride. Surely, Vincent didn't know Nefi still adored him. She wasn't like the aggressive, forward women of her generation. And if Vincent had taken one look at Nefi, he would have dropped Rose in a New York second.

"Excuse me," Blake said. "I think I'll go check on her."

Louise nodded.

Blake pushed through the nearest door to the hall. He stopped in the center of the hallway. To the right, according to the sandwich board signs, a convention of engineers was underway and beyond that, more ballrooms. Signs to the left promised the lobby, shops, and the street. He headed toward the lobby. Passing a set of doors recessed in an alcove, he heard crying behind the ladies room door.

"Nefi?"

The crying paused.

"Nefi?" He planted a hand on each side of the doorframe.

"What?"

"Come on out, please."

A tapping on his shoulder spun him around. Standing before him was a beautiful woman in her mid-to-early thirties with thick, wavy reddish brown hair loosely pinned back from her face. Her pale blue eyes and fair, freckled skin glowed with health and the outdoors. She wore an understated deep green suit with matching shoes. Her full lips formed a pout.

Blocking the door, Blake held out his hands. "Please, help me."

Nefi's whimpering carried to the hallway.

The lady planted her fist at her waist just above her hip.

"Ma'am, there's a young lady in there I'd like to talk to. Would you coax her on out?"

"Why are you calling me ma'am?" She raised an eyebrow.

He braced for a slap. "Good breeding."

A smile tugged up one corner of her mouth. She looked him up and down the way his mother examined a horse. He straightened to his full height, hoping to impress her. He was momentarily tempted to smile to show her his healthy white teeth.

"It's Miss."

Blake smiled at his dumb luck.

"You're not from the city are you?" she asked.

"I work in the city. Today, I'm attending a friend's wedding." He nodded toward the noisy ballroom.

"Is that the bride?"

"No."

"Are you the reason the young lady is crying?"

"Absolutely not."

"You'd say that even if you were." She raised her face. "No promises."

Blake stepped aside and pulled the door open for the lady.

Nefi slouched on a fancy tufted loveseat in a dimly-lit sitting area between the outside corridor and the stalls. Across from her three ornate sinks and a long granite counter gleamed under a row of tiny spotlights and a six-foot by four-foot beveled edge mirror. The sitting room light illuminated only her face, giving her a disembodied appearance that reminded her of a movie she'd watched with Martina during one of their sleepover movie marathons.

Mirror, mirror, on the wall. Who's the dumbest of them all? Two thin streaks of brown mascara ran from the outside corners of her eyes halfway down her cheeks. What did it matter now if she looked like the evil queen? Who would even care that her world had just spun to a stop?

A woman in her mid-thirties, in a stylish deep green suit and heels, shoulder-length hair the color of a new penny, eased up to the long granite counter. She leaned over to examine her lipstick then she peeked at Nefi's reflection.

"I just met a gorgeous, well-mannered man outside," the woman ventured.

How long would Blake stand out there? *Can't I have a breakdown in private?* Nefi tossed her wad of used tissues into the trash can. Doctor Sloan would be so disappointed that years of therapy came to this. Here I am all but sucking my thumb while I bawl.

The woman plucked a handful of tissues from the brass tissue holder before sitting beside Nefi. "He asked me to invite you outside to talk."

Nefi snorted. *If only talking could make Vincent's date disappear.*

The woman handed over a handful of fresh tissues.

"Thank you," Nefi said making eye contact.

Startled, the lady leaned away, then leaned closer.

People tended to stare at her golden eyes. *Yes. I am a freak.* With another tissue, she dabbed her eyes. A bawling baby freak.

"Why are you crying?"

"Disappointment." Nefi's bottom lip quivered. The image of Vincent with a date crushed her. That woman on his arm looked so...sexy. And petite. All chest and hips with the kinds of curves Nefi would have to buy.

"Did someone break your heart?"

Words clogged in her throat, so Nefi nodded. Her eyes welled up, threatening more tears than willpower could contain. Papa always said that most crying came from selfishness and not from compassion. Papa was so right, but Nefi could stop neither the crushing pain nor the tears.

"On purpose?" Her kindness touched Nefi.

She shook her head and let out a shuddering sigh. It was her own fault after all. Martina had warned her. Doctor Sloan had warned her. It wasn't healthy to obsess.

"Is it that hunk in the tux outside?"

Nefi rose and stood steady on her designer high heels. She moved to the stone counter and dampened a paper towel under the faucet. "No. Blake is one of the kindest men I've ever met."

The woman gaped up at Nefi. "Is Blake your date?"

Nefi gently wiped mascara smears from her cheeks. "No. We're both friends of the groom."

"And you're in love with...?"

"Vincent. Blake's partner."

"Partner? Oh, dear." Disappointment mixed with horror flashed on the woman's face. "That must be quite...a shock."

Nefi snorted. "Not that kind of partner. They're co-workers. They're both straight."

Smiling, the woman said, "I'm Terri Pinehurst."

"Nefi Jenkins." The ladies shook hands.

"So, what are you going to do?"

"Dig a hole and die in it."

"Please, not in those shoes," Terri said, standing.

Nefi flashed a grin. The shoes made her feel as deep-down pretty as a storybook princess. They were the most blatantly feminine things she owned she could show to the world.

Terri leaned her hip against the counter. One corner of her mouth flinched in a micro smile. "The way I see it, you have a choice. You can hide from the world every time you're disappointed or hurt by a man, or you can put on your big-girl panties and go back to the party."

In this instant-gratification world, could anyone understand patience? Nefi confessed softly. "I waited six years to see Vincent."

Terri covered her mouth with her hand. *"Six years?* Why?"

"He's older than me. I'll be twenty-one next month."

"And you thought he would be waiting for you to grow up?"

Nefi closed her eyes and nodded. *Who's the dumbest one of all?* She looked in the mirror. *I am.*

Terri crossed her arms. "Why did you think he would wait for you?"

"He gave me his dog tags." And now for the really pathetic truth. "I was waiting for him." *Oh, wow, that sounds as stupid as it feels.*

Terri bit her bottom lip. Next, she covered her mouth with a manicured hand. "Not that it's any of my business, but did anything else happen between you two?"

Like a sensible sign of commitment? No. "No sex if that's what you mean."

Nefi dabbed tissues on her eyes. Aunt Louise called it 'making repairs.' For a moment, she stared at her reflection in the mirror. *This isn't a fairytale. This is real life. I am beautiful and intelligent, and I make my own choices. I am responsible for my own happiness.*

"You know there are six billion people in the world. Let's say half of them are men. I'd bet most of them would be thrilled to go out with you."

"Maybe the boys and old men." *They certainly give me attention.*

"So maybe one billion in dating age range. Roughly the equivalent to the entire population of China," Terri said.

Fearing the woman thought Nefi was suicidal, Nefi took measure of the sheer number of men who were not Vincent.

With these empowering thoughts in mind, she refused to miss out on Ruis's wedding reception because Vincent brought a date. He was one of three-and-a-half-billion males in the world after all. How could she ever expect to work in the FBI if she couldn't handle a non-life-threatening thing like personal disappointment? Ever so slightly she raised her chin and spoke to the mirror. "I can master my feelings. I refuse to miss this party because Vincent brought a date."

Nefi's back straightened. She pulled her shoulders back. She was tougher than people knew. She'd been through worse than this. All that was really at stake was pride.

"Atta girl." Terri clasped her hands in front of her face. "In my opinion, the hunk in the tux must be some kind of friend to wait outside a ladies room for you."

She remembered how Blake had flirted with her before he recognized her. He wasn't kidding around, he was genuinely flirting. Nefi broke out a full smile. Maybe the evening wasn't a disaster after all. She hugged her new friend. "Blake?"

"It seems to me that Blake cares for you." Terri dropped her voice to a whisper, "But if you aren't interested in him, please, please, introduce me."

When Nefi and Terri emerged from the bathroom, Terri gave Blake a double-take and a grin. Nefi set her mind to matchmaking.

"Terri Pinehurst," Nefi said, "Meet Blake Clayton, a man who didn't shoot me when he probably should have."

Blake inhaled. "Now there's an endorsement you don't get every day."

"Is she being melodramatic?" Terri shook Blake's hand.

Blake said, "Perhaps you'd like to join us for drinks and an explanation?" It sounded like begging.

"I'm here for a convention," Terri said, rooted in place. "Seriously, why does she believe you should have shot her?"

"I would love to tell you that story if you have the time." He held out his elbow.

Terri glanced at Nefi.

To reassure Terri there was no territorial dispute over Blake, Nefi added, "If you come to the reception I can point out Vincent, and you can tell me if I'm wasting my time."

Blake sighed as if to remind the ladies of his presence.

"I'll take that dare." Terri slipped her hand into the crook of Blake's arm.

Helping others find happiness trumped Nefi's selfish despair. She sensed electrical heat passing between Blake and Terri Pinehurst, the encouraging stranger. Having faith in God means to trust that nothing happens by chance or coincidence. The challenge was in discerning if it was God's plan to encourage or to discourage pursuit of Vincent. Nefi sighed.

Blake offered her his other elbow then he led the ladies into the ballroom to the table where Nefi's camera and Mrs. Jenkins' purse held their lonely vigil. Blake pulled out a chair for Nefi, then one for Terri. He offered to get them drinks then he headed to the bar for a Merlot and a Ginger ale. He practically strutted.

Vincent spotted a woman in a leather skirt and silk top standing in line for the bartender. She was tall and her cropped hair stood straight from her scalp in all directions about two inches long. His pulse quickened. Nefi? He'd have to act fast to spend a moment with her before Rose swooped in. Rose tended to be insecure and suspicious though Vincent had never given her reason to be.

He tapped the woman's shoulder. "Nefi?"

The woman twisted toward him revealing artificially deep cleavage. He looked up to her eyes. Brown. Rimmed with thick black lines in Goth fashion. The makeup did not hide her wrinkles. Perhaps she was in her forties trying to look younger, or perhaps she had lived a hard life. "What did you say?"

"Sorry, I thought you were a friend."

"I can be your friend." She batted her false eyelashes.

The young bartender cleared his throat and set a gin and tonic on the bar. "Your drink, ma'am."

She stepped aside and took a sip from her glass.

Vincent spoke to the bartender. "Champagne and beer, please."

The woman sighed and stalked off.

The bartender placed Vincent's order, a glass of champagne and a beer, on the counter. Vincent dropped a ten-dollar bill into the tip bowl, picked up his drinks and pivoted toward the ballroom. The lights dimmed to near darkness as the music began.

"Getting her drunk won't help," Blake said.

Normally a gentleman, Blake refused to even pretend he liked Rose. Blake had hinted once he didn't believe Rose was in the relationship for the long haul. He had even used the term 'social climber' about her. Maybe she was though Vincent would rather get punched than admit it.

Vincent grunted. "I could get drunk."

Ruis slid up beside them at the bar. "Water, please."

The bartender plunked a bottle of water and a glass on the counter. Ruis twisted off the bottle top.

"I think it's simply poor form," Blake said, "when the groom is prettier than the bride."

"Are you saying my wife isn't pretty?"

Blake appeared properly panicked before he blurted, "She's very pretty."

Ruis laughed. "Go have fun with anyone but my sisters." He left with his water.

Blake glanced over his shoulder and waved at two women seated at the table where Vincent had earlier introduced Rose to the Senator and Mrs. Jenkins. "Got a minute? You have to meet the ladies at my table."

Vincent said, "Rose will think you're trying to introduce me to other women."

"Better women."

Vincent squinted at the ladies. The younger woman was pointing toward the bartender or was it toward Blake? She looked too refined to be Nefi, the other looked too old. "How did you find two beauties?"

"Open bar. The more they drink, the better I look."

The younger one had cascading long brown hair and looked shapely. "It could be the tux." Vincent released his pointer finger from his grip on the champagne glass and aimed it at Blake. "Makes you look housebroken."

The DJ announced the first dance of the bride and groom.

Blake told the bartender, "One rum and coke and one ginger ale, please."

Vincent raised his eyebrows. "Mother and daughter?"

The young bartender snickered.

Blake stuffed a one-dollar bill in the tip jar as he glowered at the bartender. "What are you laughing at?" He said to Vincent, "The women are unrelated, thank you very much. You really need to meet them."

"Another time." Vincent took a draw of cold, tangy beer to brace himself for the rest of the evening. Rose was on her fifth rum and coke and starting to slur her words. He prayed she wasn't a mean drunk. Holding two glasses overhead, he waded into the crowd gathering at the edge of the dance floor.

"See the man in front of Blake?" Nefi pointed. Vincent looked spectacularly manly in a tuxedo. Her ribcage felt like a wild bird, trapped and panicking, was crashing around inside.

"Wow. Okay, I wouldn't kick him out of bed for eating crackers."

Nefi was relieved when Blake headed toward them alone.

After placing the drinks on the table, he sat between Nefi and

Terri and draped his arms over the backs of their chairs as if staking territory. "Let the rumors begin."

Later in the conversation Blake reminded Nefi about the need for forgiveness, backing it up with scripture—Matthew eighteen, verse twenty-two. Forgive, it says, seventy-seven times.

Me? I should forgive Vincent for choosing that woman over me? Gritting her teeth, she decided to be the bigger, better person Blake expected her to be. She blurted, "He's using up my limit!"

Blake shook his head.

Nefi dropped back into her chair. "I suppose we're even now." She said to Terri, "Once I knocked Vincent down and threatened him with knives."

Terri leaned back in her chair. "Why?"

Blake dropped a hand on Nefi's forearm. "Technically, it was a machete and a hunting knife."

Blades, knives, whatever. Nefi shrugged then took a sip of ginger ale.

"It was a simple misunderstanding," Blake said, "Vincent had something of her father's so she logically suspected that we might have been involved in killing her parents."

Terri gasped. "Nefi Jenkins. Senator Jenkins' niece?"

Surprised anyone outside of her circle of friends and neighbors would recognize her name, she nodded.

"I remember it on the news. Your parents were missionaries in Brazil. Oh, I'm so sorry."

Missionaries, right. Big lie. Nefi sighed.

Blake must have interpreted the sigh as mourning because he reached around Nefi's shoulder and gave her a half hug against his ribs. "And Vincent, the groom Ruis, and I went down to Brazil to find her and bring her to the states. Our sweet girl was dehydrated, malnourished, covered in leeches, wearing scary looking war paint, and having a bad day when we found her." He patted Nefi's back.

At the mention of leeches, Terri glanced at Nefi.

"And none of them spoke Portuguese," Nefi added, "so there we were. I was on top of Vincent holding a machete to his neck and a knife at his ribs. Blake drew his gun on me while Ruis paged through his pocket *English/Portuguese Dictionary*."

Terri covered her mouth with her pale, manicured, right hand. Her nails were trimmed short, unlike the talons so popular with poorer women. *No wedding ring. Amen to that.* Ha. Blake noticed.

Blake rested his hand on the back of Nefi's chair. "Good times."

Terri and Nefi laughed.

"I'm glad he didn't shoot you," Terri said while looking at Blake.

"Me too," Blake and Nefi said in unison.

Ruis and Sofia stopped at the table where they greeted Blake and Nefi with hugs. Sofia's thick dark brown hair was mostly secured up with pins and glistening hairspray allowing for a few errant, artfully placed tendrils to hang loose. Her strapless gown flattered her petite curvy form.

"Happy Independence Day," Ruis said, hugging Nefi.

Pleased Ruis remembered the Brazilian holiday, Nefi smiled. It was one of the few holidays the tribe celebrated. She wondered if they still did. "Thank you."

"Speaking of holidays, I heard you went to Carnival in Rio." Ruis's left hand rested in the curve of his bride's back. That simple, intimate gesture gave Nefi a pang of longing.

"It's much bigger and louder and wilder than Mardi Gras." She and Martina had gone to New Orleans their senior year of high school on spring break.

"Don't tell me about Mardi Gras." Ruis leaned toward Terri. "Hello, I don't believe we've met."

"This is Terri Pinehurst," Blake said. "I corralled her from the conference next door."

Ruis asked Terri, "You're a chemical engineer?"

"I'm with the other convention, next ballroom down."

Standing, Terri looked at her watch. "Congratulations on your wedding. I'm sorry, but I really have to leave." She retrieved a name badge from her jacket pocket and clipped it to her lapel.

Ruis smiled. "It's a pleasure to meet you, Doctor Pinehurst."

Blake placed his hands on Terri's shoulders and gently spun her around to face him. Her tag was framed in a red border. At the bottom margin appeared another title in large white letters. "And you're the keynote speaker?"

"That's why I need to be on time." She gave Blake a kiss on the cheek and then she hugged Nefi. "Call me," she whispered. "I would love to know how this works out for you." She palmed Nefi her business card.

Blake patted Nefi on the shoulder. "I'll be right back. Save a dance for me."

"Wait!" Nefi picked up her camera from the table and aimed it at them.

Terri reached her hand into the crook of his arm and leaned against him momentarily. Blake looked grounded, secure and fully alive in the presence of this gracious stranger. They looked like they belonged together, excited and at ease at the same time. How could love be so easy for them?

Nefi took two photos of them. While she checked they were in focus, she overheard Blake and Terri talking.

"May I walk you to your meeting?" Blake said.

"Thank you."

"A doctor. My mother would be so proud of me for meeting you."

Arm in arm Blake and Terri maneuvered a path between the tables toward the double doors to the corridor. Nefi followed them as far as the doors on her way to the buffet line.

"You could come hear me speak," Terri said.

"That's tempting, but there's no predicting what Rose might do if she senses a rival for Vincent's attention," Blake said. "Rose might bluff toughness. Nefi doesn't bluff."

NORTH OF THE KILLING HAND

At that point in her unintentional eavesdropping, Nefi veered sideways and ducked in the buffet line behind two athletic-built men who looked out of place in business suits. They looked like the kind of men who never talked about what they did for a living outside of their own tight circle. Definitely Ruis's guests.

Seconds later Martina grabbed her arm. "Oh, Nef. I'm so sorry. Wow. I didn't know what to say when I realized he had someone with him. Men are so clueless. Don't kill him, okay? I think he's in his typical male-idiot phase."

The two men in front of Nefi glanced back at Martina.

Martina glared at them. "Eyes front, sailors."

They dutifully faced the buffet.

Martina in a blood red dress was a fiery vision. Angry, she came off as a dragon. "Honestly, she's not the kind of woman to bring home to mother if you know what I mean."

"His mother died over a year ago."

"You know what I mean."

"I've decided to have fun tonight anyway."

Martina hugged her. "We're going to punk the limo while they cut the cake. You want to help?"

"I'll pass. I'm matchmaking for Blake."

"Okay. Sure. He just left you know." Martina nodded to her sisters who were gathered at the double doors to the corridor. "But if you want me to kneecap Vinnie boy's date just say the word."

"I'm getting over Vincent."

"I'll believe that when you stop wearing his dog tags." Martina darted out the double doors where she nearly collided with one of her brothers.

A short while later, after Nefi wolfed down chicken wings, steamed vegetables and a huge helping of mashed potatoes, Blake returned. Nefi memorized the information on Terri's business card.

Blake coaxed Nefi out on the dance floor by saying, "Let's show

Vincent what he's missing." Blake firmly guided Nefi through a salsa dance, whispering the steps in her ear as they danced. After the first dance, he said he liked dancing with athletic women because they learn quickly without falling off their heels.

Nefi had learned the salsa in Brazil from Antonio, but she kept that information to herself. She was impressed that Blake could dance so well. His confidence and the intimacy of body contact with him stirred an unexpected reaction of lust in her. Perhaps it was the rhythm that prompted sexual thoughts regarding Blake, but as fantasy images drifted into her mind the face of the images morphed into Vincent.

"You anticipate my dance moves like you're reading my mind."

Something like that. The music changed to a slower tempo and more couples converged in front of the band on the open dance floor.

"Just so you know," he said after he caught Nefi stealing another glance at Vincent, "I'm single."

If she had never met Vincent, she probably would have fallen in love with charming, sweet, who-knew-he-could-dance Blake. Too bad he was even *older* than Vincent. He was probably younger than Terri though. She deftly tucked Terri's business card in the jacket pocket of Blake's tuxedo. She felt a square object in the pocket. It was about the size of a cell phone. Perfect. He should find the card when he empties his pockets. The tuxedo was a designer brand, not a rental. Well, well. Blake's got moves and his own tuxedo.

Blake's statement of his single status demanded a reply. Nefi knew that even if they ever, ever dated, he deserved better.

Vincent and Rose danced at the edge of the crowd.

Nefi whispered in Blake's ear, "Never settle for being anyone's second choice."

Vincent's eyes locked on Nefi and raked down her body. Nefi's breath caught. *Now? Seriously, now you notice?*

Blake sighed. "Now that is the kindest, most elegant, and uplifting rejection I've ever received. And I have received a few."

Nefi rested her head on Blake's shoulder to avoid staring back at Vincent. She didn't want him to come over to talk. She would not be able to bear seeing him up close with his *date*. Suddenly, a commotion on the edge of the dance floor caused a few couples to step away. In the gap, Vincent's date staggered, announced she didn't "want any coffee," and stalked off. Vincent followed.

Nefi continued to dance for an hour and a half before she left with her best friend Martina to wave at the limousine carrying Ruis and Sofia away to their happily ever after.

The limousine's exhaust fumes reeked of Limburger cheese, and the rattling of gravel in the hubcaps faded in the distance. White letters on the back window spelled out—*Divers do it deeper.*

. 17 .

In March 2009, leaders in law enforcement converged in Washington D.C. for the annual U.S. Law Conference and Exhibition. Representatives of the Federal Bureau of Investigation, major metropolitan police stations, academy instructors, criminal psychologists, forensic scientists, Texas Rangers, Drug Enforcement Agency directors, and assorted academics shared information on emerging technologies along three separate course tracks: Countering Terrorism, Securing Critical Infrastructure, and Strategizing Safety and Security.

Vincent shook off snow as he hiked through four blocks of the cavernous Washington Convention Center for the one meeting room out of seventy designated for the session innocuously titled 'Non-Confrontational Interrogation Techniques.' His mentor Director of the New York City's FBI office, Quinn Flanagan, had recommended it. The three course tracks were color-coded. Passing green lettered signs and blue lettered signs, he scanned for the orange ones and ducked into the room as the lights dimmed.

Using the light from his cell phone, he found an empty seat in the front third of the room where he wedged himself between the shoulders of other large men, switched off his cell phone and tucked it into his jacket pocket. Papers were handed down the row, so Vincent took one and passed the rest.

At the front of the room, on a raised platform, three women and two men wore business suits. In front of them sat four tables and three chairs. On three of the tables were open computer laptops with wires running from them to a device on a fourth table. At the front edge of the platform, a distinguished-looking black man introduced Supervisory Special Agents from the Behavioral Science Unit of the FBI. The agents raised their hands as their names were called.

"And I'm a clinical psychiatrist. My name is Ethan Sloan." He nodded at the Special Agents. He held a microphone wired to the table on stage.

It seemed odd to use antiquated equipment in such a modern facility. Why hadn't the Behavior Sciences Unit upgraded to wireless technology? Vincent remembered his tour of the Behavior Sciences Unit at Quantico. Doctor Sloan had not been there. Maybe he was a civilian consultant. The FBI agents left the platform and sat in the front row.

"Sixty years ago people laughed at the idea of building a computer that could fit on a tabletop. Then came the personal computer. Today," Sloan held up his cell phone, "people can send data from computer to computer with devices as small as this."

Three women in black, wearing large black wrap-around sunglasses and black baseball caps labeled FBI in white letters, strode onto the platform. All had their hair pulled back into ponytails that stuck out the back of their caps. The first two were stout, middle-aged ladies with short, blonde ponytails. The third and youngest, in three-inch heels, moved in long, sweeping strides. Confident, athletic, graceful, her gait captured Vincent's full attention. Her long brown hair hung halfway down her back. She moved like a jaguar. He wished her clothes fit tighter.

"Communication changes the way we live. As scientists, my colleagues and I explore how the human brain receives and processes information. We communicate with our world through our senses. We see, we hear, we touch, we taste, and we smell to gain information. Among us live rare individuals who also gain information subliminally through such keen observation that it can appear to be a sixth sense. Many times, even these rare individuals attribute their skill to psychic ability."

Muffled coughing and fidgeting broke the quiet of the crowded, dark conference room while the women in black sat behind the laptops on the stage. The hottest one took the seat on the far right. Vincent's attention was divided between the long-legged woman on the right and Doctor Sloan.

Sloan flipped a switch on the device on the table. A screen lowered from the ceiling behind the ladies at the table. After a few bluish flickers of light, the screen showed two vertical lines dividing the screen into three parts, left, center and right.

"Behind me are three ladies whose abilities have led to the capture and prosecution of violent criminals. One teaches grade school. One is a college student. One is a field investigator who holds a Master's degree in criminology. For their privacy, they shall remain nameless. They have achieved through training and natural ability the kind of observation skills used by Mossad interrogators. Rather than call them psychics, we call them readers."

Sloan walked to the left side of the platform, grabbed a microphone secured to a metal stand, and carried it to the front of the aisle by the platform. He set it on the floor at audience level.

"You might dismiss one example of this ability as nothing more than anecdotal evidence. Rather than put you to sleep with volumes of our empirical research data—which is available on my website listed on the handout—I believe you will be more impressed with a demonstration."

Demonstration? Murmuring and whispers rose up from the audience. Was this for real? Lettering at the top of the handout gave the doctor's office address in Alexandria, Virginia, and a website address. Vincent realized that the reason Flanagan had recommended this session was because he told Vincent to develop and trust his own intuition. Flanagan suggested that intuition was a reflection of the subconscious mind assembling observations into the answers to unasked questions. Flanagan suggested that learning to listen to one's intuition could save lives.

"The rules are simple." Sloan's voice quieted the crowd. "Volunteers from the audience will make a short statement about themselves and the ladies behind me will signal whether they perceive the statement to be true or false. Any statement that has both true and false parts to it will be judged as false. After the ladies respond, tell us if your statement is true or false so we can score the accuracy of their answers." Sloan swept his gaze across the room. "The accuracy of this test depends on your honesty. I'm hoping this is an honest crowd."

Chuckling sounded in the audience.

A raised hand in the third row attracted Sloan's attention.

"Yes?"

"How do we know someone isn't feeding information to the ladies?"

"I'm glad you asked. This room has been set up with signal-scrambling technology," Sloan said. "It's safe for those with pacemakers, but cell phones and other wireless devices won't work. So please step up to the microphone and say your name, then give us a simple statement."

The man to Vincent's left took out his cell phone. His screen read *No Service*.

"Doctor Hashiri, of Stealth Technologies has kindly loaned this signal scrambling equipment." He gestured to the laptops and the projector. "Volunteers are welcome to step up to the microphones located in both aisles."

A man from the second row stepped up to the microphone. "My name is Stan. My statement is that I'm the first son in my family."

The screens lit up from left to right. True. False. False.

Sloan said, "So is your statement true or false?"

"False. I'm the second son. The first was stillborn."

"Thank you for participating." Sloan used a mouse wired to the device to click on the columns with the correct answer. Two red stars appeared at the top of the center and right columns.

The next statement came from a woman in her fifties. "My name is Carol. I had a near-death experience when I was twelve years old."

The screen lit up. False. False. False.

"Wow. False. I was fourteen when it happened."

People lined up in the aisle behind the microphone. Red stars popped up in all the columns. What had begun as a solemn academic presentation gradually evolved into a sport. Questions rolled out personal tragedies, triumphs, outright lies, and embarrassments. The red stars competed. The ladies at the left and center scowled at incorrect answers and occasionally glanced behind at the screen to see their scores. The college-age woman never checked her scores.

After the thirtieth question and the thirtieth consecutive correct answer on the right section of the screen, people pointed and cheered. The woman on the right, the young one, had a perfect record. Money changed hands. Rarely shy to a challenge, Vincent donned his sunglasses and joined the line for the microphone. He had read that con men had difficulty reading their marks through sunglasses.

Vincent flipped his lanyard nametag to hide his name. At his turn, he stepped up to the microphone and squared his shoulders, the psychics reacted. One sighed. One put her hand over her heart and the youngest, inhaled sharply. He knew he looked great in his custom-tailored dark gray suit, so he was disappointed the younger woman did not react like the other two. He asked the thirty-first question.

"My name is Vincent. I'm wearing contact lenses."

The young psychic bowed her head as if concentrating on her keyboard. The screen lit up. False. True. True.

Sloan said, "Is your statement true or false?"

Vincent removed his sunglasses and spoke in a deep voice, "I lied."

The only red star shot up to the corner of the far left section of the screen. The crowd reaction was mixed. Some gasped or groaned. Others applauded. The young one on the right had finally missed one.

His turn completed, he wandered back to his seat by way of passing between the platform and the front row to see the young woman up close. He regretted tripping her up. He tried to get her attention, but she held the sides of her laptop screen in a tight grip with her head bowed. Was she hiding or embarrassed? Something about her attracted him beyond her height, and her figure. Something elemental and powerful. Being close to her felt right. Almost familiar. But that was not likely. She looked too young to have gone to high school with him. College maybe. He did not know any so-called psychics.

Another question challenged the ladies. Answers appeared on the screen. True. True. True.

A few crumpled pieces of paper bounced off Vincent as he walked back to his seat. Bets had been lost. The questions continued. Sloan ended the demonstration at question forty. The lady on the left side of the panel racked up twenty stars. The lady in the center earned twenty-two stars. The lady on the right had thirty-nine correct answers, the only miss had been his.

Sloan opened his arm toward the ladies on the platform. "Let's thank our panel."

Applause erupted in the room. Some stood to cheer. The ladies stood. The one on the far right bolted offstage.

"And the research team from the FBI thanks you for participating. We have a few minutes before the next group will need the room, so I'll entertain questions over here." Sloan switched off his microphone and pointed down stage.

A square-built woman in a navy blue suit approached Sloan.

"Excuse me, but how can we arrange to use one of these human lie detectors?"

"Send a request to the Behavioral Science Unit. They're establishing a database of them. Some specialize in certain types of investigations. For example, I know of three who specialize in missing person cases." Sloan stepped out of the way of the crew taking down the equipment.

Vincent waited in Sloan's peripheral vision. While more people flocked to the front of the room, Sloan faced Vincent. Vincent held out his hand.

Sloan hesitated before shaking hands. "You must be Vincent."

Vincent looked down and flipped his nametag around so his name showed.

"Congratulations, Agent Gunnerson," Sloan said. "You broke a perfect record." His intense stare unnerved Vincent.

"How did you know my name?"

"One of the ladies described you quite accurately."

Well, that's intriguing. "Who is the younger, uh, reader?"

Sloan said, "You have to understand her abilities come with unique privacy and safety concerns. The student in today's demonstration is one of many gifted people."

"I'd like to buy her a drink, you know, to apologize."

Sloan smirked. "If she wants to see you, she'll find you." With that, he fielded another question from another person.

Vincent waded against the flow of the incoming crowd to the open corridor for the next session on his schedule. Standing near the young woman had felt so natural and so right that it begged comparison to the constant tension he felt near Rose. As a Catholic, he suspected he should lump a psychic with those who practiced witchcraft and spoke with the dead, but if such near-psychic ability was evil in itself then why would these ladies use it to capture evil people? Though trained to rely on reason and evidence, from time to time his intuition helped him. Besides, the women didn't claim to be psychics, just trained observers. He could not reason through the fact he could tell when someone was lying, so he accepted intuition as a real phenomenon. He also knew when he was being watched. That same intuition told him loudly and often that something was missing in his relationship with Rose. He remembered a two-thousand-year-old definition of love. He decided to measure his relationship with Rose against the ideal, the one in Corinthians chapter 13.

He pulled a schedule from his jacket pocket to look up his next class. On his way to his next class, while his mind was focused on the schedule, Vincent shrugged off the wild idea that the young reader-psychic with the great legs could have been Nefi. *What were the odds of that?*

The odds of guessing had worked against Nefi. Vincent's beautiful voice, amplified by the microphone, had nearly buckled her knees. Her mind blanked. Total blinding whiteout. She noticed how broad his shoulders looked in his tailored suit, which triggered a memory of him in shirtless glory in the jungle. She never heard his question and had to choose an answer at random. The wrong one. Embarrassingly, totally, ruining-a-perfect-streak wrong.

Seeing him again six months after Ruis's wedding had knocked her off balance. The moment the presentation ended, Nefi dashed off stage. She stopped her flight response after ducking into the nearest restroom. She was about to peel off her sunglasses and baseball cap when she noticed the odd-looking low sinks that people were facing.

"If this is a hold-up," an older man said over his shoulder, "you are officially the dumbest criminal ever." He zipped up and turned around. The plastic ID badge hanging from his neck read FLANAGAN and below that NYC FBI.

The other men chuckled.

"The best-looking robber I've seen."

"Are we getting punked?" asked another man toweling off his hands.

Nefi gasped and dashed from the room. *As if this day couldn't get worse. So much for my masterful observation skills.*

She fast walked to the ladies room and secured herself in a stall. Doctor Sloan said volunteering for today's demonstration would be enormously helpful for the FBI's Behavioral Sciences Department to present their latest project. It had sounded like a great idea to help her doctor and get a foot in the door with the FBI to lift her application to the top of the pile. It had been fun until Vincent took the microphone. The conference hosted hundreds of people, hundreds of predominantly handsome, brawny men. And yet the very one she didn't want to see showed up to her particular presentation. What were the odds?

According to a letter from Terri, Blake and Vincent were hired in February of last year. A year on the job and the agency sent Vincent to this conference? Maybe Blake was here too. She could have read Blake like a billboard.

She removed her cap and sunglasses. Staring at the letters FBI, she believed that one day she would wear them for real, as an agent or employee and not as a volunteer for a demonstration. She already looked the part.

In the six months since Ruis's wedding, Nefi concentrated on her last year of college and sent out job applications. She was over Vincent. Moving on. He had his life with whatshername in New York City, and she had her own life to live on campus. Terri had Blake. Aunt Louise had Uncle Hamilton. Ruis had Sofia. Was the whole world pairing up without her? Martina was dating. Nefi plucked her cell phone from her back pocket and stepped out of the stall to call Doctor Sloan. He had mentioned something about a debriefing, and she couldn't remember where they were supposed to meet.

"Sloan here."

"Sorry to run out like that."

"I understand. I met Vincent. He seems to be your kryptonite."

"My what?"

"Sorry for the obscure cultural reference. Kryptonite is a rare substance that weakens Superman. He's a popular superhero from comic books. Anyway, Vincent asked to meet you."

Sure. Six months after Ruis's wedding and he finally thinks of me. Out of sight out of mind. "He recognized me?"

"I don't know. He said he wanted to apologize for ruining your perfect score."

"Did he call me by name?"

"No."

Nefi snorted. *And here I hoped he was thinking of me. How pathetic.* He was just trying to hit on a stranger. "What did you tell him?"

"I told him you would find him if you wanted to see him."

"Just after hell freezes."

"Good to hear you're moving on. The others are going to submit letters of recommendation on your behalf."

The others were the FBI Behavioral Sciences staff who had been working on the project. Amen to that. In her view, the Behavioral Sciences department would be the ideal fit for her skills and temperament.

"Thank you. May I skip the debriefing?"

"Is this avoidance behavior?"

"Yes, but I'm not avoiding you."

"I know. Fine. Drive safely."

Nefi pulled her ponytail through the back of the cap and secured it in place. She put on the large opaque lens sunglasses. She liked the image in the mirror very much. Her future nodded back at her.

As it was March in Washington D.C., she quickly plotted an escape route to her car through the least-populated corridors, remaining indoors if possible since she left her thick warm coat in the car. *Avoidance behavior? Let's call it evasion training.*

. 18 .

Vincent and Blake accompanied Director Quinn Flanagan to the courthouse because they had to drop off papers on a case. Flanagan was scheduled to testify, so the three shared a cab. Vincent felt a little naked without his weapon nudging his ribs, but his boss said it was quicker to enter without it. They climbed from the cab and headed toward the line waiting to pass through security.

It was a balmy seventy-six degrees on that pleasant Wednesday afternoon, and parade barricades were up on major streets for tomorrow's Fourth of July parades when Vincent spotted a woman who appeared over-caffeinated and in a hurry as she butted in front of Flanagan and stopped.

"Are you Flanagan?" she asked as if it was an accusation.

The hairs on the back of Vincent's neck stood at attention. Before he could guess why he felt alarmed, she jammed her hand in her purse. A shot cracked the air. Flanagan staggered with both hands clutching his side. Blake tackled the woman. Vincent grabbed Flanagan and eased him to the sidewalk.

Pedestrians ran screaming for cover.

Kneeling beside his boss, Vincent pressed his hand hard on

the blood spot growing on Flanagan's gut. With his other hand, he retrieved his cell phone and called for an ambulance.

A second shot banged and both Flanagan and Vincent looked at Blake, who rolled to his knees beside the prone body of the woman who had shot Flanagan. She wasn't moving, the gun still in her hand.

A patrolman ran toward Blake with his gun drawn. He shouted at Blake who slowly raised his hands and locked them behind his head.

"Hello? Can you hear me?" the 9-1-1 operator asked.

"Yes, I'm at the courthouse. I need an ambulance for a gunshot wound. Make that two ambulances." Vincent's throat tightened.

Flanagan shouted, "Clayton!"

"I'm fine sir," Blake shouted back.

"Thank God." Vincent cleared his throat. Flanagan had to survive. He had to. Tucking away fears and memories of his own father's shooting, Vincent felt warm fluid oozing through his fingers. His eyes burned. *Don't die. Don't die.*

Two bystanders described the situation into their phones. One thanked the operator.

"It's going to be all right," Flanagan said. "Take a deep breath."

"An ambulance is on the way," a voice said.

Vincent nodded.

Flanagan patted Vincent on the stomach, accidentally leaving bloody smears on his shirt. "Call Kate so she doesn't hear about me on the news."

"Yes, sir."

Flanagan whispered his home number. Vincent memorized it.

Two sets of sirens grew louder. Police and bystanders gathered as Vincent blinked away tears. He pressed as if he could push blood and tissue back into place where it belonged.

Flanagan grimaced. "Ruined my shirt."

Vincent chuffed. He could hear his own pulse thumping in his ears. "Do you recognize the shooter?"

Flanagan shook his head.

Two EMTs elbowed through the spectators. One dropped to his knees beside Flanagan and placed gloved hands on him. The other prepared a gurney. After a quick assessment, they asked if he could stand and he agreed, so they hefted him to his feet. One EMT held a wad of gauze on the wound. The crowd parted to allow the EMTS to rush him to the back of the ambulance. Vincent followed. He was torn between climbing in with Flanagan and checking on Blake.

"We're taking him to Presbyterian," said the EMT in the back.

The other slammed the doors and ran to the driver's seat.

Vincent stood by the curb until the siren faded into the traffic. The flashing lights of the second ambulance and two patrol cars pulsed across the walls of the courthouse and the gawking bystanders. Praying for Flanagan's safety, he placed the life-changing call to Kate Flanagan. His training emerged, reminding him to deliver the news incrementally and calmly as he walked toward Blake and the officers flanking him who were jotting notes in their pads.

Ring.

A flash of white lights announced the arrival of a news crew. Vincent reached a shaking, blood-sticky hand into his jacket for his sunglasses.

Ring.

"Hello," Mrs. Flanagan sounded heartbreakingly cheery.

Vincent donned his sunglasses and angled away from the camera. "Hello, Mrs. Flanagan, this is Vincent Gunnerson. I work with Quinn."

"He asked you to call didn't he?"

"Uh, yes, ma'am." *Remember, O most gracious Virgin Mary, that never was it known that anyone who fled to thy protection, implored thy help or sought thy intercession, was left unaided.*

"Let me guess, he's going to be late for dinner?"

Vincent took a sideways glance at Blake, who jerked his

thumb in the direction of Flanagan's ambulance. He mouthed the word, "Go."

Vincent nodded and marched toward a cab that was letting out a passenger. "As a matter of fact, he will."

"Trial running long?" her Irish lilt tugged at Vincent's heart.

"Not exactly. I'm on my way to your place in a cab. Could you meet me downstairs?" He climbed into the back of the cab.

"Aye. What's he up to now?"

After covering his phone with his hand, he told the wide-eyed cabbie Flanagan's address. With his gaze locked on Vincent's chest, the cabbie vigorously shook his bearded head. Looking down, Vincent realized he was wearing a crime scene. He pulled out his badge.

"Quinn asked me to pick you up."

"Oh, all right then, Agent Gunnerson. I'll meet you downstairs."

The cabbie jerked the shift into gear and pulled away from the curb. On the ride to Flanagan's Vincent buttoned up his suit jacket to cover Quinn's bloody handprint. He didn't want to alarm Mrs. Flanagan. He also knew how important it was to have a shoulder to lean on when she got the news. His mother had the worst moment of her life when two uniformed officers knocked on her door around dinner time. Dad's partner whispered at the funeral that he should have been the one to tell her. Everyone knew he couldn't have been the one to tell her because he had been shot as well and had spent that fateful day unconscious in surgery.

Vincent would do his best to minimize Mrs. Flanagan's trauma. He prayed invoking the name of St. George that the gunshot was a clean through-and-through with no major organs ruined. If she needed a shoulder to lean on, he would be there. He'd served this role before.

The cabbie handed back small packets of hand wipes. "You better not be bleeding in my cab."

"Your compassion is underwhelming." Vincent wiped his whole face and hands so he wouldn't miss any blood.

Meanwhile at Harvard, Nefi wiped sweat off her face with the back of her hand. Like other graduates, she was thumb-typing messages on her phone. One of the commencement speakers, a morning television show host named Matt Lauer, was telling the crowd to have children because they keep parents humbled. Lauer said that while he was interviewing President Obama, his own son was off-camera with a finger up his nose. Nefi wished she had been across campus at the ROTC Commissioning ceremony listening to General David H. Petraeus instead of a talk show host. She tugged at the collar of her gown. It had been a long day of lining up and being directed, followed by this long sit.

Martina was back at the house directing the caterers for the next day's party in McLean, Virginia. Her text message: so y r u still wearing his dog tags?

Nefi thumbed: reminder 2 stop waiting 4 life. Carpe diem.

Martina replied: Fish god?

Nefi: Did u sleep through Latin class?

Martina: Just kidding. C U tomorrow.

Uncle Hamilton and Aunt Louise had convinced Nefi to participate in graduation ceremonies. Seated in the spectator's gallery, they were probably nostalgic about their own graduation. They claimed that these could be the best days of Nefi's life. It was a singularly depressing thought. College had been rewarding and challenging. She had enjoyed group activities, like pickup games of volleyball on the lawn, but these couldn't be the best days. *Please no.*

She'd been on a few dates since Ruis's wedding. To a man, they each expected sex on the first date. Fortunately, all but one took her 'no, thank you' as a gentleman should. The one who challenged her discovered the true stopping power of mace. If she could have reached the taser in the bottom of her purse first, he would have been more violently convinced what 'no' meant. In retrospect she wished she had been able to use the taser, touted to last for ten years. At this rate, spraying Hands-on Harold could be the biggest sex-related thrill in her life.

And so it was that she planned to celebrate her graduation at her uncles' home in McLean, Virginia, with friends and family as a single woman. Aunt Louise was growing increasingly distraught over the fact her niece wasn't bringing home any important male for her to render a verdict on.

"You got a job lined up?" the graduate sitting on her right asked. They had shared a chemistry class freshman year. His girlfriend Anne lived in Nefi's dorm.

Nefi had an appointment at Quantico set for the Friday, July 3, 2009. The day before Independence Day. That gave her exactly a month to prepare. "An interview. Next month. How about you?"

"UBS hired me. Ever been to Switzerland?" he asked.

"No."

"Great skiing. Amazing chocolate. Terrific people."

"Is Anne going, too?" Nefi felt safe asking because Anne was seated five rows away.

"On our honeymoon."

"Sounds wonderful." Good for them.

A few sniffling graduates around her whispered about nostalgic lasts on campus: last cafeteria meal, last exam, last night on campus, last kiss, last dance, and last beer at the Club Casablanca, better known as CasaB. Nefi couldn't wait to leave for her firsts.

. 19 .

In the heat of that mid-morning in July, Damiano rode in the right front seat of a plumbing company van with New York license plates. Hate, fueled by a need for revenge, seethed through him. Tightness in his chest spread to his shoulders. He had threatened and beaten and killed as part of his business. Today was personal. Today was a statement. Today was—as the American's say—unfinished business. He blamed the missionaries for the loss of his hand. Sure, the Indians had cut off his hand, but he would not take revenge on them. He feared them more than he could admit. The missionaries were the reason he ventured into the jungle. Since he couldn't punish the dead, he could punish the last of their flesh and blood—their family. He bounced his artificial hand on his thigh in rhythm to salsa music he alone heard.

Close behind was a second similar van. The panel signs on the sides and back of the vehicles advertised 'Theo's Reliable Plumbing, Depend on this Greek to fix your leak' under a cartoonish face with a heavy black mustache and thick eyebrows. The lead van stopped at the entrance to an upscale housing development in McLean, Virginia. The guard, a gray-haired man carrying a clipboard, stepped out of the small brick booth and approached the driver of the first van.

The driver held out a work order scrawled with illegible handwriting on a pre-printed Theo's Plumbing invoice. Damiano leaned forward to see the guard's reaction to the papers.

The guard checked his clipboard. "I don't have you on the schedule."

"No one," the driver said, "schedules a sewer pipe break."

The guard looked at the second van.

Two cars rolled into the entrance behind the second van, forming a line.

The driver said, "Take your time, old man. I can double my price if I have to pump out the basement."

"I'll write you in," the guard groused as he scribbled on his clipboard. He checked his watch then climbed back into his booth.

The wide black metal gates to the subdivision swung open. Damiano settled back into his seat and breathed deeply. Both plumbing trucks breezed through to the far end of the subdivision where the houses were the largest. It was Friday, July third. The plumbers told Damiano that many of the families would be out of town the day before the big national holiday called Independence Day. Fewer witnesses around, they said.

Lush green lawns flowed from the manicured flower beds to the paved driveways. He wondered how many servants lived in each house to protect the property from robbers. In Rio, such houses would have armed guards at the gate instead of an old man. At the end of the driveways sat squat masonry mailboxes matching the houses. He read the brass numbers on the side of the mailboxes. He pointed to a brick mailbox topped with black roofing shingles. The driver had found photos on a real estate website that matched the Jenkins' home exactly.

He ordered the driver to pull into the driveway as close as possible to the side of the house. The driver mowed down a bed of three-foot-tall pink trumpet lilies sending their scent airborne.

Damiano and the driver climbed out of the first van, trampling the rest of the lilies. The driveway continued into the back of the property to an open two-car garage containing a green compact Toyota.

"Go ring the doorbell," Damiano told the driver.

The man pivoted on the pavers and marched toward the front of the house. Damiano dashed to the garage. Peering into the windows of a compact car, he found books, a pink sweater, and sandals. His heart pounded with hope. Maybe the Jenkins girl was in the house. Americans didn't travel a block without driving.

He was the luckiest man alive.

He spun around in time to glimpse a shadow moving across the upstairs window. His heart raced as his breath caught in his throat. The doorbell played an odd little tune that seemed to be amplified through the house. He stepped into the shadowed area of the garage and watched the windows for more movement. Someone hid behind the curtain. *Yes, stay right there and hide.* Moments later, the driver walked down the driveway. He looked around the tree-shaded backyard.

Damiano stepped into the light.

"No answer, Mr. Guerra," the driver said.

"Hurry." Damiano pushed the driver down the sidewalk, past the first truck to the second truck.

The man in the front passenger's seat of the second truck flung open his door and jumped out. He held the door for Damiano, who climbed in. Once all three men were inside the rear truck, the driver started the engine. The man in the back held a disposable cell phone with only one phone number in it, the number of another phone set to trigger the bomb. The vehicle backed away from the house to the street. There were no other cars moving or parked on the street.

"Are we safe from here?" Damiano asked.

The car eased down the street.

"*Si.* We should activate the bomb from the highway." The

driver gripped and re-gripped the steering wheel. He then looked in the rear-view mirror.

"*Si*," said the man in the back.

Damiano understood that people whispered he was crazy. It did not offend him. In fact, it reassured him that they would not dare challenge his authority or disobey him. It was the kind of respect that demanded obedience. In the end obedience cost either money or lives. Hiring stupid men cost lives because they had to be disposed of. Hiring smart men cost more money. Dispose of one stupid man in front of a group of smart men, however, and the smart ones remembered the example.

"We must do it immediately," Damiano hissed. A rush of excitement flooded his chest. He expected being blown apart would hurt worse than having a hand cut off. No more Jenkins.

The driver continued toward the subdivision's exit.

Damiano pressed his artificial hand on the driver's chest. "Stop!" He twisted to face the backseat. "Blow up the house!"

"But, Mr. Guerra—"

"I have to see it." His body shook with urgency. He had told his boss Cortes that the bomb was a political statement. Cortes could never know the girl might have been a witness. He considered climbing over the seat to convince the man in the back.

The man with the cell phone clenched his teeth while he pressed the numbers, triggering the other cell phone in the truck left behind.

An explosion rocked the van. Bricks and wood shot into the street. It was the most satisfying fireworks Damiano had ever seen. With his ears ringing from the blast, he took a deep breath and let out a sigh. His skin tingled with joy. No more witness. That, he told himself, would teach the mighty Jenkins family a second lesson. With his luck running hot, the samba music in his head resumed in bold, burning celebration of his victory. He nodded to the driver.

By the time they reached the gate, the guard was busy on the phone, shouting frantically. Triggered by the weight of the van, the exit gate automatically opened slowly, allowing the van to pass through while the guard faced the smoke plumes that rose above the oaks. Damiano's luck made them invisible to the guard.

"Will you miss your job?" Damiano addressed his question to the man wiping fingerprints off the cell phone.

He snorted in reply. From the back of the van, he said in Portuguese, "You see how we get treated? Even that guard looked down on us like every Latino is an illegal Mexican."

The driver laughed.

"What is funny?"

"I don't know about you, Mr. Guerra, but we are illegals."

"But I'm not from Mexico," said the man in the back.

The men laughed while sirens wailed in the distance.

Meanwhile in his Manhattan apartment, Vincent endured Rose's wrath. It was Friday night, the day before Independence Day and Rose was still upset about the previous Saturday. The argument was all the more awkward because Blake had shown up saying he wanted to talk, so Vincent had directed him into the living room where he settled into the sports-watching sofa. The apartment was roomy by New York City standards, but sound traveled easily through the walls. Vincent strode back to the kitchen to calm down Rose. She was all wrapped up in her important feelings and aggrandizing them for dramatic effect. She didn't care whether or not Blake could hear her. For all her talk about feelings, did she ever consider anyone else's?

"A simple phone call is all I expected," Rose whined, "when I spend good money on tickets for the best show in town."

Vincent wasn't sure if her fury had been triggered by having to go to the theater alone or that she had spent her own money on tickets.

Inconveniently detained while capturing a felon last Saturday night, he had not taken the time to make a quick call. He and Blake had done quite a great job that night, but crime-fighting was not high on Rose's short list of contributions to society. Being seen at the Gershwin Theatre's Saturday evening performance of *Wicked* must have ranked higher on the Rose scale of value than crime-fighting. Vincent wanted to say — *it was almost a week ago, for crying out loud, get over it.*

"I have apologized," Vincent said. If she wanted more than an apology, she would be disappointed. He had not asked her to buy the overpriced tickets.

"Fine," she shouted.

Vincent understood when a woman said that she meant exactly the opposite. The front door slammed, punctuating Rose's departure. He knew she'd be sulking until the big party tomorrow. For the rest of the day, he could enjoy peace and quiet. He carried two open bottles of beer to the sofa. He eased into the deep cushion and handed a bottle to Blake.

Blake held up his beer. "Thanks, I think."

The label named a microbrewery in Detroit. "Remember the wine of the month club?"

Rose's idea. Blake had also witnessed Rose's temper tantrum after she found the cases stacked in the basement storage bin, gathering dust. She had not accepted Vincent's excuse about allowing them to age.

"I told her I prefer beer." Vincent took a sip. Ugh. It had an aftertaste akin to burnt plastic. Not all microbreweries were up to the challenge of competing with the big companies.

Blake took a swig of beer and grimaced. "You shoulda been far more specific."

Vincent shrugged. Thirsty, he took another swallow of the yellow swill and decided the taste mattered less that the fact it was ice cold. Perfect for a summer evening. "I just don't understand her."

"I do."

Vincent grunted. "Sure you do."

"Rose," Blake said, pointing toward the door with the mouth of his beer bottle, "is a non-load bearing wall."

"What on earth do you mean?"

"A non-load bearing wall can be removed without damaging the structural integrity of the building."

Vincent lowered his bottle.

"In short," Blake added, "a non-bearing wall is less than it appears to be. Form without function. Take it away and nobody will miss it."

"Okay."

"Style without substance."

Blake didn't have to drive the point any deeper. "I get it." Vincent glared.

"I'm just saying, the next time she threatens to leave you forever," Blake said, emphasizing the last two words individually, "Let. Her."

"Advice from the lovelorn."

Blake peeled off the label on his beer bottle making it a generic beer identified only by its peculiar flavor. He dropped the label on a stack of magazines. Next, he rooted under *Sports Illustrated* magazines and pulled the television remote from the center of the swimsuit edition that showed women wearing painted on swimsuits.

"If I'd have known about this," Blake said pointing to the model, "I would have gladly chosen an art career." He plucked the remote from the magazine and switched on the television.

With the sound down low, Blake clicked through channels.

A show about people eating bugs. *Click.* Gardening. *Click.* A panel of women debating whether or not a movie director was the father of a younger actress's child. *Click.*

"So what did you want to talk about?"

Blake said, "I'll get to that in a minute. Humor me. I want you to imagine a future without daily arguments, without screaming phone calls, without the ever-present demands and drama."

Click. Sports news. An announcement about the next day's Coke Zero 400 race in Daytona, Florida, scrolled across the bottom of the screen, that actor Tom Cruise would drive the pace car. Kyle Busch and Tony Stewart were the predicted frontrunners. Blake lowered the remote to his lap.

Why was he talking about relationships? Vincent sighed. "Okay. I can imagine that."

"If you could date the most amazing female you've ever met," Blake said, "Who would that be?"

Since he hadn't actually met any *Sports Illustrated* supermodels, Vincent decided to play along with Blake's probing conversation. Hypothetically, if he was going to be honest, the most *amazing* female he'd ever met was "Nefi Jenkins. But now that she's graduated from college, I'm sure she's over me." Vincent raised his chin and crossed his arms over his chest.

He had sent a bouquet of yellow roses to her uncle's house for graduation. Yellow to match her eyes. Her thank-you note, handwritten in print instead of cursive, had come to the FBI office. In the note, she wrote that she had plans to work in law enforcement.

"Well, you aren't as good-looking as me," Blake said, "but I think you should stop fooling around and find someone—Nefi perhaps—to get serious with. I want you to be happy like me."

Aha. That's why Blake wanted to talk about relationships. Either he wanted to tease him once again about Nefi, or Blake was in a relationship. "Are you dating?"

"Why do you sound shocked?" Blake waved off his own question. "Never mind. Not only am I dating, but I'm in a steady relationship. That's why I came over here. Do you remember the lovely lady sitting with me at Ruis's wedding reception?"

"The mother or the daughter?" Vincent smirked. Both women had been very attractive.

"The redhead."

It had been so dark at the reception, Vincent remembered the older one had shoulder-length hair, and the younger one had long hair, but he had not noticed hair color. Was Blake dodging the question? "And you got a second date?"

Blake leaned back on the sofa and crossed his arms over his chest. "This is exactly why I haven't talked about her before. If I want to be ridiculed, I have four brothers—"

"Sorry," Vincent said. "Go on." Must be the older one.

"We've been dating for ten months, thank you very much. Her name is Terri Pinehurst. Doctor Pinehurst to you."

Huh. "A doctor? Good for you." Vincent admired Blake's ability to keep a secret.

"She's a veterinarian. Specializes in large animals."

"That explains it." Vincent downed a swig of beer out of habit and regretted it.

Blake closed his eyes and shook his head. "We've set a date."

Vincent made a small choking sound and set his beer on the coffee table. After waiting a moment for the punchline, he realized Blake was serious. Maybe it was the younger one, the one he danced with.

"I would like you to—"

"So that's why you wanted me to come meet the ladies at your table. You must have swept her off her feet at Ruis's wedding. Who knew you could dance?"

"What? I didn't dance with—" Blake's face slackened as if in panic for a moment, then he feigned a smile and shook his head. "Terri."

"I saw you. Tall with long brown hair. You'll make beautiful babies."

Color drained from Blake's face. His hand shook as he moved the remote from his lap to the coffee table. He closed the *Sports*

Illustrated magazine as if to remove temptation. Blake shook his head, letting it drop on his chest. After a sigh, he looked up at Vincent. "I told you right after the wedding that I saw Nefi and that she was still pining for you, but in the interest of full disclosure, I have to tell you the rest of the story."

"You already told me that you met Terri because you enlisted her to talk Nefi out of the bathroom."

"Right. Because Nefi saw you with Rose and ran out. But *before* that," Blake said as if weighing his words, "I...hit on Nefi."

That statement snapped Vincent's attention back to the present. Blake was single. Nefi was single. He was dating Rose, so he shouldn't be jealous. So why was he? "You flirted with her?"

Blushing, Blake ran his fingers through his hair. "It was more than that. I gave her my full A-game charm offensive."

Heat spread through Vincent's chest as a tug of war began inside him. Half of him wanted to know if Blake did more than flirt; the other half did not want to know. Blake had attended her high school graduation party, so maybe she got to know him better. "How did she react?"

"Ah, she seemed surprised. And then amused, I think."

Vincent took another swig of his beer and cringed at the plastic aftertaste. Then he remembered the two women at Blake's table again. He swung his hand to Blake's shoulder and grabbed it. "Was Terri the older woman at the table?"

"She's only a few years older than me, but yeah."

"Then the younger one was...*Nefi*?"

Blake nodded.

Vincent slouched back into the sofa. He brought his hand from Blake's shoulder to his beer and picked at the corner of the label. "I never would have recognized her. She looked so, so grown up." Womanly, in fact.

"She's twenty-one."

"Already?" Vincent subtracted the years since they found her in Brazil. Seven years. No kidding.

247

"So are you going to be my best man?"

"So why did you dance with Nefi?"

"Oh, for pity's sake." Blake drew in a deep breath. "You made her cry. I tried to cheer her up."

"So that was Nefi you were dancing with all that time at Ruis's wedding?"

Blake shrugged. "Terri had to leave early, on account of being the keynote speaker at her conference." He stared down at his hands. "I was trying to cheer up Nefi."

Vincent sensed the temperature in the room drop. He had no right to be upset about Nefi dancing with anyone. He held no claim on her while dating Rose. So why did he feel such a sense of lost opportunity? And raw jealousy.

Vincent rubbed a hand over his beard stubble creating a noise like sandpaper on wood. The ceiling fan, slightly out of balance, made a soft *whump, whump, whump* sound as the blades swung. The television newscaster discussed the upcoming race at Daytona.

What would it be like to date Nefi? If he had even a chance to find out if her feelings were more than juvenile infatuation, then shouldn't he? She was amazing at fourteen, and though he had only seen her at a distance at Ruis's wedding, she had grown into a beautiful young woman. No longer jungle jailbait, she had looked…refined. She could manage ballroom dancing in heels. With Blake. *Let it go.*

"When's your wedding?"

"October. We haven't decided on a location yet."

Vincent's cell phone buzzed. "I accept the challenge of being your best man on one condition."

Blake's face lit up. "Name it."

Vincent pried his cell phone out of the holder on his belt. "Invite Nefi."

"Deal." Blake smiled. "With so many thorns to cope with, I sense the bloom is off the Rose."

After checking the caller ID, Vincent answered his phone. "Hey, Ruis. Blake and I were just using your name in vain."

Ruis's voice was businesslike. "Turn on a news channel."

Vincent's heart rate accelerated. He hadn't spoken to Ruis in months. What was going on? After a moment of silence, he glanced at his phone and saw the call had ended. With one hand, he stuffed his cell phone in his pants pocket. With the other hand, he snatched the remote from the table and clicked through channels to the Cable News Network channel. He pressed the volume up key on the remote.

A male reporter shouted into his microphone over the sound of sirens. A fire truck stopped behind the reporter then firefighters swarmed the truck, pulling off hoses and equipment. Strobe lights in red, white, and blue flashed over the scene. The reporter stepped to his left revealing a large house on fire.

"Witnesses say two repair trucks pulled into the driveway just before the explosion." The reporter held up a hand toward the camera and pressed his other hand on his earpiece. "Just a moment, I understand the homeowners have just arrived on the scene." The reporter moved quickly off screen.

"Don't ya hate when reporters ambush people?" Blake said. "Is this Ruis's case?"

"He didn't say."

The camera bobbed and swayed until the reporter came back into view beside a tall man and woman facing a raging fire. The reporter tapped the man on the shoulder, who squinted teary-eyed at the bright light from the camera and then at the reporter.

"Senator Jenkins, sir, who do you think may have targeted you in this bombing?"

Vincent inhaled sharply, and he realized he was standing. "Oh, Lord." A chill spread through him. Wasn't the senator pushing a drug crime bill?

Mrs. Jenkins spun around with a firm grip on the sleeve of a firefighter. Her voice carried to the microphone. "Have you seen my niece? That's her car." She pointed to a smaller fire where the garage used to be. In the foreground, the undercarriage of a charred vehicle blocked the driveway alongside the house.

The camera view widened to show Mrs. Jenkins and the firefighter. "I don't know, ma'am. Right now we're trying to get the fire under control."

Mrs. Jenkins covered her face with her hands and dropped to her knees on the wet street. Senator Jenkins knelt beside her.

Vincent glanced at Blake, standing beside him with an expression of stoic horror. It was the same look he had exhibited after the Osprey crashed in Arizona. It was exactly how Vincent felt. Seeing the blazes in the background, the firemen racing across the screen, and Mrs. Jenkins falling to her knees sent hot and cold blood coursing through Vincent. As the flames swayed, he caught a glimpse of burning trees. "Maybe it isn't as bad as it looks."

"Those big trees are in the backyard," Blake's voice rasped. He held his hands in a position of prayer.

But the Jenkins had a two-story home. Vincent's apartment floor seemed suddenly soft and unstable like sand. The remote control slid from his grip and thumped on the carpet by his foot. He emitted a groan that formed into a word. "Nooo."

She can't be...gone. The images on the screen seared into his mind.

The television reporter awkwardly faced the camera. "Ah, it appears that the family has not yet accounted for their niece."

. 20 .

July 4, 2009

Damiano watched Cortes check the container numbers against the numbers stored in his cell phone. Three containers, offloaded from a ship with a Liberian registry, were stacked amid the hundreds of others in a maze of short-term storage. The three containers shipped in Damiano's name were to be loaded on Monday onto semi-trucks for delivery. Two would go upstate to Buffalo and one to New Jersey. It wasn't as if he needed Cortes to supervise. Damiano understood his boss sometimes liked to pretend he was one of his men getting his hands dirty doing the work that had to be done. Logging the arrival of the containers was as close as he would get. So why had he come all the way from Brazil?

"Does it always cost so much to unload a shipment here?" Cortes spoke in English which meant he expected Damiano to do the same.

"Today is a national holiday, Independence Day. That means fewer men to handle the shipment, but I have to pay them twice their usual fee." He liked the idea of having fewer people handle the containers. Fewer people meant less security and almost no chance for a random inspection.

The last container, a dull blue one, descended into place atop the first two. Men below shouted into radios to the crane operator to detach the cables.

"Did the Senator get our message?" Cortes jabbed a small smooth stick back into his cell phone.

"He is a broken man," Damiano said. "I saw him on television. His great mansion is ashes. His niece, dead."

"That should convince him to abandon his anti-drug bill." Cortes pocketed his cell phone. "So who will you put out of business this month?" *There it was. Cortes was bored.*

"There is a Russian supplier in New York City," Damiano said, "who dropped one of my delivery men in the East River."

"Your delivery man cannot swim?"

"The Russian tied him to a boat engine." The man's screams echoed in Damiano's memory. The Russian had let Damiano live so he could relay the message to his boss. Again his luck had saved him, but his luck was not strong enough to save the delivery man.

"What? No warning?" Cortes had never dealt with the Russians before. Nor the Asian gangs.

"That was the warning." Damiano respected the Russians.

"Is there a way I can watch when you set him up?"

Damiano knew this was not a request. Cortes did not accept a 'no.' Saying 'no' to him meant you wanted to be cut off from him forever, to be instantly shifted from the short list of people who could be trusted to the never-ending list of potential victims.

"I could arrange something, but if you're too close," Damiano said, holding up his artificial hand, "and things go wrong I will not be able to protect you." His claim that he could not protect his men years ago near the Juruá River rested on the proof of his lost hand.

Cortes tucked his hands into his suit jacket. "Watching is enough. So how will you get him to meet with you?"

"I told him I want to work with him. He will buy from me and sell it to his people. That means fewer people are tied to me. We meet Sunday night."

Cortes rubbed his hands together. "This gives me time to take a bite of the Big Apple."

He could have guessed which parts of the city Cortes wanted to explore. None of them were on the vast list of places recommended by the tour guides, but Damiano knew a concierge who could arrange things. Tonight's celebration of the shipment would begin at one such place.

Because one did not dare tell Cortes what to do, he offered a suggestion. "I found a very exclusive party for tonight if you're interested."

"What kind of party?"

"Like the one in Cartagena last spring." Though Cortes's peculiar sexual appetite repulsed Damiano, it was vital to keep him entertained. When bored, Cortes tended to let his imagination grow until he suspected everyone of cheating him.

"Ah," Cortes said, pointing to Damiano's chest. "You are making yourself at home here."

"You warned me to stay away from our product, so I found other entertainment."

Cortes switched to Portuguese to ask for details.

Damiano explained that two women, posing as undercover police, would present badges and escort him to a black van. From there, they would take him to their secret headquarters for interrogation of the most physical kind. Cortes liked rough play so much that he occasionally fondled his scars and sighed. When the interrogation finished, the women would deliver him back to his hotel.

"How," Cortes asked in Portuguese, "will I recognize them?"

"One is blonde, the other brunette." To add to the description, Damiano held his hands inches from his chest indicating the measure of the women's prominent assets. "They will approach us at a club called Don't Tell. Do you want me to arrange it?"

"Us?"

"They know to look for me," Damiano said, "but they will take you."

Cortes squinted at him. "How well do they know you?"

He would never understand how Cortes could share a prostitute with hundreds of unknown strangers, but curl his lip up at any prostitute Damiano had ever used. Did he think he would catch something? "They have the same boss as a girl I hire," he said. "One girl I hire is...tame."

Cortes smiled and stepped away from the shipyard toward his limousine. Damiano followed. This promised to be a deeply satisfying day of violence for both men. It was Cortes's turn.

Doctor Sloan greeted Senator Hamilton with a manly embrace, complete with back patting. "I was surprised when your secretary Betsy said you were here."

"I stopped in today to reschedule the next few weeks." Hamilton ambled back to his great mahogany desk and sank into his chair.

Sloan followed and took one of the burgundy leather chairs facing the desk. Silence settled around them like a shroud. Both men had learned how to be comfortable in silence from Nefi, who had a way of filling the quiet with her presence. Rather than exchange awkward pleasantries about death and mourning, they shared an understanding of loss in reverence.

Just outside the office threshold, sounds of clerks, aides, congressmen, and lobbyists rushing through the corridors of power reminded them that the world would continue without Nefi.

Sloan placed a flowery moleskin notebook atop Hamilton's neatly prepared calendar on the desk.

Hamilton opened the first page to scrawled sentences in Portuguese, and closed it, laying his hands on the cover.

"She made me promise to deliver it to you. It starts out in Portuguese, but the majority is in English. I'll translate whatever you'd like."

Hamilton cleared his throat. "We loved her like a second chance. Such an extraordinary girl." He broke into sobs and lowered his head onto his arms.

Betsy appeared at the doorway, shifted files in her arms, and shut the door.

. 21 .

July 6, 2009

Bone tired, she had nearly fallen asleep against the door, on the cold steps of a brownstone in Manhattan, when a yellow cab squeaked to a halt at the curb. A tall, rangy man in his fifties stepped out and then struggled to hoist another man out of the back seat to his feet. The nearly unconscious man was Vincent.

She rushed to help by taking Vincent's right arm over her shoulders. When she reached around his back with her left hand and grabbed Vincent's belt, the older man was startled.

"What happened to him?" she asked.

"That depends on who's asking," the man said. His voice had an Irish lilt to it.

The two of them hefted Vincent up to the front door. The older man fished keys from Vincent's coat pocket and unlocked the front door to the apartment building.

She propped the door open with her foot while they hoisted Vincent through the doorway. She helped lug him to the elevator. Vincent was trying to walk, but could not manage a straight line.

"Are you his girlfriend?" the man asked, sizing her up.

"No."

"His ex?"

"A friend."

The man pressed the elevator up button. It illuminated and dinged at the same time. The doors opened, allowing the threesome to stagger into the small space inside. The gentleman, on the wrong side of the elevator to press the button for the floor, waited.

She stared at the panel. This was Vincent's building, but that was all she knew.

"And how long have you known him?"

"Seven years," she said.

The doors to the elevator closed. She stared at the four choices on the panel.

"You don't know which floor he lives on?" The man's voice sounded sarcastic. He grunted as he adjusted under Vincent's weight.

"This is the first time I've been here."

"In seven years." The man squinted around Vincent's chest at her.

"Ever."

"When was the last time you saw him?"

"At a friend's wedding last year."

"While I'm grateful for the help, I hesitate to trust a stranger who has nothing better to do than loiter on apartment steps in the middle of the night. Prove you know him. What's his name?"

She let go of Vincent's belt and reached into the front of her shirt. The scent of smoke rose from her when she moved. She held up a set of dog tags on a long shot bead chain. The man leaned forward to read them.

He blushed, and with eyebrows raised, he said, "Press four."

The ancient elevator lurched and creaked slowly to the fourth floor where the doors opened onto a wide carpeted hallway with four doors. They hauled the mumbling drunk to a door marked Suite 402. The older man unlocked the door. He guided the way to the bedroom where the two of them flopped Vincent onto a king-size bed. Sprawled on his brown silk quilt, Vincent opened his eyes momentarily at the man.

"Just call me a cab," Vincent mumbled. He raised his hand toward the tall man and then let his hand drop.

"Fine. You're a cab." The older man pried off one of Vincent's large black leather shoes and handed it to her. "Do you recognize this young lady?"

Vincent snored.

The clock on his nightstand read 2 a.m. Vincent could sleep for a few hours before he had to report to work. She envied him because he had a place to sleep and a friend like this man to protect him.

She set the shoe near the cherry wood end table under the window. The older man tossed her the mate, and she set it beside the other. She stood to stare at Vincent. She had never imagined him as a heavy drinker. But then, she would never have imagined him with any flaws. She sighed.

The older man tugged her elbow toward the door. She walked out to the living room and looked around at the deep leather sofa and large chairs, the sturdy low coffee table and the big black television screen set between two-floor-to ceiling bookshelves. On one shelf sat framed photos: Vincent as a teenager with another younger boy, an older couple, a framed flag folded into a neat triangle, a portrait of an older man in a police uniform, and a copy of the photo of her with Ruis, Blake and Vincent taken outside the U.S. Consulate in Manaus. The fact that he kept the photo nearly brought her to tears.

She shifted the strap of her satchel that hung across her torso. This satchel was fine-grain leather, unlike the canvas one in the photo. She recalled how much she wanted to keep wearing her tribal face paint when Ruis caught her re-applying it. It felt like a lifetime ago. *Let go of the past.*

"Why is Vincent drunk?"

"He showed up at my bar. The only thing he said all evening was 'she's gone.'"

A smile bloomed on Nefi. "His girlfriend is gone?"

The man smiled back. "His colleague said she was a high-maintenance kind of gal."

"Sounds like something Blake would say."

"And so it was," he said holding out his hand. "I'm Quinn Flanagan."

She shook his hand then slumped into a dark green leather recliner. It was rude not to give her name, but she wasn't sure she should.

"What brings you here?" Flanagan sat on the sofa near her. His keen eyes assessed her as if he was trying to determine her sanity.

She hoped she didn't appear as desperate as she felt. She had come for help, but Vincent's condition was more than disappointing. She needed immediate help from someone she could trust, someone who understood life and death stakes. Maybe she should have found Blake. "Mr. Flanagan, do you know where Blake Clayton lives?"

"Yes. I could call him for you, but this is an alarming hour to call." Flanagan cleared his throat. "Don't you have a cell phone?"

"I lost it." She blew out a breath. "I need someone as trustworthy as Vincent." Someone sober.

"Are you in trouble?"

"I'm chasing it. And I need help."

"I used to be FBI Assistant Director, headed up the New York Division. Vincent reported to me."

"You speak in the past tense."

"Injured on the job." He patted his side. "I'm retired now."

He was sober. He was connected. Vincent trusted this man, so she decided she would. "The man who firebombed my uncle's house is in the city."

Flanagan's countenance changed as if she had morphed into a

crazy person. In a calming voice, he asked, "And what is your name?"

It certainly wasn't the first time someone treated her like that. She fished her Virginia driver's license from her satchel and handed it to him.

His eyes widened. "Your uncle is Senator Jenkins?"

She nodded.

Somberly, he handed the license back to her. "I can take you to the bureau."

"I can't go to the authorities," Nefi said. "Not yet."

"And why not?"

"My name would come up in the news. If this man knows I'm alive, he'll come after me again."

"What makes you think he's after you?"

"Seven years ago he killed my parents."

Flanagan's features softened as if she needed to be humored, as if she'd come to a false conclusion, as if she were a self-absorbed child who believed all events in the world revolved around her. "Now why would he go and do such a thing?"

"I intend to ask him." Or beat it out of him.

"You think he's after you because he killed your parents?"

"I was a witness."

"Seven years ago." Again, his tone of disbelief challenged her. Something in his voice reminded her of her father, enticing her to trust him more.

If she told him everything, even the things she would never tell Vincent, he would help. This man who once led the New York office of the FBI, this man whom Vincent and Blake trusted, this man would understand. Wouldn't he? She wished she had her cell phone so she could verify his title.

"I'm a bartender now. It's like being a priest, in a way. People confess all kinds of things to me. So what is it you're not telling?"

Is he reading me or guessing? She was exhausted from hitchhiking, she was hungry, and she'd used up the last cash in her wallet. She smelled like smoked homelessness. After all the risks she'd taken, she knew she couldn't do everything on her own, so she decided to trust him completely, hoping the truth would set her free, or earn his trust. Or both.

She took a deep breath. "There is another reason he wants me dead. After he killed my parents," Nefi's voice dropped to a whisper, so Vincent couldn't possibly overhear, "I hunted him and...cut off his right hand with a machete."

To his credit, Flanagan didn't flinch. "I can see how he would hold that against you." He cleared his throat and added, "Not everyone handles disability with grace."

There. Her deepest, darkest secret uttered, she felt lighter. "You're the only person I've ever told."

Flanagan's eyes pinned her. "Why didn't you just kill him while you had the chance?"

That was not the reaction she expected. As if his presence drew truth from her, she confessed more, "I was fourteen years old. I wanted to kill him. When I found him and the others asleep, I prayed for God's guidance. Then I remembered a verse that said if your hand sins; cut it off. It's better to go to heaven maimed than to go to hell."

The corners of Flanagan's mouth pulled downward. "Hold on a minute. He kills your parents, and you're worried about his soul?"

Nefi snorted. "He's a psychopath. I cared about *my* soul, about breaking one of the Ten Commandments. I also thought I wouldn't survive attacking him. I figured that if he bled to death, then it was worth it."

"How did you survive?"

"It was a moonless night. While they slept, I moved their weapons behind a tree. I had the advantage of surprise because I grew up in that area of the jungle."

"What about the others you said were with him?"

"After I cut off his hand, he screamed and hid behind a tree.

Yeah, the tree where I put the rifles. I climbed another tree to hide in because city people never look up. When the others woke up, he panicked and shot them."

Flanagan dropped his chin. His eyes were shadowed by his eyebrows. "Your aunt and uncle have been on the news. They fear you're dead."

Nefi's eyes brimmed up to the limit. "As long as the news says I'm missing, the Pirarucu Man will leave them alone." She blinked, spilling tears.

"That's his name?"

"He was a fish buyer. That's what everyone called him."

"So you came here to find Vincent and hide from the what's-it Man?"

"I came here to hunt him again."

Flanagan's eyebrows rose. *Ah, young people think they can take on the world.* "This is a big city."

"I have a few tactical advantages. First, he thinks I'm dead. Second, I followed the evidence. And," she hesitated, "third...the third advantage you wouldn't believe."

"I'm Irish. I love a good story." He toyed with his wedding ring.

She sat up, all business. After a sigh, she said, "I'm a reader. It's kind of like being psychic." While she stared at him, she recited what he was thinking. "And no I'm not crazy."

Flanagan sucked in air. The hair on his arms stood at attention.

Her gaze penetrated his brain like sunlight through a new window. "Go ahead, genuflect if it will make you feel better. Wave a rosary at me if you want."

Flanagan covered his forehead with a hand as if drawing a curtain over his brain.

Nefi sat back in the recliner. "My father called it a gift from God. My uncle is ashamed of it and made me promise to keep it secret."

"Does Vincent know about this?"

"Not directly. I just came here to ask for a place to stay. I wasn't going to tell him about conducting surveillance either."

And then, just when he was about to believe her, she rang the craziness bell again. "Hold up now. You can't follow a killer around."

"I already have."

"Are you out of your mind?"

Nefi rubbed her hands together, spreading dirt more evenly on her skin. "I had to gather evidence. I've hunted this murderer before."

"But this is different," she said in unison with him.

"Stop that, please. My first wife finished my sentences. It drove me up the walls."

The air conditioner kicked on with a low hum. The cool breeze from the vent nearly lulled Nefi to sleep. He watched her eyelids close in long, languid blinks.

She rallied and sat up. "Will you help me, Mr. Flanagan?"

"I can't leave you here. I tell you what; my wife is visiting her sister this week. You can stay in the spare room while I see what I can do."

Nefi nodded and stood.

"Are you always this trusting of strangers?"

"You're a friend of Vincent's." Her matter-of-fact tone was like an audible shrug.

"I'm still a stranger to you." He stood. "I could be a pervert or a rapist."

She chuckled. "You love your wife so much, you'd look away if I walked naked through the house."

"How do you know that?"

"You blushed when I pulled out the dog tags. And you play with your wedding ring."

"That is a wee bit creepy gift you have." He headed toward the door to the hallway.

"I'm glad we don't have to involve Vincent." Nefi followed Flanagan, pausing for one last glance at Vincent sprawled on his bed. This was not how she had so often imagined him in bed. Not even close. She sighed.

Flanagan, waiting by the front door, raised his eyebrows at her.

"I don't want him to know I cut off a man's hand," she whispered.

"I see." Flanagan set Vincent's keys on a small table by the front door.

Nefi dropped her head. She had attacked Vincent once with a machete and a knife. Wouldn't he be afraid of her if he knew about her maiming a man? Any sane man would.

Flanagan opened the door to the corridor. "Well, now. Answer me this—what is your relationship with Vincent?"

With her eyes downcast, she shrugged. Trudging into the corridor, she wondered what to call their relationship. Rescuer and lost girl? Mercenary and deliverable? Federal Agent and wanna-be Fed?

"You love him?" It seemed Flanagan knew a thing or two about reading people.

She gave him a quick nod and pushed the button to the elevator.

Locking the door from the inside, Flanagan left the apartment and shut the door. He tried the knob. He met Nefi at the elevator, where he said, "You would be amazed at what a man can forgive a woman."

"For example?"

"Oh, the temptation of a good listener. I could spend days telling you all the things my Kate has forgiven me for."

The doors to the elevator chimed and opened. They both stepped in.

"Doesn't Vincent have to go to work today?"

"He's young, he'll be fine." He combed his fingers through his wavy black and gray hair. "But let's get back to you and Vincent. How old are you?"

"Twenty-one." Nefi pressed the button to the street-level.

"Ah, to be young and in love. And how do twenty-one-year-olds define love these days?"

The elevator sank slowly through the building.

"Most confuse it with lust." Nefi sighed. "My parents taught me that love is patient, kind, doesn't envy, doesn't boast, isn't proud, or rude, and it always trusts, always hopes, and never fails. That's how I feel about Vincent."

"And how does he feel about you?"

Sorrow draped around Nefi like a thick, damp cloak. She shrugged.

The elevator groaned to a stop. The doors slid open. They stepped into the darkened lobby and continued through the security door down the steps to the sidewalk.

"I live two blocks from here." Flanagan opened his arm eastward and led the way.

A siren echoed through the concrete canyons of the city. The crisp summer night's air wafted the smell of garbage and asphalt from the road. Yellow cabs flashed between the hunching silhouettes of buildings as they shot across a busier street in the distance. The grumbling traffic echoed. Nefi had often thought of New York City because of Vincent. Back in high school, she wrote a paper on it. Being here, she marveled at the scope of the Manhattan, where over one and a half million people within twenty-three square miles seemed to constantly migrate from the top of cloud-high buildings to the maze of underground tunnels and subways. Even in the deepest hours of night lights glowed from windows as far as she could see. Natural light from the moon and stars could not compete with man-made lights. Nefi calculated the population density of Manhattan at 62,000 people per square mile. There were barely 620 living in the twenty-three square miles around her village in Brazil.

Within a mile of Vincent's home lived tens of thousands of women. *And I thought I had a chance with him. Such hubris.*

Nefi's stomach grumbled.

Flanagan hiked alongside her on the uneven sidewalk. "So tell me about the bombing."

After her parents had picked her up at Dulles International Airport, Martina Ramos whimpered to sleep in the back of the car. Between her bottomless grief, her shock and the seven-and-a-half-hour-long flight from London, exhaustion flattened her. She awoke, near the end of her ride home, to the smell of smoke, afraid her dorm mate had left her curling iron on again. As her eyes focused on the window of her parents' luxury sedan, she glimpsed the charred skeleton of a house. Suddenly aware of where she was, she sat up.

"Stop!" she shrieked, scaring her parents into simultaneous gasps.

"Let's see it in the morning," Admiral Ramos pleaded. He slowed the car.

It would have been the sensible thing to do, but then, it was two a.m. and Martina was not feeling at all sensible. She opened the door and stood in the middle of the abandoned street. A balmy summer night breeze stirred ashes into a knee-high swirl that quickly died. Neighborhood pole lights cast a bluish glow over balloons, stuffed animals, letters, signs, damp candles, and a

NORTH OF THE KILLING HAND

poster-size photograph of Nefi that lined the sidewalk in front of yellow ribbons of crime scene tape. Others had begun a make-shift memorial. Martina vowed to organize a formal one at church that people would remember. Nefi deserved to be remembered; her loss mourned.

Arms enveloped her. Martina rested her head on her father's chest. The carnage, framed in a plastic fence of yellow crime scene tape that flapped in the breeze, spread out before her. The second story was gone. Bricks and glass lay scattered far outward from the foundation. Beyond the foundation, the garage and Nefi's car melted into a great black heap, and the leafless, blackened backyard oaks testified to the heat of the fire.

No wonder the firemen couldn't recover Nefi's body.

Martina's eyes burned anew at the unspeakable void. The smoky Nefi-ness.

Nefi had come far from that feral teenager in face paint who broke into Portuguese when she got excited. Martina had introduced Nefi to high school, shaving, fashion, makeup, sleepovers, video games, all the extended Ramos cousins, cell phones, computers, driving cars, swimming and more. Nefi had introduced Martina to self-defense classes, Portuguese slang, reading the Bible, and breaking from the pack to become an individual. Nefi challenged every aspect of teen culture to force Martina to see the pack mentality for what it was—the surrender of one's identity and will.

Martina remembered how she tried to help Nefi assimilate that first week of high school. Her parents had coordinated with the Jenkins so the girls would have all the same classes together. Martina eagerly agreed to escort and translate for Nefi, first of all, because her big brother Ruis asked her to, and secondly because she enjoyed the celebrity status of accompanying the most exotic student in the school. The red and black stains of Nefi's tribal paint had not completely faded, so whispers followed the girls through the halls.

A snapping sound drew Martina back to the present. The remains of a six-foot tall bookcase crumbled onto piles of ash that coughed out puffs of fine grit. All those stories lost. Lost like Nefi. Ashes to ashes. Dust to dust.

Father and Nefi were right. The world was a very dangerous place. It only took a few to ruin it for the rest. All it took was one crazy man with a bomb to destroy a home, a community's sense of safety and a noble life. Her shock transformed into burning fury in her chest, Martina took a deep breath of cool, sooty night air and wailed.

On the walk to Flanagan's brownstone, Nefi got her second wind. Like she used to experience when she ran track, untapped energy flowed through her when she should have been tired. Although it was three a.m. she was energized and alert.

"I was getting ready to leave for a job interview when I heard a vehicle in the driveway," Nefi said. "I looked out the window and saw two plumbing company vans. Aunt Louise would have been home if she had scheduled repairs. I was about to go downstairs when two men got out of the first truck, and they were speaking Portuguese. That's when I recognized the Pirarucu Man in my backyard."

"What else do you remember?"

"The Pirarucu Man sneaked to the garage like he was going to steal my car. I tried to get my cell phone off my nightstand, but it was by the window. He said something in Portuguese to another man about a bomb. I found my camera, so I held it up to the window and took a picture of him. He saw me in the window so I dropped to the floor and crawled to the master bedroom. I had time to take only one thing with me onto the balcony, so I grabbed the big album from the closet."

"An album you say?" Flanagan scratched the back of his neck.

"My cousin Jason died of a drug overdose before I came to America. The album is all they have of him."

Flanagan sighed. "To lose a child must be devastating."

It's devastating to lose parents, too. Nefi clenched her jaw and took a deep breath before she continued. "The killer told his driver to set up the bomb. That's when I opened the door to the balcony and threw a towel over the zip line."

Flanagan stopped walking. "I'm sorry. The what?"

"It's a metal cord used to ride through the canopy of the rain forest." She spoke as if everyone had one as she came to a halt on the pavement. "It was a gift from my best friend. The line runs from the upstairs master bedroom to the far oak in the back yard. I didn't have time to attach the harness, so I used a towel instead."

"So that's how you got out without being seen." He resumed walking.

Nefi strode alongside. "I tucked the album under my shirt and rode the line to the far side of the yard. I climbed down. The second van backed down the driveway, so I ran to the other side of the house to see the license plate. I counted three men in it. They drove to the end of the block and stopped. Then the explosion shook the house. Flames shot into the back yard, bricks fell like hail. I ran through the smoke to the tree. I wrapped the album in my sweater and hid it in the neighbor's pool house. They never lock their pool house."

"Did you get a license plate number?"

"The side of the van read Theo's Plumbing. It had a New York City phone number on it."

"Good. And then what happened?"

Nefi pursed her lips as if tasting a lemon. After admitting to maiming a man, she shouldn't be shy about telling him the rest. She sighed.

"Out with it," he said.

Nefi squeezed her hands together. "I stole my neighbor's bike and went to the park to think. That's where I met a student with a cell phone, the kind that has wireless internet connection. When I found out the plumbing company was in New York City, I rode the bike to the Farragut North Metro Station and took the Metrorail Red Line to Washington Station."

"The bombing was on Friday," Flanagan said. He climbed four steps to a brownstone. He pressed a code on the keypad and the door clicked open. He held the door open. "Where have you been all weekend?"

"Tracking people down." Nefi walked into the entranceway of a single-unit brownstone.

Flanagan stepped by her and poked numbers on a second keypad mounted on the wall above a lovely antique table. He flipped on a light and led the way through a narrow passageway that opened into a cozy living room. Aromas of furniture polish and rose potpourri permeated the apartment. She took in the room. Homey, and inviting, it had burgundy and emerald green flowered chintz curtains, roomy matching brown sofa and loveseat, two leather recliners, and real wood tables adorned with aged carving topped with lace doilies. And books. Built-in bookshelves lined every wall. She felt like a scruffy stray in the middle of this warm sanctuary, this lived-in home.

"Go on," Flanagan said.

"I waited outside Theo's Plumbing until yesterday morning. The driver of the van showed up and lied about how his truck was stolen. His boss fired him. I photographed him and the beat-up old van he left in. Then I met with the manager and got the man's name and address."

"He just *gave* you this information?"

"I told him I was looking for my uncle. I described him and spoke a little Portuguese..." Nefi batted her eyelashes.

"Go on." Flanagan rolled his eyes.

"I went to the creep's address and took his picture when he was standing beside the driver. They were talking about meeting up with someone to get paid, so I climbed into the back of his van."

"You shouldn't have entered that van." He waved toward the sofa.

Nefi sank into the soft cushions. She longed to curl up and sleep, but she dragged her mind back into the conversation. "I know. It was filthy—full of clothes, tools, plumbing supplies, tarps, and fast-food trash. What a pig. He couldn't see me. I heard him on a phone talking to someone he called Mr. Cortes. When the van stopped, and everyone else climbed out, I did too. I hid behind a barrel and took their pictures. We were at the docks. The Pirarucu Man was waiting there. He paid the other two men and then they drove off leaving the Pirarucu Man behind."

Flanagan plopped into a recliner. "What did you do with the photos?"

She pulled her small digital camera from her satchel just enough so he could see it. She then tucked it safely away. "I haven't downloaded the photos yet." She longed to curl up on the sofa and sleep. Was it really Monday already? She yawned.

Flanagan scrubbed his hand through his salt and pepper hair.

"I also took photos of Cortes. He showed up in a limousine. The Pirarucu Man acted like Cortes was his boss. I heard them talking about a club called Don't Tell. They talked about a Russian, but I missed some of that because a crane was unloading containers. They left in the limousine and, yes, I took a photo of the license plate." She smiled. "And last night I went to an internet cafe and searched for Vincent online."

Flanagan scowled. "Just like *that*, you found the personal address of an FBI agent on the internet?"

Nefi snorted. "Of course. Do you own a computer?"

"I have one at my office in the back of my restaurant."

"Okay." Nefi pulled her camera from her satchel and handed it to him.

"You are quite a tracker." He took the camera and set it on the end table. "Have you eaten today?"

"I haven't eaten since Friday."

"I tell you what; I'll cook while you freshen up. The bathroom's there. You can stay in the room on the right."

Exhaustion caught up with her as her adrenaline faded. She was as Martina called it "running on fumes." Thinking of Martina and how she must have heard the news, Nefi's eyes welled. She looked up at Flanagan, who was watching her. "Are you always this nice to a stranger who has nothing better to do than loitering on apartment steps in the middle of the night?"

"Miss Jenkins, you're a friend of Vincent's. That's good enough for me."

True to his word, by late morning on Monday, July 6th, Flanagan reviewed the evidence collected by Nefi. In the back office of his pub, he downloaded photos from her digital camera. The first photo showed a short, ugly, dark-haired man looking up from a paved driveway. She had photos of two men wearing uniform shirts that read Theo's Reliable Plumbing. Behind them was a parking lot full of company vans. More photos showed three men entering a tenement building, followed by grainy shots of two men at Brooklyn's Red Hook Container Terminal, a marine shipping and storage facility on the Hudson River. A handful of neatly written notes identified the subjects of the photos with details of time and place and the license plate labeled with a note 'white limousine.' Who but a criminal, a celebrity, a young bride, or teenagers would use a white limo? He scanned the photos and notes into his computer then he locked the originals in the restaurant's safe. He copied the scans and photos onto a key drive.

One of the men in the photos, the one Nefi called the Pirarucu

Man looked vaguely familiar. He was just ugly enough to stick in Flanagan's memory, but not familiar enough to attach with a name.

Flanagan used the internet to research the names from Nefi's notes using various spellings. He also searched the Interpol database for photos of wanted Brazilian criminals. One Interpol photograph matched Nefi's Pirarucu Man. His name was Damiano Guerra. Of the seven types of notices issued by Interpol, Guerra's was a Red Notice—to seek the arrest of a wanted person with a view to extradition.

Connected to this notice was the name and photograph of a known associate, Victor Alexandre 'Cortes' Rodrigo Cortes, suspected leader of a cartel. Cortes had a Blue Notice issued—to collect additional information about a person's identity or activities in relation to a crime. Both notices, issued a week earlier at the request of Brazil, referred to cocaine trafficking and human trafficking. It comforted him that Nefi was safely tucked away in his apartment and no longer chasing around after the Guerra fellow because he was a deadly sort of person to have as an enemy. Nefi was right to keep her survival a secret.

Flanagan called the new assistant director of the New York City bureau, Sam Watson, who showed up half an hour later. They had been friends and colleagues, so when Flanagan left, Watson easily moved into the position.

Flanagan served Watson his usual order, a plate of lamb stew, and a cold ginger ale. For a man of British descent, Watson had a voracious appetite for Irish food. But then, British food, well...British restaurants were few and far between in the rest of the world for a reason.

Flanagan sat across from him in the back booth with his laptop. There he angled the screen so only Watson could see the images copied from Nefi's camera. "I got a couple hits on eye twenty-four seven on these two blighters."

A few regulars at the far end of the bar argued amiably about the Mets. A lay person eavesdropping would not have understood Flanagan's reference to Interpol's secure global police communications system known as I-24/7.

Flanagan reported he had a witness who named Damiano Guerra as the killer of missionaries by the last name of Jenkins. That same witness, he added, named Guerra as the McLean, Virginia bomber.

Watson reviewed the evidence and washed down the last of his lunch with ginger ale.

"This Guerra fellow, he'll have a stub or a prosthetic right hand," Flanagan said. A memory teased the edges of his consciousness. Had he seen Guerra before? Probably a mug shot. Thousands of faces over the years were tough to keep straight. Plenty of blighters to go around.

"Why didn't you bring your witness to me?"

Flanagan explained the whole gruesome story as Nefi told it to him, about the murders, the maiming, the bombing, and her request to stay 'dead' until Guerra was captured. He ended the briefing with "and the witness doesn't want Agent Gunnerson to know about the maiming. She's sweet on him."

"And where is your witness?"

"Tucked away safely at my house. I'm the only one who knows she's there because Kate's out of town at her sister's."

Watson wiped his mouth. "I'll need a copy of your evidence."

Flanagan slid a 2-gigabyte jump drive across the table to him.

"How is it your witness was at crime scenes in two countries?" Watson leaned back in the booth.

"I'll need your word you won't reveal the witness's name until the bastards are in custody."

Watson nodded.

Flanagan slid Nefi's driver's license across the table.

Watson's mouth fell open. He clamped it shut as he reached for his cell phone.

Flanagan tucked the driver's license in his shirt pocket.

"I need to make two calls in private," Watson said.

Flanagan tucked his laptop under his arm. He guided Watson to the back of the restaurant and up a small staircase to his office. He stood just outside the door and was about to close it when Watson pulled him into the office.

"I want you in the loop." Watson made two calls, one to his second in command, and the other to his contact at the Brazilian Embassy. He set his phone on speaker mode and set it on Flanagan's desk.

A woman answered, and Watson asked for something that sounded like Cheetah.

"And whom may I say is calling?"

"Watson."

The call was transferred.

"It's really Conchita, but she prefers Chita," Watson whispered to Flanagan.

"Director Watson, how good to hear from you. How may I help you?" The woman's smoky voice purred when she rolled her Rs.

"Damiano Guerra and Victor Cortes are in New York City. I have photographs and a witness. The witness also names Guerra in the murder of the missionaries named Jenkins."

"I have two agents in the city on another case. Can you arrange a meeting with your witness at your office, say tonight?"

Watson glanced at Flanagan.

Flanagan nodded and checked his watch. He figured that if Nefi wasn't still sleeping, she might have her clothes out of the dryer. The restaurant was short-handed so he couldn't be home until closing. All Nefi had to do was stay put and rest while the professionals took over.

"Tonight will be fine," Watson told Chita.

"We would like to work with local authorities," Chita purred, "in the apprehension of these men. Cooperation between our agencies increases the likelihood of success. I also would like assurances that we may deport them after you question them."

"Guerra's been named a suspect for bombing a Senator's home," Watson said, starting negotiations from the get-go.

"I see. Keep your witness protected. Cortes and Guerra have a reputation for making people disappear," Chita said.

Watson crossed his arms. "Understood. What are the names of your agents?"

A sexy laugh came from the phone. "Giada and Lucille. Men turn stupid around them, so beware. I'll have them contact you."

At noon, Nefi was rested, back in her own clean clothes, and talking on the ancient landline phone in Flanagan's living room when the apartment door creaked open. Remembering that most robberies happen during daylight while people are at work, Nefi froze. Mr. Flanagan had said he would be back after dark. Nefi set the handset on the sofa cushion as far as the curled cord allowed. She then sneaked into the kitchen where she grabbed a French knife from the butcher block knife holder on the counter. Her aunt Louise had taught her that the French knife was designed to cut vegetables, but it was also the kind used in horror movies. Tracking the intruder through the corridor to the master bedroom, Nefi stepped around the corner and shouted at the back of a five-foot-two figure.

"Raise your hands!"

The startled woman dropped her suitcase and reached her hands over her head. She slowly pivoted to face Nefi. A bosomy fifty-something-year-old, sporting wild gray and reddish blonde shoulder-length curls, she wore a deep green dress with a ruffled lace collar. She looked as Irish as a leprechaun. Spotting the French knife, she shrieked.

"State your name," Nefi said.

"Kate Flanagan. You'll be in a world of trouble for this. My husband—"

Nefi gasped. "I'm so sorry." She lowered the knife to the countertop. "Mr. Flanagan told me you'd be gone all week."

Kate dropped her hands to her waist. "Oh, he did now? So he let you in?"

Nefi pulled the dog tags from under her shirt for Kate to see. "I'm a friend of Vincent Gunnerson."

Kate peered at the dog tags. "So you are it seems. Now would you mind telling me why you'd be in my house waving a knife?"

Nefi, unsure of whether or not to involve Flanagan's wife, hesitated to answer. She had endangered her aunt and uncle and Mr. Flanagan by association. Even revealing her name to Kate might set in motion a series of questions and answers that law enforcement professionals would share only on a need-to-know basis, according to Nefi's studies. There was so much Kate did *not* need to know that Nefi had to scramble to find something she could tell her.

"Quinn!" Kate's voice cut through the house. She walked toward Nefi.

"He went to work." Nefi backed into the living room.

"Vincent doesn't strike me as the kind of man to hire a working girl," Kate said, "but tell me now, is that how you know him?"

Working girl? "I'm unemployed."

"That doesn't answer my question." Kate planted her hands on her hips.

Nefi read her body language and sensed fury gathering like a storm. Struggling to find something truthful to say, she said, "Vincent is my...friend. I have a Bachelor's of Science in Social and Cognitive Neurosciences from Harvard. I'm looking for a job in law enforcement." *And I'm a babbling idiot.*

Kate crossed her arms under her ample bosom. "My husband

retired from law enforcement. By any chance was he interviewing you here?"

"No." Nefi's confusion ran deep. The FBI did not conduct job interviews in people's homes. Flanagan was retired and, therefore, had no hiring authority. Or was 'interviewing' a euphemism?

"Tell me this. Were you supposed to be gone before I returned?"

"Yes, ma'am." Nefi suddenly recognized jealousy and betrayal in Kate's behavior. Whatever the reason, this woman felt threatened. Territorial, if Nefi read her properly.

"Well. I'm home." There was no mistaking the finality of Mrs. Flanagan's statement.

"Yes, ma'am." Nefi stuffed her few things into her messenger bag while Mrs. Flanagan followed. Nefi's driver's license was missing, so she checked around the end table quickly. Gone. "I'm sorry I upset you. For my safety, please don't tell anyone I was here. Not even Vincent."

"You don't even want your friend to know you were here?" Kate stepped toward Nefi.

"No, ma'am." Seeing herself through Kate's perspective, Nefi would have been just as suspicious. No matter what she said, she sounded either suspicious or crazy. Nefi backed into the narrow corridor that led to the front door.

"And you won't tell me why you're here?" Kate continued toward Nefi. Though smaller and softer, Kate had an imposing presence.

Nefi pulled the strap of her messenger bag over her head and backed into the front door. "No, ma'am." She reached back and opened it, afraid to show her back to the furious leprechaun, and backed out of Flanagan's apartment.

"Then be gone." With that, Kate slammed the door.

On her lonely march down the sidewalk, Nefi realized she had left Flanagan's home phone off the hook while on hold. She also left the phone book on the end table beside the phone, open to a listing of local escort services. She had circled in red the ones who had Portuguese-speaking escorts. *Oh, no.* She cringed, but there was no going back.

Quinn Flanagan arrived home that evening at nine eager to tell Nefi the good news that the FBI and the Brazilian Federal Police were searching for Guerra and Cortes. Kate greeted him with a spatula in her hand. She scowled at him from the doorway to the kitchen.

"Welcome home, love," Quinn said. As he moved toward her for a hug, she raised the spatula at him like an accusing finger.

"I got tired of hearing my sister badmouth men, so I came home early and found she's right."

"Your sister's choice in men is a self-fulfilling prophecy." Flanagan should have expected Kate to come back from her sister's like this. That spiteful woman spread bitterness like a disease. He hoped Kate had only a mild case of it this time. He headed to the living room. "Where's Nefi?"

"Oh, so that's her name." Kate's tone reminded him of a flash of distant lightning.

"Where is she?" His throat dried up.

"I think the better question is who is she?" Kate's voice rumbled like thunder threatening rain.

Was that a wounded look in her eyes? He stepped up to Kate and gently gripped her shoulders. "What's the matter with you?"

"With me? Ha! If I hadn't come back early, I never would have known." Kate's bright green eyes welled up. Kate swatted her husband away and pointed to the phonebook. "The minute I'm gone you're calling up escort services!" She stormed from the room and slammed the bathroom door.

What the hell? Flanagan inspected the phonebook. Sure

enough, it was laid open to listings of escort services, a few circled in red ink, with a note in the margin—*Portuguese*. Was Nefi searching for Guerra through escorts? He dashed to both bedrooms calling for Nefi. He prayed she had not gone to the escort services to ask questions.

Not shy of danger that girl. She might try to stake out the club. He called Assistant Director Watson. If he couldn't locate Nefi, maybe he could locate Guerra and Cortes. Nefi had mentioned the club Don't Tell. Watson didn't answer, so Flanagan left a message.

He couldn't let the girl face those monsters alone. He needed to go to the club, but first, he had to save his wife from pointless, wrong-headed hysteria. He marched to the bathroom and banged on the door.

"Kate, you are my one and only true love. I am deeply offended you would leap to conclusions that defame me. And the young murder witness I was protecting. You egregiously underestimate your effect on me if you think a child could turn my affections."

The whimpering stopped.

Flanagan held his heart in check and his breath inside awaiting her response. He pressed his ear to the door. Kate blew her nose. He felt the door vibrate, so he stepped back. The door swung open.

Kate fell into his arms and spoke sobs. "She's a murder witness? Oh, lordy. What have I done?"

He hugged her firmly. *Praise the Lord.* After his heart had steadied, he held her at arm's length. "Did you by chance send her on an errand?"

Kate bit her lower lip, gave it quick chew, and let it go. "She refused to tell me her name or why she was here. Oh, no. Oh, no. My sister's ranting bent my mind to her way of thinking. I ran the girl off."

Flanagan heard his heartbeat thudding in his ears. "When?"

"About noon."

Flanagan groaned. Ten hours ago! He ran his fingers through his wiry hair while he paced the living room. He tried calling Vincent, but the call went to his voicemail. He dialed Blake's number as well. Same result.

In a moment of stillness, a memory appeared in clear detail as if Flanagan was standing in the tech booth at 23 Federal Plaza. The photo of Guerra reminded him of an informant he had approved, an equally ugly fellow who had presented a passport. Silva. His name was Silva. Flanagan had warned FBI Agent Lenny not to trust the informant because he sensed a reptilian coldness from Silva. Like he was the kind of man who might kill for pleasure. He signed with his left hand because his right hand was a prosthetic. Then as if Flanagan had broken through the surface of deep water, he gasped for air. Silva is Guerra.

"What was Nefi wearing?"

"A white shirt, smart gray slacks, and low heels. Oh, and she had a leather messenger bag draped across her." Kate gestured with one hand from her shoulder to the opposite hip. "Looked like she was going to a job interview."

"I have to find her. If she's going where I think she is, she'll get herself killed."

Kate stood to kiss him then she gave him a little shove toward the door. "Don't get shot."

With his cell phone in hand, he bounded down the front steps to the curb and used his free hand to hail a cab. He found Agent Lenny's number and prayed he was keeping track of his informant's whereabouts. He couldn't blame Lenny, the man had followed protocol. Flanagan blamed himself for approving the ugly weasel as an informant. He vowed to protect Nefi from his terrible decision.

. 22 .

Vincent and Blake, dressed for undercover duty, sipped soft drinks at a small table in the middle level of the Don't Tell Club. The club's dark interior included carpet on the walls to baffle noise and four tiers of booths and tables surrounding a glass block dance floor. Colored lights flashed from under the dance floor, illuminating the dancers. Extending past the dance floor was the bar in the center, with bathrooms and a kitchen off to the left and the club entrance to the right. The club was a small arena of sorts designed for watching and playing the mating game. Neon strobe lights illuminated plenty of flesh. The lights pulsed to the tempo of the music.

Vincent's three chief complaints about this kind of place: one, after enough beers in the dark everyone looked good, and two, the noise level reduced communications to pantomime, and three, it was the kind of place where he had met Rose. Not on a weeknight, but still, he would have preferred to be at home. He stretched his legs under the table. His silk navy blue shirt billowed at the waist though it fit him snug across the chest. Assistant Director Watson had often warned him to wear a dark shirt instead of a T-shirt so he didn't look like a bouncer when he was meeting with or following informants. Blake's dark shirt contrasted with his pale skin and red hair.

Blake appeared less redneck and much more like a New Yorker in black.

Vincent could have fallen asleep on any flat surface, even concrete, if given the chance. He traced the start of his weariness to Friday, the day of the bombing. Since then he had seized every opportunity to hear or see the news on it. On Saturday, he and Rose had attended a formal Fourth of July party hosted by her friends. An old boyfriend of Rose's arrived in a Ferrari, and that was that. On Sunday, Rose announced she needed to find herself. *In a Ferrari, no doubt.* The accumulation of bad news knocked Vincent off his feet. He went to Flanagan's to get out of his empty apartment, to vent, and to have a drink or two. Rose's departure had not been the worst news of the week.

"Vincent," Blake said, "you look terrible."

"Rose left." Vincent let that excuse stand because he couldn't bear to speak of Nefi's death. After all, even though Blake said Nefi harbored a crush on him, he would never confess that he secretly hoped they would meet again after Nefi grew up. The greater tragedy was that Nefi lost the chance to grow up. *She deserved so much more life.*

"You can't drink a woman out of your system."

"I started out celebrating Rose's departure."

"How many drinks did this celebration last?"

"You'd have to ask Quinn. I think he dragged me home." Vincent had flashes of Quinn and some woman hoisting him up the front stairs of his apartment building. The landlady? No, younger. Stronger.

Blake raised his glass. "To absent friends."

They drank to the toast.

Agent Lenny's description of his informant was apt. Look for the ugliest man in the room. Sure enough, he was it. Blake confirmed Silva-the-ugly by a file mug shot on his cell phone. Lenny had another engagement, so the babysitting job fell to newer agents. The weasel was supposedly meeting with a Russian to become a supplier for him. He wasn't wearing a wire. He just wanted protection during the meeting. Neither Vincent nor Blake wanted to be in a sleazy club on a Monday night, but here they were.

The fact that Blake had not mentioned the firebombing or Nefi made losing her more acutely painful. With two rooms of the house vaporized in the blast, there wasn't even a body to bury. No doubt, the Senator would have a memorial. Vincent longed for a strong drink as much as he longed to be able to stay home and mourn. But duty called to watch one drug-dealing weasel make a deal with another drug-dealing lowlife.

The informant sat at the focal point of a prominent U-shaped booth, one level up from the dance floor, with a Russian drug dealer called Rykov. The informant had promised a big fish. Rykov reminded Vincent of a crocodile from his wide-set eyes to his large yellow teeth. According to his reputation, when Rykov opened his mouth bloody things happened.

The parade of women at the club ranged from professionals to lonely college girls. Some stopped to flirt and chat, unintentionally helping Vincent's cover. Blake, however, got irritated when they blocked his view. Vincent took this as a serious sign that Blake's heart beat only for Terri. How wonderful would it be to have a relationship without drama? Months ago when Blake offered his opinion about Rose, he suggested in specific terms that Vincent mistook drama for passion. The problem was that Vincent felt the passion; Rose felt only the drama. He knew he would not miss Rose's shouting. The loud, thumping music reminded him of Rose. Regular, monotonous, driving, but lacking meaning, the noise was, like Rose, drama without passion, loud and insistent.

"Rykov's men are stationed at eleven o'clock and two o'clock," Blake reported.

"Two o'clock is the no-neck at the bar?"

"Yep."

"How do you know?" Vincent toyed with his drink.

"When he reached for his glass, I spotted a tattoo on his wrist that looked like Cyrillic."

"*Gesundheit,*" Vincent said.

"Russian alphabet."

Vincent grinned to let Blake know he knew what Cyrillic was. "This surveillance is pointless. We can't even record the conversation."

"All we have to do," Blake said, "is protect the little rat."

"Have you noticed he keeps looking over our heads?" No one had their backs in this seedy place.

"Probably leering at college girls, but I'll take a look." Blake stood and stepped down the platform that held a row of tables at his level, one level above the dance floor across from the informant.

Dancers gyrated and swayed on the dance floor. A few danced with their faces aimed up at the strobe lights. Ecstasy users found lights stimulating. Vice cops called it safe sex. Blake waded through the crowd on the dance floor toward the glowing glass block bar and the restrooms.

Vincent flagged down a waitress. She wore the club's uniform, a hot pink spandex top stretched over large breasts, and a short black skirt covered with an even shorter pocketed black apron. Carrying her empty tray, she pranced over in high-heeled ankle boots.

"What can I get you?" She did not write down orders. She somehow remembered them despite the thundering music and dozens of patrons. She was the same waitress who had served them for the last two hours. Her nametag claimed Rita. Easy to remember, Rita as in Margarita. She looked old and tired up close.

"I'd like a ginger ale and bring a coke for my friend. Please, no straws. We don't want to look like lightweights."

"One day at a time," she said. She winked and cleared away the empties.

At the bar, Blake leaned toward the female bartender. They chatted for a while. Blake probably poured on his Southern charm.

New York women seemed to respond to it like a foreign accent. Blake walked back to his table.

"The bartender said the man at the table two levels behind ours is a high-roller from South America. Calls himself Alexandre Cortes. The other tables are college girls. Rumor has it last night Cortes left with two prostitutes."

"Two?"

Blake sneered. "That's his story."

The thumping music synchronized with pulsing colored lights, giving a strobe effect. Under strobe lights, the dancer's movements appeared jerky and disjointed, like on a surveillance tape with five-second interval recording. His mind tried to fill in the gaps.

A vibration at his waist signaled Vincent of an incoming call or text message. Vincent pulled out his phone and read the small screen. A text message from the Assistant Director. He was about to read the message when a movement in his peripheral vision distracted him. A tall young woman in dress slacks and a white oxford shirt passed on his left. Far too preppie for this dump, she had a purse strapped across her torso, like a messenger bag. Something in her gait, in the shape of her legs, in her long brown hair, and her height demanded Vincent's attention. She moved purposefully like an athlete, but with a hint of a predator. *Jaguar.*

Her gait looked so familiar that Vincent suspected she worked at the bureau. This club had a reputation for attracting models and actresses, thanks to its proximity to Times Square. Perhaps she had been on television. Was she a tennis player or a model? Wishing he was off-duty, Vincent watched the woman in case she turned her head.

His view was suddenly blocked by cleavage. Rita set two sweating tumblers of soft drinks on the table. She obscured Vincent's view of the tall beauty for a moment. Vincent placed a fifty-dollar bill on Rita's tray. "Thank you, keep the change," he said, dismissing her.

"Thank you," she said, moving out of the way.

The jaguar crossed the dance floor toward the few occupied tables on the opposite side. Instead of stopping at the table of young construction workers, she stopped at the informant's.

Vincent groaned. Civilians got in the way sometimes. The young woman talked to Rykov, but he waved her off. Maybe she worked for Rykov. Had the informant arranged a date? The brunette persisted. Rykov backhanded her across the face, causing her to stagger back a step. If it was a set-up, the informant shouldn't have used a woman. An assault charge would not keep Rykov in jail for long. When her long brown hair flipped out of the way, her profile revealed she was in her twenties. She pulled something from her purse and straightened up. She extended her right arm at Rykov, who convulsed violently then pitched face down on the table. *Taser. Served him right for hitting a woman. Clear cut case of self-defense.*

Blake stood up so fast his chair fell back. He yelled something over the roar of the music then he hopped down toward the dance floor. Vincent stood. Did Blake think the informant was in danger? The informant scooted away from Rykov while he shouted at the young woman. Rykov's bodyguard from the bar shoved his way through dancers toward the table. The sober dancers stampeded away from the bodyguard.

Suddenly, the bodyguard dropped out of sight, revealing an older man standing behind him. The man looked old enough to be the young woman's father. He also looked familiar, but colored strobe lights obscured his features.

Rykov's other bodyguard grabbed the young woman by the arm. Screams rose from the dancers who surged away from the fight. Against the flow of traffic, Vincent charged onto the crowded dance floor. Still a few feet away from the young woman, he saw her elbow the second bodyguard in the nose. A moment later, the bodyguard became airborne and landed so hard on the floor he bounced. *Wow. That had to hurt.*

The young woman faced the informant, who climbed over the table to jump on her. She grabbed his shirt and twisted, catapulting him to the floor at Blake's feet. She dropped to a knee on the informant's chest and drew back a fist. She was holding something pink in it. Blake grabbed the fist and lifted her to her feet. She pivoted and fell against Blake's chest.

Blake looked so shocked that Vincent feared the young woman had tased him or stabbed him. She broke free and bolted toward the bar. Seconds later, Vincent reached Blake and spun him around to look for blood.

"I don't believe it," Blake said.

"Are you hurt?" Vincent shouted over the music.

"No."

Vincent dashed after the young woman. With her help, they could nail Rykov on assault. To his right, a thirty-year-old Hispanic man leaped down from a higher level of tables. Cortes? The man pushed a college girl to the floor on his way to the front door. Vincent sensed that this man had been watching the informant and the Russian. Was he armed? The man suddenly ducked into the crowd and headed to the back toward the bar. Two women in their thirties strode through the crowd toward the Hispanic man. Must be Cortes. One of the women carried a gun low in front with both hands. FBI Agent Lenny followed closer behind her than a shadow.

Vincent pursued his own suspect past the bar to the narrow hallway toward the restrooms and the kitchen door.

Lenny called out to "stop that man."

In the narrow hallway, Vincent body-checked Cortes against the wall hockey style. In his peripheral vision, he saw the man crumple to the floor. The kitchen's double doors swung shut. Vincent shoved open the door on the right and stepped over a waitress sprawled on the floor. The young woman, the jaguar, fled through the back door to the alley. She was fast.

Vincent lost sight of her when the door to the alley closed. He shouldered it open and drew his weapon. He didn't want to get Tased like Rykov. Had it been long enough for the Taser to recharge? A movement in the shadows of a doorway caught his attention. He approached the doorway by gliding along the wall. Had she run because she was an illegal? Or a prostitute?

"I'm Agent Gunnerson of the FBI. Come out with your hands up. I saw what happened. You were clearly defending yourself." He waited a moment then he shouted, "*Soy agente Gunnerson del F-B-I. Salir con las manos arriba.*"

He eased one step closer to the shadowed doorway. His heart pounded. He sucked in a deep breath to steady himself. Panting sounded from the shadows. He suddenly wished he had worn a bullet-proof vest. He was a huge target at close range. He remembered Flanagan's warning to trust his intuition. He could use his size to intimidate. Stepping in front of the doorway, he leveled his weapon at the shape in the shadows.

"Show your hands." A sensation of *déjà vu* flowed over him. He sensed the woman in the shadows was emotionally overwhelmed, but not by fear. This moment resonated as vital and life-changing to her. Vincent knew in his soul that the next few moments mattered. He hoped this *déjà vu* sensation was a warning against shooting. He willed the woman to obey his command. If she Tased him, the electrical charge would cause his muscles to contract involuntarily, and he would shoot at random, unable to release the gun.

Come on. Come out. Come out.

Two shaking hands emerged from the shadows. Vincent took a step backward crunching glass underfoot. The figure eased out of the darkness into the bluish glow of the alley's pole light. The woman's face was wet and her eyes closed. She extended her arms, open-handed, slowly raising them above her head.

Her eyes remained downcast as she spoke. "Are you going to arrest him?"

"Yes. Why did he hit you?"

"I provoked him."

His pulse pounded in his ears. Is this what college girls did for fun? Vincent raised the barrel of his gun to the sky. "Why?"

Her eyes opened. "So someone would call the police."

"You could dial 9-1-1." He clicked the safety on his gun, holstered it and snapped the leather flap in place under his jacket. Her voice, her height, seemed familiar, but he could not name her. She looked too young to work at the bureau. She was nearly eye level with him, something he rarely experienced with a woman.

"Vincent, you learned Spanish."

Wait. How does she know my first name? He struggled to recognize where or when he met her before. After growing up in New York City, he knew thousands of people as familiar and hundreds by name. *Who is she?*

"The man who bombed my uncle's house is here." In the light, her eyes glowed like honey.

No wonder Blake looked stunned. "Nefi? You're alive!" He embraced her. "Oh, thank God." Relief washed over him, leaving a residue of utter confusion.

The door to the club banged off the brick wall. The commotion behind Vincent caused him to release Nefi and spin around to shield her. Cortes staggered out and took a few steps before a woman caught up with him and shoved him into a brick wall. He dropped to a sitting position and put his back to the wall.

Oddly, Cortes seemed to be enjoying it. He held out his hands. "You will handcuff me now?" he said, laughing.

The woman slung him face down and swiftly handcuffed him.

"Who are you?" Vincent asked.

"Brazilian Federal Police," the woman said. "Who are you?"

The man on the ground laughed harder.

"FBI," Vincent said.

"Clayton, Gunnerson, or Flanagan?" The woman pressed a knee on the man's back. When she straightened her back, her ample chest stuck out, straining shirt buttons.

"Gunnerson," Vincent said. Nefi pressed her hands and face against his back. She was alive and well, warming his back, but why was she here of all places?

"I'm Giada," the woman said. "And this," the shapely brunette nodded toward the handcuffed man beneath her, "is Victor Alexandre Rodrigo Cortes, of the Cortes cartel." She rolled her Rs.

Cortes said, "I don't want this man involved. Only women." He craned his neck at Nefi, leering at her. "She can stay."

Vincent's whole body heated up at the way Cortes looked at Nefi. He balled his fists. It made sense that a drug dealer would bomb the Senator's house because of the Senator's drug bill. The bill had died in a previous vote, but this time around the bill was gaining traction. By bombing the Senator's house, Cortes probably helped the bill. But then, criminals weren't known for being smart.

Cortes addressed Nefi, "Call me Xano, pretty girl."

Giada sneered at the prostrate man. "I'll call you whatever I please. Now shut up, adults are talking here." Her accent came through despite her Americanized vocabulary. She frisked him thoroughly from the ankles up. After discarding a knife hidden in his sock, she checked his pockets and crotch.

"Yes, there, there," Cortes said.

What kind of idiot flirts while he's being arrested? Nefi took hold of Vincent's hand. Her gentle touch eased tension from him. He squeezed her warm, soft hand in reply. *Thank you, God, for sparing Nefi.*

"That man bombed your house?"

"No, the other one," Nefi said.

The Russian.

At that moment, the door flung open, again banging against the brick wall. Flanagan hopped off the doorstep onto the concrete alley. When he saw Cortes handcuffed on the ground, he smiled. "Giada?"

The woman nodded.

"Quinn Flanagan at your service." He strode to the handcuffed man, grabbed a fist full of shirt, and hoisted him to his feet. "Cortes I presume?"

"No men," Cortes told Giada. "I'm not paying for them."

"What is going on?" Vincent gaped at Flanagan. Didn't he have a pub to run? The night was beginning to feel like a stress dream, the kind in which whatever you try to do doesn't work, like running through hip-deep mud, and everyone speaks in gibberish.

"We have warrants for Guerra and Cortes," Giada said. She searched Cortes's torso and arms.

Between his joy at discovering Nefi was alive and his surprise at seeing Flanagan, he wanted a timeout to get his bearings on the situation.

"We need to talk," Flanagan told Vincent.

Giada wrestled Cortes through the door to the club.

Cortes's voice echoed from the kitchen. "Where is the other woman?"

Flanagan, Nefi, and Vincent watched Cortes and Giada until the door swung shut. Flanagan and Nefi laughed. Cortes's reaction to being arrested was the first time Vincent had seen a suspect so entertained by it. Was the man high?

Nefi squeezed Vincent's wrist. "I'm glad Mr. Flanagan called you." Her golden eyes bore through him to his heart.

Vincent desperately wanted to deflect questions. Even in daylight, this wasn't a safe place for Nefi. "What? Wait. You know each other?"

Flanagan opened his palm toward Nefi then he used his handkerchief to pick up Cortes's knife from the ground. "Please let's go inside."

Vincent positioned himself so he could keep his shoulder holster and Nefi on his left. Placing his left hand on the small of Nefi's back, he walked her to the back door of the club. She was taller than he remembered. Her posture seemed athletically graceful and confident. Her face had matured beautifully, just as he had predicted back in Brazil. He imagined her high school littered with broken hearts. He hoped she still wore his dog tags.

Then he thought of Senator and Mrs. Jenkins. They should be told Nefi is alive.

Vincent followed Nefi's long, lean silhouette through the kitchen. Flanagan gallantly opened the door and waved them in. His smirk told Vincent that he'd caught him assessing Nefi. The inside of the club, without the pounding music and synchronized strobe lights, could have been a different place than the one they ran from minutes earlier. Beyond a few overturned tables and chairs, two dozen people sat in clusters being interviewed by police and FBI. On the dance floor, five men lay face-down in handcuffs.

Giada and another woman held down Silva and Cortes. The Russian's two thugs were quietly seething while Rykov moaned. Cortes raged in English and Portuguese at the informant Silva.

Vincent parked Nefi behind the bar where the wait staff huddled. He leaned over her and said, "Stay here."

"If Flanagan didn't call then why are you here?" Nefi whispered in Vincent's ear.

"I can't say." His neck tingled.

Rita, his waitress all evening, eyed him and gave him an approving nod. Flanagan stayed with Nefi and the wait staff, blocking their exit from behind the bar.

Vincent strode to the dance floor where an hour-glass shaped woman stood with her boot on Silva's back. His left hand was handcuffed to his right ankle. Though unorthodox, it was effective. An artificial right hand rested on the floor beside him.

Giada held the hysterical Cortes face down on the floor with her knee between his shoulder blades. Giada pointed to the hand on the floor. "Damn, Lucy, you broke him."

"Oh, he was already damaged goods," the other woman said. Her familiarity with Giada gave Vincent the impression they were partners. Brazilian Federal Police.

FBI Agent Lenny checked the Russian's neck. "What happened to this guy?"

"A Taser." Blake rose from a chair. He held an ice pack on his face as he addressed Vincent. "A pink Taser if I'm not mistaken."

Vincent smiled with pride for Nefi. His gift had served her well.

"So which one of you carries a pink Taser?" Giada looked from Blake to Vincent.

Blake and Vincent answered in unison, "Nefi."

"What happened to you?" Vincent asked Blake.

"A little disagreement about jurisdiction," Blake said. His glance accused Giada's partner.

The woman grimaced. "So sorry. I thought you were protecting Guerra."

"Who is Guerra?" Blake asked.

Vincent shrugged. He scanned the faces of the remaining clubbers giving their statements to patrol officers. They were mostly white college preppies and two black couples.

"Didn't Assistant Director Watson call you?" Giada asked Vincent.

"I got a message about the time all hell broke loose in here," Vincent said. "Blake meet Giada, Brazilian Federal Police."

Giada pointed to her partner, "And my partner is Lucille." When she turned, the badge clipped to her waistband showed.

Blake lowered his ice pack and turned toward Lucille. "I'd say it's nice to meet you, but I'd be lying."

Rykov moaned.

"Who's Nefi?" Lucille asked no one in particular.

"I'll tell you that if you'll tell me who Guerra is," Vincent said. His feet hurt, and a low-grade headache compressed his temples.

Lucille, still holding down Silva with her boot, pointed down. "And that's part of him too." She indicated the prosthetic hand.

Blake's mouth fell open. "There can't be two men that ugly. That's Silva."

NORTH OF THE KILLING HAND

Vincent wanted to ask Giada about the warrants, but it would be smarter to discuss the suspects when they weren't listening. He had so many questions he wanted to ask about the warrants, about Flanagan's presence here, but most of all about Nefi.

Agent Lenny stepped forward. "Let's separate these jokers and cart them in for questioning." He glared at Blake and Vincent as if to signal them to protect Guerra's or Silva's informant status.

Vincent glared down at Rykov. If he bombed the Jenkins' home, his drug-dealing days were over. He could be charged with terrorism. And then there was the crazy Cortes creep who seemed amused by Giada. Lenny's scum informant—Guerra, Silva, whatever he wanted to call himself, well, his protected status was shot. As Vincent stared down at the prosthetic hand, a long-dormant memory stirred, churning a deep-seated surge of anger. As the emotion grew, he recognized the memory. A hand. A hand recovered in the jungle with two whole bodies near Nefi's village. His heart skipped as a chill ran through him. Guerra was wanted by the Brazilians, maybe for more than drugs. Murder? When he looked up, Blake had a vacant expression, his eyes aimed at the plastic hand.

Lenny started directing incoming FBI agents and the Brazilian Policewomen.

When agents hauled Guerra to his feet, Vincent picked up the prosthesis. "Where did you lose your hand?"

Blake closed in behind Guerra.

"Give a lady a hand?" Lucille reached out a gloved hand, took the artificial hand from Vincent and dropped it in an evidence bag.

Vincent turned and jogged to the bar. "Nefi, which man bombed the house?"

"The one with the killing hand." Nefi glowered at Silva, the informant, as two agents escorted him away.

Animal rage distorted Silva's already gross face as he passed

Nefi. He clearly recognized Nefi and hated her. Silva was Guerra.

Lenny's voice boomed across the room, "The employees behind the bar have already given statements. They can go."

Flanagan escorted them out.

The bottom of Vincent's world sank lower. He searched for words to form an apology on behalf of the FBI for practically harboring the man who bombed her uncle's house, the man who killed Nefi's parents. Before he could voice them, Blake sidled up to the bar.

"We got him, Nefi," Blake whispered. "If we had known who he was, we never would have been sitting here all night protecting him."

Nefi's eyes widened. She sidestepped from behind the bar to stagger away from them.

"We didn't know." Vincent headed down the length of the bar toward her.

She stood at the opening of the bar. With her lip quivering, she backed away from Vincent. "You were protecting *him*?"

Vincent eased toward her. In a few more steps, he would be able to reach her, to block her from the back door. "You're safe now. We need you to make a statement to…" He slowly reached out to her, but she held up her hands as if swatting at an invisible attacker.

Nefi shook her head and bolted to the alley.

Vincent's previous joy crushed, he chased after her. By the time he leaped out the back door, over the single step down to the vacant alley, she was out of sight. He continued down the alleyway and stopped to listen for the rhythmic sound of shoes on pavement.

"Nefi! We didn't know." He dashed to the street where agents loaded the suspects into the back of vehicles. He then ran the other way down the alley to the other side of the block. Breathing heavily, he stood in the center of the road and searched for moving targets. He was alone. The sidewalks were empty for three blocks in both directions. Traffic echoed from blocks away.

He ran checking between parked cars until his phone chimed. Flanagan's name glowed from the phone.

"Where's Nefi?"

Vincent was too winded to speak. He managed a cough. In the background of the call, he heard Blake's voice.

"He went after her."

"She's...too...fast," Vincent ground out.

"Come on back," Flanagan said. "She had a shock that's all."

Vincent considered going to the nearest roof to sing "Amazing Grace" at the top of his lungs. Instead, he choked back sorrow and trudged back toward the flashing lights. *I'm so sorry, Nefi. I didn't know.*

Nefi stopped running six blocks from the Don't Tell Club. She gulped air between sobs. Sirens echoed off buildings. Headlights of a turning police cruiser arched over her then the car raced past her in the direction of the club. She wiped her eyes with the back of her hand and headed toward Times Square, where she could blend into packs of strangers out on the summer's night, where she could be another anonymous sad face in the crowd, where she could figure out why the axis of the earth shifted and turned the world upside down. Disillusioned, betrayed, alone, she continued on the sidewalk in the direction of heavy traffic.

Her plan had been to provoke Damiano to attack her so the police would arrest him. Then she could tell the police who he was and what he had done so he would get locked in a small dark cell for the rest of his hateful life. She had not counted on a Russian brute interfering. She never would have imagined Vincent and Blake involved let alone *protecting* the Pirarucu Man! Was he an informant?

She mentally retraced her actions in desperation to pinpoint how her plan had failed so spectacularly.

After waiting seven years to face her parents' killer, she had approached his table and politely suggested the Russian man should leave. No need to involve him. He slapped her, so she calmly Tased him to eliminate the distraction and to show the Pirarucu Man her seriousness. The Russian's bodyguard attacked, so she defended herself. When she finally spoke to Damiano, she asked him why he killed her parents. He said he didn't remember killing anyone. Goading him, she asked if he remembered losing a jaguar-head ring along with his hand. Enraged, he climbed over the table at her. She used his momentum to catapult him to the floor where his fall broke loose his artificial hand. She dropped to one knee on his chest and pulled back her right fist. Years of pent anger wound up in her like a spring set to kill him. She yearned to drive his nose into his brain, but she hesitated.

At that moment of indecision, someone grabbed her wrist and hoisted her to her feet as if she weighed nothing. She spun around and collided with a wall of flesh. Blake. For an instant, standing in a dance pose, she was transported back to Ruis's wedding. He looked as stunned as she felt. What if Blake had not been there to stop her? Looking beyond Blake's startled face, she saw Vincent charging toward her. She dropped her Taser. She twisted her wrist free and ran out of pure instinct, out of fear and guilt at being caught in a murderous rage.

Vincent chased her with powerful, frightening speed like a train. The floor shook under his feet. She ducked into a dark doorway. Then the unthinkable happened, Vincent glared at her over the barrel of his handgun. Nothing could have prepared her for having the man of her dreams aim a gun at her heart. If only he had pulled the trigger, she never would have heard he was protecting the Pirarucu Man, the one Flanagan called Guerra, the one Vincent called Silva. The words cut through her like bullets.

A whisper of rustling leaves caught her attention. Surprised to find a garden, Nefi stepped off Fifth Avenue between 49th and 50th streets into a mini park and stared up at the largest tree. As she had done in childhood, she climbed as high as she could into the sheltering arms of a tree to quiet herself and shut out the upside-down world. There she prayed.

Verses from the Book of Proverbs bubbled to her consciousness. They admonished her to trust in the Lord instead of in her own understanding. The Proverbs also reminded her to shun evil. It was easy to shun evil like the Pirarucu Man. He embodied hatred. Hatred, her father once told her, consumed those who fed it to their hearts. She recognized burning hatred in the Pirarucu Man because the same fire consumed her from the inside out. The bombing had rekindled it. This realization horrified Nefi. Shame swelled inside her, forming tears.

Hate had brought her to this place, to this time, to this horrible situation. He killed her parents, so she cut off his hand and stole his ring. He then bombed her uncle's house, leading her to attack him in a bar. She was caught in a cycle of violence with a sociopath. She begged for God to make it stop.

In the endless noise of the city that never sleeps, Nefi listened for what other students and her professors had denounced and mocked. The consensus had never influenced her beliefs. She knew she was different, and she embraced her individuality. Though she had never heard God's voice like Moses had, when she prayed and listened, oftentimes verses whispered truths she needed to hear. This time, the truth came from the Book of Luke.

Do not judge, and you will not be judged. Do not condemn, and you will not be condemned. Forgive and you will be forgiven.

Forgiving was the hardest part. Nefi whispered, "For seven years I've judged and condemned him. He is yours to judge, not mine. Please, Lord, even if he escapes the punishment of man's law for his crimes, he is yours to judge. Please forgive me. And please keep him far from Uncle Ham and Aunt Louise." She sealed her prayer with tears. Peace washed over her as the burden of hatred lifted from her.

She knew what to do and whom to trust. Uncle Ham and Aunt Louise loved her unconditionally. They deserved to know she was alive. Ruis and Martina treated her like family. Surely, they missed her. And Vincent. Oh, Vincent. She pulled the dog tags up to her lips. *Love is patient. Love is kind.* Her eyes stung. She inhaled deeply against a crushing feeling in her chest. *Love does not demand its own way.*

For seven years, she wanted him because, like her, he heard the unspoken. Like many, he dismissed his gift as intuition. She also wanted him because he was kind and good and so, oh, magnificently male. But did he want her? Quelling her pride, she asked herself more questions. And was she the person God wanted Vincent Gunnerson to love and cherish for life? Did she serve his best interest? Her tears flowed. Her heart sank like a crushing weight on her chest.

Maybe not. Maybe he doesn't want me. Love does not demand its own way.

She let his dog tags drop the length of the chain on her chest. She finally, completely let go of Vincent.

Resolved, she climbed down from the shelter of the tree and trod to Times Square. A shell of temporal flesh, her body moved at her command, out of duty instead of passion. She asked a passing couple if she could use their cell phone. When they hesitated, she offered her watch to them. Refusing the watch, the man handed Nefi his cell phone. She pressed the keys to one of the few phone numbers she ever memorized. It rang four times.

"The number you have reached is not in service at this time. If you feel you have reached this number in error, please hang up and dial again."

She handed back the phone. The house burned. The land line was not forwarded. Where would Aunt Louise and Uncle Hamilton be? Nefi wandered down the street. Crossing the street toward her was a pair of Hispanic men wearing red berets, black pants, and white t-shirts. Their t-shirts read Guardian Angels. Once again strangers arrived when she needed angels.

"Excuse me," she said, stopping them on the sidewalk. "Can you tell me where to find the nearest police station?"

"Have you been mugged?" the older one asked.

So I look as bad as I feel. "I want to turn myself in."

"Have you committed a crime?"

"My name is Nefi Jenkins."

The older Guardian Angel pulled a smartphone from his back pocket. He quickly accessed a website and held his phone up, glancing from it to Nefi and back. "Where do you live?" he said. It was a test.

"I don't have a home anymore," Nefi said.

"Where *did* you live?"

Nefi recited her uncle's McLean, Virginia address.

The man lowered his smartphone and nodded to his companion. The younger man pulled a cell phone from his pants pocket. He pressed one number and held it down before he put the phone to his ear.

"Where have you been?" the older Guardian Angel asked Nefi.

"I don't want to talk about it."

The man raised his eyebrows. The younger man talked into his phone, giving a quick description of his location. He then described Nefi and her clothing. When he was done, he stuffed his cell phone in his pocket. "Now we wait."

Nefi leaned against the wall of a souvenir store. Traffic flickered, raced, roared, thumped, and honked on both sides of the boulevard. To her, the traffic no longer represented people on their way to places, but sound and light and the smell of exhaust fumes. Flattened paper cups billowed over the curb. Stunted dirty trees poked up through concrete, and a partially crushed drink can rattled along the curb. Glass shards glittered from the pavement as passing headlights shone on them. A man in a tight black top, miniskirt, high heels and makeup, walked by arm-in-arm with another man. They stopped and lit a cigarette in front of Nefi, who stared.

The man in the skirt squinted at Nefi. "See something you like?"

"I have those same heels," she said. Same color, same size. She had worn them to Ruis's wedding to impress Vincent. They had made her feel pretty in a grown up way. They must have burned with the house.

The cross-dresser's expression softened. "You have good taste."

A dark sedan pulled up to the curb, its red strobe light flashed on the dashboard. A man and woman wearing dark suits emerged from the car. The woman spoke on a walkie-talkie.

"We're there." The woman lowered the walkie-talkie. "Miss Nefi Jenkins?"

"Yes."

The couple with the cigarette scooted out of the way to watch.

"Cancel the BOLO on Jenkins. Over."

Nefi's chest muscles tightened. Someone had issued a Be-On-the-Look-Out notice for her. Had someone declared her dangerous? The man from the sedan pulled a thin wallet from his suit jacket. He held it up to the Guardian Angels and to Nefi. The wallet had a metal shield on one half and an identification license on the other. His photo resembled him in the way a younger brother might. "I'm detective Black, and this is my partner, detective Sanderson."

Nefi braced herself for the possibility the detectives would arrest her. In an upside-down world, anything was possible. Since the FBI protected killers like the Pirarucu Man, perhaps they would prosecute her for attacking him. She reminded herself to surrender to God's will.

Weary, fearless, she had lost a battle against evil from her past.

The man she loved and had hoped to share her future with had threatened her at gunpoint. That left an empty, uncertain present. Her aunt and uncle might rejoice she was alive only to mourn her disgrace for being arrested. If only Vincent had shot her in the alley, she would be with her parents in heaven, instead of being stuck in this nightmare.

"Thank you, gentlemen," Black said to the Guardian Angels. "Miss Jenkins? Please, come with us."

Nefi handed her purse to Sanderson. She then turned and held her hands behind her back.

"What are you doing?" Sanderson asked.

"I stole a bike," Nefi said. "I assaulted three, no four men and I interfered with a federal investigation."

The cross-dresser slowly shook his head and said, "Now that's a bad day."

It wasn't just a bad day; it was the second worst day of Vincent's life. Nefi, who trusted and adored him, thought he had betrayed her. Flanagan's briefing on the ride to the field office brought the full impact of the situation into painfully sharp perspective.

According to Flanagan, Nefi had waited on his doorstep when she needed help. That was the night Rose walked out on him and, taking Blake's advice, he let her. Then he went to Flanagan's pub to drink until he could no longer make a fist, but it wasn't losing Rose that drove him to drink. He could admit it now that it was fear that Nefi had been killed in the blast. That night he feared she was gone forever. Diving into the bottomless well of stupidity, he swallowed alcohol faster than his liver could process it, drinking himself into a dreamless stupor. During that time, a girl he often thought of, dreamed of and fondly hoped to meet again had helped haul him from the cab to bed. And he missed it. If only he had not been drunk, he could have given her the help she sought. He could have offered her shelter and comfort.

If only he had never met Rose, he could have danced with Nefi at Ruis's wedding. If only he had known what Damiano Guerra was doing when he wasn't under surveillance, he might have been able to prevent the bombing. The informant was extremely lucky, or foolhardy, or smart enough to trick his usual contact. Probably lucky. Creeps like Guerra were rarely smart.

If only Vincent could find Nefi, he would embrace this one opportunity after squandering the others. Would she head for the park? It was midnight, an unsafe time to be in Central Park. Did she have any cash? Was she still running to get as far from him as possible? She didn't appear injured, but after the house blew up she might not be in her right mind. How much tragedy could she take before losing her hold on sanity?

Unable to sit at his desk, Vincent paced the clearing by the elevator, cell phone in hand, praying for Nefi. Where was she? He longed to get back out to search for her. She might feel at home there in Central Park. He had to find her and explain how things were not what they seemed. He needed for her to know how terrible he felt about all his missed opportunities to help her.

Blake stood up from his cubicle and shouted, "NYPD found her!"

. 23 .

In Times Square, Sanderson applied handcuffs. "The BOLO said she was wanted for questioning." She felt Nefi's purse. "What do you have in here?"

"A knife. I lost my Taser."

Sanderson scowled at Nefi. "Okay." She patted Nefi down for other weapons.

Black opened the back door of the sedan in a gesture of duty, not chivalry. Nefi climbed into the back seat. The back doors locked with a metallic *clunk*. The detectives climbed into the front seats and started the car. The air conditioner blew on Nefi's face, chilling her tears. Otherwise, she floated in a general numbness that distanced her from her body. Where joy and hope once lived, hollow spaces grew. Freed from burning hatred, she also felt devoid of love. She could no longer convince herself that Vincent loved her the way she loved him. She watched people and cars and buildings blend into a blur of colors, shapes, and light through the smudged passenger side window. The backseat reeked of sweat, hinted of urine. The stained seat absorbed her tears. It was a bad day. A very bad day in a series of very bad days.

She whispered to herself in Portuguese. "Though God forgives me, I accept the consequences of my actions. Let no one else be harmed because of me. I am a fool." She had saved herself for a man who almost shot her in the alley behind a sleazy dance club. *What good is honor and purity in this world? I let go of my will and turn my fate over to you, Lord.*

When the car stopped at twenty-six Federal Plaza off Broadway, the detectives climbed out. The door opened. Black put a hand on Nefi's shoulder to guide her toward the open plaza. A low square building with dark windows sat on the far side of the plaza. Looming behind it was a taller building of forty or so stories. The windows of the Jacob Javits Federal Building zig-zagged at different elevations so that the white frames and the dark windows appeared to be giant zippers set side by side up its height.

She thought the huge building must be the main office of the New York City Police Department. She hoped she might have her own cell in lockup.

Sanderson and Black flanked Nefi as they strode through the plaza and passed a low, black curved wall. On the surface of the black stone, Nefi spied her reflection as a tall, indistinct shape of light and dark moving across the blackness. Like a ghost.

Sanderson opened the door and followed Black and Nefi into a large atrium featuring a set of uniformed guards behind a desk. Blocking the main corridor to the elevators was a series of security scanners. Sanderson and Black showed their identification to the guards. One of the guards lifted a phone receiver.

"Please inform Agent Gunnerson that Detectives Sanderson and Black are here with the girl."

What? The floor tilted and swayed underfoot. Emotional and physical exhaustion slammed Nefi. This was not the police station. She backed away from the guard desk into detective Black. "No. No. No." Her resolve weakened under the effects of exhaustion, hunger, and hopelessness. She couldn't face Vincent. She fought to breathe. Gasping, she saw darkness squeeze the world into a pinpoint of light then she pitched forward into bottomless blackness.

⚬══✦══⚬

Vincent rushed down the hallway toward the security scanner on the east side of the plaza entranceway. He spotted Nefi in handcuffs, falling face-first toward the floor. A man and a woman caught her just as her knees touched the floor. He reached the couple seconds later as they eased Nefi to the floor.

A guard leaned over the reception desk. "Is she drunk?"

Vincent scowled at him.

Detective Black checked Nefi's pulse at the neck. "She fainted."

"Take off the handcuffs," Vincent said. "She's a witness."

"She told us she assaulted four men and interfered with a federal investigation," Black said fumbling for her key.

Vincent's heart sank because Nefi assumed blame. "Self-defense and accidental."

Sanderson opened Nefi's purse and showed him the hunting knife.

"That was a gift." As soon as he said it, he realized how absurd it sounded. It was a weapon.

Black removed the handcuffs. Vincent knelt on the floor where he cradled Nefi in his lap. Nefi generated warmth where her body touched his. Her long hair draped over her shoulder and down her back. He brushed the hair from her face. A hand-shaped bruise on her cheek marked where Rykov had struck her. Her skin was soft and warm; her breathing regular but shallow. He gently patted her face on the unblemished side. Her eyes were closed, but he saw her face as it had looked the moment she stepped into the light in the alley, confused and vulnerable, surrendering to

307

him at gunpoint. If only he had recognized her earlier, he would never have frightened her. *If only.*

"Shouldn't her feet be higher than her head?" Black said. "You know, to get blood to her brain?"

Vincent didn't want to let her go again. He had missed too many chances already.

The security guard handed Vincent an oblong wad of gauze, so Vincent pinched the gauze to break the small glass vial inside. He waved the intense-smelling vial under Nefi's nose.

She rallied and lifted her hands to her face. Her breathing became rapid as she looked up at Detectives Sanderson and Black. Struggling to sit up, she planted her hand on Vincent's knee. She looked up as if to see whose knee it was.

"You're safe now." Holding her close, Vincent wanted to hold her until the world stopped spinning.

Nefi pulled her hand off Vincent's knee and eased out of his hold. Detectives Black and Sanderson lifted her to her feet. She wobbled, so they steadied her by draping her arms over their shoulders, Black on one side and Sanderson on the other. Vincent climbed to his feet. He led the group to the scanner. He removed his watch and badge and set them in a plastic bin. He strode through the scanner and waited on the far side for Nefi.

Nefi did not look at him. Leaning on the counter by the scanner, she removed dog tags on a long shot bead necklace and dropped them in a bin. Blake had said that she wore them, but Blake often kidded him about Nefi. Sanderson put Nefi's purse in the same bin. Sanderson and Black unloaded their weapons and badges in the bins and followed Nefi through the scanner.

The security guard held up the hunting knife. "I'll have to keep this here. Someone can pick it up later." The guard tagged the knife with a number and dropped a matching tag on Nefi's purse.

Vincent gathered his belongings, returning them to their places. He then picked up the bin that held Nefi's purse and the dog tags. Nefi slung the purse strap over her shoulder, leaving it hanging on the opposite hip. She wandered toward the elevator before he could hand her the dog tags, so he followed her.

Sanderson and Black came along. Vincent held the warm dog tags in front of Nefi. She turned away. Nefi's refusal to take the dog tags cut through him worse than Rose's shouted insults. Stung, Vincent pocketed them. The four rode the elevator in silence.

The elevator doors opened to reveal Quinn Flanagan, two women, another man, and Blake discussing protocol. Blake held a cloth-covered gel pack over his left eye. Nefi avoided eye contact with Quinn and Blake. She couldn't bear to see their disappointment in her. Conversation stopped as everyone turned toward her. Quinn introduced Nefi to the new Assistant Director, Samuel Watson, and Brazilian Federal Agents Giada and Lucille. Giada held a folder in her hand. Detectives Sanderson and Black introduced themselves to the group. Watson gave the detectives a quick briefing on the arrest of Rykov, who was theirs for the taking on an assault charge. Flanagan brushed back Nefi's hair to show the bruise handprint on the left side of her face.

Detective Sanderson took a photo of Nefi's injury with her cell phone. A man entered from the hallway with a large digital camera and what looked like half of a stainless steel picture frame. He sneered at detective Sanderson's cell phone.

Vincent rolled a chair up to Nefi, so she sat. "I'll get water," he said and left the group.

"Hold still, Miss Jenkins," the stranger said. He handed the metal piece to Sanderson.

Sanderson held the small metal ruler to the side of Nefi's face while the stranger took photos. Nefi held still while the attention given to the bruise mocked her. Sure it throbbed, but the real damage, her broken heart, cut like glass at her insides.

The photographer told Detective Sanderson that he would forward the digital images to her if she gave him her email address. They drifted away from the others to scribble contact information on paper.

Vincent handed Nefi a cold bottle of water. She took it without looking up and acknowledged his kindness with a nod. She twisted the top off and took a long drink to prevent another embarrassing blackout. She couldn't bear being comforted by Vincent again. His presence reminded her of another loss in her life.

Watson announced that though Rykov had no Interpol notices, three other warrants came up matching his fingerprints: two from New York State and one from New Jersey under different aliases. His bodyguards also had outstanding warrants in Connecticut. Watson directed detectives Sanderson and Black to where they could pick up Rykov. Sanderson and Black left.

Giada, Lucille, Quinn, Watson, and Vincent talked among themselves. Blake eased up close beside Nefi. He handed her his gel pack. His swollen eye had begun to change color.

She knew that to refuse the gel pack would hurt Blake's feelings, so she held it on the left side of her face. She was too exhausted to argue. "I'm sorry," Nefi told Blake. His swollen eye, she believed, was somehow her fault.

Giada, a shapely woman in her thirties, rolled a chair up toward Nefi. "The evidence you collected will help our case," she said. "I need to take your statement about how you know Guerra. Are you up to it?" She sat.

Nefi nodded. Being treated like a victim instead of a criminal put her at ease.

"What do you know about Guerra's business here in the states?"

"He and Cortes have a shipment of three containers at the docks," Nefi said.

Watson, standing with his arms crossed over his chest, grimaced and added, "At the Redhook Terminal."

"Who was the other man at the club?" Nefi said.

Flanagan said, "The man you Tased is a Russian drug dealer, named Rykov."

"I interrupted their meeting." Silence confirmed Nefi's suspicion that she had ruined the informant's set up, and that she had interfered with FBI work.

Flanagan spoke barely above a whisper to Watson, who nodded.

What now?

Director Watson addressed Vincent and Blake. "Gentlemen, because of your previous association with Miss Jenkins, you should step away from this business with Guerra. I'll assist the Brazilian officials with the interviews on this case. Bring me your reports in the morning."

"Yes, sir," they answered. Vincent stepped closer to Nefi.

Watson, Flanagan, and the Brazilian agents huddled to discuss the interviews.

Vincent dropped to a knee in front of Nefi and spoke in warm, deep tones, "I didn't know Silva was Guerra. I am so sorry."

Nefi nodded at the floor in her struggle for composure. Vincent's presence drew all her senses to him. His aftershave wafted against her. Aramis. Her favorite. Her pulse quickened when he stood. She longed to touch him while his shadow covered her like angel's wings. He distracted her so much it clouded her mind. She couldn't allow herself to read his body language. His shoes pivoted away from her.

She had to shed Guerra and vengeance from her life. She had to turn him over to God and the FBI. Guerra's business threatened thousands. She measured her needs and desires against the living danger of his crimes. It would be childishly selfish to put her feelings ahead of the investigation.

She glanced at Vincent on his way to the elevators. His left hand was on his face. Was he rubbing his eye because he was tired? Was he disappointed in that girl he once rescued? The image of him walking away became one last memory of him to keep. She prayed for God to forgive her for bringing chaos and sorrow. He was a good man. God would choose someone for Vincent, someone who wouldn't bring him trouble, someone who would treasure him. Someone...else.

Nefi looked back down. The weight of frustration over her parents' murders eased with the realization that Damiano Guerra was finally in custody. Though it cost her dearly, the day had at last arrived when she could let go of guilt. She had found the murderer. Droplets landed near her feet. *I fought a good fight.*

Blake patted her back and said softly in her ear, "Vincent is still in the sixties, right?"

Nefi grabbed Blake's sleeve. She would forgive Vincent whether or not he forgave her. She nodded slightly. Vincent was not the problem. Soon all would know that she set the series of violent acts in motion by one of her own. She tried to let go of the last of her hope for Vincent's love. She hoped for his love and longed for it, but she didn't know if he felt the same way. She didn't have the chance as long as he thought of her as a child. She regretted her naïve selfishness. *Love does not demand its own way. Let him go. Let him go.* She realized she was still holding Blake's sleeve. She looked up at his eyes.

"Thank you," she whispered, "for stopping me...at the club."

"If I'd known he was the one, I would have let you whup him," Blake whispered.

"I would have killed him," she confessed, releasing his sleeve.

Blake's lips parted. He took in a quick breath. "That would have put him out of his misery, but it wouldn't end yours."

Nefi heard his words as if they echoed through Blake's soul. It was a distinctive sensation to hear someone voice a deep, personal lesson. Nefi knew he had served in combat. Certainly, he had wrestled through the distinctions between murder and killing, and between the duties of being a Christian and being a soldier. He understood. He has taken a life.

Blake glanced at Vincent and the elevators.

Nefi nudged him, "Go."

Flanagan and Watson, standing a few feet away, turned toward Nefi and Blake. The elevator chimed. Blake dashed to it.

Nefi turned her face from the elevator so she couldn't take one last look at Vincent. Soon after, the doors closed. Vincent and Blake were gone.

Vincent imagined the walls closing in, ready to crush him. He wiped his sweaty palms on his pants. When the elevator opened to the lobby, relief flooded through him. He activated his cell phone and, staring at it, sighed. "The only number I have for Senator Jenkins is his McLean home number." Emotionally gutted, he rubbed away tears before stepping out of the elevator into the corridor. The lobby was mercifully empty except for the night guards.

"What about Ruis's parents?" Blake asked. "They're neighbors and friends."

Vincent nodded. They were more than neighbors if Nefi and Ruis's little sister were best friends. He could have called the Virginia State Police, but notifying Senator and Mrs. Jenkins required a personal approach. He called Ruis. Whatever time zone Ruis was in he would take the call or listen to the message as soon as he could. At least someone would be happy after all this.

Vincent spoke after Ruis's automated answering message beeped. "This is Vincent. Nefi's alive and well. Please tell Senator Jenkins that she's at the New York office of the FBI. Have him ask for Assistant Director Watson." He tucked his phone into his pocket, where it clinked against the dog tags.

Blake patted Vincent's shoulder. "There you go. Ever faithful, ever thoughtful."

An odd thought brought a chuckle out of Vincent. "You know, the most dangerous person we encountered in the Amazon was the teenage girl we were sent to rescue."

Blake nodded.

Nefi was out of Vincent's hands, but not his heart. Nefi had let him go. From being idolized to being despised, he had achieved the fastest descent rate possible in freefall—terminal velocity. It was like his jumpmaster once said while checking his parachute, "It isn't the fall that kills you. It's that sudden stop at the end."

"How long until the translator arrives?" Assistant Director Watson said into the phone. "Thank you." He hung up. "Twenty minutes."

"I can interpret," Nefi said. She spoke Portuguese fluently, and she could read their body language and facial expressions.

Patronizing smiles broke out on the others.

"We have to use a translator who isn't involved in the case," Watson told Nefi.

Flanagan spoke to Watson. "That's not what she means. Remember the Patrone case in ninety-three?"

"Sure."

"And how we broke it?"

The Assistant Director's eyebrows rose. "That Mossad interviewer?"

"Nefi can do it."

Nefi saw their smiles fade.

"I don't know. Juries don't trust voodoo psychobabble about reading body language and micro-expressions. She's still involved in the case."

"But it can point us toward concrete evidence," Flanagan said.

"Can you read a subject from the other side of a mirrored window?" Watson addressed Nefi.

"Yes, sir."

Watson turned to Giada and Lucille. "Interview them one at a time. You wear an earpiece. Miss Jenkins will be in the booth with Quinn and me."

Giada planted a hand on her hip. "If she knows something, she can tell me now."

"Guerra shot and killed two of his own men in the jungle," Nefi said. "It might have been accidental because he was panicked."

"How do you know this?" Giada said, opening the folder of reports sent to her from Brazil on the Jenkins murders. She had not had time to read them.

"I was there."

"When?"

"Seven years ago," Nefi said.

"What? When you were twelve?" Giada asked.

"Fourteen." Nefi remained calm in the face of disbelief. She could prove her ability if given the chance and winning that chance depended on convincing everyone involved.

"Where?" Lucille asked.

"Twenty kilometers up the eastern bank of the Juruá River from where I lived."

"Why were you there?" Watson asked.

"I was hunting him because he shot my parents to death."

"How do you know that?" Watson asked.

"I witnessed it." Nefi closed her eyes a moment then opened them. She tamped down emotions and images that threatened to unravel her. In a silent prayer, she asked for God to grant her the strength to endure a little longer.

"Those murders aren't even on our warrant," Giada said to Lucille.

Lucille addressed Nefi. "You were hunting armed men in the jungle?"

"Who else was with you?" Watson asked.

"I was alone." Nefi dug into her messenger bag and handed a gold jaguar head ring to Flanagan. It looked like something a pimp would wear, flashy, gaudy and gold. "This belongs to Guerra."

Flanagan lifted the ring off Nefi's hand. "Did you take it from him before or after you cut off his hand?"

"After."

Flanagan just had to ask. "Why?"

She recalled how he searched for his hand. He couldn't just pull it back on, so she wondered why he was trying to find it. Then she saw the gold ring. "Because he wanted it."

Lucille and Giada gaped at the ring.

"And my fingerprints are on the rifles found near the bodies of his men." Nefi's words had the weight of a confession.

Nefi had told Flanagan she handled the guns.

"That's easy to prove." Lucille fingerprinted Nefi and scanned the prints into her laptop.

While the group waited for the results, a well-dressed, sweating bald man arrived who identified himself as Mr. Cortes's lawyer. He was escorted to the interview room where Cortes was held.

While they waited for a reply from the Brazilian police and the translator, Giada and Lucille read the files on Cortes and Guerra. They marked notes on the papers. Watson carried a fresh cup of coffee to his office.

Flanagan pulled up a chair near Nefi, who slouched in a desk chair. "I wish you had waited for me at the house."

"Your wife was so upset. She saw me as trouble. That's what I bring to everyone."

"Those men in custody are the problem," Flanagan said. "You are the solution."

Lucille checked her laptop. "Nefi's fingerprints match the unknown prints found on the guns."

Flanagan asked Lucille, "Where exactly were the unknown fingerprints found?"

"On the handles and barrels."

"On the trigger?" Flanagan asked.

Lucille pointed to the screen of her laptop that showed red arrows where the unknown prints were located on the weapons.

"Just to be clear," Flanagan added, "whose fingerprints were on the triggers?"

Lucille smiled. "The gun used on Guerra's thugs and the Jenkins couple had Guerra's fingerprints on the trigger."

Flanagan clapped his hands and hugged Nefi.

"So," Giada said to Nefi, "the evidence says you were there. I'm willing to believe you cut off his hand. Now, how can you help us prove that Cortes and Guerra are working together?"

"I can tell you what people don't say." Nefi's calm, steady gaze at Giada was the same as the one Flanagan had experienced when he doubted.

He grinned. "Go ahead, show her."

"You think this is," Nefi stated, "a phenomenal waste of time and resources."

"Exactly."

"If we learn anything useful then it won't be a waste." Nefi stood half a foot taller than Giada. "You don't like owing favors, so humor Assistant Director Watson by paying him a favor now."

Giada mumbled, "I do hate owing favors." She closed her eyes and said, "What am I thinking right now?"

Nefi snorted. "You think American coffee is disgusting."

Giada's eyes popped open. "Good guess."

Lucille piped in. "Guess what I'm thinking."

"You wish I had cut off Guerra's head instead of his hand."

Lucille backed up a step.

Flanagan handed Giada the gold ring. Giada glanced at Nefi as if reassessing her.

Watson emerged from his office. "The translator's coming up." He strode through the room toward the elevators.

The rest of the group crowded into the booth between the rooms where Guerra and Cortes waited separately. Through one-way mirrored windows, Cortes was visible at a table with a lawyer beside him; through the other window, Guerra sat alone. The recording officer, who sat at a panel of screens and dials inside the booth, handed an earpiece to Giada. Giada poked the small device into her ear canal.

Watson opened the door to the control booth.

Lucille held up two files. "Which one first?"

"Guerra," Watson said. He then escorted the translator into Guerra's interview room and introduced the translator to Guerra.

Nefi touched Giada's arm. "I still don't know *why* he killed my parents."

Giada and Lucille looked at the file transmitted from Brazil. They had scribbled notes in the margins of the report.

"He came to our village to buy fish," Nefi said. "We called him the Pirarucu Man."

"Is *pirarucu* Portuguese for ugly?" Flanagan asked.

"It is a type of fish." Giada closed the folder and placed a hand on Nefi's shoulder. "In two-thousand-two police received a tip from an American in Manaus about a suspicious shipment of Arapaima. The port authorities intercepted that shipment. It contained two hundred pounds of whole fish packed with cocaine."

Nefi exhaled as if experiencing an epiphany. She closed her eyes and covered her face with her hands.

To Flanagan, Giada added, "The tribal people call it *Pirarucu.*"

Her parents died because of cocaine.

Flanagan draped an arm around Nefi's shoulders. "Does it help to know?"

Nefi nodded and leaned against him. "The legend of the

Pirarucu tells of a vain, violent man who mocked his elders and the gods. The gods struck him with lightning and turned him into a giant ugly fish. You've heard of piranha?"

"Vicious little buggers," Flanagan said.

"*Pirarucu* eat piranha." Nefi turned toward Giada. "I overheard Guerra and Cortes talking about hiring prostitutes to role-play being abducted and interrogated."

Lucille entered the conversation. "Did you get a sense of whether the men were the aggressors or the submissives?"

"I called escort services for Portuguese-speaking escorts. One company offered a dominatrix pair."

Giada and Lucille swapped smiles. Giada stood in front of Nefi. "Are you ready?"

Nefi nodded and stood by the one-way window facing Guerra's interview room.

Giada left moments later to appear in Guerra's room, where he was handcuffed to a steel table that was bolted, like his chair, to the floor. His left hand was back on the stump of his forearm; his feet, shackled and chained to a metal brace on the floor. Giada sat on a rolling chair on the other side of the table from him.

"What brings you to New York City, Mr. Guerra? Business or pleasure?"

The translator began to speak, but Guerra cut him off.

"I am not stupid. I understand English." Guerra leaned back in his chair.

"Are you in town for business or pleasure?" Giada asked.

"Both."

"What did that girl do to make you so angry?"

Guerra rolled his shoulders back. "She electrified a man sitting by me."

"So you care about this man?"

Guerra sneered. "I took offense."

"Did you take offense because you recognized the girl who cut off your hand?"

Guerra's eyes widened. He lowered his chin to his chest and glared at Giada. "Is that the lie she told you?"

"How did you lose your hand?"

Guerra's nostrils flared, and he squinted. "Why do you care?"

"I don't. I was just curious." Giada held up the ring long enough for Guerra to get a good look at it then she shrugged and put the ring in her jacket pocket. Guerra watched her and continued to stare at the pocket. Giada tapped the table. "We have your boss Cortes in custody."

She tapped her pen tip on the table. "Mr. Cortes is really upset with you," Giada said.

Guerra raised his face. His mouth and eyes opened wide.

"He's angry that my partner and I aren't hookers. What's that about?"

"Let me speak to him!" Guerra's face flushed. He tried to stand, but the chains restricted him to a stooped position.

"Mr. Cortes is consulting with his lawyer. Where is your lawyer?"

Guerra sat.

In the booth, Watson groaned. "Why did she have to say that?"

"Oh, he didn't get you one?" Giada raised her eyebrows in mock surprise. She opened one of the folders and held it up so that Guerra could not read the contents. She lowered her folder to her lap. "Your business in town probably has something to do with three shipping containers that arrived under your name."

Guerra placed his hands palm down on the table.

Watson's voice came through Giada's earpiece. "The shipping manifest lists the cargo as detergent."

"Since when do you ship detergent?" Giada said coyly. "I guess one white powder looks like another."

Guerra said, "I am an informant for the FBI. I am protected."

"Did you read the contract you signed?"

"Of course."

"He's bluffing," Nefi said into the microphone.

"Was your contract in English, or Spanish or Portuguese?" Giada asked.

"I don't remember." Guerra shrugged and crossed his arms over his chest.

Giada pulled a paper from her file. "Is this it?"

Guerra looked at it and nodded.

"Really? You signed your own Interpol notice?" Giada turned the paper around and made a show of examining it.

Nefi was glad Guerra was chained to the table. Giada's goading was bound to set him off eventually. Criminals generally have weak impulse and anger management skills.

"What charges do you have against me?" Guerra said.

Giada read the list of crimes and their country of origin. After reading the Brazilian warrant, she pointed to the bottom with a red manicured fingernail. "And then there's the matter of murdering the Jenkins couple and two Brazilian citizens. I guess the typist missed that. Don't worry. I'll get those added right away."

"Is that what that demon-eye bitch told you?" Guerra spoke in a growl.

"You mean the one who cut off your hand?"

"She lies," his voice grew louder, "Everything she says is lies."

"You have quite an arrest record. How did you end up living on the streets?"

"I am *meninos de rua*, an orphan." He jutted out his chest as he said it.

"You lie," Giada said.

In the observation booth, Nefi nodded. Guerra was lying and proud of it.

"I lived on the streets since I was eight years old." He stabbed the table top with a finger.

"Our records show your parents threw you out." Giada glanced at the file. "The police interviewed them seven years ago because one of the men shot in the jungle was your cousin."

"They are liars. I have no parents. You cannot trust the Rio police."

"I didn't say anything about Rio."

Guerra's nostrils flared. "I have no family! I have nothing to say to you."

"Okay, then I'm done with you for now," Giada said. "Was there anything you would like to tell me about the shipping containers now? Or do you want to wait to be charged when we follow the containers to Buffalo and Pennsauken?"

Guerra's face slackened. Horror set in. He looked like a man condemned.

"If you want to cut a deal, now is the time, because Cortes will let you take the full blame." Giada had her pen poised over a paper in the file. "Especially when he learns that you shot his men after you shot the Jenkins couple."

Guerra sat back, looking stricken. His attention darted to the door.

"No?" Giada slapped the folder closed. "You've been such a help." Giada left.

Nefi walked to the one-way glass. At Guerra, she whispered, "*O, Deus puni-lo-a.*"

"What does that mean?" Flanagan asked.

"God will punish him."

"So you no longer want to kill him?"

Nefi turned her back to the interrogation room to face Flanagan. She shook her head. "He is a small, empty man. He is already a ghost. And when he dies, no one will mourn."

Watson was on his cell phone talking to investigators at the Red Hook Container Terminal. It was six a.m. "Test for cocaine. Pick up is at nine a.m."

Watson's actions meant that the warrant had come in. The door to the observation booth opened.

Giada stepped back into the recording booth and hugged Nefi. "I don't know how you did it, but do it again."

Nefi nodded. This had to be the longest night of her life. Flanagan pitied and admired her. Giada treated her like a magician. Watson wanted to keep her away from the investigation, and Lucille seemed slightly jealous of her. Nefi had waited a long time for justice. If only Vincent had not been involved, this could have been the best night of her life.

"Quinn, bring the translator to Cortes's room," Watson said.

"Yes, sir." Flanagan escorted the translator to the other interview room. The attorney and Cortes refused the services of the translator and signed a form to that effect. The attorney said he would translate, if necessary. Flanagan returned to the control booth.

Giada looked through the window at Cortes. She unbuttoned the top three buttons of her blouse. "Lucille? Care to join me?"

Lucille unbuttoned her blouse to reveal deeper cleavage. "Why not?"

Watson held his hand over his cell phone while he told Giada, "We need to connect Cortes to the shipment. The containers originated in Macapa, Brazil under the name Damiano Guerra." Into his phone, he said, "Sample the containers and install tracking devices. Tail them. Arrest the buyers."

The ladies strolled from the sound booth. Flanagan and Watson exchanged a raised-eyebrow salute to the women before Flanagan grabbed two chairs and followed the ladies. He set the chairs in Cortes's interview room and left. The ladies strutted in and arched their backs while they eased into their chairs.

Flanagan returned to the recording booth for the show.

Nefi elbowed him.

"What?"

"Quit drooling."

"No harm in enjoying one's work," Flanagan said by way of apology. "You know I'm partial to redheads."

Nefi grunted. She sat beside the recording agent who had a distant look in his eyes. "You too?"

The recording agent apologized in his own way. "Hey, I'm paid to watch."

Watson shook his head. Fortunately, the Brazilian agents sat with their backs to the window for the interrogation of Cortes. Giada assumed the lead. She sat on the left, Lucille on the right across the table from Cortes and his lawyer. Giada took the ring from her jacket pocket and set it on the table by the file folders. She clicked her pen and opened the top file, lifting it so that only she could read the contents.

Cortes eyed the ring.

"Mr. Cortes, I'm sorry to disappoint you earlier this evening. Lucille and I really are Brazilian Federal Agents. This isn't a role-playing game as your lawyer can prove. He has copies of our warrant." She flipped through papers in the file.

"My client does not have to speak with you," the lawyer said.

"Frankly, I don't care if he does or not. The FBI tells me that before I can take possession of my prisoners, I have to ask your client a few questions."

Flanagan glanced at Watson's reflection on the one-way window. "Will they get extradited?"

"It's in the works," Watson said.

A measure of relief and joy washed over Nefi. The FBI could charge Guerra with the bombing, but the Brazilians could try him for multiple murders. The Brazilian penal system had a stronger reputation for punishment than the United States did.

"You think you're too good for me," Cortes said.

"It isn't that I'm too good for you," Giada said, "I just don't think I'm bad enough."

Cortes smiled with one side of his mouth. He immediately glanced at Lucille. The insult flattered him.

"He prefers Lucille," Nefi said into the microphone.

Giada slid the file and pen to her partner. "Since I interrogated Guerra," she said in her deep, soft voice, "Lucille, would you brief Mr. Cortes on what we've learned so far?"

"While working for you, Mr. Guerra shipped three containers from Macapa." Lucille pretended to search the papers. "To the Red Hook Terminal here in New York City. Two containers of detergent are supposed to be picked up at nine this morning for shipment by semi-truck to Buffalo, New York."

Giada toyed with the ring. Cortes's gaze followed it. His jaw muscles bulged as he clenched and unclenched his teeth. He wore a similarly gaudy gold ring shaped like a coiled snake with diamond eyes.

"And the third container is supposed to go to Pennsauken, New Jersey," Lucille said.

Giada held up the ring. "Did you give this to Mr. Guerra?"

Cortes slung his back against the back of his chair.

"How sweet," said Giada. "Is this an engagement ring? Or a promise ring?"

Cortes snorted. His attorney reached over to pat him on the shoulder, but Cortes pulled away and glowered at him.

The attorney folded his hands on the table. "My client does not have to speak."

Lucille said, "I wish he wouldn't. That will only slow down this process."

Cortes began tapping his heel at a fast pace.

"Careless of Mr. Guerra to lose such a valuable gift." Giada weighed the ring in her palm. "Solid gold, diamonds and what?" She held it up for Lucille.

Lucille squinted at the ring. "Hematite."

"How sad," Cortes said, "two beautiful women don't know their gemstones."

Giada closed her hand on the ring. "So what's the black stone?"

"Jet. Far more valuable."

"Whatever," Giada pocketed the ring. "I suppose Mr. Guerra told you some grand story about how he lost the ring along with his hand."

Cortes stiffened. He clenched and unclenched his hands.

"Something about being outnumbered and outgunned no doubt," Lucille said. She shook her head. "Men."

Cortes leaned forward, set his forearms on the edge of the table, and folded his hands like his lawyer. "And what story do you have?"

The attorney cleared his throat.

Cortes glared at him.

"A fourteen-year-old girl chopped off his hand with a machete," Lucille said.

Cortes laughed vigorously. "So you do engage in fantasies."

"How else would she get this ring?"

"He likes prostitutes," Cortes punctuated his statement with a wave of his hand. "She probably stole it from him in his sleep."

"This girl isn't for hire," Lucille said.

"So you say. Who is she then?" Cortes made his lawyer squirm by speaking.

"The one who frightened you out of the club last night." Lucille folded her hands on the table.

"I was not frightened," Cortes said. He slid his arms off the table to his lap.

"You ran like a frightened man."

"Your American nightclubs are known for violence. Rappers shoot each other. I heard that twenty-one people died in a stampede in a Chicago nightclub. Knifings, fires." He shuddered. "Only a fool would remain after a fight starts in an American nightclub. I am no fool."

"So what kind of business do you conduct with Mr. Guerra?" Giada asked.

"I manufacture detergent."

"Where?" Lucille asked.

"What?"

"Where is your factory?" Lucille sat with her pen poised over an open file.

Cortes waved a hand in the air. "I have many factories."

"Name the location of one," Lucille said.

He squinted at her then shrugged. "My attorney handles such things."

His attorney blanched.

Lucille waited. Twenty seconds passed in silence.

"Perhaps I should have brought my accountant," Cortes said in clipped English. "In Brazil, I am like your Donald Trump. I own many, many, many properties."

"But you don't know where they are?" Giada said.

"Not even one?" Lucille said. She sounded positively disappointed. She clicked her pen and clipped it to the folder. "I don't think he's been half as helpful as Guerra."

"If we find anything other than detergent in the containers your employee shipped," Giada said, "then we will charge you both with smuggling."

"I am a businessman," Cortes said. "Damiano has taken advantage of me if he ties my name to his drugs. You cannot believe what Damiano says. He was beaten by police when he was very young. It damaged his head."

"Were you also beaten by police?" Lucille said.

"No. Why?"

Lucille spoke softly, "Because we never said anything about drugs."

Cortes leaped to his feet.

His attorney raised his arms as if to protect himself.

"You did!" Cortes pounded the table with his fist. "You said you would charge me with smuggling."

"In Brazil, we prosecute people for smuggling wood, people, rare plants, birds, snakes, and fish as well as drugs."

Both women stood and headed for the door. Flanagan dashed to the interview room door and opened it. As they passed him, Giada winked at him. The door locked behind them.

As the door clicked shut, Cortes backhanded his attorney out of his chair. "You idiot! You are supposed to protect me."

"And you're supposed to shut up and let me do the talking." The attorney scrambled to his feet.

"You're fired."

The attorney knocked on the door. Flanagan bolted from the observation room and freed the attorney. Nefi peered into the corridor as Flanagan escorted him toward the elevator. The attorney, his face red, ripped off his visitor's pass and threw it on the floor.

Watson met Flanagan and the attorney at the elevator. "Are you planning to fight his extradition?"

The attorney eyed Watson and Quinn. "For my safety, he must believe I stirred up a paper storm."

Watson picked up the visitor's pass and handed it to the attorney. "And we will officially curse your name in front of Cortes and Guerra."

The attorney turned the badge over in his hands as if examining it. "If you let him cool off in a cell, he'll call me back tomorrow."

"We can do that," Watson said. He nodded at Flanagan.

"Who's representing Guerra?"

"He hasn't asked for an attorney," Flanagan added.

The attorney pulled out his wallet and from it, he plucked a business card. "Let him know about this lady. I'll call her and get her up to speed on the situation, just in case."

. 24 .

Evening had fallen by the time Senator Hamilton Jenkins pulled up to the guard's booth at the entrance to the old McLean, Virginia neighborhood. It was the first time Nefi had been back since the bombing, and she was eager to apologize to Martina for letting her believe the bomb had killed her. Though it had only been five days since the bombing, it felt like much longer. The entrance guard stepped up to the driver's side window of the rental car and did a double take.

"What a joy to see you, Senator and Miss Jenkins!" Mr. Dawson placed a hand over his heart. "Not much left of the house. No, sir. Sure hope they catch the criminals who did it."

"Thank you, Mr. Dawson," Hamilton said. "The FBI and the New York City Police arrested them last night."

"I'm so glad to hear it." He nodded, stepped back from the car and buzzed them through the gate.

They drove halfway through the neighborhood and parked along the curb.

"I believe you should see it."

"It's up to you, Uncle." Having lost a home before, she was prepared for a shock. She had not lost as much in the bombing as her aunt and uncle did. Perhaps he wanted to show her the consequences of her actions.

"Things can be replaced." He patted Nefi's arm. This time, he did not cry like he had at the FBI office.

The bombing could have easily been a far greater tragedy. Nefi refused to imagine what would have happened if Aunt Louise had skipped her weekly Bridge game.

Uncle Hamilton resumed the direct route to the Ramos house, slowing as he passed the charred frame of his once-beautiful home. The yard was cordoned off with yellow crime scene tape. Along the sidewalk mounds of flowers, stuffed animals, burned out candles, and a poster-size portrait of Nefi adorned the sidewalk. The makeshift memorial choked Nefi up. Students had left notes, flowers and photos all over the front lawn. *This time—praise God—the tributes were not a memorial after all.*

Uncle Hamilton wiped away tears and parked the car.

Poor uncle. Nefi lowered her window and rested her face on her forearm. Perhaps a similar tribute had been made after Jason committed suicide. She took in a deep breath. She was awed by the display. Sniffling, she quickly wiped her eyes and sat back in her seat.

"The house was a rental," Hamilton said.

Houses were replaceable. He and Louise had a primary residence that Louise called their real home. They had returned to their real home after the bombing to wait for news about Nefi. She had visited the home when the Senate was in recess a few summers ago. It had a breath-taking garden of herbs and flowers.

Uncle reached into the back seat and handed a Moleskine notebook to Nefi. "Doctor Sloan gave this to me after the bombing. I haven't had the courage to read it."

Nefi eyed the journal. She had written her deepest thoughts, and dreams in it since her first meeting with the psychiatrist. The one secret she had never committed to ink was the one that led to the destruction of the house. She never sullied the journal with any mention of the Pirarucu Man. In many ways, Dr. Sloan knew her better than anyone else could. Just as she had asked him to, the good doctor had given her journal to Uncle Hamilton, believing she was dead. It felt peculiar to see it again under the circumstances.

"Why didn't you read it?"

"I wasn't ready to accept that you were..."

Nefi planted a hand on his forearm. "Let's go."

Having flown into New York City that morning, Uncle Hamilton said he had planned to rent a hotel suite near Washington, D.C., but the Ramos family insisted they stay with them. Aunt Louise had flown directly to Washington D.C. Martina, he said, had dropped her summer classes to come home to prepare a memorial service.

Cars filled the Admiral's driveway and both sides of the street. They parked as close as possible. Nefi reached her hand in the crook of her uncle's arm to escort him to the front door and to anchor them in the reality of the moment. They were stepping off the driveway onto the paved walkway when a shriek sounded. Martina leaped off the front porch steps, down the front yard, and threw herself against Nefi, hugging her.

Nefi barely recognized Martina with short-cropped hair and a nose ring that practically shouted "rebellious phase." Martina's sweet enthusiasm contrasted her tough-girl appearance.

More of the Ramos family and other friends and neighbors swarmed out the front door. Anna, one of the Admiral's grandchildren, wrapped herself around Nefi's knee and would not let go until Nefi picked her up. Anna flung her arms around Nefi's neck and squeezed so hard Nefi coughed.

"I told God," Anna said, "He had to send you back so Aunt Martina would stop crying."

"Thank you, Anna," Martina said. Eyes welling, she pried the toddler off Nefi and carried her on her hip.

The whole procession trooped into the house and spread out

into other rooms. In a swirl of activity, the neighbors, friends, and family brought out food and chairs and drinks while dozens of lively conversations overlapped. All asked for news from Nefi, but she deferred to Hamilton. He had been briefed by Assistant Director Watson, so he reported the key information that Nefi had helped identify the bombers and they were being deported to Brazil for trial on more serious charges.

Nefi hugged Aunt Louise, each of the Ramos family members, and high school friends who crowded into the house. Notably absent was Ruis, so Nefi assumed he was at work. One of Martina's sisters followed Nefi around the room, photographing the greetings on her cell phone until Admiral Ramos blocked her phone with his hand.

"This is not for public consumption," the Admiral said.

"We owe thanks to Sam Watson, in particular, for leading the investigation and for assisting in the deportation of the bombers." Hamilton glanced at Nefi's Grandfather Ted Wright. "He is Assistant Director of the New York City field office of the FBI."

Grandfather Wright nodded and turned away, cell phone in hand. Ever the newspaper publisher, he had news to print. Good news merited publication this time.

The crush of attention overwhelmed her, so Nefi slipped away with Martina upstairs. Martina and Nefi hugged again in the privacy of Martina's old room.

"I forgive you for not calling me. I don't know how I'd get by without my cell phone," Martina said.

Nefi snorted. "I lose everything but the clothes I had on and you think I missed my cell phone?"

"I'd miss mine." Martina pulled a sweater-wrapped album from her closet and handed it to Nefi. "This was right where you said it would be."

It smelled of smoke. "Thank you." Nefi held it to her chest, hugged Martina, and headed back downstairs. She crossed the room to her Aunt and Uncle, who sat side by side on a loveseat. She handed it to her uncle.

"What's this?" Uncle Hamilton peeled off the sweater to reveal a thick leather-bound scrapbook. His breath caught in his throat.

Louise had lovingly collected mementos, photos, and hair clippings to document Jason's childhood. After his suicide, the album had become evidence of the fragile, fleeting nature of life. Louise caressed the familiar smooth leather cover. Her eyes welled as she covered her mouth with her hand.

Uncle Hamilton spoke to Nefi. "How?"

Nefi said, "I had time to grab one thing."

Aunt Louise rose from the sofa and hugged her. "Thank you." She held Nefi until she could compose herself.

"Nef called me before you picked her up," Martina said. "She told me to get it from the Swanson's pool house."

Their retired neighbors, the Swansons, traveled every summer, leaving their house vacant.

Aunt Louise embraced Martina. "Thank you, dear."

Nefi whispered to her uncle, "Before the Swansons get back, I need to buy them a bike."

Hamilton nodded.

Once again, all she owned was what she wore and carried in her satchel. Amid a house full of celebrating people, she considered her future. Being alive meant she had a future, but then what? Having missed her job interview at the FBI without so much as a courtesy call to cancel, she knew that opportunity was irretrievably gone. Another dream crushed.

. 25 .

Vincent had glimpsed Nefi on the television during a press conference in Washington D.C. in which she thanked the New York City Police Department, the FBI, and the Guardian Angels for their help. While the rest of America seemed to be talking about the death and funeral of singer Michael Jackson, Vincent mourned his severed ties to Nefi. In the week since the arrests and deportation of Guerra and Cortes, he had filed reports and handled smaller tasks assigned by Assistant Director Watson. He was returning from an errand when he overheard his name in the lobby of the Jacob Javits Building of the FBI.

"Is Agent Gunnerson here? I'd like to see him." A short dark-haired woman in blue jeans, a deep V-neck red cotton top, and hiking boots stood at the reception desk. She swung a woven, bright-colored backpack with leather trim onto the granite counter. The silver buckles clinked on the counter top. Vincent detoured to stand behind her.

When the guard glanced up, Vincent shook his head at the guard.

"I will need to see some form of identification," the guard said. Tall, black and muscular, he had a military posture that normally intimidated people, but not this young woman with the spiked hair.

334

She unfastened the strap on her backpack and dug out her wallet and passport.

After the guard took a second comparative look at the Virginia Driver's License and the woman, he finally nodded.

"Yeah, yeah. I changed my hair. Get over it."

A second guard of similar build watched her from his post at the counter.

"Do you have an appointment?" asked the first guard.

"No."

"And what is the nature of your visit?" The guard eyed the passport and then her. "Miss Martina Ramos?"

"Personal. And quit looking at my chest."

"One moment, please." The guard picked up a telephone receiver and pressed numbers on the phone pad. He slid the passport and driver's license back to her slowly enough for Vincent to peek at them. "This is the reception desk. I have a young lady here to see Agent Gunnerson."

Martina Ramos. Ruis's sister?

Martina tucked her driver's license into her wallet then she stuffed it and her passport into her backpack. She drummed her dark green acrylic nails on the counter top.

The guard placed his hand over the mouthpiece. "Are you also called Rose?"

Martina huffed. "No, and I can't believe he is still seeing that—"

"That's a no," the guard said into the phone.

"Tell him I'm here to kick his ass," Martina said. "He'll understand."

"The young lady said she's here to kick his ass and that he would understand." The guard spoke in flat tones as if delivering a message about the weather. "Yes, sir, Agent Clayton." He hung up.

Martina's fingers stopped drumming. "Blake," she enunciated it like a swear word.

"Do you know it's a crime to threaten a federal agent?" the guard whispered.

"Whatever. I'm not threatening him in his capacity as an agent. I'm threatening the man."

After a glance at her backpack, the officer said, "Are you carrying a weapon?"

"No."

"Agent Clayton is on his way down."

"Close enough." Martina slung her backpack strap over one shoulder barely missing Vincent. She marched toward a large window.

Vincent dashed over toward the security turnstile and ran his badge through the sensor. He melded into a group of men by the elevator and stepped out of view of the lobby to wait for Blake.

Traffic in the lobby picked up, mostly outgoing. Through a reflection in the window, Vincent watched Martina pace the lobby. When Blake marched out of the elevator, Vincent pulled him aside.

"I think Rose is here to make a scene," Blake said. "Want me to run her off?"

"It's Ruis's sister, Martina."

"Is she armed?"

"Why would she want to hurt me?"

Blake's mouth fell open, then snapped shut. "You're kidding right?"

"What have I ever done to her?"

"You broke her best friend's heart. Twice." Blake combed his fingers through his hair. "She probably wants to vent. Go hear her out."

Vincent nodded.

Blake snorted. "I'll block, you tackle."

They headed to the lobby.

⚬━✦━⚬

Martina spotted Blake first, followed by Vincent. She tried to swallow, but her mouth dried up. Vincent was even bigger than she remembered from the wedding. A giant in a suit, he wasn't even as good looking as Blake. What had Nefi seen in him? Sure, Nefi's height probably led her to seek taller-than-average men, but Vincent had to be six foot two or six foot three.

"Well, lookie here," Blake said. "If it isn't Ruis's baby sister."

"How are you, Martina?" Vincent asked.

"What did you do to her?" Martina clenched her fists.

"Let's talk over lunch," Blake said. He stepped between Vincent and Martina and put his hand on her back, easing her toward the door.

"Fine," Martina said. Besides, this was not the place to avenge her best friend. Too many witnesses and cameras.

They walked in silence to a pizza buffet, ordered drinks and pizza by the slice, and settled into a table at the back of the crowded room. Martina sipped her Dr. Pepper. Slouching in a cheap metal chair, she crossed her arms over her chest. She had learned from Nefi how to use silence. Actions, after all, did speak louder than words. Sometimes, silence shouted.

Blake dug into his lunch as if at a baseball game, watching opposing sides square off.

Vincent pitched the first ball. "How is she?"

"Devastated. Again." Martina held back the urge to cry. She had warned Nefi about building unreasonable expectations. "First, you miss her graduation. Then you bring that skank to Ruis's wedding."

"Hey," Vincent said.

Blake held up a hand, "Missing graduation was not his fault. His mother was dying."

"Oh. Well, he could have called. God knows Nefi would have forgiven him. But last week? Last week she turned up at my house in tears and refused to talk about her trip to New York. This is your third strike."

"Her trip to New York has been all over the news," Vincent said. "Why do you need her to tell you about it?"

Martina had expected Nefi to confide in her about everything. Ruis assured her that Nefi would talk when she was ready. It really sucked to be out of the information loop. "I'm talking about whatever happened between you and her. She won't talk about any of it. All she said to me was 'thank you for the zip line. It saved my life.'"

"That's a fact," Blake said. "Most folks might call it a coincidence that you gave her the zip line. You probably even think it was your idea, but it looks to me like God had a hand in there somewhere."

Martina's glare stifled Blake.

"Did she tell you she caught the man who killed her parents?" Vincent asked.

She caught him? "No." Was it true? *Why hadn't Nefi told her?* She looked at Blake, who nodded. "That's great. So why is she depressed?"

Vincent loosened his tie and cleared his throat. "Blake and I were protecting him as an informant."

Martina covered her mouth with both hands. *"Oh, Dios mio."*

"Of course, we didn't know he was a killer," Vincent said. He rubbed his face with his hands. "He gave us an alias."

Martina dropped her hands to her lap. "She never knew his name. She called him the Pirarucu Man. Said he was a fish buyer."

Blake said, "He shipped cocaine in the fish."

"His real name is Damiano Guerra," Vincent took a sip of his drink. "The Brazilians took him into custody for murder. All we had on him was the bombing."

"Tell me Brazil has the death penalty," Martina said.

"Their death penalty only applies during times of war, but we've been told the prisons there are brutal compared to ours," Vincent said. "He could live a long miserable life in prison."

"I knew it was bad when she came back without the dog tags."

Martina studied Vincent for his reaction. "Did she lose them?"

"She gave them back to me. You're welcome to hit me if it makes you feel better," Vincent said. "It can't make me feel any worse."

Vincent's sad brown eyes and full lips made him somewhat attractive. At that moment, Martina glimpsed what Nefi adored about him. Kindness. Nefi had a way of seeing the real person while ignoring appearance. It had baffled Martina. Why had Nefi bypassed Blake for Vincent? Both were big hunks. Both lived the Marine code of honor. Both behaved as gentlemen. Both liked Nefi, as far as Martina could tell. Maybe Nefi chose Vincent because he wasn't as good looking as Blake. There would be less competition for him, and it would be easier to earn his devotion.

"She deserves to be treated better," Martina said.

"She won't answer my calls," Vincent said. "My letters to her uncle come back unopened."

"Are you just trying to apologize?" Unwilling to let him off yet, she pushed for more information about his feelings.

Vincent looked stricken. "I can't stop thinking about her."

Infatuation was not enough. Nefi deserved his total devotion or his total absence. "Do you love her?" Martina demanded.

"I hardly know her. What I know I admire." His honesty impressed Martina. He had not mentioned Nefi's beauty, only her character.

Blake made a slurping sound with his straw in his empty paper cup.

Vincent said, "When you see her, please tell her I'm sorry." With that, he left the restaurant.

Blake nabbed Vincent's untouched pizza slice. "It's killing him that she's mad at him."

"Good." Martina bit into her slice of warm, cheesy pepperoni pizza. She had a long flight ahead. Comfort food was just what she needed. Up until the moment Vincent crossed the lobby, she had anticipated a real chance to apply her martial arts training.

She could have brought him down just as surely as David took down Goliath. Vincent wasn't at all the beast she had expected. It galled her to admit she had misjudged him.

"By the way, did you lose a bet?" Blake asked.

"What do you mean?"

"I'm just saying, that chainsaw haircut isn't your best look."

What a flirt. "Like I'm going to take style advice from a Fed?" Martina took another bite of pizza.

"If I invite Nefi to my wedding, do you think she'd show up?" Blake asked.

"You're getting married?"

"Try not to sound so shocked. I am quite a catch, you know." A splotch of sauce hung on the corner of his mouth.

"Most man whores think they are." Martina sipped her drink.

People at nearby tables stole glances at Blake.

"What did you call me?"

"A man whore," Martina said. "A player. People your age probably say playboy." She enjoyed teasing him about his age. *He could dish it out, but could he take it?*

"Why would you say that?" He had not denied it. He took a giant bite of pizza.

"I saw you at Ruis and Sophia's wedding. You were flirting with Nefi *and* an older woman." She spoke loud enough so the people at nearby tables would not have to strain to eavesdrop.

"That older woman is my fiancé." Blake continued to eat Vincent's pizza. "Will Nefi come to my wedding in October or is she mad at me, too?"

"I don't know." Martina sipped her drink.

"I'll send her an invitation. Being a man whore, I'll send you one, too." Blake smirked. "Just so you know—Vincent is serving as my best man."

Martina took the hint. Did Blake share her intentions for Nefi and Vincent? "Is he good enough for Nefi?"

"Yes." Blake swallowed the last of the crust. "I happen to

know that since Nefi gave back the dog tags, he's been wearing the choker she made for her father."

"Are you freaking kidding me?" Hope sprang up in Martina. Maybe Vincent and Nefi were made for each other in their own odd way.

"I'm just saying he kept it all these years," Blake said. "Now he wears it."

She felt a hitch in her throat. "That's so weirdly romantic. You better not be lying."

"On my honor as a gentleman," Blake said. His attention dropped from her eyes to her cleavage.

"Quit stealing glances at my chest."

"Soon as you quit exposing it."

Men.

"So are you going to convince Nefi to come to my wedding?"

"I can try. She left for Brazil last night on a one-way ticket."

. 26 .

Nefi sat at one end of a seven-foot-long mahogany table in the prosecutor's office. To her right a gentleman sat with fingertips poised over a stenotype machine for her testimony. She had already agreed to return to testify at the trial, but this preliminary testimony would serve as evidence for the trial. Lawyers filled the rest of the table. Half of them represented Cortes, one represented Guerra, and the rest were part of the prosecutor's team.

After answering a series of questions from each lawyer, she was told to describe, in her own words, what happened in the village along the Juruá River on August third, two-thousand-two.

Memories long-ago seared into her mind rose to the surface again. She closed her eyes and voiced them.

Her father's rule had been that she was not allowed to go beyond the sound of his voice. She had borrowed her father's binoculars to see what she could from the top of her favorite strangler fig tree, shouting distance from the village.

She watched the Pirarucu Man and two others walk into the village from the river. Their boat was not in sight. In the dry season boats couldn't reach her village, so merchants parked downstream and hiked the rest of the way. As usual, at the arrival of strangers, a bird call sounded, and children ran to their hiding places.

At the warning call, Nefi focused the binoculars at the Pirarucu Man, who pointed to her mother and father. For whatever reason, they knelt in front of him as the villagers circled. The Pirarucu Man lowered his rifle from his shoulder and aimed it at Nefi's mother and father. Two bursts of gunfire sounded. Colors exploded from the nearby trees, followed by frantic flapping.

Nefi opened her eyes at the table of lawyers to ground herself in the present. "I screamed and dropped the binoculars." She took a long drink of water.

The prosecutor nodded for her to continue.

She closed her eyes and returned to the nightmare. She described witnessing the murders through binoculars, scrambling down the tree and running toward the village.

Wailing greeted her when she reached the village. As if a giant invisible hand slammed against her chest, she stopped near the huddled crowd. Sucking air, she plowed through a wall of fear. The shaman shook his walking stick overhead so that the monkey paws tied to the top snatched at the air. Nefi elbowed through sweaty, bare, brown shoulders and stopped barefoot in a puddle of warm blood. She dropped to her knees near her father's back and rolled him face up. His arm dropped away from her mother's body. *So much blood.* Nefi gulped air by the mouthful. How could their bodies hold their souls without blood? She cried out and shook her father's body, but it remained warm and still. Her father couldn't hear her. Blood had seeped from holes in his chest and neck. She hugged him and moaned. Her mother's unblinking eyes faced heaven. Her parents were gone. *Gone to God.*

If this had been an attack from another tribe, every man would have taken machete in hand and fought until every attacker was dead and the pieces of their bodies scattered in the river. It was understood in the jungle that no one challenged men who had guns. The men with the guns gave orders; those without guns obeyed. She was angry and confused that the Pirarucu Man killed her parents.

The family cook, Mali, draped her thin arms around Nefi and tugged her, calling for her to stand up. Nefi complied with the old woman and gradually realized Mali was speaking in Arawak. The tribal sounds tangled through her crooked teeth. She repeated that the ugly frog-faced man killed them.

Nefi's voice quavered when she asked why the Pirarucu Man would do such a thing. Mali said she didn't understand his foreign tongue. Nefi asked her if it sounded like the Bible language Mother taught. Mali shook her head, denying the sound of Portuguese. Was it, she asked, the language of the boatman who brought supplies? Mali shook her head. Not Spanish?

Mali said the killer spoke the love language, meaning the language Mother and Father used in private. *English.*

Nefi asked which way the Pirarucu Man left. Mali pointed toward the northbound trail that ran alongside the river.

The elders proclaimed they would take the bodies to Manaus by boat and all others agreed. One elder ordered Nefi to be a good daughter and pack everything for the trip. He said she would go to Manaus and then be sent to her tribe in the U.S. He insisted it was what her parents wanted. Mali patted Nefi's arm in confirmation. Patting her arms and back, they pushed Nefi toward her hut.

Numbly, she pulled open the plank door to her three-room hut. It was a home, a sanctuary from the rain. It was a school where her parents taught her about the outside world of governments and wars, about the natural world of science, and about God. With fresh eyes, she saw books, pots, clothing, and furniture, pictures in frames, oil lamps, tools, mother's scarf and father's hat. She debated what to pack as she stared at the stack of Bibles and other books her parents treated so tenderly. Familiar treasures all, but her family was destroyed, gone. She was, in effect, being banished from home. The elders wanted to ship her like a box of supplies to America to grandparents, Nana and Papa Wright, whose faces smiled from frames on the wall.

All her life she had longed to go to America. Though born there, she remembered nothing about the country. Her parents had promised that one day, they would move back to live near Nana and Grandpapa. She yearned to meet them to thank them in person for their letters and gifts and clothes. Staring at their pictures, torn between known and unknown worlds, she believed the elders spoke the wishes of her parents.

The idea of packing her family's belongings was like trying to chew boiled Chicle tree sap. No matter how long one chewed, it had no flavor, no texture, no nourishment. It delayed hunger. It did not satisfy it.

She fell to her knees by her parents' bed. Interlacing her fingers in front of her face, she tried to pray. With each breath, she inhaled familiar scents, her mother's perfume, and her father's boots. *Oh, Father God...* She pried open her hands, sticky with blood, and stared at them blurred through her tears. She couldn't pray. She couldn't pack. She paced in a stupor.

Her gaze fell on father's *Bible*, open to a story about a shepherd boy who faced down a giant who had insulted God. The boy, armed with a slingshot and small rocks, risked his life to defend the name of God. There would be no more stories read by her father.

Nefi sighed. Surrounded by things that reminded her of her parents, she let tears burn and fall, blink by blink. Lifeless things. She didn't want things. She wanted what the Pirarucu Man took from her. An unfamiliar sensation, strong, urgent, and primal, grew in her. The intensity of this sensation convinced her that it was right. This evil act awakened the warrior within her. It grew louder in her as she embraced it. She stood and slowly clenched her fists.

She strapped her father's hunting knife to her leg. Placing her satchel strap over her head and shoulder, she filled it with a box of matches, three bananas, a package of dried fish, a small pouch of unripe *Jenipapo* fruit, a small pouch of spiky copper-colored *urucum* fruit, and her compass. She grabbed the sharpest machete by the door and paused. Turning on her bare heel, she faced the window at the back of the hut. She strode to the window, lifted the palm frond flap, and climbed out.

She opened her eyes and found all eyes in the room on her.

The prosecutor cleared his throat. "And where did you do then?"

"I tracked the men to their camp." She then told them about amputating Guerra's hand and hiding up in a tree while he panicked and shot the other two men.

Cortes's lawyers whispered among themselves at the far end of the table with Guerra's listening in.

"How is it you came into possession of this ring?" Cortes's main attorney asked.

"I took it off the Pirarucu—Guerra's—hand."

"The one you cut off?" he asked.

Let him try to make her sound like the barbarian, but the truth was that Guerra was a murderer three times over. "Yes."

"Were you taking a souvenir?"

The prosecutor scowled at Guerra's lawyer. He then turned to Nefi and said, "Why did you take the ring?"

"Because he wanted it." It stung to admit to such petty cruelty, but she had sworn to give a truthful account. She would do her best and leave the results up to God.

Her testimony was followed by two more hours of questions. By the end of the day, she had a strong sense of the prosecutor's skill and the mounting evidence against Cortes and Guerra. The prosecutor's assistant escorted her to the front door.

"I'll give you as much notice as I can for the trial date, so you can get time off from work."

"Thank you, but I'm unemployed."

"I heard that you were planning to work for the FBI. If it might help, my boss could write a letter of recommendation for you."

"It couldn't hurt," Nefi said softly.

A black limousine with diplomatic flags on it pulled up to the curb. The driver, Antonio Morales, came around and opened her door. He was still working as his uncle's chauffeur. Ambassador Morales insisted she stay at their villa while she was in town.

The Prosecutor's Assistant gazed at the gleaming limousine.

"Thank you, sir. It couldn't hurt." She smiled at Antonio. "I'll be out of reach for a few weeks. I booked a boat from Manaus to take me back to the village."

The prosecutor's eyebrows rose. "Be careful, Miss Jenkins. I hope you find what you're looking for."

. 27 .

The Clayton family farm extended across two-hundred acres of rolling hills, watered by a spring-fed lake, bordered on the east by woods and on the west by the Smoky Mountains. The October woods glowed in oranges, flame reds, and bright golds.

Vincent scanned the crowd moving toward the reception area tents, specifically; he was searching the crowd for Nefi. The bride, groom, and others in the bridal party fidgeted through the requisite posed photographs, eager to join the five-hundred guests under the white tents to dine and visit. The photographer, in a race against the setting sun, nagged and cajoled people into place for photos against the stunning autumn backdrop. Finally, the photographer dismissed them, so the group dispersed toward food and friends. Vincent headed toward a table where he saw Quinn and Kate Flanagan.

The wedding reception spread across the fresh-cut lawn between the main house and a giant red barn. Other large buildings clustered in a cove slightly downhill and east of the main house. Vincent guessed these buildings housed farm equipment though he had not seen crops on his way down the winding driveway from the country highway. On the far side of a

348

group of tables that were laden with peach tablecloths, candles, and flowers, Vincent spotted Ruis and Sophia Ramos with the Flanagans. He hoped one of them had seen Nefi.

Blake had promised to invite her. Had she accepted? Ruis said that Martina couldn't come to the wedding. That news dampened Vincent's mood. He believed that if Martina came, Nefi would. He clung to diminishing hope.

Vincent was halfway through the crowd when Blake's father, a robust bald man in his sixties, blocked his path.

"Are you having a good time, Agent Gunnerson?"

"Please, call me Vincent."

"Well, thank you. I'm sorry we didn't have time yesterday to give you a proper tour of the property, but if you're free tomorrow, I can show you around. Do you ride?"

"I've been on a four-wheeler before."

"I meant horseback." Mr. Clayton grinned.

"Does a pony at the fair count?"

"I suppose it does as long as it wasn't a wooden one going in a circle. Riding is the best way to see the farm. I have a gentle Belgian that could support you."

"I'm unfamiliar with horse breeds," Vincent said.

"Think of a Budweiser Clydesdale, only blonde."

By any standard, Blake's family was wealthy. Had Blake's fiancé been as surprised as he was to discover that Blake could have lived off a trust fund instead of taking up a career in law enforcement? "What kind of farm is this?"

Mr. Clayton's wry smile resembled Blake's. "A stud farm."

Well, well. What a surprise. "Blake never mentioned that."

"My boys got ribbed about it in school, but as they grew up, all that teasing nonsense stopped." He waved it off.

"I bet." Considering the size, number, and build of the Clayton sons, it made sense that only a fool would dare mock the family business. At the rehearsal dinner, they had told plenty of stories about Blake that explained a few of his scars and his history of broken bones. The brothers recounted the nurses at the local emergency room by name. As the youngest of the five brothers, Blake endured the wariness of teachers, neighbors, and other townspeople who were pleasantly shocked that the last of the Clayton boys was smart enough to learn from his brothers' mistakes. Nonetheless, the way the sons behaved around their father spoke of his firm, fair authority. In that, Mr. Clayton reminded Vincent of his own father.

"I'm very proud of Blake," Mr. Clayton said. "These days he's doing honorable work. He's also demonstrating sound judgment in his choice of friends and his wife."

"Have you told him you're proud of him?"

After a blink, Mr. Clayton said, "He knows he's doing well." His quiet humility suited a Southern Christian gentleman.

"Sir, I believe you underestimate how much your opinion means to him."

Mr. Clayton's glance swept over the crowd. "Very sound judgment in his choice of friends." He reached up and patted Vincent's shoulder then he walked into a huddle of small children who squealed to "pretty please" let them pet the horses.

Vincent headed toward Flanagan's table.

Blake owed his newlywed happiness to two friends who weren't on speaking terms. To put it bluntly, they had issues. Misunderstandings, poor timing, violent reactions, you name it. He firmly believed that his own wedding day was the day to spread happiness, so he intended to help his friends come to terms with their relationship issues. Blake and his bride Terri had a plan to bring them together. It was as simple as that, so the moment after the wedding photographer freed him from the last of eight family group shots, he whispered to his bride, "You detain Vincent. I'll find Nefi."

While the maid-of-honor reached under the back of Terri's lacey ivory wedding gown for something, Terri smiled at Blake. "Don't worry about Vincent. I'll detain Vincent. I'll show cleavage if I have to."

The maid of honor glared at Blake as if he had suggested such a brazen thing.

"He's a friend and we owe him a favor." Blake's explanation sounded more reasonable in his head than spoken. He blamed the distraction of the maid of honor's actions. *What on earth is that woman fishing for under Terri's dress?*

"Go," Terri said with a wave that flashed sunlight off her ring. Her shoulder-length hair had been twisted and pinned and sprayed in place under her veil so that only her bangs gleamed like a new penny on her forehead. Her dress captured her perfect curves and flowed off her hips, obscuring her shapely legs.

Blake enjoyed a view of Terri's ankle as her skirt was hiked up. "Can I help with whatever she's doing?"

The maid-of-honor huffed before deftly hooking a small loop to a button on the back of Terri's dress. "Tada!"

"You meant to bunch it up in the back?"

"Now the train won't drag behind her," the maid of honor told him as if explaining it to a child.

The train? Women had their own vocabulary, especially when it came to clothes. "Then why not just make the dress the right length to begin with?"

Both women stared for a moment before laughing.

Terri said, "That's so manly."

He could live with being manly. It kind of took the sting off being laughed at. After a longing gaze at Terri's cleavage, Blake strode across the lawn of his family's ranch toward the reception area.

Tables, decked out in black and white patterns with fussy centerpieces of red roses and lacy white sprigs, spread out over a quarter acre of lawn between the back porch and the horse pasture for the three hundred guests. Gleaming pickup trucks, cars, and a few golf carts lined the open field along the white rail fencing and beyond the fence horses grazed. Guests herded over the lawn, some huddled amid the tables between the three bartending stands and the buffet. The early fall weather felt made to order at a perfect seventy-two degrees. Heavy, late summer rains had created flooding that pushed water down into the valleys, effectively drying out the higher elevations. It was October fourth and in the rolling mountains surrounding the Clayton Ranch, the maples had already burst into bright oranges and reds. Today turned out not too hot, not too cool with zero chance of rain. Catering staff scurried around the buffet table while waiters carried trays of finger foods to guests.

Nefi, Nefi, where are you?

Blake owed Nefi for introducing him to Terri. He also wanted Nefi to have another chance to meet Vincent under circumstances that didn't involve machetes or guns. He rose on tiptoe and spotted Nefi at a table near the bartender's stand. A guy in a tux was leaning in toward her, signaling to the world with body language that he was attempting to stake a claim. Blake marched quickly toward them. As he neared, he recognized the guy as a thinner, younger version of Vincent. *Oh, no you don't.*

Vincent's brother Oscar looked up at Blake and flinched. His smile fell away. "Hey, Blake."

"Hello, yourself." Blake stepped between them and turned toward Nefi. "Nefi, please come with me." He held out his hand.

"You're killing me," Oscar said, tapping Blake's back.

"Always an option," Blake muttered over his shoulder. He spotted Terri floating in a cloud of white fabric toward Flanagan's table. He then returned his complete attention to twenty-one-year-old Nefi, who looked all grown up in an elegant lavender dress, with her long brown hair draped over her shoulders in loose curls. *Almost domesticated.* Nefi's amber eyes were framed with a thin smudge of black. *Terri will be so proud of young Nefi in makeup and a dress!*

Nefi had raised an eyebrow at Blake before she held out her hand. "Why are you acting so rude?"

"First, *he's* not right for you. Second, Terri wants to see you," Blake said. He had arrived before the two swapped phone numbers.

"It was a pleasure to meet you," Oscar said, leaning around Blake's back.

Noting that Oscar didn't even call her by name, Blake grinned. They hadn't even traded names. *Whew! That was close.* He nabbed Nefi's hand and led her up the lawn for a better view of the tables. From there he recognized Vincent taking a seat beside Terri. Others at the table were couples from the FBI and the US Marshals Service looking elegantly off-duty in formal wear. *Well, well, the gang's all there.*

Blake threaded the crowd, occasionally stopping to hug and kiss neighbors and relatives without letting go of Nefi. At five-feet-ten, Nefi easily kept pace with him. "You know I invited Martina."

"She's in London for a job interview. She said it's a fun, part-time job she can do while she's working on her master's degree."

"Good for her."

"I have good news." Nefi's voice barely carried through the cacophony of the crowd.

Blake paused and turned his head toward her. "Oh?"

"I'm going to Hogan's Alley."

For a moment, her enthusiasm reminded him of the first time he saw her smile. The Brazilian Ambassador had left a gift for her at the U.S. Consulate in Manaus. She didn't know how to operate her new camera, but she wanted to take a photo of the men who had escorted her from the jungle after her parents were killed. Blake, Vincent, and Ruis humored her and stood for a photo. It seemed like longer than seven years ago, yet here she was all grown up and headed to Hogan's Alley for training.

Of course, the FBI had accepted her application. She had the heart of a lioness and spoke four—or was it five?—languages. He was relieved she didn't have an announcement about dating someone. Blake turned his back to their destination, shielding Nefi's view of the table where Vincent sat with Terri. Sure, it stung a bit that Nefi had developed a crush on Vincent, despite Blake's efforts, but life had a way of getting in the way of plans. Nefi once told him he shouldn't settle for being anyone's second choice. Now he was Terri's first choice, and Terri's was his. God worked in mysterious ways.

It was time for Nefi to be happy. Blake gambled that his plan would do just that, but he needed to know one thing first. He didn't want the past to haunt his future. The fact that she came to the wedding meant more to him than he could put into words. Was it possible she had forgiven him for protecting that informant? Both he and Vincent had been assigned to protect the creep. They could not have known he was the man who had murdered Nefi's parents. From the moment she identified Silva as Guerra the Pirarucu Man, all protection ended, and he was extradited to Brazil for trial for murder and smuggling and other crimes.

He took Nefi's hands in his. "Do you forgive me?"

Nefi raised her amber eyes toward him. After a deep breath, she nodded.

A mantle of guilt lifted off his shoulders. To his surprise, his eyes burned and blurred. "Thank you." He wiped his eyes with the back of his hand. If she could forgive him, surely she could forgive Vincent. *Please, God. Please.*

A waiter, balancing a tray of champagne flutes, each with a strawberry at the base of the bubbles, shouldered his way through the mob. Blake released Nefi's hand and plucked two flutes from the tray as the waiter passed.

"Terri wasn't sure you'd be here, so I want to surprise her. Stay close behind me, okay?"

"You're a good man, Blake," she whispered it like a secret.

For a moment, he felt like a very good man. *Redneck nobility at your service, miss.* Blake turned and led her toward her future happiness. Her hand on his back told him how closely she followed. He stopped short of the table in a position directly behind Vincent's back. Across the table from Vincent and Terri sat two couples: Quinn and Kate Flanagan, and Ruis and Sophia Ramos. It was a year ago at Ruis's wedding where Blake first met Terri, thanks to Nefi. *And what a year it has been.*

Vincent reached Flanagan's table. Seated beside Ruis was his wife, Sophia. Quinn and Kate Flanagan, in the midst of animated conversation, stopped and welcomed Vincent to their table. As the only single, he settled in beside Kate, who greeted him with a firm hug.

"I was just telling Ruis and Sophia about how you were the first one at the hospital when Quinn got shot," Kate said, releasing him.

"I ordered you a drink," Quinn told Vincent.

"Thanks." Vincent leaned over the edge of the table. "Have you seen Nefi?"

The others at the table shook their heads.

A corner of Quinn's mouth tugged up. "Do you expect her here?"

"Blake invited her," Vincent said. *Was she angry at Blake, too?*

Bearing a tray of drinks, a young waiter arrived at the table.

Kate directed him while she pointed with her open hand. "A glass of Merlot for Mr. Ramos, sangria for Mrs. Ramos, a margarita for me, beer for my Quinn, and the root beer for Vincent."

"Root beer?" Vincent asked.

Quinn said, "I'm getting too old to cart you around."

Vincent laughed. He hadn't had root beer in ages.

Quinn and Ruis stood, looking behind Vincent. He turned and saw nothing but lace. Looking up, he recognized Terri, so he stood, trying to give the impression of being pleased to see her instead of Nefi. Terri could have been a model in her strapless wedding gown.

Terri smiled warmly at the men. "I never get tired of that."

Ruis said, "Of what?"

"When gentlemen stand for a lady."

Sophia nodded. Kate declared an "amen." Terri gathered her dress to sit in the empty chair by Vincent. As she sat so did the men.

"I'm so glad all of you could be here," Terri said. Speaking to Ruis and Sophia, she said, "Thank you for letting me crash your wedding last year. It changed my life."

Sophia cuddled against Ruis and gave Terri a shy smile. "You look beautiful and very happy."

Terri leaned over the place setting and said, just loud enough to carry to the far side of the table, "I'm very happy. Meet Blake's brothers and you'll know I got the pick of the litter."

To that, all glasses raised and clinked together. Vincent took a deep draw on his root beer. The taste of it reminded him of happy days in childhood. Back when life was simple. He looked around for his brother Oscar. He was somewhere in the crowd, probably waiting for the garter toss.

"Where's Blake?" Quinn asked.

Terri waved her hand toward the crowd. "Probably greeting his twenty-five cousins. I suspect half the town is related by blood or marriage."

"Where are you going for your honeymoon?" Sophia asked.

"Paris after one night's stopover in Atlanta," Terri said.

Kate said, "How romantic."

Quinn added, "Great food." For that, he got an elbow from Kate.

"I'm relieved Blake didn't get hurt at his bachelor's party. I heard about the crazy things he and his brothers used to do." Terri turned to Vincent.

"What?" Vincent said.

"Yeah, I'm looking at you, Mister," Terri said, "Your brother Oscar told me about your creative use of plaster."

"I learned that from Blake," Vincent said. "Be warned, he considers April Fools' Day a family holiday."

"Sure, now you tell me."

Ruis said, "Speak of the groom and he appears."

Vincent turned around to see Blake carrying two glasses of champagne with strawberries in them. He handed one to Terri.

"Quit flirting with my wife."

"I can see now why you kept her to yourself," Vincent said.

"Stand up and say that."

Vincent stood. He caught sight of a bare shoulder close behind Blake.

"While you're up, let me introduce you to a guest." Blake grinned at Vincent.

All the men at the table stood. Vincent realized he was holding his breath, so he willed himself to take deep breaths and exhale.

Vincent glanced toward Ruis and Quinn for signs that they were in collusion with Blake. Both looked surprised. Did their surprise mean the guest was a stranger? That the men stood merely indicated the guest was a woman. He sent up a quick prayer that Blake was not trying to match him up with a cousin. People in love tended toward matchmaking, but such intentions often caused hideously awkward situations. He braced himself to meet an ugly cousin before he turned around to face Blake.

In Blake's place stood a tall, lovely young woman in a simple lavender-colored dress and heels. *Nefi. Wow.* She took two steps toward Vincent, invading his personal space. The scent of lavender wafted against him in her wake. His pulse quickened. *Now or never.* He seized the moment. He remembered the tribal saying—silence makes words meaningful. He didn't need a single word to communicate his feelings for her.

He tugged his bow tie loose and unbuttoned his tuxedo shirt collar to reveal the stone and leather choker he had worn since she had given back his dog tags. It was the choker she gave him years ago, the one she had made for her father, the one that once triggered her to attack him with a machete and a hunting knife. Holding the choker, he had often hoped—since that awful night at the office—that she might speak to him again. A *Bible* verse that had confused him became clear—*Faith is the substance of things hoped for, the evidence of things not seen.* He admired the beautiful substance and evidence of answered prayer standing before him.

In the heat of Nefi's full attention, Vincent felt challenged to prove himself worthy.

In the last seven years, he had been close enough to hold her three times, two that he remembered. He was ashamed of all three encounters. According to Quinn, during the first encounter, he was too drunk to know she had come to him for help. On the second one, he threatened her at gunpoint. In their third encounter, she rallied from unconsciousness and gave him back his dog tags. How or why she wanted to face him again defied explanation. This time, he was sober, and she was conscious. This time. he wanted to help her, to comfort her and to apologize to her. This time, he hoped he wouldn't fail her. She was old enough to decide whether or not to trust him again. This time, he realized he was dead on in his prediction that she would grow up to be beautiful. *She is magnificent.*

Blake handed off his champagne glass to Terri. He watched Vincent and Nefi at last within arms' reach of one another, and because of their silence; he feared that their proximity invited violence. Love and fury were strong passions. Which emotion did Nefi feel at this moment? The situation reminded him of something his mother used to say about her sons, "Putting them together threatens the furniture." Most big Clayton family gatherings involved a trip to the emergency room or a visit from the police; however, none of the family members tolerated altercations between men and women. Did Nefi want to settle the score? She had attacked Vincent before. At age fourteen she had been scary fast. She looked awfully fit at twenty-one.

Blake stood by in case he had to intervene. He couldn't allow a fight at his wedding. If it came to a fight, though, he would bet real money on Nefi. She was faster and seven years younger than Vincent and handy with blades. Of course, she was in heels so that counted against her. Toe to toe she stood, unflinching and disturbingly calm, facing Vincent.

"What are they doing?" Terri whispered.

"It's a warrior thing," Blake whispered back. *Dang. They're close enough to breathe for each other.*

Vincent reached under his tuxedo jacket and removed his Glock from his underarm holster. He handed it to Blake. *Disadvantage Vincent.* Moments later, Vincent pulled up his right pant leg and removed his backup handgun. He handed it to Blake. *Further disadvantage Vincent.* Was it chivalry or recklessness? Vincent outweighed her. All the heads at the table pivoted toward Nefi, who stood dangerously close to the newly disarmed Vincent.

Nefi reached behind the nape of her neck under her thick, long hair. She pulled out a sheathed hunting knife. Terri inhaled sharply.

"I gave that to her," Blake told Terri.

"Why?" Terri asked.

"High school graduation."

Terri expelled a puff of air. It was Terri's way of saying the gift was wildly inappropriate, but she barely knew Nefi. He realized he could never tell Terri what Nefi once did with a machete.

Nefi handed the knife and sheath to Blake, all the while keeping her gaze on Vincent at almost eye-level. She then reached under the hem of her dress—of all places!—and pulled out a pink Taser. Blake and Terri exchanged a glance under raised eyebrows.

As if to justify his own gift, he told Terri, "Vincent gave her the Taser."

Nefi handed her Taser to Blake, who backed to the table and parked himself in the empty chair by Terri. He clunked the weapons on the table. She heard only her pulse *thud-THUD thud-THUD thud-THUD* in her ears as if five-hundred guests suddenly disappeared.

Disarmed, she stood almost eye-to-eye with him, waiting for him to speak. After years of longing and disappointment, she knew she didn't need him, but she wanted him. He should understand that the fact she was at the wedding meant she had forgiven him. If he needed to hear the words, well, then he'd be waiting awhile. She held her ground.

Vincent's pupils widened. An artery throbbed in his neck. Was his pulse quickening from fear or arousal?

He slowly reached his hands under Nefi's ears and cradled the back of her head in his shaking fingertips. Nefi reached under Vincent's tuxedo jacket around his waist and felt his lungs expand. Leaning into her, he closed his eyes and covered her mouth with his lips.

At last, she felt at home. She melted into his embrace.

THE END

coming soon

West of Famous

by Joni M. Fisher

West of Famous will be released in the spring of 2017. For a preview, sign up at www.jonimfisher.com to Subscribe to Book News. You will also be asked, when the time comes, to vote on cover art choices.

ABOUT THE AUTHOR

Author **Joni M. Fisher** is a reformed Yankee with a B.A. in journalism from Indiana University in Bloomington who lives with her husband Maury in central Florida and North Carolina. When she isn't writing, she can be found flying, hiking, writing for aviation magazines, reading, or at church. An active member of the Women's Fiction Writers Association, the Florida Writers Association, and the Kiss of Death and TARA Chapters of RWA, she is hard at work on her next novel.

Connect with Joni online:

Official website www.jonimfisher.com/books/

Goodreads (Author Page) www.goodreads.com/jonimfisher

Amazon (Author Page) www.amazon.com/author/jonimfisher

Facebook www.facebook.com/jonimfisher

Google+ www.plus.google.com/+JoniMFisher

CPSIA information can be obtained
at www.ICGtesting.com
Printed in the USA
FFOW02n0037171216
30375FF